Eating Blackbirds

by

Lorraine Jenkin

HONNO MODERN FICTION

Acknowledgements

For Huw, for Charlotte and for Maude again.
With many thanks to all those who have helped make this a better book.

Chapter 1

Reduce, Re-use, Recycle, Steal from Work

Godfrey Palmer passed the time of day pleasantly enough with the woman, as she flitted a duster around the office. She emptied his waste paper bin, the majority of its contents neatly ripped into four equal squares, into her black plastic bag.

"Don't work too late," she smiled as she paused at the door. "No one'll thank you for it – well, they certainly don't me!"

"No, just finishing off now," replied Godfrey, his pen still in his hand as if he were politely waiting for her to leave so that he could return to his life's work. The woman departed and scuttled down a dreary corridor lined with filing cabinets that were filled with documents that no one could bear to go through and dispose of – far easier to simply order a new cabinet and start a new system.

Godfrey waited until the swing doors had creaked shut and then tossed his pen down and stretched. He sauntered to the bottom of the corridor to the staff kitchen (that had, when the building had housed a wealthy family, been merely a cupboard). With the familiarity belonging to regular routine, he yawned as he filled the kettle to the brim and turned the hot tap on to flow into the washing-up bowl, adding a generous splash of washing-up liquid. Bowl brimming with bubbles and tap turned off, he returned to his office and collected the holdall that was kept behind the door and which was the butt of more than a few jokes from his colleagues:

"Big lunch today, Godfrey?"

"You still not drowned them kittens yet, God?"

He would smile patiently, knowing that the guffaws would be even louder if they knew the truth.

With the exactness of a careful man, he bumped the holdall onto the kitchen counter and undid the zip. He took out two Thermos flasks, immersed them in the suds and washed out the dried-on remains from the night before. He rinsed them, and then filled them with hot water from the tap to warm their insides. A small Tupperware beaker was dropped into the bubbles and then allowed to drip dry.

As the kettle chugged slowly to boiling point, he took two teabags from the communal box and put them into his own small plastic box, followed by a twist of coffee in a torn off corner of an envelope. He poured the water out of one of the warming flasks, took out a bag of macaroni from his holdall and measured out a mugful. He poured this into the clean flask and topped it up with boiling water.

Godfrey set the kettle to boil once more and, taking the milk bottle from the fridge, he hummed quietly to himself as he filled the beaker and placed it carefully into his bag. It had leaked a few weeks ago – the seal was beginning to perish – but he felt it still had life in it, as long as he was careful about transporting it. The second kettle was poured into the second warmed flask and this too was put into the bag.

He carefully put the zipped bag over his head and shoulder (like a mum who doesn't want her son to leave his bag on the bus) and adjusted it to make sure it was upright and comfortable. He took a last look around him to make sure he had left no trace, but, as usual, all was as it should be. When one has been doing something for as long as Godfrey had been doing this, a certain amount of attention to detail is inherent. A quick visit to the toilet would save on a metered flush at home and then he would be done.

He hummed an extract from Handel's *Messiah* as he strolled back down the corridor, leaving the kitchen's and his own office light on and the computer whirring. As with many 'careful' people, Godfrey was extremely generous with bills that others had to pay.

He walked slowly home through the drizzly December evening; the twenty minute stroll being nearly enough to turn the dried pasta in his Thermos into swollen macaroni. Perhaps not what the River Café might enthuse over, but when he considered the benefit of having the ingredients for his evening's two cups of tea and a slightly lukewarm coffee in the morning to hand, al dente was not a requirement that particularly bothered him. His motivation was the seventy-six pence that was thus saved and he thought of his future plans coming seventy-six pence nearer, with a glow that never failed to warm his heart. And all in work time, to boot…

Chapter 2

A Lounge Laid with Carpet Samples

Mansel Big Face flopped onto the leather sofa that held pride of place in his bland semi on the Lake estate. He plonked a large pile of toast onto the table at his side. He clicked on the television that groaned under the weight of his school cricket trophies and tapped in the directions that would bring up the golf. He loosened his tie and kicked off his shoes and they landed in the large pile of other shoes at his feet. He decided against getting up again to shut the curtains and began to tuck into his pre-dinner snack.

Mansel felt that he should be thinking, "Ah, peace at last!" but actually there was no need. His job at the Council was pretty easy and because he was the only one that did it, he had no other officers to compete with over speed or efficiency. It didn't matter that he had a pile of complaints to work through; everyone in the Council did and the powers that be knew that clearing in trays was an impossible target. As long as he looked busy, he tended to get away without being over-supervised.

He was also lucky in that no one really knew exactly what he did do. He had slipped through re-organisation after re-organisation and had now ended up in the Community Charge

4

section, simply because he was a member of the union and didn't want to be moved up to County Hall where all the other stragglers had been grouped. He had therefore been donated to his new boss, Sandra Burton, as poor compensation for losing two efficient administrative staff. He'd lost all chance of promotion under his previous boss when he'd said, "No wonder we're not allowed to bring partners to the Christmas party!" on meeting the man's wife, and Sandra didn't seem to be pushing for it at the Management Team Meetings either.

He was known internally as the "Slides and Dogshit Officer" or if he was unlucky, the "Duck 'n' Dogshit". He, however, knew that he was a Recreation Parks Quick Response Officer, and so he would spend his days in different play areas and parks throughout the county, wiping off a bit of sexual graffiti here, or chucking a dead goose over a hedge there. He dealt with complaints and he tended to find that by the time he went to investigate, they had either been faded by the sun or had decomposed. Thus his targets were high but often achievable without undue effort, and on a good day he wouldn't even have to get out of the van more than once or twice.

Therefore as he lay on the sofa that drizzly evening he couldn't quite shake off a feeling of boredom. Usually he ate so much toast that he didn't have enough blood left in his head to think anything, but he had been having this feeling more and more lately. He was beginning to wonder if there should be more to life than this?

He met the boys every Thursday night and that was always a good laugh. He still turned out occasionally for the reserves on a Saturday if he answered the phone from Thursday night onwards, and of course then there would be the after-match night out and the aftermath of that would usually wipe out most of Sunday.

His mates were settling down around him, and Mansel was finding that there wasn't as much need for a bloke who was always up for an invitation as there used to be. No one really called round the house anymore – the last ones probably being the kids on the estate who called to ask whether he would like to play slide football with them again. He'd thought at one point that a kitten might be a good idea, but had blown that. "I love kittens, they're so soft to sit on," he'd said to the concerned and committed lady at the cat rescue centre.

Suddenly he became sick of the golf and flicked through the channels. How many were there and *still* nothing to watch? He turned the TV off and sighed deeply. Perhaps he could clean the early mid-life crisis sat out on his driveway – it might be fun to use the new power washer again? Nah, raining. He did need to do some ironing? Nah, he wasn't that bored. Perhaps he could check out the prices of that new golf driver? But then, he hadn't played golf for about three years now – that particular hobby probably didn't warrant another new piece of kit just yet.

Luckily, just then the carbohydrate in the last piece of toast sucked the remaining blood from Mansel's head and dragged it to his stomach and he lay back into the cushions and clicked the TV on again. Ahhh, peace at last.

Chapter 3

Knitting the Fluff from your Turn-ups

Audrey Gloucester pulled up outside the Council building, completely ignoring the polite cluster of notices that marked her chosen bay as being reserved for the Chairman of Council.

"Hush now," she ordered to the two chocolate Labradors that were hauling themselves from the blanket in the back of the old Rover in anticipation of a walk, "you stay here, boys. Guard the car." She gathered her coat, hat and voluminous bag from the passenger seat and scrambled from the car, not even noticing that her keys were still in the lock and that the door wasn't properly shut.

"Where's the rates office?" she barked at a young man in a suit with an armful of files.

"If you go into the main reception and explain what you want, they'll call down the relevant officer to meet you, Madam," he began helpfully, but she'd already stalked away and was trying to get in a door that was clearly marked "Staff entrance only – all enquiries to the main reception" in both Welsh and English and in a large plain font, accompanied by a helpful directional arrow.

She was eventually delivered to the main desk where a

helpful soul extracted what she really wanted and called the Council Tax office.

Godfrey Palmer strolled slowly down the stairs to meet his charge, happily filled with a cream cake from a colleague whose birthday it had been. The receptionist pointed to his new client with a raise of his eyebrow and Godfrey put on his pleasant customer-greeting face and walked towards the lady who was rummaging in her bag and making the row of wool-covered seats dog-hairy on contact with her posterior.

Godfrey saw an inherently elegant woman with classically good features, sat so near the Christmas tree that needles were falling onto her shoulders every time she nudged it. Her long greying hair was swept into a plait and secured by a large bejewelled clip. Her burgundy wool jacket was of a fine cut, but, as with the rest of her wardrobe, could do with being separated from her dogs a little more often. Her wine-coloured tights clashed with her navy shoes, but Godfrey didn't notice this, being completely unaware that his own tan brogues clashed horribly with his late father's mustard-coloured socks.

"Mrs Gloucester?" enquired Godfrey with a smile, trying not to notice that she resembled his old French mistress, the wonderfully stern Madame Laurette whom he'd fancied for the whole of his school career.

"Ah, yes, Audrey, Audrey Gloucester," she said in reply, shaking his outstretched hand firmly but briefly. "Now, I want to get this blessed rates tax sorted out – and you are?"

"Godfrey, Godfrey Palmer."

"Well, sit down," she said, patting the chair beside her and dislodging a few more dog hairs and then proceeded to spew out a torrent of phrases that described her position perfectly adequately in her own mind – any lack of clarity being wholly the fault of the poor listener, in this case Godfrey with his notepad and pen poised.

"Tŷ Mawr, Bryn Coch, is ours...husband Jerry was brought up there...bloody mess – paperwork as well as the blessed farm...bills everywhere, mostly unpaid, probably mostly unwarranted... Well I'm taking over, trying to make sense of it all – probably been paying for things five times over...bloody crooks all of you. It seems we've been paying rates on this bloody great house, as well as two others... Good God, we're not made of money you know – and now it's finally up to me to sort it out."

Godfrey put down his pen and stared hard, trying his best to glean relevant fact from irrelevant ranting fiction. He liked cases like these; in his own ordered life he knew exactly where every penny went and why, and he was always certain that it should go there – he was prepared to bend but never break the rules. That is why he was completely at peace with the tea fund issue: he paid into a weekly fund for the provision of tea, coffee and milk. No mention was made in the unspoken rules that the goods should only be for consumption in the office, therefore...

He'd always thought that he would relish being a debt counsellor, showing others how to be as sensible and orderly as he was. It was another thing on his list of intentions for when he took his early retirement; he was too busy to give it the time it deserved now. Anyway, it wouldn't be long now and he would be able to do whatever he liked with his days

– and *still* be young enough to start a whole new lifestyle.

After letting Mrs Gloucester vent until her phrases were less urgent and she was simply shaking her head in disbelief at her husband's stupidity, Godfrey squared his pad onto his knees and wrote "Mrs Audrey Gloucester" in a firm hand and then underlined it twice with a ruler that he produced from his jacket pocket.

"Now, Mrs Gloucester," he said, as if having disregarded her previous information, "let's sort this out and get you the best deal we can, shall we?"

Audrey was about to bluster and protest that she had just told him all that he needed to know, but seemed to run out of energy and hence succumbed gratefully to this gentle man, his paunch rising softly over his belt and with a curling beard that reminded her of her husband's. Jerry Gloucester's beard was, however, a style choice, rather than being solely based on an estimated forty-two pounds of savings a year on blades and shaving foam.

A neat line of details was soon scribed onto Godfrey's pad after which he was able to tell Audrey that the Council offered a 50 per cent discount on second homes for Council tax, to account for the fact that second home owners didn't make full use of Council services. "Although, do remember that the bin lorry still visits your gate, regardless of whether there is a bin there for it to empty or not," Godfrey warned, trying to prevent the usual tirade of "Why should we pay when we don't use much," that usually entered such conversations.

"So, what I need to know in order to process your claim is evidence that it is indeed a second home and then we can put all this into order, get a new bill sent to you – and you can even get a further two per cent off if you pay by direct debit!" he beamed happily, knowing how much he himself cherished that additional two per cent saving and had proudly been the first person to sign up for it.

"Evidence? What do you mean evidence? How can I prove that it's not where I live, apart from it's a great monster of a place that will probably have a three-month-old pint of milk in the ridiculously large fridge-freezer that runs day and night to keep solid half a frozen pig that Jerry bought on impulse from some local farmer that he met in the pub." Audrey raised her hands into the air in exasperation and her thick gold bracelets clattered down her thin wrists to nestle in the cashmere sleeves protruding from her jacket.

Godfrey began to list potential evidence at which she waved him away, "Oh, I can't find those – Jerry…well his papers are in a complete state, which is probably why I am finally being allowed to do something with them. In the meantime, I'm paying a bloody fortune for a place I don't even visit. Plus another place I get to visit even less. Look, I'm going to Tŷ Mawr now actually. Come with me and see for yourself and when I find those blessed other forms, I'll send them to you and you can tick your boxes or whatever, but, in the meantime, I'll have my discount please."

She picked up her bag and began walking off, leaving Godfrey with little option but to scuttle after her. It really was quite irregular, but part of preparing to retire was doing things that weren't specifically task-efficient and, besides, Godfrey knew of Tŷ Mawr; it was an eighteenth century farmhouse that rented out its land to a neighbouring farmer

11

and stood on the outskirts of Cysgod y Ffynnon. It was hidden from the town by a woodland that had been planted by Jerry Gloucester's ancestors a few generations ago to block the view of the settlement that had sprung up from next to nothing into a thriving Victorian town, built to allow wealthy city dwellers to sample the healing qualities of the sulphur and saline springs.

Godfrey had always been interested in Tŷ Mawr, as it was just visible from his house in winter when the trees were bare. When he'd been younger, he'd imagined himself living there with his chosen wife, his father standing next to him at the gate with his arm around Godfrey's shoulders saying, "Well, my boy, you've done it! Well done: I knew you'd get there in the end!" He'd read about how it used to be the local Lord of the Manor's house, and he'd always wanted to know what it looked like inside and how grand it really was.

So, Godfrey's interest in local history overcame his integrity and soon they were hurtling down the lane leading to the house, Godfrey clinging to the door handle as the Rover swerved around the worst of the potholes and splashed through the unavoidable ones. The dogs sensed their impending freedom and were standing up, their great heads hanging between Godfrey's and Audrey's, breath panting sourly into Godfrey's ear.

"Sid-down," roared Audrey and the dogs obeyed momentarily, but soon returned to their prior position, lurching and swaying in order to stay upright as the car rumbled along.

Audrey pointed out features as they went, a part-dug pond that Jerry had plans for, the good salmon river, a pile of timber that was supposed to have been made into a hide two years ago and a bulldozed clearing in front of an old barn.

"Jerry loves this place," said Audrey, "always means to spend more time here, but we never get round to it – too bloody far, you see. A three hour drive from Bridlon – no bloody good. Two hours max' a second home should be, otherwise a complete waste of money – just like this place. There are plans for a country retreat – holiday cottage in that far barn, complete with fishing rights, a pond, a hide etcetera and then to do up the big house and let that too – you know, to friends, all his work cronies etc. But, when does a barrister have time to organise anything in his private life, let alone drive three hours to see it?"

"You mentioned another place," asked Godfrey, "where is that then?"

"Oh, not far. That takes care of itself really. No need to worry about that one. Now *here* we are!"

Godfrey nodded silently as the car skidded to a halt in a large yard.

"Huge you see but, well, we'll keep it, no doubt," she added, softening, "he does love it you see. Brought up here he was. Half hoping that our kids would run it as a farm again, but they're not interested, are they? Far too bloody busy buying sports cars as far as I can see. No bloody work ethic there I am afraid, so it's up to me to sort it out now." She opened the door and climbed out, the dogs taking their cue and piling out around her, ignoring her brusque cries of "Gently boys, gently!"

Godfrey stepped out and as he stood there brushing the hair and dust from his previously neat trousers, he looked

13

around him. Tŷ Mawr was an imposing stone farmhouse. Double-fronted, with a large stone porch, its bay windows no doubt rattled for months on end in the harsh Welsh winter.

The dogs rushed from pillar to post, spraying every corner or step, finally settling on an open patch of the yard to discharge their bowels. Huge doors, that looked as if they would collapse the next time they were opened, marked the entrances to the barn that ran along two sides of the yard.

"Perfect for conversion," snorted Audrey, "but Jerry wants to keep them as barns, the bloody idiot. What on earth do we want with a barn, I ask you? Especially when it's full of someone else's tractor! Man only rents the land from us, but he's still more than happy to fill our barns with his rubbish!"

She walked briskly round the side of the house, through a rickety wooden gate, climbing over a collapsed tangle of rose briars that obviously once trailed in a beautiful arch, the struts of which had long since decayed and collapsed under the weight. Godfrey closed the gate as best he could, seeing the sheep that were kept in the garden in order to keep the grass down, their droppings gathering on the path showing where they lay in order to keep warm thanks to any sunshine that the path absorbed.

Audrey stopped at another porch, this one less grand than the front porch, but still substantial enough to allow a farmer to have a seat whilst he removed his boots before entering the kitchen. Godfrey watched as she took a large key from under the eaves and unlocked the door. She shouldered the black peeling paint and the heavy old door groaned open.

Godfrey followed her in, stepping over a pair of green

Hunter wellingtons. The woollen over-socks that were sticking out of the tops were no doubt occasional homes to Jerry's weekend feet and more often a home to earwigs if not mice.

The kitchen that they stepped down into was huge. The flag-stone floor dipped at the doorway, evidence of the volume of traffic that it had carried before only-child Jerry sought the comfort of the Bar. A few leaves had squeezed in through gaps and now shifted as the closing door caused another gust of wind. Bit musty, but not damp thought Godfrey, his nose attuned to such things.

A long, sturdy wooden table ran the length of the kitchen, grand carver chairs sat at both ends and a mixture of benches, settles and chairs along its sides.

"Enough for, oh, twenty-five people on a good day," reflected Audrey as she ran a finger through the dust that now covered it. "Supposed to be twenty here for Christmas dinner – that's why I've popped down, to try and get everything ready in advance. How on earth am I going to make this dusty old place look inviting and festive in just two days, I ask you?"

A large inglenook fireplace took centre stage with two battered leather winged chairs either side. "The draughts are such that you really do need the wings," observed Audrey more quietly. "This is Jerry's place pretty much all weekend when he comes. He just loves to sit here by the fire, a bundle of papers gathering ash at his side – God knows what his clerks think when he returns them to the office! See, that's his pipe – he only smokes it here, never bothers in Bridlon."

Godfrey looked down to see a magnificent carved creation

lying on the hearth, a penknife, presumably to clean it, open at its side. The ash from the fireplace had spilled out over the hearth and would no doubt reach Jerry's pipe during the next gale. The vast chimney funnelled a draught down, even on that relatively still day. A whirring sound clicked on from the corner of the kitchen and Godfrey turned to see a large larder fridge whose motor had just kicked in.

Audrey clattered over to it, opened it despondently and shook her head as she gazed at its contents. "Yes, I was about right, but this milk is, let me see, oh, five months old. And what other delights do we have – tomato sauce, oh that's still in date, that's good. God only knows what this started out as…" she said as she pulled out a clear plastic bag with a greenish pulp in the bottom. "And I don't think I'll be using these to bake a cake with," she said as she gestured at a tray of a dozen eggs.

Audrey suddenly looked tired and she slumped down into one of the leather chairs, oblivious to the dust that would now be busy nestling into the fibres of her clothes. Godfrey pulled up a carver chair, removed the faded cushion that was on it revealing clean, polished wood and sat. Audrey mistook the gesture as one of reverence to Jerry's chair and smiled gratefully at him.

"Well, is this evidence enough for you?" she laughed, waving her hand around the room.

"Yes, I think so, for the time being," he replied, trying hard not to sound too officious, "but if you *could* forward the documentation that we discussed earlier in due course, that would be very helpful.

"What do you think you will do with the house long term?"

Godfrey asked, thinking about the huge depths of resources that were obviously flowing into the property.

"Oh, God only knows," she said, her voice still weary as she wiped dust onto her forehead. "I haven't the time to do anything particularly constructive here and Jerry certainly hasn't, so I think for the short term, we shall have to keep shelling out. Such a waste to keep a place this size heated day and night, when there's no one here to enjoy it, but so be it. I've got other things I want to enjoy when I come to Wales; I don't want to spend my time mucking about bleeding thirty-five radiators all weekend..."

Godfrey felt his insides lurch as he considered her statement. He thought of his neat semi-detached house, heated only to ten degrees; a warm vest and a thick woollen jumper making up for the additional eight degrees that other people considered minimally comfortable.

"We have time switches all over the place, to make it look as if the place is inhabited," she continued. "Lit up like a bloody Christmas tree it is – as if people don't know! Christ, when Jerry does come back, it's always such a performance, clattering into the local in Bryn Coch, entertaining old friends etcetera, that I am sure the whole valley knows when we are here and when we aren't." Again, Godfrey reflected on his own home, low energy lit room by thermostatically controlled room – his neighbours could trace his exact movements around the house, should they have cared. But, they didn't care, because they knew next to nothing about him. He was pleasant enough they would say, always waved and passed the time of day, but never took it any further; friends and relationships were something he felt he would cultivate after he retired – he didn't really have time now that he was working. He had other plans that he needed to crack on with …

Godfrey looked about him; he could imagine himself in a few months time sitting in a kitchen like this. His early retirement was looming and he had been thinking about what he would actually do with himself, when the time came, for nearly thirty years. He had scrimped and saved and postponed and lost out simply to make sure that he could attain his dream existence, and now that it was imminent he was glad that he finally knew what it looked like: his new friends would be gathered around a roaring fire, holding cut glass tumblers with generous tots of whisky in them. The talk would be lively, laughing at the escapades of the day's fishing in the river or hunting in the forests. He, Godfrey, would be cooking on a large modern gas range that lined the opposite wall, joining in the banter as he attended to the day's catch. Ah, yes, life would be good when he retired – only four months to go and that would soon pass and then all the scrimping and saving would have been worthwhile and a sensible investment of his energies.

"Perhaps I'll ask Eira Howard to do a bit more," Audrey said. "She comes in and just keeps an eye on the place every month, does a bit of dusting type thing. Jerry has an arrangement whereby he posts some money on the first day of every month to her here and then he *knows* that she will come in to get it! Yes, he's canny he is. There's also an arrangement for her husband to do occasional odd jobs. He sends a note back with the details and then the next envelope contains a little more – but, saying that, I can't see what he has done over the past few years. Mind, I can't really see a great deal of evidence of a cleaner either, but there we are. I don't know why he insists on employing them; should have been sacked years ago, the pair of them if you ask me. Some bloody misguided schoolboy loyalty, I suppose. But then, it's only thirty pounds after all."

Godfrey resisted the "only?" that threatened to burst forth. Goodness, he'd do an hour or two with a duster for thirty pounds a month – think of the boost to his pension fund that that would give. Twelve times thirty pounds, well, that would be three hundred and sixty pounds per year. Invest that in his Super Saver account…not a bad little sideline. Pay more than stuffing envelopes of an evening ever did.

"Right then, Mr Palmer," she said brusquely, standing up, "I'd better get you back to your office; let you sort out a few more financial muddles etcetera?"

Godfrey smiled at her and reluctantly put his chair back under the long table, carefully replacing the cushion. He had hoped for at least a cup of tea, powdered milk would have been fine, and surely a house like this would have had some shortcake holed up in an airtight tin somewhere?

Audrey locked up and returned the key to its hiding place. Then they set off round the back in search of the dogs, having heard them bark.

"Oy!" she roared, her elegant features contorting in annoyance. "Ged 'ere, boys! That'll be those bloody cyclists," she said. "Your bloody Council wanted a cycle route from Bryn Coch to Cysgod y Ffynnon and Jerry, being a benevolent soft touch, granted access along our back lane – so now we have bloody cyclists disturbing our peace.

19

Well, we could have, but nobody uses it; complete waste of bloody taxpayers' money I say, bloody nonsense. Let them cycle in Bridlon and then they'll see how safe these bloody roads are."

Godfrey shrugged his shoulders in mild disagreement; he quite liked cycling – why spend eleven pence per mile driving when you can walk or cycle for nearly free. Walking to work over the past thirty-two years had boosted his coffers hugely, he reckoned.

Chapter 4

Giving Blood to Get a Biscuit

Mansel breezed into the pub, smiled and rubbed his hands to warm them, glad to be out of the cold December night. "Right, let the evening commence!" he laughed to anyone who might be listening. He glanced around, catching people's eyes, looking to receive their greetings. "John!" he acknowledged. "Where's Bren tonight? Slimming Club night, hopefully – is it?" John nodded, grated out a smile then looked down. "Dar! How's tricks? Still single?"

"Yeah. You?"

"Er, yeah. S'pose."

Then a figure at a table in the corner caught his eye. A young woman sat on the settle alone. She looked nervous and was rubbing something imaginary from her finger.

"Don't worry!" called Mansel. "He'll turn up! Eventually!"

Everyone listening winced, knowing Mansel only too well, but the girl burst into laughter, a big toothy smile spreading across her face. "I doubt it! Not if he has any sense!" and she turned back to her smudge.

Mansel spotted the boys in their usual place by the dartboard – this time with a mean twist of tinsel wrapped round the outside of it – and strode over. "Hi boys, how's it going?" They all grunted their greetings and carried on with the game, telling Mansel that he would be on Fat Git's team if Daniel turned up.

"What about Howard? Where's he tonight?" Gary's face cringed a little as Mansel paused, obviously having something important to say. "Don't tell me, he couldn't come out as his mum hadn't got round to ironing the Thursday pants that she gave him last Christmas!" Mansel looked round the pub again to collect his laughs and saw the woman in the corner giggle in spite of herself.

"No, er, his, mum died last night. He's had to go over to help."

"Oh," said Mansel deflating, "that's really tough." Gary threw the dart and then chalked his score on the board as Andy offered Mansel a pint.

But Mansel was not looking at the scores, nor was he beaming at the head on his pint in the way that he usually did. Instead he'd glanced again at the lone girl in the corner. She was checking her phone for the umpteenth time. It looked like she was going through and deleting old text messages. He thought she was beautiful.

She was petite with long brown hair and small mousy eyes. He could imagine her in a television game show, running through an assault course in a Lycra one-piece, her hair escaping in tendrils from a red crash helmet. At the end of the course, the host would interview her and it would become clear that she had little tiny freckles sprinkled over her nose and cheeks …

She must have felt his eyes on her because she looked up.

She smiled again and looked back down. She had a clingy fawn-coloured top on and wore tawny-red lipstick. Boy, was the late guy missing himself a treat; he, Mansel, would have kissed that off in seconds.

For once, Mansel took a back seat from the conversation that was going on around him. He positioned himself in the corner so that he could see the woman's table without having to make it too obvious. He'd never seen her before; he felt sure that he would have remembered her petite face, framed so beautifully by that glossy brown hair.

He watched as she began to gather her things together. She checked that her necklace was straight and that her bag was closed. His heart began to beat faster – he couldn't let her go without saying something. She drained her glass and put it back onto the beer mat and pushed it to the middle of the table. She seemed reluctant to leave; she'd obviously been let down big time, but she didn't seem sad, or even annoyed – more *resigned* to her fate. What could he say to her? What should he do to keep her here? He'd never successfully kept a woman anywhere, let alone in a place that she had obviously decided to leave.

She started to put her jacket on. Mansel licked his lips, trying to summon up courage. As she stood up and smoothed her hands over the back of her skirt, he pushed through his circle of friends: he had ten paces in which to decide on how to make an impression.

He walked across the dark carpet, his eyes fixed on her as she flicked her hair out of the neck of her jacket. He didn't see the short stool until his legs were wrapped around it. He fell the remaining five paces as he crashed full-length onto the carpet, with the Christmas tree that he'd grabbed at for support landing across his back. His arm was stretched out in front of him and it threw the last third of his pint over the woman's shoes.

"Hi," said Mansel from his position on the floor, "I'm Mansel Batten. I'm sorry I just ruined your shoes." He turned to the barman who was running over to his aid, "Sorry to ruin your tree an' all; it was quite a nice one too." The barman lifted the tree off his back, fairy lights and needles dripping down around him. Mansel dragged himself to his feet and looped two runaway baubles round his ears. He put his hand out to the woman, who shook it laughing, and said, "I like to make an entrance. Can I buy you a drink for you to throw on my shoes, or can I take your shoes into the gents to waft under the hand-dryer?"

"Lucy-Ann," giggled the woman, shaking his hand. "My name is Lucy-Ann. No, I won't take my shoes off 'cause my tights have a hole in them. I'd love a drink though."

Mansel's friends stood in amazement as he fetched two more drinks from the bar and sat next to the woman, pine needles standing out from his back like a porcupine's spines. They watched in awe as the man who was famous for putting his foot in his mouth, sparkled away. It appeared that Mansel's idea of witty conversation had at last not only found its spiritual home, but had taken off its shoes and put its toothbrush on the shelf.

Chapter 5

Slitting Open the Toothpaste Tube

Georgia Harrow gripped the headboard of the hospital bed and shrieked in frightened pain once more.

"It's OK, love, I'll be with you in a minute, we're just having a few problems here," shouted the midwife from the next room. She was busy trying to pacify an angry husband who kept insisting that *somebody* should be doing something more.

"Sir, your wife is doing more than enough; I suggest we just leave it in her capable hands now, shall we? You've been to the classes? Well, Sarah here seems to know exactly what she is doing."

Georgia wept in frustration as pain tore through her and the contractions gripped her exhausted body. Although it was a strong body that was used to hardship and neglect, the last few weeks of pregnancy had taken their toll.

Previously she had considered that the squat she shared with friends had been a haven, a real little community in which the fourteen or so members looked out for each other. But, when the chips were down – as they most certainly were at this moment – it seemed that she was on her own.

She thought back to the time when her pregnancy had

been a fresh, even exciting prospect. The father was almost certainly one of three candidates and she instinctively knew that none of them would ever either believe that the resulting child was theirs or take any more than a passing interest, and so had not told them about it.

She had told Hannah, her best friend in the squat, of her suspicions in a nightclub toilet and Hannah, ever the party girl, had whooped with joy and laughed, "Now we'll be a real family! This baby's gonna be, like, sooo lucky! It'll have at least fifteen parents – God this is gonna be sooo good!" And she had swept Georgia back to the dance floor and, as they rejoined the crowd of sweating youngsters with wild eyes, Hannah had held Georgia's hands in the air. They'd bounced up and down in time to the music and she had yelled, "I'm gonna be an aunty! I'm gonna be an aunty!"

And Georgia had believed her. Although it seemed to her now that she'd been as stupid and oblivious to the realities as she'd been to the urine washing about on the floor of those toilets.

And then she fell to thinking about how she'd come to be friends with Hannah in the first place…

Georgia had been described as a pretty girl with everything going for her when she had left her Holsborough home at fourteen after an incident with her mum. In fact, she'd been miserable for years, irritated by her mother, Annabel, and not getting on with Annabel's controlling partner, Ray, who'd been living with them since Georgia was ten.

The rows had increased in regularity and severity since she was eleven and her mum seemed to have finally come round to Ray's whispering campaign that Georgia was "odd" and Annabel had "spoilt" her and that Annabel shouldn't allow a spoilt teenager to ruin her own happiness, simply by trying to get all the attention.

Siding with Ray had eventually seemed the easier option for Georgia's mother and had at least allowed her to have good relations with someone. Therefore, Annabel had begun to notice that the things Ray said about Georgia were, actually, true: Georgia was told that she *was* lazy and she *didn't* help out round the house in any other way than her specified chores, which she carried out with *very* bad grace. She apparently was also sulky and seemed to want to spend more time with her friends or alone in her room than she did with her own mother.

Annabel would reproach Georgia for any aspect of her behaviour, behaviour that Georgia's friends' parents would consider typical for a girl of her age. It enraged Georgia to be told off by her mother who sat engulfed by the sofa, clutching Ray's hand for support. For her part, Georgia tried first compliance, then withdrawal and then complete rebellion as Ray's stares and smirks widened the gulf between the generations. Georgia particularly hated the way Annabel looked weakly at Ray for approval after such a remonstration and he would put his hands up in a "No, Annabel, you're her mother, you must do as you see fit; I am only your boyfriend and would never presume to project my thoughts into a family issue" kind of way. But Georgia could see what Annabel couldn't, the smugness on Ray's face as he relished in her being disciplined and mocked her inability to reason with an adult.

As twelve turned to thirteen, Ray's stares changed. Rather than smirking into her face, his eyes kept dropping to her chest. Georgia, in her burgeoning sexual confidence, felt she could control it and began provoking him by keeping on her school uniform after school, but just undoing a few buttons in order to relax. Her friends thought he was a good laugh and that, as stepdads go, she was lucky to have him. Annabel continued to look on in distress, trying to please everyone and ending up pleasing no one as Ray's attentions slithered from her to her daughter.

Georgia had begun to get on better with Ray, particularly when her friends were around. They practised their flirting techniques on him and he was only too willing to reciprocate. As time passed he had seemed to be more fun than her mother; he'd fix Georgia and her friends glasses of vodka and Coke or Malibu and pineapple juice when they came round in the evening and chat to them in the sitting room as if they were adults. He would also tell Annabel to leave them alone when she'd frowned her concerns about this.

Feeling empowered, Georgia had sought control in other elements of her life. She teetered on the edge of bulimia, enjoying her mother's concerns as she guessed something was going wrong but seemed unable to confront her daughter.

The situation had leapt forward several leagues when Ray had caught Georgia looking at his pornographic magazines.

She had come home from school to what was usually an empty house and had, whilst grabbing a pile of clean washing as a decoy, sneaked into her mother and Ray's bedroom to flick through the recently discovered stash. She was alternately intrigued, aroused, repulsed and flooded with guilt as she turned the pages and gazed at the images. In her eyes, the women were glamorous, powerful and in control. However, her newly feminised awareness also picked up shaving rashes, cellulite and the faint scars from breast augmentation that even heavy make-up couldn't hide.

She had turned with a start as she'd sensed a presence at the bedroom door. To her horror, Ray stood leaning on the door frame, a smile spread across his handsome features, his arms folded in smug delight.

Georgia had jumped to her feet and started to babble, "I was just... I was putting the washing away... I was only looking. I'm sorry." Ray had walked forward slowly and picked up the magazine that had fallen to her feet in her fright. He had put it back on the bed, the brunette holding herself open for Georgia's frozen gaze and clashing horribly with the rather twee floral bedspread.

"It's OK," he had said casually, "there's nothing wrong with a bit of a look. We've all got bodies, we just want to see what other people's look like. See," he said, "I think this girl is actually really pretty – see, look at her eyes; they're beautiful aren't they?" In hindsight, Georgia could see what he had been trying to do. By keeping her in the bedroom, keeping her talking and stopping her running away, he had hoped that something more might have developed from their mutual interest in the female sex.

Georgia had dragged her eyes away from the bits of the girl that she had so obviously been focusing on before and sought the dark brown pools that showed the depth of the person who paraded her nakedness for the pleasure of others.

Ray must have guessed at her hesitation and quickly turned the pages again. A young blonde in a school uniform gazed out innocently, sucking on her lollipop. She was a million miles from the school girls that scuffed their heels past Georgia's house twice a day, their saggy jumpers covering sluggish figures, laden with heavy school bags and even heavier periods; showing any flesh was the last thing on these girls' angst-ridden minds.

"Yes, she's quite pretty, but not a patch on you!" he had said. "You look far better in your uniform than she does – even with all that airbrushing and professional lighting. Go on – give me a pout like hers!"

Georgia had blushed and laughingly given a wide-eyed pout as Ray clapped and chuckled and then suggested that she leant forward as she stuck her butt into the air. Relieved at not receiving the yelling at that she'd expected, Georgia began to let her guard down. Ray had pretended to snap photos of her laughing and pretending to be as sexually powerful as the women on the bed between them.

Georgia hadn't heard the front door unlock. She hadn't heard the step on the stairs or the farting about with coats and handbags. Her mother never came home early; she was a creature of routine. It shouldn't ever have been an issue.

What Annabel would have expected to see as she walked into her bedroom would have been a neat Laura Ashley counterpane covering a bed with a white padded headboard and two small bedside tables, hers piled with creams and magazines, Ray's with golfing books and a wooden-backed hairbrush.

What she really wouldn't have expected would have been

to see her daughter kneeling on the floral print, her mouth pouting open, red with the application of her mother's lipstick. Her white blouse had been undone a few buttons revealing a push-up bra, the buying of which Annabel herself had debated for sometime. She would have never have dreamt that the navy blue pleated skirt that she spent so long ironing each Sunday night would be hitched up round her daughter's waist for the benefit of the pretend camera that her own boyfriend appeared to be running off rolls of non-existent film on.

Georgia remembered that the first scream that her mother's mouth made, never really made it into noise. She remembered thinking that her mum was so useless that she couldn't even scream properly when her daughter was posing for her mother's boyfriend. Her second scream, however, had worked.

Georgia had leapt from the bed, brushing down her clothes and fumbling with her buttons. She remembered pushing Ray out of the way and realising as he turned away that he had an erection tenting his trouser fly. Annabel would have seen that too and that was probably why her third scream had been so loud.

"Wha'?" he had stuttered, obviously not seeing the bigger picture. And that was the last she had seen of him, standing holding his make-believe camera, his erection pushing out his trousers as if there were a bunch of bananas hiding in there. She remembered pushing past her mother who still had her mouth open and a bewildered look on her face that had haunted Georgia every day since. And that had been the last she had seen of her as well.

*

So, as Georgia lay on the hospital bed her hands gripping the metal bedpost behind her, she recalled the shame she'd felt and what it had driven her to. She would love to have her mother beside her at this time, teaching her, willing her to do what was needed. She would love to simply not be there at all, but she was, and she was on her own. And that may just be how things were going to be from now on...

Just seventy-two hours later, Georgia gingerly pushed open the plywood sheet that semi-covered the otherwise open window. She stepped into the darkness, feeling the familiar grind of broken glass and slimy rubbish beneath her feet. She clutched the tiny warm bundle, wrapped in hospital clothing, to her painfully swollen chest and felt her way slowly towards the skylight-lit stairwell.

The silence in the house told her that it had been a heavy night, but instead of looking forward to the tales of the adventures and escapades that an evening fuelled by drink, drugs and young hormones never failed to bring, she yearned for the silence to remain in order for her to deal with her newborn bundle at her leisure.

She stepped over a pool of dried vomit that had adhered to the bottom stair and groped her way upwards, struggling to balance with her baby in one arm and a bag of clothes and nappies given to her by a sympathetic midwife in the other.

The stench of fusty bodies emitted from one room as she crept past the door-less opening, but this was soon overtaken by that of urine from the "bathroom", which people insisted on still using, even though no fresh water had passed through its pipes for years.

She finally reached what had been "her room" for the past eighteen months and wearily pushed open the door. Against all odds, she had made it relatively comfortable; she had an old mattress on the floor and a number of blankets and an ageing sleeping bag. Her clothes were neatly stacked in a cardboard box and a pile of tatty magazines was placed next to it. An ex-boyfriend had done a mural on the wall, but she had recently improved upon the smashed window by nailing up some board and therefore it was usually too dark to do the picture justice.

Georgia hadn't really thought how she might accommodate a baby within this room and certainly not within a waterless house. She had had delusions of her friends doing up her room in her absence and had felt sure that on her return from hospital, she would be led upstairs by the others skipping round her in excitement to a pastel bedroom. It would have clean curtains with clowns on and a cute little cot with a mobile hanging over it. As she walked up the stairs, her expectations dropped. Hopefully there would be a cardboard box lined with a blanket for Jocey. Perhaps the expected level of frills was not so necessary, but it would be good to have something to help her out.

How could she have not been better prepared? The days since the birth had been a whirl of pain, tiredness and anxiety. How could such a little thing be so difficult to dress? She was used to late nights, but she was also used to sleeping things off and suddenly that seemed a luxury that was not likely to happen for a while.

As soon as she stepped into the room, she sensed that

something wasn't right; wasn't the same as it had been when she left it just a few days ago. The smell was different and there was someone else's breath coming from the bed. She put her bag down and fumbled for the candles and matches that she kept by the door. The sound of the match and the feeble glow of the candle was enough to wake the bundle tucked up tightly in her bed: "What the fuck are you doing?" it demanded. "Turn the fuckin' light off for fuck's sake."

"Who are you?" she demanded in return. "And what the fuck are you doing in my bed?"

"Trying to sleep before I was so rudely awakened," it growled, "now, fuck off."

"But, this is my bed, my room, my stuff," she cried, her easy emotions beginning to wash over her as the pain and exhaustion of the last few days sapped her energy.

"Well, some mate of yours said I could use it as you weren't coming back. You're supposed to be in hospital or summit."

"I was, well, I am, but I had to leave...they needed the bed," she wailed, the baby sensing her distress began to whimper.

"Oh, fuck up the noise will ya; I can't bear it," and the bundle turned over in a huff, pulled the blanket over his head and made as if to sleep once more.

Georgia was overwhelmed. She dissolved into tears and, clutching her baby and bag of goodies, she reversed out of the door. She walked along the hall, oblivious to the rubbish on the floor and the damp that soiled the ancient ragged wallpaper. She knocked gently on the next door, the sound barely penetrating the thick wood that had miraculously withstood the numerous phases of looting that the once-grand building had endured.

She knocked again and then sobbed, "Hannah, Hannah," desperately needing the warmth of a friend. "Fuck off," groaned a male voice from within over a giggle from a girl.

"Hannah," she sobbed again, louder this time, "it's me, Georgia, can I come in? I've got the baby." She tried the door but it was wedged shut.

"Fuck off, I said," shouted the male voice again, laughing as he clutched his hangover into his head.

"Yeah, fuck off!" laughed the girl (who lay naked beside him, trying so desperately to please him that she was able to spurn her best friend in her time of need). "We're busy!" Hannah added, trying to make it sound less callous and also hoping that they soon would be.

This was the final straw for Georgia. Hannah was the mate who had bounced her round the nightclub floor after having heard her news, telling her, reassuring her, that it would be OK – persuading her not to have a termination as the baby would have a ready-made family. But then, this was also the mate who had left her hospital bedside when Georgia had needed someone to dig her nails into, making feeble excuses about not knowing that it would take so long and that she didn't want to let the others down by not meeting them at the stated rendezvous. And now, when she had intended to present "the family" with their new bundle of joy, this: a piss-head in her bed and her best mate more interested in a bloke that she probably met less than twelve hours ago than in Georgia and her new baby.

Tears streamed down Georgia's face as she stumbled

down the stairs in desperate need of the banisters that had been burnt so many winters before. Baby Jocey was now bawling, probably as much as from being squashed as from needing a feed or a fresh nappy, and this just increased Georgia's desire to escape – to escape the miserable squat that had been a dirty, cold, damp home for two winters and to escape the life that had kept her there.

Her thoughts turned to home, to clean sofas and cups of tea brought indulgently to her warm bedside, but even in her desperate state, she couldn't do it. Couldn't face a mum whom she had betrayed in such a terrible way. No, it would have to be another saviour, and yes, perhaps it had better be Uncle God …

Chapter 6

Straightening Nails

Mansel stood in front of his bedroom mirror and sucked his stomach in. Most of it refused to budge. He turned to the side and tried it again; it was worse in profile. How had he not noticed how out of shape he'd become?

Now, a shirt. He opened the wardrobe and reached for his trusted favourite – a white open-necked shirt with three blue buttons at the top above the usual white ones. He looked awful. He smoothed the expanse of cotton over his stomach, but there was no hiding the beast below. He dropped to the floor and heaved himself into ten sit-ups, but the horse had bolted, so he undid the stable door again and threw the shirt onto the floor.

He looked at the clock. Half an hour until he was picking her up, with the table booked for eight thirty. He rummaged in his wardrobe again. The blue shirt? No, that had curry stains on. The red one? No, it highlighted his perspiration problem. Stripes – no, too officey – spots, no, more curry. Why hadn't he been more careful? Why hadn't he checked or washed and ironed a few backups?

At ten to eight he started on t-shirts, but they were either jokey or free from the building trade. He couldn't sit opposite the most beautiful woman in the world and look like he'd already "eaten the Jewson lot" …

Five to eight came and went in a flurry of polo shirts and at ten past eight, Lucy-Ann opened her door to Superman.

She screamed in laughter and her hands rushed to her face. "You didn't tell me it was fancy dress!"

"Didn't I? Sorry. Do you have anything? We've still got time for you to get changed if you want to?"

"Oh my God!" she laughed. "Um, I'll have to go up and change. Hang on, wait there, I'll be five minutes." Then she looked again at Mansel, already cold in the winter weather, his Superman costume not offering much in the way of warmth – but then a woollen Superman costume wouldn't have had the same appeal. "Oh, OK, you'd better come in. You can wait in the hall; I won't be long." She waved him past her, and left him shuffling awkwardly by the door as she raced upstairs. "Five minutes, OK, five minutes!"

Mansel stood in the hall and shivered; it wasn't really much warmer than outside. The door to his left was ajar and when he peeped through, he could see a fire blazing in its stove and it looked too inviting not to go and stand beside. He went quietly in and walked straight to the fire where he rubbed some life back into his hands. His nipples were erect from the cold and he desperately wanted them to calm back down in case she noticed that they were not quite as high on his chest as they should be.

Being a bloke, he noticed her television first, then her stereo and then had a look at her CDs – not bad, he thought. A little too much Carly Simon, but not bad. He liked the glittery Stetsons hanging from a nail on the wall, and the feather boas hanging from a hook on a beam.

But he wasn't so sure about the animals.

All over the lounge on shelves, on the sideboard, on the hearth and on the floor were cages filled with various scuffling creatures – white mice, gerbils, hamsters, even a couple of rats. The bigger cages held guinea pigs and a couple of chinchillas. Mansel was bemused; perhaps she was looking after them for a friend, for lots of friends. They surely weren't all hers, were they?

There were a few photos on the wall of Lucy-Ann with the animals – holding rabbits or with a gerbil on her head or a hamster peeping out from her sleeve. There were many more of just the animals – seemingly on days out to the park or the woods. The books on the shelf ranged from tattered child's guides such as *Looking after Hammy* to newer, more technical volumes for example *Behavioural Patterns in Cavies*.

He'd peeped at the books, as apparently books were always a good indicator of a person's personality. He was hoping for *How to Please Your Man in Bed*, but unless it was hiding behind a book about *Diagnosing Health Problems Via Stools*, (and he didn't really want to touch the book to check and see) it didn't look like it was there – but perhaps she kept it upstairs...

Mansel wasn't a great animal lover – he'd had two gerbils when he'd been younger, but had soon tired of them and eventually he'd killed them (manslaughter) by building Airfix models alongside their accommodation and using too much glue. He'd never understood the attraction of pets and if he were honest, he really couldn't be bothered with the upkeep of them. However, it wasn't his place to be judgemental. If they were a friend's, then they'd be gone soon, and if they were hers – well, he wasn't in too great a position either, owning far too many remote-controlled cars for a man of his age.

So, once reconciled with the notion of a rodent-lover for a lover, he could go back to the excitement of the night. He still couldn't really believe that he was here! He'd always been gauche where women were concerned. Playing the clown was easier than laying your soul on the line, so usually he tried to take the women he dated to meet the boys in the pub and would play it cool, so that it wouldn't matter when they remembered another appointment at nine-thirty. If he liked a woman, he rarely got round to asking her out; he could just never find the words. Sometimes he was sure that they liked him too, but his lack of progression of the situation tended to allow someone else to step in. He was sure that he had lost a number of potential girlfriends to other (bigger) idiots around the bar, simply because they had had the gall to ask a few questions.

However, with Lucy-Ann it had been different. He'd felt confident in a way that he'd never known before. He didn't worry about risking being a prat, because he didn't feel a prat with her. He felt funny at last – not a "nearly made it" funny, but a genuine funny that made her laugh. Even stranger, he'd also felt that it might be OK not to be a comic genius all night and they'd actually had a few sensible conversations about bigger things – work, music, camping holidays they'd had as children.

Even on that short evening in the pub, he'd felt she

understood him and therefore he might able to be himself. With previous girlfriends, it was as if he always knew he was on borrowed time before he was rumbled as being an arse, and therefore his safety mechanism was not to invest too much of his soul into the relationship. Better to be laughed at later in the week by a table-full of women for making a few gaffes, than it was to be laughed at for telling the truth. He'd never felt quite ready for that...

Since that night in the pub, he'd thought about little else other than Lucy-Ann's smile and her laughter. They had had a wonderful evening chatting and giggling in the bar, smiling at each other during gaps in the conversation and her not moving when he wriggled just a little bit closer towards her. (Although in hindsight, he now understood the look she'd given him when she had asked him whether he liked guinea pigs and "things like that" and he had said that he did, but he couldn't eat a whole one.)

In addition, he'd felt quite confident in suggesting that he walk her home. It wasn't that he was trying to get into her house or her pants; he simply felt that she was too precious to risk being hurt by drunks wielding kebabs and bags of chips. His previous dates had usually fled by the end of the evening, or found someone else who was going their way. Either that or they seemed to think it preferable to run the gauntlet of Toss the Kebab alley alone, than have to have a piggy back from someone who thought it amusing to pretend to be an aeroplane.

He had held Lucy-Ann's arm as they had walked the ten minutes to her house and had chatted and laughed all the way. She had not invited him in and he had not hovered around waiting to be asked. He had simply stated that he would like to take her out to dinner and had been over the moon when she had agreed. He had waved and walked away leaving her standing smiling at her door.

After an acceptable twenty yards, he had allowed the smile on his face to burst all over his body and he had jumped in the air. Feeling silly after he landed, he had looked back sheepishly. She had still been there and stood laughing at him as she waved once more. But he hadn't felt a prat. He hadn't felt stupid – he'd just worn his heart on his sleeve and her seeing it wasn't such a bad thing.

So, that is how he had gotten there, standing in her lounge looking for more signs that told him what she was about.

Overall he liked her lounge; the ambience was cosy rather than stylish, and he could imagine the two of them cuddled up on the sofa together. Even the smell of the animals was not apparent, more of a smell of fresh hay, which was quite pleasant and better than the *"eau de lost Chinese takeaway foil dish"* that tended to impregnate his lounge. He rarely went to other people's houses, as he met mates in the pub and so he had little idea about what his contemporaries might be doing. However, here, he liked what he saw and felt comfortable that his own lounge, after a little spring-cleaning, probably wasn't too far off the mark either.

There was a clomp clomp down the stairs and he held his breath. It seemed a shame that he'd suggested the fancy dress as she'd looked stunning in that black dress – he hoped that she wasn't going to have changed into a troll's outfit or be the back end of a chinchilla or something.

To his delight, Minnie Mouse skipped, blushing, into

the room. Her little red and white spotted dress revealed beautiful legs and tiny white shoes. And her black mouse ears framed her face perfectly.

"Minnie," he said, pushing back his cloak and kissing her hand, "you look fantastic."

The restaurant was full and people smiled at them as they were shown to their table. Both enjoyed the attention.

Mansel hadn't been on a proper date in years and he had always been pretty crap at them when he had, but this time it was as if he suddenly knew what to do.

He asked for the wine list and at Lucy-Ann's request chose a sensible option. Usually he'd have ordered a couple of cherry brandy and lemonades or mugs of ginger beer for a laugh and the poor recipient would gag her way through the drink wondering if she could skip the pudding and get home quick. They shared a starter as Lucy-Ann said she had a small appetite. Mansel said that he did too, but had had to put on the weight around his middle so that he would look good in his costume.

They laughed and chatted easily over their steaks and then shared a pudding.

"By the way," asked Mansel, chewing on some sponge with sticky toffee oozing around his lips, "what's with the zoo?"

Lucy-Ann stopped with her spoon midway to her mouth. "Oh, you saw? Well, nothing really." She shrugged. "Rescued a couple of furries from a kid down the road that weren't being treated properly and then sort of got carried away. You know how it is."

"I do indeed," said Mansel. "Sounds just like me and beef burgers. Confiscated a couple off a kid once too. He was mistreating them – smothering them in salad cream would you believe. They were much better off with me: I respected them, gave them real tomato relish: I've been collecting them ever since."

Lucy-Ann laughed and finished her mouthful and the awkwardness – if it had been awkwardness – was gone.

They sipped their coffees as all the other diners were leaving. The waiter finally came with the bill. "So, where are you off to next?" he asked.

"Oh yes," said Lucy-Ann, "I never got round to asking! What is it? A fancy dress party or something?"

Mansel looked down and bit his lip. He still hadn't thought how he was going to play this one. "Um, no party," he whispered. "I was just going to drop you back home."

"*What!*" she exploded, her eyes glaring at him in amazement. "You are joking? You made me take off that little black dress that I spent all day yesterday shopping for and a week's wages on? You made me dig out my old Minnie Mouse outfit and wear these crippling shoes for *nothing*? No party, nothing?"

Mansel nodded sheepishly and looked at the table. Oh no. Had he really pissed her off that easily?

"Well?"

"I, er, I – well, I didn't like my shirt and my other one had curry sauce on – I looked like a darts player you see – so I thought if I wore this it'd be OK, and then you suggested that you should dress up, didn't you? Oh, I can't remember – but – I'm sorry. I just wanted to look good for you and it wasn't going to happen any other way…" he tailed off in a whisper.

The waiter looked on in disbelief: he wasn't going back to the kitchen without hearing what happened next in this one.

Silence.

Eventually Mansel raised his eyes – he couldn't bear to see her puzzled face, feeling that sick feeling, knowing that another woman was going to walk out on him on their first date, just when he was so sure it had been going well. Her mouth was pursed, then just as his glance reached her eyes, she exploded into laughter. Tears ran down her face as she laid her head on the table and groaned. She took the mouse ears from her hair and threw them at him. He put them on. The waiter shook his head and walked away, just as she was boxing Mansel's ears with her two sizes too small shoes.

All the kitchen staff pressed their faces to the window in the swinging door as Mansel gave Lucy-Ann a piggyback out of the restaurant, both of them giggling like fools.

"Fuck me," said the waiter, pleased with his tip and the packet of Fruit Pastels that Mansel had produced from his cape and pressed into his hand, "a match made in heaven those two. Stupid heaven, mind, but heaven none the less."

Chapter 7

Minesweeping!

Godfrey leant back in the chair in his usual spot by the crackling log fire. It was the second Thursday in the month and therefore he was at the gathering of the Cysgod y Ffynnon History Society. It was the only real social engagement in his diary and, being one of the founder members, he enjoyed the nights in the Llew Ddu in the nearby village of Bryn Coch. Tonight the group had taken over the snug and the landlord had laid on a few sandwiches and a log fire in mistaken generosity, expecting as he was similar returns over the bar to those he took from the local darts team.

Godfrey cherished his warming pint of dark and listened half-heartedly to Margaret Graceman's account of the spa waters of Eglwys Fach. Margaret was a relative newcomer to the group and this was her first attempt at leading the debate. Godfrey didn't have the heart to tell her that Eglwys Fach Spa wasn't as undiscovered as she thought and that it had actually been done twice since the beginning of the society's meetings.

Each month, a different member took their turn to conduct the research, deliver a talk and lead the debate and, in fairness to Margaret, hers was as interesting as most – well researched and she had obviously spent some time in producing the talk, rather than just shuffling through a collection of facts like some of the others did; Rolf Raven's talk about the history of the mount at Bryn Du, for example, had been interminable.

Godfrey felt his mind slip, uninvited, back to the earlier message that he'd found left on the rarely activated answer machine at home. The line had been bad and there was the sound of traffic and something crying in the background, but it had sounded like Georgia and it seemed like she wanted to come and stay …

Georgia was Godfrey's only niece and his only ever reason for indulgence. He and his sister, Annabel, hadn't been close as children; he was five years her senior and had never really been the type for her friends to fancy and therefore their poor but proud upbringing had brought two more stereotypes into the adult world. Godfrey unable to form relationships, apart from…well, that was a long time in the past, and Annabel so desperate for affection that she latched onto anyone who might provide it.

Once they had matured into adults, Godfrey and Annabel's contact was formal and dutiful, particularly after the deaths of their parents. But, with Georgia, it had so nearly been different. She'd always been an open child, willing to climb uninvited onto her uncle's lap and she had a way of demanding fun and affection that persuaded him to indulge her. And so he had doted upon her and spoilt her from afar. Birthday presents of Premium Bonds and investments had dwindled and girly pink fluff arrived in the post for her instead.

He passed on his love for history and together they would wander around castles or ancient burial sites and he would tell her tales far more exaggerated than those he had managed to find out. She was the reason he had bought a car, so that they could explore places that were not on bus routes. Annabel was usually glad for the day's reprieve and although she would occasionally have a stab of jealousy at the way in which Georgia responded to her uncle, she also appreciated the time and effort he put in.

The contact had diminished slightly as Georgia had entered her teens; he'd mistakenly thought that she wouldn't want to spend time with a dusty old bugger such as himself when she had plenty of friends and daily after-school activities, but he had been wrong and Georgia would have liked to have remained close to her uncle, but had heeded her mother's warning of not making herself a nuisance.

Therefore, Godfrey had been vaguely aware of, but had not known the depth of, his niece's difficulties with Ray. Annabel had certainly not alluded to them and Godfrey, not one for reading the red tops, never really guessed that the garden was anything other than rosy.

Annabel had phoned in distress a couple days after Georgia's disappearance, but had simply said that there had been a row, a misunderstanding, and if Georgia were to turn up at Godfrey's house, then he was to explain that all was forgiven and for her to return home.

Godfrey had been upset at the news given Georgia's relative youth, but had just assumed that she just wanted a little peace; that she wanted to make her own way in the world and had therefore not thought a great deal of it. He had received cards on (well, around) his birthdays from her, postmarked Tavsham, so he wasn't worried for her safety, but apart from a couple of lines of chat about living with a bunch of friends and thoughts of trying for college, he'd heard nothing and had no real insight into her situation.

In time, Margaret reached her conclusions about the Eglwys Fach waters, informing her small but polite audience that it was only really a twist of fate that Eglwys Fach had remained a settlement of ten houses and a mountain, whereas Cysgod y Ffynnon had exploded into a town of fifteen thousand people and a dozen struggling hotels. She blushed and fiddled with her pendant as the small audience gave a ripple of applause and thanked her greatly for the interesting in-depth insight that she had provided.

Everyone, save Godfrey, who was on a budget, retraced their steps to the bar to lubricate their passage into the debate. Godfrey took the opportunity of being alone and whipped out a plastic bag and stuffed a selection of the buffet's remaining sandwiches into his folder, once more allowing his warped sense of conscience to wipe out the extravagance of the earlier pint.

The debate passed without any real interest, mainly because all the arguments had been resolved at previous airings, unbeknownst to Margaret who would have been distraught had she been informed of her faux pas. The minimal business of the night was dealt with and the following month's details were confirmed: Godfrey sighed inwardly as Rolf Raven proudly announced his intention to regale all with the events and happenings that led to the shaping of the nearby village of Glan-yr-Afon.

Godfrey rounded up the night by clapping his hands together and thanking Margaret once more for her delivery and wishing people a safe journey home. As usual, they chuckled as he was the one with the bicycle with the dim dynamo-driven lights on a wide but rural road and they were the ones with cars. He left them to enjoy the social element of the society as they lingered for a chat over their drinks and the remaining curly sandwiches. Godfrey thought that he really didn't have the time to afford such luxuries as chit chat, what with work tomorrow and all Margaret's notes to write up for the log book whilst it was still fresh in his mind. After he had retired, well, it would be a different story then and he was looking forward to stopping for a pointless chinwag.

He took his usual time to pack his rucksack and assume his cyclist's attire, during which his fellow society members quickly forgot about him, closed themselves into a circle and began chattering and laughing in a way that always surprised him considering the sobriety of the meeting that he had just chaired. Eventually, rucksack on, Council reflective vest tightly Velcroed in place and helmet fastened securely under his chin, he bid them all goodnight once more and disappeared into the darkness.

It was a cool night with a beautiful moon as he clambered onto his bike. As he set off on the quiet main road to Cysgod y Ffynnon, he saw the Sustrans sign pointing to the newly-opened cycle route that passed Audrey and Jerry Gloucester's Tŷ Mawr; the one that Audrey had rubbished so readily when he'd met her a few weeks before. Relishing the idea of turning off the light's dynamo, which slowed his progress on the hills, he slipped into the quiet lane and set off, curious to see where the route took him.

The lane wound narrowly between two high hedges and as he passed the openings to two farm tracks, he heard the barking of dogs unused to passers-by at this time of night. He could feel the surface of the lane deteriorate under his tyres as weeds grew in the centre of the tarmac, but this actually helped him to locate the route in the moonlit night and he happily meandered along enjoying the solitude and mild adventure.

The road eventually bore to the left where it would end up in another farmyard and he saw the cycle route sign pointing off down an old green lane that had been part re-surfaced to enable safe and easy passage for its new cycle traffic. This must be the section that Audrey mentioned – the one that, in her opinion, cost more per user, per linear metre, than the Mall.

Through the trees, he could see a blaze of lights and eventually he pulled up at the rickety wooden back gate to the vast stone property he recognised as Tŷ Mawr. Lights were on throughout and as Godfrey stood and looked, the hallway and stairs section clicked off. Godfrey started and he felt rightly guilty for being a voyeur until he remembered Audrey's words about the numerous time switches. After a few minutes he felt his inquisitiveness overtake his manners and he looked at the fastening of the rear gate and saw how simple it was. Tentatively, he pushed at it and then bumped it round as it had dropped on its hinges. He wheeled his bicycle into the garden and leant it against the thick overgrown hedge – another job that the cleaner Eira Howard's husband had neglected to tender for, tutted Godfrey: what a wasted opportunity.

Godfrey sauntered over the rough lawn and crept up to a lit window. The Gloucesters' security system left a great deal to be desired as Godfrey was able to peer through the large window and study the goods on display behind the glass. The room he was looking at was an overtly male domain that appealed to him. It had a sturdy oak desk with a leather inset. A green shaded desk lamp threw a warm glow over the room and Godfrey traced the wire to a battered socket with a gleaming white time switch giving the game away all too easily. Godfrey looked enviously at the many shelves filled with books that had been amassed over generations.

Books were Godfrey's passion and the older, the better. They were one of his few financial Achilles' heels and he would allow himself an afternoon trawling Hay-on-Wye's eclectic book shops every six weeks or so, whereby he would loiter for hours before his careful purchases were made. Indeed, it was the main reason he allowed himself to keep his car. It was nearly impossible to get a bus to Hay and back in a day and the thought of missing a connection and having to fork out for a taxi or, God forbid, a night in a hotel, had clinched the decision to retain it.

His alcoves at home were filled with a mishmash of shelves, cobbled together from various offcuts of wood, MDF and ply, and painfully screwed into the walls with the help of his father's bradawl and hand-powered drill. These shelves were stacked high with second-hand purchases that he would read from cover to cover, absorbing every detail as he went.

His main interest was local history and this was the reason that few of the presentations at the History Society gatherings were new to him. As every avid reader will understand, his gaze scanned disinterested over the paintings, the stuffed animals in their dusty glass boxes and the carved wooden ornaments as he squinted to read the titles of the books.

The books had no particular order and ancient encyclopaedias were stacked next to John Wyndham, who was leant on by *Fish of the Wye*. Godfrey's eyes finally fell on a rare treasure in the shape of *The Elan Valley: a History of Greatness and Sorrow* by T R Hope and his avaricious juices flowed. He had spent hours in Hay-on-Wye looking for this book, of which there had been only a limited number of copies printed.

He had once found a splendid version, but its perfect hardback condition had commanded a high price, one that Godfrey was not prepared to pay (and the shop owner was too fed up with the cautious dusty bloke who had cluttered up his aisles and freely drunk the complementary coffee all afternoon to accept a half price offer). Godfrey had later regretted not making the purchase. There were many simple archives about the experience of the Elan Valley, a rural farming community some ten miles east of Cysgod y Ffynnon that had been flooded and a series of dams built to collect clean water. Leaflets could tell him that the project had been built between 1893 and 1904, and still today piped clean water seventy-three miles to Birmingham, but he had wanted more substance, more details of the history and the experiences of the people who had had their livelihoods and way of life compulsorily purchased from under them for the purpose of sending water from their hills to people that they would never meet.

He had intended to use the Elan Valley as his next personal topic at the History Society, but wanted more than the usual tales, to dig a little deeper than the descriptions on display in the Elan Valley Visitor Centre. Godfrey stood looking at the book, its dustcover doing a valuable job and showing that it hadn't been touched for months, if not years. He was not a devious man by nature and certainly not a thief, and he knew that someone who collected books such as Jerry Gloucester obviously did, would be more than happy to loan them to a fellow collector, someone who would look after them and appreciate them as much as he did. He would be *bound* to lend them, knowing that the precious copy would be returned in due course without having to be asked for.

An idea flitted across Godfrey's mind, was dismissed and then allowed to flit back once more. He knew where the key was. He (sort of) knew Mrs G, and was actually helping her sort out her affairs and he felt he knew Jerry well enough by proxy to know that he wouldn't mind. A week's loan would probably be enough, if not then definitely no more than two. He also knew that he was trustworthy enough to simply borrow that one book without being tempted to rummage through Jerry's personal belongings, or disturb anything in a way that would cause distress to the house's owners – indeed, they were used to strangers in the house, and pretty useless ones at that, in the form of Mr and Mrs Howard. No, what they didn't know wouldn't hurt them and if they weren't there to grant permission, what was he to do?

And so, Godfrey crept round to the side of the house,

being careful to stay on the grass, so as not to leave prints in the mossy path. The outside light at the side porch easily lit his route and he peered through the kitchen window just to double check that no one was at home.

The vast kitchen was as soulless as it had been on his previous invited visit and the leaves in the middle of the stone floor convinced him that no one had entered since. He felt for the key and found it easily – almost an open invite for all, he justified to himself. He pushed at the door, unwilling to shoulder it as roughly as Audrey had in fear that a bang would set off any farm dogs unused to such a noise. Luckily, Audrey's shouldering seemed to have been for her own satisfaction or haste and wasn't actually necessary; Godfrey's calculated and steady pressure did the job.

Godfrey stepped quietly into the big room and stood for a while listening out for noises that he knew wouldn't be there. He'd lived alone since he'd left his parents' home and therefore emptiness had never been an issue for him and he well knew the creaks and groans of a vacant house. He looked around at the kitchen at his leisure, noticing the dusty crockery displayed on the Welsh dresser, the large china bowls filled with the general clutter that even a second home gathers and the dust that hung in feathered pendants next to the full fly papers in the corners of the yellowed ceiling. The Christmas tree that Audrey had muttered about having to get for her Christmas guests stood leaning at an angle, looking decidedly sad with half of its needles on the floor. Bad luck was storing up in this house, it being long past Twelfth Night; Audrey had better get back here pretty quickly …

Godfrey's distinctive morality became evident once more

as he quickly decided that to look at things that were clearly on display was acceptable, but to rummage behind closed doors would be without invitation. Therefore, he was happy to study the china and memorise the make and style in order to value it out of interest later, but it would have been wrong to open the dresser drawers that bulged with correspondence. He leafed through the selection of Barbours and raincoats on the rack of pegs running the width of an alcove, but he would not venture into their pockets. He tutted with incredulity at the ninety-watt bulb that lit the lampshade on its fine oak pedestal and wished he had the authority to swap it for a low energy one and to reduce the hours on the time clock: really, those hours were excessive, even for this time of year.

Closer inspection of the nearest time-clock showed him that he only had about ten minutes of lit time left and he moved quickly to his goal. Godfrey clunked open the latch on the dark wooden door that led from the kitchen and he stepped out into the now dark hall. The smell of musty dampness hit him with greater effect; this area of the house didn't have the benefit of under-door or chimney ventilation and the thick but worn carpets retained the moisture from the air.

He felt his way along the wall, noticing the soft plaster under many layers of wallpaper and made for what he presumed would be the study, the light shining round the outside and through the cracks of another old door.

He pushed it open and suddenly felt the intruder that he was. It dawned on him as to how exposed he was to any passer-by – such as he had been – perhaps someone would be out walking their dog last thing? Perhaps Mrs Howard wasn't as useless as she had been given credit for and looked in on the house as she walked past on the way back from checking the stock? Maybe someone was asleep upstairs?

He quickly sought and then grabbed the book on the Elan Valley, then loosened the regiment of books surrounding it so that its absence wouldn't leave an obvious gaping hole. He mentally noted the book's neighbours in case there was a system – it had sat between *The War Years in Radnorshire* and *Tickling Trout and Snaring Hares; a poacher reveals all*. He fought the desire to grab both of those books as well and instead, fled. Although still careful to leave everything as he had found it, by the time he wheeled his bike back into the lane, Godfrey was running like a child afraid of being caught scrumping.

Chapter 8

Second-hand Sanitary Wear

Godfrey whistled softly as he cycled into his road; it was a quiet estate of 1950s semi-detached houses, each with a good-sized garden. It was respectable to the point of boredom and was deserted at that time of night, the few street lights being little more than adequate to light the way round the estate loop for mid-evening dog-walkers. The ambience suited Godfrey. He had bought his house with a mind to it being the ideal place to bring up his family, but well, that hadn't come to fruition quite yet...

Godfrey swung his leg over his saddle and glided to a halt in his short drive in the way that children try to do in order to mimic men of Godfrey's age. Easily too mean to leave an outdoor light on, Godfrey rummaged in the zipped pocket of his rucksack for his keys. The additional weight of the book in his bag still troubled him slightly, but the short journey home had allowed his conscience to return to that of a passionate book-lover, rather than of a deceitful thief.

He hummed softly to himself as he approached his side door until he stubbed his toe on something that made him start. The bundle at his feet made a sound and this made him stumble back in shock: "Who's that? Who's there?" he said, his voice high with not quite believable bravado.

"Uncle?" it returned quietly and then broke into sobs, "Uncle God?"

As they sat in the kitchen, Godfrey passed Georgia a second cup of tea. Seeing that she had easily finished the two rounds of cheese sandwiches that he had given her, Godfrey went back to the counter and extracted several more of the landlord's best ham sandwiches from his folder.

She looked dreadful. Her face was swollen from tears and exhausted from the events of the last few days, which had come on top of the general stress and drama of giving birth to a first child at an unsupported sixteen years old. In his quiet and gentle manner, Godfrey hadn't pushed for information, allowing her to sob quietly, hugging the foul-smelling baby in her arms.

Her long brown hair was greasy and in no particular style, her skin was spotty and pale and an untreated cold sore sat painfully on her upper lip. He took in but didn't judge her clothes, her jacket cheap and unable to cope with her newly engorged chest and sagging stomach, and her jeans grubby from general grime and baby related substances. Godfrey's calm and methodical manner helped Georgia feel at ease and she was soon reaching for the third sandwich, this one spiced up with a little ketchup.

Although few people had bothered making it into Godfrey's kitchen, those that had, had found it old fashioned and charmless. When he had bought the house in the late 1970s, its modern pine fitted units had been one of the vendor's main selling points, but although they were still clean, they were tired, and the items within them were functional and uninspired. No one in this house had ever felt the need to write anything funny in fridge magnets, or even bought a frivolous Christmas gadget to grace the Formica work surfaces. It was a DIY enthusiast's dream project, a speculator's dinner party tale and the miserable abode of a man who had never known the pleasure of treating himself once in a while.

As Georgia began to look more relaxed and secure, so she started to release her grasp on the bundle in her arms and eventually Jocey Willow was introduced to Great Uncle Godfrey. Six and a half pounds and surprisingly content, Jocey stared vacantly at Godfrey and his heart flushed with warmth. His arms instinctively went out to her and Georgia awkwardly relinquished her charge, still not confident in her ability to hold, carry or pass over a baby correctly.

Godfrey was amazed at how comfortable he felt, the little scrap in his arms seemed happy to be there and he cradled her head in his hand and cooed. He'd always wanted children – he still did – and he always thought that he would be a good dad. His own father had been austere and so worried about what other people thought of him that he was unable to do anything that might be considered unmanly or puerile. Godfrey and Annabel had grown up in a humourless house, with little joy or frivolity. However, Godfrey had always thought that he would be more than happy to do his share of rolling around on a carpet, walking the miles with a pram or pushing swings.

He knew little about the practical care of babies, save what he'd gathered from the trials of parents in his office, but he did know that there was rarely time to do anything but be prepared for the next phase in the feed, clean, sleep cycle. He could also see that Georgia was exhausted and needed immediate attention herself.

Cradling Jocey in his arms, he led Georgia to the bathroom, dug out a couple of ragged towels and set the shower running. The fact that his shampoo and soap was supermarket own-brand may have dismayed the Georgia of two years ago, but for someone who had spent their time since feeling grubby and trying to keep clean via public or shop toilets and the occasional snatched bath at a friend's, to have a hot shower, a locked door and two towels to wrap oneself in at the end, was bliss.

As bidden, she shamefully left her soiled clothes outside the door and Godfrey, in return, left a luxurious dressing gown and some thick flannel pyjamas that had once belonged to his father and which he had been saving for best. The harsh soap and astringent shampoo soon worked their magic and Georgia's young, tough body began recovering from the trauma of the past few days.

In the meantime, Godfrey assessed the smelly baby in his arms and the provisions that Georgia still had in a large carrier bag. Enough nappies for a few days more, a couple of vests and Babygros, some cardigans knitted up by the good fingers of the Friends of the Hospital (who would have felt their endeavours to be more than worthwhile had they seen the pitiful scene waiting outside at Godfrey's door that cold night).

Godfrey was a careful but practical man; years of living alone and making do and mending had left him with a methodical and reasoned approach to any problem and thus he set about the baby's needs in the same manner as he would a repair to his bicycle's gears.

He laid Jocey on the work surface and unwrapped the crocheted blanket, checking it for grime. It was grubby, but not soiled and it would certainly do for a while without a wash. Not so with the next layers and as he peeled them off, he was amazed to see how such a small baby could make such a fantastically-coloured mess. Despite the smell, he noted how the nappy was positioned and fastened before he removed that too and he pushed around the remaining faeces with his not-particularly-absorbent value toilet roll.

The sink was clear of dishes – the night's "eating out" had not necessitated dirtying any crockery and, using a freshly boiled kettle, he ran a bowl-full of water with a small squirt of washing-up liquid and cooled it to a temperature he thought suitable for a baby.

Those who stipulate the need for extensive classes in child-rearing would have been amazed at how simple he made it look as he held Jocey's back and head in one hand and gently splashed soapy water over her with the other, cooing while he did so. Inspired by his efforts, he ran another, less soapy, bowl to rinse her off and then wrapped her in the more luxurious of his tea towels and gently patted her dry.

He put Jocey's and Georgia's soiled clothes in the washing machine, correctly guessing at Georgia's embarrassment at her uncle handling her most intimate items and thinking them best out of the way. He was unable to break his rule of "full loads only" and foraged around in his own bedroom for the remainder. When Georgia eventually came out of the bathroom, baby Jocey was snuggled up on Godfrey's chest, clean and sweet-smelling in a new set of clothes with her tufts of hair sticking straight up and Godfrey's large hands keeping her warm and safe. Georgia began to weep again, with relief as much as anything, and Jocey's restless snuffles broke over into hungry cries with just seconds to spare.

Godfrey settled Georgia into his old leather armchair and passed her her daughter. He wrapped them both in a big blanket and left them in peace as Jocey suckled contentedly at her mother's breast and Georgia, not really knowing about the debates of breast versus bottle, but having been aware that there would have been no way she could have bottle fed her baby from the squat, did exactly what the midwife had told her and felt calm and at ease for the first time in just over nine months.

Chapter 9

Unravelling Jumpers

Godfrey sat at the kitchen table, tired-eyed and feeling stiff after a night of interruptions. It was six-thirty a.m. and he sipped at his coffee after having taken Georgia a cup to drink as Jocey fed from her. Jocey had woken three times in the night and each time he had gone in to check all was well. He had changed her once and then walked her up and down the dark hall until she settled and he was able to return her to her sleeping mother's bed.

His life had never known such disruption. A man of routine, he went to bed at the same time each night, read for an instinctively fixed period and slept soundly for eight hours, waking only once at three-thirtyish in order to empty his bladder. His waking routine was similarly fixed, rising over the period of a particular news programme, drinking his office-sourced coffee, packing his bag and leaving the house at eight-twenty. For nigh on thirty years, his life had consisted of this, with his weekend routine swaying perhaps an hour either way with maybe a late night film, or a bit of a lie-in.

Inherently, Godfrey was a caring man, albeit one without much practice at caring for anyone other than himself and his main concerns that morning related to Georgia and Jocey. Whereas Georgia had seemed to have decided that to get to Uncle Godfrey's would be enough in itself, in reality the logistical problems were just starting.

Georgia had been hazy about her life for the past two years and Godfrey had not felt it his place to pry at this time. She'd skipped over her journey from Tavsham to Cysgod y Ffynnon, having apparently spent the night in a motorway service station's toilets – plenty of room to lie down in a disabled toilet, hot water, padded changing mat for Jocey to sleep on and relatively undisturbed too. One thing she had been adamant about, however, was that he must not contact her mother, Annabel. He had agreed to this, seeing how important it was to Georgia's ability to feel safe and comfortable for the night, but only on condition that they discuss it another day.

Hearing movements from the small spare room, Godfrey drained his coffee and, feeling he needed every ounce of caffeine that it had to offer, hauled himself stiffly to his feet and set off to see if he could help.

Godfrey's colleagues were concerned when at eight forty-five, his usual place in the kitchen was not filled. It was his habit to delay the start of the real working day as long as possible and this had been quite easy to do since the introduction of flexi-time. People would drift in from eight o'clock onwards according to their particular lifestyles. Hywel, an ex-military man from Debt Recovery would arrive at 07.58 hours, shoes shined and hair greased into place and by 08.05 he would be determining his schedule for the day having scanned the news headlines and had a slick and time-efficient shit. He would then make himself a cup of black coffee in a gleaming mug that was not entrusted to the rigours of the general kitchen, but was instead kept, polished, at nor-nor-west on his desk.

Angie, Anwen and Eleri worked a rota between them of delivering and collecting their kids to and from each other's houses and then on to school to allow them the most from their obsession with making-up flexi-time. None started work until all had arrived, but for at least two out of every three days, they were able to clock in by eight. The younger, child-free staff used the purpose of flexi-time to the full and dragged themselves to their desks at unpredictable times and in unpredictable states, depending on the frolics of the night before.

But Godfrey: not in and no word by eight forty-five? Yes, Godfrey took sickies, but even these were predictable and were due to a lack of motivation, rather than a lack of health. The administrative staff were usually given notice of the impending sick leave by about lunchtime the day before – when he would saunter into their office, stand at the window and either blink at the bright lights (headache to migraine) or stroke his painful neck (sore throat to chest infection). This would happen again at mid-afternoon tea and then before home-time in deepening degrees of severity and so, by the next day, a phone call by eight-thirty would be both expected and forthcoming.

But today? By nine a.m. nearly the whole section was in the reception office – phone round the hospitals? Any news of car accidents? Someone must go round to his house, and so, amongst giggles, straws were being prepared for pulling as people guessed at the possibilities.

"I'm not going," laughed Anwen. "He'll be naked, trussed up, with an orange in his arse and his dominatrix's leather boot in his mouth."

"No, no," said Angie, "the police'll have had him – it'll be for all those disappearing puppies that have been in his bag for so long."

"Oh don't," tutted Sandra. "He could have had a heart attack, could be there now, gasping his last breath. Go on, get his number, I'll ring to check."

As Angie reached for the personnel file, the phone rang and everyone looked at it. Sandra growled as no one made to pick it up, and finally dived for it herself. "Good morning, Council Tax. Oh, hello, Godfrey, are you OK? Me? Lunch? Well, of course. I'll be there at 12.30ish? What number? OK. See you then. Goodbye."

Everyone stood gaping at her as she put the phone down. Enjoying the suspense she looked up and said, "Right, well, God's fine, he's having a couple of days off, and I'm going round there at lunchtime, apparently to give some advice!" They all stared, desperate to know the ins and outs, "Oh, and…" she said as she swept out of the room with an armful files "…I'm sure I could hear a baby crying in the background—" and as she closed the door on her office next door, she smiled as she heard the tumult explode into a hundred questions and theories. Not much going to be done today she surmised. Correctly.

Sandra spent a distracted morning. She had set aside the

day for drawing up effective Performance Indicators for her section following a course the previous week and was struggling. Her attitude prior to that session had been "just work as hard as you bloody can and it'll be fine" and that had seemed to do the job. Yes, they had good periods and lean periods and there would always be lazy folks in every office, but now the Just Get It Done attitude was no longer sufficient to the task.

Therefore, in the name of increased productivity, she had sat through a two-day course that, minus the role play and ice breakers, could easily have been completed in a morning. The upshot was that she had to compile a list of indicators that could prove how well her section was running and provide ammunition against any member of the public hacked off by the size of their Community Charge bill. For the third time, she crossed out "answer phone within five rings" and clutched her hair in futility.

Her mind drifted easily back to the earlier phone call and meandered over its content and what it might mean. Godfrey and an unplanned day off? That was strange in itself, but to ask her for lunch and to have to take the morning off to prepare for it? Surely the request for advice was a bluff? Could it possibly be that the feelings that had been growing over the last couple of years were reciprocated?

Sandra had worked with Godfrey for nearly eight years. In that time she had gone from being a competent mum of two and very much the wife of Dave, police officer and captain of the local darts team to single mum whose pants now needed two clothes pegs when hanging on the washing line. Her way of life had changed radically when Dave had walked out three years ago, leaving her and their two teenage children to their "life of blandness" while he chose "freedom and adventure" and moved in with Hayley and her two teenage children. Hayley was captain of the ladies' team; she could sit at a bar on a stool by herself and hold her own. She wore animal prints and had a devil-may-care attitude to smoking too much that Dave apparently admired.

The separation and resulting divorce had rocked Sandra's whole existence and her feelings of shock, shame and indignation had taken months to work through. Godfrey had been a gentle source of comfort during that time. Not that he meant to be, it was just that he didn't gossip, would listen non-judgementally to the things she said – as long as he was standing next to the kettle – and he was the even keel that she craved.

It was the whole package about Godfrey that she found so enticing, not just individual elements of him. She loved his broad shoulders, his large hands and his look of contentment. He never rushed, he never panicked, he just went about his daily life in a haze of quiet self-assurance. It was if he were waiting for something to happen – and knew that it would and that he was just keeping his head down, quietly getting on with things, until his turn came. For someone as rushed and in demand as Sandra, Godfrey's calmness was a paradise to aspire to.

As a younger woman, she would never in her most fantastic dreams have been attracted to a man such as Godfrey, preferring the excitement of racier catches like Dave. However, her recent experiences had made her question what she looked for in a man and now she found herself drawn to Godfrey and often made up situations in which he would reveal hidden depths which would allow her to have the last laugh over Hayley – who was actually well on her way to alcoholism, with Dave now following close behind. She would spend pleasant hours imagining scenarios involving the capable, calm Godfrey. Her Performance Indicators course tutor would be impressed at her ability to role play, an ability that she really hadn't let rip at the seminar. But these scenarios didn't involve a harassed member of the public and an overworked council officer; they were of Godfrey cycling round a corner and finding her with a puncture and not only mending it, but whisking her off for a weekend away – after having organised someone to look after the kids and put the piles of washing away.

Sandra didn't require animal prints on lycra jockstraps; two pairs of comfortable pants hung from their four pegs, blowing side by side in a good breeze was all that she sought from a future partner. Shared responsibility and a hand with the garden. Not too much to ask from life, surely?

Glad that she had an office to herself, she brushed her hair throughout the morning and smoothed down her tailored trousers, carefully arranging and re-arranging her blouse to cover the elasticated panels at her waist. At ten past twelve, she re-wrote "answer phone within five rings", added "must say 'Good Morning / Afternoon, Council Tax Section, XX speaking. How may I help you' in both English and Welsh and thought, "Sod it." She walked out the door, making sure she used the back stairs, previously intended as the servant's staircase, in order to avoid stares and requests for further information.

Chapter 10

Borrowing from the Collection Plate

Godfrey had been quite relieved to abandon the house and its new residents on a gallant quest to source provisions. He set off leaving Georgia and Jocey snuggled up in front of morning television, its trivia being the ideal undemanding companion. He took the unusual step of stopping off in a café and ordered first just a coffee and then thought "hang it" and started tucking into a full breakfast, reading the café's chosen red top and, in doing so, learnt more about the female form and psyche than he had done in a decade of day to day life.

Over an indulgent second coffee he deliberated upon his next moves. Asking Sandra to come over had been a good plan. He had always liked Sandra; liked what she stood for and her gentle way of life, and much more so after her abandonment by Dave and his insatiable dart – particularly after the unnecessary "get a life" comment that Dave had off-handedly thrown at him at the office party a few years back when Godfrey had declined the offer of being in a round.

He was slowly coming to the conclusion that Sandra was his kind of lady; one that he could see himself settling down and having a family with, if previously-made plans went awry. Godfrey still firmly believed that there was plenty of time in life to do all the things that he had aspired to, but never been in quite the position to instigate, as far back as his teens. He still felt that he would make a good dad and husband; he also felt that when the time was right his dream woman and, soon after, a family would drop into his lap without any effort or discomfort on his behalf. His current problem was that the person who he had lined up for such a lifestyle hadn't contacted him for thirty-two years and he didn't really know many other suitable candidates to size up, deliberate on and when the time became right, encourage to allow what would be, to be. However, that would obviously all change when he retired – indeed, he had just that morning noted that for a fallback position, the café may be a good place to strike up a pleasant conversation with a pretty lady and let nature take its course.

And so Sandra was happily put on the back boiler for the time being; someone to remain convivial with before it was definite that his existing plans weren't going to happen or until it was no longer inappropriate to mix work with pleasure. It didn't bother his male ego that she was his boss; he knew that the job could easily have been his should he have slipped out of his comfort zone for long enough to fill in an application form, and so he harboured no real grudges toward Sandra, although he had been somewhat surprised that he hadn't been handed it regardless of such nonsense as application forms (but in a bureaucracy such as the Council, when did anything sensible ever make sense?).

She was a little mumsy for his tastes, which hadn't really changed since they'd been formed in the seventies. Therefore she didn't really fit in with his ideal, which came in the guise of a beautiful woman with long blonde hair hanging around her face. She would have burnt her bra (which would have been a large one) or done at least *something* terminal with it, and be wearing something like a Pan's People costume. Even at the time when such a woman existed, it had never occurred to him that he was not something that looked as if he had just fallen out of Saturday Night Fever; he simply did not see himself and his life in the same judgemental way that others did.

Therefore, he felt completely adequate when at twelve twenty-seven the front door was tapped and he opened it, clothed in his weekend garb of work clothes, minus the tie and with a home-knitted fawn cable jumper instead of a jacket. He welcomed Sandra and, with the moderate discomfort of someone who rarely has guests, shuffled about a bit asking her if she would like a cup of tea to go with her sandwich.

A squawk from the sitting room brought an immediate gush from Sandra, and Godfrey was forgotten as she rushed in to coo over the little treasure. An exhausted Georgia was more than happy to hand over her bundle to an obvious expert, who immediately settled the little scrap to her bosom. Georgia looked the same as every other proud parent as Sandra gushed at how beautiful Jocey was. Sandra also knew how terrible Georgia would be feeling physically and her vocal empathy allowed Georgia to dissolve into tears.

Twigging quite quickly that Godfrey was out of his depth, Sandra took charge and ordered the kettle to be put on. "Get her a glass of water as well; she needs to drink lots if she is to feed this little darling." She could smell that the baby needed changing and asked if she could have the honour, to which Georgia gratefully agreed. Sandra rummaged in Godfrey's bags of provisions, found the bare essentials and set about deftly returning the baby into a bundle of joy. Godfrey mooched about in the kitchen as Sandra talked with Georgia, reassuring, asking and answering questions and generally cooing. She then came into the kitchen to address Godfrey.

"Right…she seems OK considering what she's been through. The baby seems OK too, but I'm no expert. She needs to see a midwife as soon as possible – if not, a doctor. And then she'll need regular checks and advice. She also needs a list of things as long as your arm – it's OK, God," Sandra smiled, misreading the alarm in his eyes, "she'll be fine. She's not the first woman it's happened to and she won't be the last."

Sandra then borrowed a biro, which looked suspiciously as if it had started life in the office's stationery cupboard, and scribbled a list on the back of an envelope. Halfway through, a thought came into her head and a tingle tingled in her gut. "Oh, hang on, I think I have at least some of these in the attic at home. They use them for such a short time that they'll still be as good as new – you can come and get them if you want to?" Again, she misread the look in his eyes. "I'll look them out tonight. Come around tomorrow evening if you want them …"

She gave a few more tips, a bit of advice and some orders, quite relishing her new position of matronly authority and then took her leave, not noticing that she had left her sandwich behind uneaten, but knowing damn well that she'd left her scent-squirted silk scarf.

Sandra bluffed her way through the afternoon, trying to dismiss the inquisition with, *Ooh, just a bit of advice for a family friend, now where's that report?* She decided not to work to her usual five-thirty that night and slunk off with a pile of files and an excitement-induced headache at four.

Sandra was an efficient, practical lady, but she was also a dreamer. By the time she reached home, she and Godfrey had been trapped in the attic by a dodgy loft hatch and she was sleeping with her head in his lap, his big strong hand stroking the soft hair that he had secretly yearned to caress.

She greeted her children, Daniel, fifteen and Sophie, thirteen, in their usual after-school position: on the sofa, feet on the coffee table, a large plate of cheese sandwiches each balanced precariously on their respective sofa arms. They grunted in reply, waiting for the usual "Homework!" tirade which didn't arrive.

"She's on the blob," sneered Daniel.

"Don't be disgusting," retorted Sophie, "she doesn't have things like that any more, stupid." Her face creased with revulsion at the thought of it.

Sandra changed quickly into old clothes and reconnoitred the attic – better to make Godfrey help her down with things rather than have them in a pile by the door – keep him in the house longer. She rummaged around and spotted the crib, baby bath and pushchair, all wrapped in plastic to keep the dust out; she'd always wanted a third child, but Dave had never been keen. She also spotted a box labelled *sheets* and knew that it was full of baby linen and towels. Great – now she could look as if she weren't trying too hard but that she still kept a tidy attic. She threw a mackintosh over a dusty exercise bike and once more rued the lack of commitment she had shown to it. She then climbed down, replaced the hatch, and cleaned the house from top to bottom. Just a quick wipe around the inside of the vacuum cylinder and she would be done.

Her final act when she stood back to admire her handiwork was to whip a large pair of plain white pants off the radiator, and suddenly the whole room seemed a little warmer …

Chapter 11

Reading by Street Light

Mansel was excited. He had been up early and cleaned all the burger boxes out of his car and it was smelling almost fresh – or at least would have been had he not trodden on a tomato sauce sachet in the footwell of the passenger seat. He'd had a shower and had made an effort to clean himself, rather than just stand in it and hope. He'd arranged with Lucy-Ann to pick her up at ten-thirty and he was feeling on time. Just a quick swing by the florists to pick up the flowers he'd ordered and he was ready for a great day out.

He was so excited at how things were going with Lucy-Ann. He'd come to realise that she was a reserved person who liked her own company and didn't go out much. So far, aside from the Superman meal out, they'd had just two more dates and a walk in the park on a drizzly January afternoon. In Mansel's terms, they'd gone really well.

He'd tried to curb the excitement that usually made him prattle, but he'd found that Lucy-Ann really didn't seem to mind. She would laugh at his comments and smile at his coltish behaviour, as long as it didn't go on for too long. "Man-sellll," she would warn and he then knew it was time to calm down, take the item, whatever it was that time, off his head and change the subject.

Today he had high hopes that they would both enjoy their day. He'd spent a long time deciding what they might do, as he'd promised her a special time – and all she had to do was open her door at ten-thirty with a coat and a smile.

Lucy-Ann was already waiting outside her small terraced house when he turned up, although he was early, clutching her bag and wearing a red coat. "Hello!" she chirped and jumped into his car, slipping a bit as she stepped on the remainder of the sauce. "How are you? I'm very excited about today – am I allowed to know where we're going to go?"

"No," said Mansel, "it's a surprise – I think you'll love it!" He wanted to bend over and give her a kiss, as he'd managed to sneak a couple in on their last date, but he sensed she was a little shy again and instead he smiled at her and pulled away down the road.

They chatted quite happily for a while about what they had been up to that week and their jobs. Mansel had cleaned four marker-pen "sex"es from a slide, picked up two condoms and a tampon inside a wendy house and pushed a rotting badger a little further under a park hedge. Lucy-Ann sold advertising space from her office at home and had made 124 phone calls, written 57 letters and had sold £5,874 worth of adverts, exceeding her target by £1,874. It made Mansel feel a bit of a lazy shite. "That's because you are one…" smiled Lucy-Ann. It was her first *"many a true word said in jest"* joke, but Mansel didn't mind: it meant that she was getting to know him yet *still* wanted to spend the day with him.

They stopped for a hot drink on the way and sat on a café

veranda enjoying the weak winter sunshine on their faces. "It's just so lovely to be outside," said Lucy-Ann, turning her little pointy nose upwards towards the sky, "I don't think I've been any further than the postbox all week."

"Really?" asked Mansel. "How come? Don't you need to buy milk, talk to people, make sure that they know that you're still alive? I'd be like one of those old people queuing outside the post office at seven-thirty in the morning just to have a chat if I didn't see anyone for a day! How do you manage?"

"I talk all day to people, you know, on the phone. I get sick of talking sometimes – sick of the sound of my own voice! Sometimes it's nice just to shut the door and keep the rest of the world out." Mansel shrugged, not really knowing how to answer – was she dropping a hint? He'd missed so many in the past. However, she must have read his mind, as she quickly turned to him and took his arm, "Present company excepted, of course!" Mansel glowed as he drained the rest of his cappuccino with marshmallows, grated chocolate and whipped cream.

"Come on, let's get going, still half an hour to go before we get to the surprise!"

"I can't wait," she said. "As long as it is nothing to do with those football medals you seem to carry everywhere…"

Mansel was having a quick listen to the sports report on the car radio and Lucy-Ann had drifted into her own world when they turned in to Cae Du. Mansel pulled into the nearly empty shingle car park and had slid into a space before Lucy-Ann realised that they were stopping. "Oh, is this it? Are we here now? Sorry, I was nearly dropping off – where are we? I didn't catch the signs."

"Aha!" said Mansel, keen to prolong the anticipation. "Come on, out you get, you're going to love this!" He jumped out the car and ran around to her door and whipped it open. He helped her out and told her to shut her eyes. He carefully put her coat on her, brushing a few guinea pig hairs from the back before he did so and pressed her bag into her hands. "Right then. Ready?"

He walked her slowly over the shingle, enjoying her leaning on his arm, still with her eyes shut. Finally they were standing in front of the entrance and Mansel said, "OK, you can open them!" and he blew a little fanfare on a pretend trumpet that he found in his coat pocket.

The entrance was a carved wooden archway that had "Cae Du Petting Zoo" painted over it. Mansel stood with his hands outstretched "Ta da!" he shouted and waited for her to burst into laughter.

It went silent.

Lucy-Ann looked at him: she wasn't laughing. She looked again at the entrance and then back at him. He sensed something was wrong but he wasn't sure what on earth it could be.

Lucy-Ann shook her head and turned to him, and spoke in a quiet, wobbly voice. "OK. Very funny. Now can we go home?" He felt his guts loop the loop. "Do you know," she said, sadly, "I thought you might be different, but you're the same as *all* the rest."

Mansel was in shock. "What d'you mean? Don't you like it?"

She looked at him and her face was set. Tears welled into her eyes and one rolled down her beautiful cheek, past her freckles. "How could you? It's just all a bloody joke to you, isn't it? Well, they're the best friends that *I've* ever had, and that goes for you as well now, doesn't it. Come on. I want to go home *now* please." And she turned around and walked steadily back to the car, her head held high even when she slipped on a piece of shingle.

Mansel stood still at the entrance, looking about him, desperate for inspiration as to how to deal with this one. "Lucy-Ann," he called, "it's not supposed to be a joke; I really thought you'd like it! Lucy-Ann…"

"Yeah, yeah. Home now please." She'd reached the car and was standing dead upright, looking straight ahead. Mansel ran over to her, slipping on a loose stone as he did and falling in a pile on the dust. She didn't even look at him. He picked himself up and carried on, until he'd reached her.

"Lucy-Ann, it's not a joke. I really thought you'd enjoy it. I thought, well, you liked guinea pigs and things and therefore you'd like a place like this. It's got rabbits and—" He was brushing the dust from his clothes as he spoke to her back and picked the tiny bits of grit from his grazed palms. She carried on looking straight ahead.

"Lucy-Ann. On my life, it was never meant as a joke. I really thought…" he walked around in front of her to plead his case and was distraught to find tears pouring down her face. "What's the matter?" he asked gently. "Please tell me. I don't understand, honestly, I don't."

Lucy-Ann shrugged. "Well, it's you lot isn't it? You lot.

You think you like the look of me, and take me out. We get on OK, and then – you see my animals. You see how I live with animals people think of as kid's pets and then you think it's OK to take the piss. Well, I'm sick of it. Really sick of it." The view continued to interest her and the wind blew gently in her face, drying her tears and fanning her hair, making Mansel urge to touch its softness.

"*I* don't mind that you live with lots of animals." Mansel said quietly. "You can live with who you like. I'm just glad you wanted to spend the day with me, that's all." Now *he* was looking straight ahead and *his* voice was beginning to go a little wobbly.

Lucy-Ann turned and studied him. Then she returned to the view. She brushed the tears from her eyes and held her hair out of the way as she turned to Mansel again. "Do you mean it? Are you *honestly* saying that you didn't bring me here to humiliate me? To have a day out that you would then relate to all the boys round the bar and then stand me up on our next date?"

"Well, yes."

She pursed her lips and stared at him, obviously turning over what he had just said. "Well, now I've embarrassed myself even more, haven't I?" she said, and the tears started again. "Now I just feel so, so stupid …"

Mansel wrapped his arms around her and engulfed her in a bear hug. He was so big in comparison to her that he enveloped her whole body and rested his chin on the top of her head. He loved her scent, her smell and her fragility in his big arms. He could hear her crying softly, and he squeezed her tight, trying to stop his own tears, trying to make her feel better. Then the noise changed and finally he realised that it was a squeak for help. Quickly, he released her.

"*Phew*!" she gasped, "for one moment, I thought I was going to die in there!"

"Sorry," he smiled, "I got a little carried away!" He held her shoulders and tipped her back to look at her. "Are you OK?"

She nodded and took a deep breath. "Shall we go in?"

"Are you sure you want to?"

"Yes, I'd love to – as long as you really want to?"

"I'd love to. I've not hugged a hamster in weeks…"

Chapter 12

Ordering Macaroni Cheese

Mansel screeched to a halt in his drive and dived out of the car. He had forty minutes. Forty minutes to turn his shithole of a house into a palace fit for a young lady to dine in. *Forty minutes.* He slammed the car door shut and wrestled with his Deputy Dawg key ring to find his front door key. After losing two valuable minutes in his haste, he fell through the door and stood hyperventilating in the hall, trying to take stock.

Right. The whole place was pretty grim. He didn't have much clutter as television viewing and PlayStation gaming didn't really generate a great deal. It was more of the mountains of shoes, dirty plates, piles of hairy razor blades by the sinks etc. So, he needed an action plan. Was it best to start in the kitchen where they would be eating, or in the rest of the house so that he could clear the kitchen whilst they were preparing food?

Get the most offensive stuff out first, was his gut reaction. Yes. Some things would put off even one's own mother.

Therefore, first stop, the bathroom. He grabbed a bin liner and sprinted up the stairs. After much flushing, squirting and binning, that was soon passable. The bedroom – well, just in case, eh? Best to be over-confident than under-prepared! Wasn't that one of his Cub Scout mottos, he mused as he scraped old underwear into the wash-basket, chucked piles of coppers into a mug with an inch of cold coffee in and tucked it under the bed and did a quick dust with a used t-shirt, feeling that his old Akela would be very disappointed in the way that he had turned out.

His bed was made and then stripped and made again with clean bedding and then he sprinted back down the stairs to tackle the lounge. The piles of shoes, and plates with toast crumbs on, were soon dispatched to make a mess somewhere else and moraines of leads and game consoles were scooped to the side of the room.

The kitchen was just beginning to fill its second bin bag when the doorbell rang. Mansel was exhausted, sweaty and shaking with effort. He was not the suave picture that he wanted to be when he opened the door to his belle.

She laughed at him and he hid a bin bag with three pizza boxes sticking out the top behind his back. "Having a little clear round, Mansel?" she grinned.

"Rumbled. Guilty as charged," he said. "I had a spot of bother setting the scene. You know, finding the candles, the pink light bulbs …"

He waved her into the hall, kicking a pair of Smurf slippers out of her way as she passed.

"I instinctively knew that this place was yours," she said, "didn't have to look at the number on the door."

"I know, those neatly edged lawns are a bit of a giveaway aren't they…"

"No – funnily enough, it was the line of garden gnomes

sitting on the roof of the upstairs bay window that clinched it."

"Do you know," said Mansel as led her into the kitchen, "I'd forgotten about those. Toby and Fat Git put them there when I was away one weekend. Said it was because that's about all I'd done on the football pitch in the previous week – I might as well have been sat fishing!"

Lucy-Ann was given a seat at the breakfast bar and offered a drink. Mansel then opened the fridge door to a stack of cans of Brains, a tub of half-fat margarine and some Cheese Stringers. "God, I'm really sorry, I thought I had some wine." He was beginning to regret offering to host the evening; he'd instinctively felt that she might not be comfortable with him at her house after their earlier altercation, but he still wanted it to be nice for her and it was beginning to look as if he might have made a mistake.

"It's OK," she said, "part of only venturing out of the house once a month is having a full store cupboard," and she pulled a couple of bottles of red wine out of her bag.

"Wonderful!" he said and rummaged in the cupboards for some decent glasses, beginning to question the amount of cocktail shakers and boxes of willy-shaped ice cube trays he had on his shelves.

Against all odds, an hour later they were finally sitting down to a relatively decent supper. Lucy-Ann had stopped by the shop on the way up and bought a fillet steak and between them (but mainly under her guidance) they cut it into strips and found enough ingredients in his cupboards and (mostly) her bags to make a tasty stir-fry. It was washed down with plenty of wine and soon the two of them were sat at the breakfast bar satiated, slightly inebriated and feeling that all was good with the world.

Over a bowl of raspberry ripple ice cream, spiked with a couple of soft wafers, Mansel took a risk and plucked up courage to ask about the morning and what had she been so upset about.

They'd had a great day when they'd finally got into the petting zoo and once Lucy-Ann had relaxed a little and cheered up over a chocolate muffin, they'd gone around all the pens, looking at and stroking the animals. Lucy-Ann had raved about the rare species and had chattered away to Mansel, telling him about the lives that the animals would lead in their natural habitats and what their little quirks would be. At some points he was even quite interested.

When he stepped back and very nearly annihilated a dwarf rabbit, Lucy-Ann realised that he was nearing his fill and they headed off back to the car. In the car park, she had reached up on her tiptoes and given him a little kiss on the cheek. "Thank you!" she had whispered and they had walked the remaining journey to the car hand in hand.

After asking his question, Mansel put down his glass, not really knowing whether he had gone a step too far too soon.

Lucy-Ann took a deep breath, then blew it back out. He could see her thinking carefully about her response, looking at him as if to assess his trustworthiness. "Let's just say," she said finally, "let's just say that I had a few problems when I was a kid, you know, with other kids. Bit of bullying I suppose you would call it and that sort of thing. Guinea pigs just seemed to give me an easier ride. Then I got into them and it's sort of grown from there really. I enjoy them. When you work from home, it's nice to have company. You know – little noises in the corner when you're getting barked at by some git on the phone for wasting her time, even though her secretary told you to call back that afternoon." She shrugged, indicating that her revelation was over.

Mansel nodded. "I see. I can see what you mean." He sensed that she wasn't going to tell him any more and so he just smiled at her, topped up her drink and said, "Do you mind if I just start the washing-up whilst you're sat here – otherwise it'll be there for ever more! No – you just sit and enjoy your drink, sounds like you've had a hard week and deserve more of a break than I do – scrubbing "Recreation Parks Quick Response Officers Are Tossers" off park benches isn't too taxing in comparison!"

Astutely, for Mansel, he'd realised that Lucy-Ann needed a little break from the evening and as he pottered about washing the easier of the dishes and setting the pans up for a five-day soak, she sat quietly in the semi-darkness, sipping her drink occasionally and humming quietly to the music in the background.

"Do you know," she said softly, as he finished the bits of washing-up that he could do without breaking into a sweat, "I would like to stay here tonight."

"Really?" gulped Mansel, his thoughts jumping to the spare room; a single bed that occasionally had a pissed friend sleeping in it, and a floor piled with the things that had been on his bedroom floor until about three hours before. "It's a bit of a state in the spare room – look, I can get you a taxi?

Or you can have my bed and…"

"Mansel! Silly! Are you going to make me spell it out?" Obviously he was. "I would like to, you know, sleep with *you* – not necessarily in a sex kind of way, but perhaps a cuddling, snuggling kind of way?"

"Wow," he said, not really as coolly as he would like to have in such a situation. "Bloody hell."

"Well, is that a yes or a no?"

"Oh a yes. Without doubt a yes." Then he added a "Yippee" and threw the damp tea towel over his shoulder, knocking over a dead spider plant as it landed. He did a little dance and then tried to calm down, but could barely contain his happiness as he walked over and kissed Lucy-Ann on the cheek, "You're wonderful!" he whispered.

"And you've caught my hair in your watch strap," she whispered back.

As they walked up the stairs to bed, hand in hand, to clean sheets and a clean duvet cover, but to an alarm clock that was going to wake them with a claxon at seven-thirty, Mansel felt the happiest and most at peace that he'd felt in his whole adult life.

Chapter 13

Walking in another Man's Shoes

After a couple of weeks of her being in Cysgod y Ffynnon, Godfrey felt it was time to address what had happened to Georgia between the time of leaving home and acquiring her current status of mother. She had seen a midwife and the health visitor had called three times, so he was confident that the immediate health and well-being of her, and Jocey, were in hand. He now felt that he needed to address a few longer-term issues, and for that to happen he had to know what had gone on in the past.

Coincidently, Annabel had phoned for a routine chat and had tearfully said that she still had no news of her daughter and that it had been two years since she had gone now. God had clucked sympathetically but hadn't broken Georgia's confidence. However, he now felt it was time for Georgia to put Annabel out of her misery.

He waited until Jocey had gone to sleep and he took Georgia a cup of tea and a couple of biscuits. She was nestled up on the sofa watching something about the so-called *Leylandii Wars* and she turned it down before Godfrey could mutter his usual derisive comments such as, *"Huh, more Celebrity Sink Unblocking?"*

Godfrey shuffled about a bit. He was not good at prying and he tended to afford other people's business the same privacy that he wanted for his own. However, there were more people than Godfrey at stake here and he felt a moral obligation to help.

Georgia watched him shuffling – surely it wasn't that difficult to get comfortable in a chair that you sat in every day of your life? He had the same look that her mum had had the day she had tried to talk to her about sex. I bet she wishes she'd tried a little harder, thought Georgia bitterly. She watched Godfrey a little more and then put him out of his misery.

"Uncle God, you want me to tell you what's happened don't you? And you want to tell Mum that I'm here?"

Godfrey looked down at his worn trousers. "Yes," he said quietly. "And yes, again. Georgia, your mum is still very upset about you. She needs to know you're OK – it's been two years now."

"Tell me about her," whispered Georgia, "is *he* still there?" Ah, thought Godfrey, so Ray *was* involved. He'd assumed that, due to the lack of detail from Annabel about *"the argument"*. Annabel was usually the complete opposite to Godfrey in that she would happily give chapter and verse on any topic of her life, whether the listener wanted to hear it or not. Bowels, grocery lists and wool/acrylic mixes would be discussed with her friends with no conscience as to delicacy or interest.

"He's still there," said God quietly, "but he may not be for much longer." Georgia looked up, her eyes hopeful.

"What d'ya mean?"

"Well, just that your mother and he are, er, having difficulties."

Georgia drank in the information and swilled it around. Her mum she could probably face again – they would talk about the incident briefly, her mum would dismiss it with one of her nervous laughs and then it needn't be mentioned again – but *him*? No, Georgia thought back to that horrible face leering as he held his make-believe camera up, giving her directions as if it were a game. She could not bear the thought of seeing him again. Despite some pretty promiscuous moments in the squat, which had made her realise that what she and Ray had done wasn't really the worst thing in the world, the feelings that she had about the episode were still those of fourteen-year-old Georgia. Guilt, disgust and shame. And how could you possibly feel worse about discussing those things than with your own mother? No, she couldn't go home again – if she'd preferred the squat to there, she could certainly prefer Uncle God's.

"No," she said, "*he* mustn't know I am here and therefore *they* mustn't know I am here." She looked deep into Godfrey's eyes, "Promise me, Uncle, promise me you won't tell her I'm here?"

Godfrey thought hard. "OK," he said, "you have another month and then we'll talk again. But you must let me phone her and tell her you're safe. I'll say you called and left a message, OK?"

Georgia nodded miserably, "OK, just a message."

And so it was that that evening when Annabel was sat on the sofa diligently enjoying the football, the phone rang.

She hauled herself wearily out of the chair and went into the kitchen to answer it; Ray hated her chit-chat interrupting his programmes.

Annabel wasn't sure what she thought of Ray anymore. His overbearing nature gave her little control over her household and if she ever raised any hint of discontentment, he would hammer it down immediately with a tirade of a dozen different things that she did that he didn't like, but put up with, until eventually she had learnt not to bother. Now, as long as the television was on, their relationship could function – but she didn't always want the television on.

She had held the cards for about ten days after *"the incident"* during which he had apologised, flattered and cajoled until he knew that she wouldn't throw him out. On day eleven, he managed to call her daughter a slag and get away with it and then he just seemed to despise her all the more.

Annabel had thought of asking Ray to leave, but she didn't know how. He'd also made her aware that he was now entitled to half her house through his contributions to a few bills and the occasional takeaway that he bought and therefore she didn't dare take the risk. If Georgia ever tried to come home, this is exactly where she must be. Same house, same address, same job, same phone number.

Their sex life had dwindled to nothing and this suited Annabel. Any amorous suggestions from him brought back an image of her beautiful daughter who, until that fateful day, had been innocence personified in Annabel's eyes. At least Ray had had the decency not to moan about her newly-acquired frigidity: he had plenty of other methods of releasing his burden.

She picked up the phone. She was tired, but she still had that spark of hope within her that she would hear the quiet little words, "Mum? It's me." But as usual her heart sunk as her brother's weary tones said, "Annabel? It's Godfrey."

She pulled the kitchen door to as she greeted him. Ray rolled his eyes whenever Godfrey was mentioned and asked after each phone call what the tight old git had to say for himself this time. Annabel usually muttered a truthful answer of *"not a lot really"* and this would bring a sneer and a chuckle of derision that she didn't know how to deal with.

After the pleasantries, Godfrey took a deep breath and looking straight at his niece, who insisted on being in the room when the conversation was being held, said, "I've had a message from Georgia."

Annabel gasped and clutched at the mouthpiece, "What? When? Tell me Godfrey, tell me."

"Well, it was left on the answerphone; I was at work. She just said hello and that she was fine. She just wanted to let us know she was fine. Also, well, also…"

"What?" screeched Annabel in an urgent whisper. "What else?"

"Well, that she's had, er, had a baby."

Georgia could hear the scream from where she was sat across the room and she rose to come and listen. God let her share the receiver and they both listened in silence as Annabel burst into tears.

"Oh my God, oh my God, a baby? Are you sure? Is she OK? Did she sound OK?"

"Yes, she sounded fine. She said that the baby is fine and

that it's called Jocey."

"A little girl, oh, a little girl, oh *my* little girl has a little girl." She babbled through her tears and the sound of her voice brought tears to Georgia's cheeks as she clutched the phone.

Godfrey felt helpless. Lying to his sister about anything was against his grain, but about something as important as this… "She also said to tell you that she loves you and she wanted to know whether Ray was still there. But, obviously, I couldn't tell her yes or no as she only left a message."

Georgia stared at Godfrey intently, not knowing whether to be cross or to hug him.

The line went quiet and the seconds flicked by. Godfrey wondered whether he had been fair. He never meddled in other people's business, but he'd always thought his sister deserved better than that overbearing parasite and surmising that Ray had had something to do with Georgia's leaving, made him sure.

"Well, you know that he is," said Annabel quietly, "but I think he will be leaving this evening, yes, tomorrow at the latest. I must go now, Godfrey, but if she phones back, tell her he's gone. Gone forever and then please, please, tell her to phone me."

Godfrey quietly put the phone back in its cradle. "Did you hear all that?" Georgia nodded, the tears streaming unchecked down her face. "She's doing that, now, for you. Ring her? In a few days, ring her…" Georgia nodded and went back to her chair in the sitting room where she realised that she didn't give a shit whether the *Leylandii* were felled from in front of the swimming pool or not.

Chapter 14

Turning Off the Lights

Annabel squared her shoulders and walked back into what was going to return to being *her* sitting room. "Who was that?" asked Ray. It clearly irritated him that Annabel now took her calls out of his earshot; even though it irritated him when she took them in front of him, he still liked to hear what was going on.

"Godfrey," said Annabel. Ray craned round to look at her, but his look changed as he saw her face. It was as if he was about to make a quip, but having seen the look on her face, suddenly thought better of it.

"What's up? Is he OK? Does he want to borrow a fiver or has he received an electricity bill for more than twenty-five pence?" he smirked then returned to his football.

Annabel shook her head in disbelief. It was as if a veil had been removed from her face. Who was this fool she'd been living with, shouldering for so long? He quite clearly didn't like her and she finally realised that she didn't really like him. It just made the job she had to do all the more uncomplicated.

"No," she clipped. "But if he had wanted to borrow a fiver or have me pay *all* his electricity bills, I would happily do so. Anyway, Ray, we have to separate. You have to move out. Tomorrow."

"What!" Ray blazed, the remote clicking off the television for a few seconds whilst he stared at her to make sure he'd heard it correctly. "What the fuck are you going on about?" Then the football clicked back on.

Annabel felt a strength that she'd lost many years before flood back into her. She walked round the sofa and turned the set off at the wall. "I said we're separating. You're leaving. Tomorrow." She watched him trying to comprehend. After so many years, she did owe him an explanation, so she sat down on the coffee table, blocking his view of the television so that he couldn't be distracted by its silence.

"Georgia's rung Godfrey. She wants to come home." Annabel watched Ray's eyebrow raise as if another smirk was coming on. "She's had a baby and she wants to come home.

"Yes, she *and* her boyfriend. They've been living together all this time; nice flat in Bath apparently, but now she wants for them to stay here for a while. So you'll have to move out. I'm sure you can stay with a friend for a while whilst you sort yourself a place?" Annabel barely felt the enormity of what she was doing; she only felt a knot of nervous joy in her stomach at the prospect of seeing Georgia again soon.

"I'll go and pack your clothes. You can sleep in the spare room tonight. I'll pay for a taxi to take you tomorrow as your van is still off the road. What will you do? Go to Brian's for a while?"

Ray nodded. "S'pose," he whispered. Like the archetypal bully, he gave way at the first sign of rebellion in his victim.

"Yeah, Brian's will do," he said matter of factly and craned his neck round a little to see around her.

Annabel stood for a while and surveyed the bloke that she had thought to be her saviour when he had turned up to paper her hall so many years ago. He had charmed her, made her laugh, mended the leak under her sink and eventually bedded her, making her feel human again after the painful divorce from Georgia's father. He had been a fresh start for both her and Georgia. He had been fun, lively and so helpful – doing all those little jobs around the house Annabel couldn't manage. He had brought life and people into a dull and exhausted household.

Slowly it had turned into a distant and then into a meaningless, relationship. And now, when two minutes before she had told him that it was all over, Ray was back to wanting to watch the football as if she had instead mentioned that she might have her hair cut in a different style. Annabel was more than happy to oblige and clicked the switch back on and went upstairs to air the spare bed and get her oldest suitcases out of the attic.

The overriding thought that ran through both of their minds was, "Was that it, then? That should have happened years ago."

98

Chapter 15

Reading Last Week's Newspaper

Ray had slept in late having had a restless night. Instead of the usual cuppa in bed as Annabel busied herself getting ready for work, Ray had lain there in the spare room trying to work out what the unusual noises were.

She had obviously taken the day off work otherwise she would have been gone by now. He'd heard the sounds of coat hangers clanging together and then of suitcases zipping up. He'd lain in the clean sheets of the spare bed and listened as Annabel had clumped up and down the stairs presumably taking his possessions to the front door.

He'd heard videos and DVDs being slid off the shelves in the sitting room below and being packed into some kind of box and then the sound of his golf clubs being taken from under the stairs and put into the garage. Bitch had better be careful with those, they'd cost him a bloody fortune.

At about nine-fifty, by the bedside alarm clock, the door was knocked and Annabel had come in. She'd passed him a cup of tea, but without any of her usual humble smiles. It was as if this particular bed and breakfast client was stopping her from getting on with her day.

Ray had sat up, feeling naked under her stare despite the

fact that he still had last night's t-shirt on. He'd taken the tea and actually muttered his thanks for a change.

"I've phoned Brian and Kathy," she'd said, "and they said it was fine for you to go there for a while." OK, he'd nodded, as if they'd agreed to give him a lift to work. "You can come back for your van, your tools and your other things when you are ready." He'd nodded again – at least with the van broken down on her drive, she wouldn't want him to live in that!

And that had been it. She'd laid a pile of fresh pile of clothes on the foot of his bed – and in fairness she'd made a good choice – and walked out of the room saying, "Taxi's booked for eleven," over her shoulder.

Ray had stayed there for another hour – the tea had been cold, but there would not have been any point in calling her back to tell her. He'd watched the digital clock's numbers flick their way towards his eviction.

He didn't know what to think. He had the feeling that he should be thinking *something* – this was surely a momentous occasion, but his mind perused its normal topics in its normal bored way and the time that he should have spent negotiating a stay of eviction, he had instead spent lying under a floral nylon counterpane trying to guess when the digital numbers would flick to the next minute.

At ten to eleven, Annabel had shouted, "Taxi's here!" Fuck it – it was early. He dived out of bed and into his clothes, not knowing what to do with yesterday's outfit. He spent a few valuable seconds debating whether to take them with him or put them into the wash basket, but in the end just left them on the floor.

At the bottom of the stairs sat four suitcases in a neat row. Annabel couldn't have got them any nearer to the door if she'd tried. The taxi driver had beeped again –as if *surely* they weren't going to make him get out of his cab and ring the bell in this cold weather?

Ray stood next to his belongings and sensed Annabel behind him. He turned to see her leaning against the kitchen door frame, a fresh cup of coffee in her hand and a glow about her face that he hadn't seen in years.

"The rest is in the garage. Ring me when you're ready to collect it." Ray had nodded. He opened the door and started to decant the suitcases. His situation had then suddenly become real.

"Hang on, Annabel love, surely we can sort this? Georgia can—"

"No, Ray." The reply had been curt as if he'd been a child asking to play with a lawnmower.

"But I've been here for years. This is my home!" His wail had grown emotional.

"It was Georgia's home first, Ray, and it will be her home for as long as she wants it, now off you go; don't keep the taxi waiting."

Ray had followed the taxi driver down the drive, miffed that the man had chosen the two lightest cases. By the time he'd settled himself in the seat, the front door had slammed shut and Ray had been left staring at the leaded light glass tulips in the white UPVC door that had signalled home for the last five years or so.

Somehow he managed to chat to the driver about the footie, the boxing and the new landscaping at the third hole at St. Andrews and by the time he'd arrived at Brian and Kathy's, if he'd swapped his four suitcases for a crate of beer, he would be feeling his usual fine self.

Kathy Hansford was not pleased as she opened the door to Ray. She'd always thought him a prick that outstayed his welcome and brought out the worst in her husband, Brian. Annabel's phone call had caught her off guard and she'd agreed to the lodger out of a sense of duty to her friend and the hope that someone else would take Brian off her hands when her time came.

"He's got until next weekend," she'd snarled on the phone to Brian's mobile as she relayed Annabel's request. "No more. Next weekend, all right?"

"All right, love, all right. That'll be fine anyway," oozed Brian, "plenty of time for him to get a place of his own by then."

"Hi Ray," Kathy grimaced. "How *are* you, love? I *am* sorry to hear your news. Come on in."

Ray mumbled and followed Kathy's fitted jeans into the house. He'd never felt particularly comfortable with Kathy, but she did put on a good spread, you had to give her that.

"Brian's at work, love. He won't be back until later, so settle yourself into the spare room next to the bathroom. Then, when you're done, come down for a coffee. I've got to push the Hoover through now, love, so excuse the noise."

Ray nodded and dragged two of his suitcases up the stairs, aware of Kathy's sharp intake of breath as he banged her paintwork. "Good job I'm a painter and decorator, eh!" he quipped, but spotted her I-wouldn't-let-you-near-it-if-you-were-the-last-painter-and-decorator-on-earth look and sloped off to his new home.

The spare bedroom next to the bathroom was not their usual guest room – that one had a queen size bed and pelmets. This bedroom held the ironing board, a clothes-horse and a small single bed. Ray put down his suitcases and wondered where he would put the larger two, which were still downstairs. The wardrobe was full of Kathy's coats, and boxes of shoes filled the space under the bed. He eventually piled all four suitcases onto the bed. There was just enough room beside them for him to sit and read *101 Dinner Party Speeches,* which he found on the bookshelf. He'd wait until Kathy had finished vacuuming and then he'd give her five to get the coffee on. His mouth started to water; he hoped she'd been baking...

Chapter 16

Selecting the Value Range

Georgia walked along the pavement pushing Jocey in her pram. It was a bright January day and the frost sparkled on the ground in front of her. She looked to any passer-by like any other mum, albeit a rather young one, taking her baby for a stroll. For Georgia, it was the most surreal moment yet of the past two years. Until now, all the events had had a lead up and were a reaction to something else that had happened – the incident with Ray, the arrival in Tavsham, meeting Hannah and being taken back to the squat – all may have been unpleasant, but they had made sense and had been do-able because she only had to look after herself.

Yet, suddenly, within just a three-week period, she had gone from being runaway Georgia struggling to keep warm and fed in a revolting house to being transported into a clean suburban mother pushing a pram with a leaf pattern on it, on her way to a Parent and Toddler club.

Her baby was dressed in a white Babygro, with a lacy cardigan and was wrapped in three white crocheted blankets, all courtesy of Uncle God's friend, Sandra. Georgia knew it was a ridiculous thought, considering the trouble she'd had keeping *herself* clothed over the past two years, but she wished that she could dress Jocey in slightly cuter, funkier stuff – a bit less home-made crochet, a bit more stripy tights.

Before, when she didn't have a mirror, she got quickly used to not noticing how she dressed and would pile layer over layer in the hope of keeping warm. As people moved on from the squat, their leftover belongings would be rifled through and she'd had a great, sloppy, blue jumper from Bumper and a fantastic ankle-length dress left behind from Dopey Sue – both of which were probably now being worn by Hannah or that bastard in her bed – well, perhaps not the dress, although it had been *very* cold this January.

She would have an image in her head as to how she looked each day and it was usually quite good, but then she would catch sight of herself in a shop window as she walked past and would barely recognise the skinny girl with the greasy hair and dirty white puffa jacket over the top of her clothes.

Other times she would have gone into a shop and tried on a few things, just to pass the time and would be shocked at the state of her skin and her hair and spend the time that she should have been trying on a pair of jeans, trying to rub a grimy tidemark off the side of her face or removing blackheads from her forehead. When other girls her age were experimenting with fashion and having too many spray tans, she was just trying to keep warm.

So now, walking along in a pair of pale denim jeans and one of Sandra's daughter's cast-off jackets, she felt as if she were giving quite the wrong impression about the person she was. It would seem wrong to ask Uncle Godfrey for any more money – especially for frivolous things such as fashion, when there had been so much "doing without" for so long. He would think that she should think herself lucky to have *anything* bought or given to her; there was no need for specifics. The health visitor had helped her fill in some forms to collect benefits, but it might be a while before any money came through. Until the time that she could buy things for herself, she felt that if she were going to be neat and clean, then at least she would like to be neat and clean in her own ways and with her own touches.

She rounded the corner and saw the sign for the church hall and she slowed her pace. Was she really going to a church hall Parent and Toddler group with a baby? Was she really going to sit with a bunch of other women moaning about a lack of sleep, stretch marks, ripped perineums and the latest twist in Eastenders? The health visitor had near insisted that she go, so, here she was – but this wasn't how it was supposed to be …

Throughout her pregnancy, she'd visualised being sat in the squat with her friends all taking it in turns to help her with her baby (who would be an absolute angel to look after), then she'd pop Jocey onto her back in some kind of sling and life would carry on much as usual – only warmer. She'd certainly not imagined herself wearing pastel colours and white trainers, pushing a pram with leaves on. Progress? Probably, but it didn't necessarily *feel* like it.

A man marched towards her with walking boots and canvas trousers on with a baby in a sling on his front protected from the wind by a Goretex mountaineering jacket.

"Hi," he said, turning into the hall porch, "are you coming in? Once you've made it through the door, that's the hardest part over!" Georgia mumbled and bashed her pram up the small step and followed him in.

Once inside the church hall, which smelled of church hall, she stopped and surveyed the scene in front of her. A dozen or so women sat around on chairs or on the floor either looking at their babies in front of them on a mat, or trying to ignore their toddlers who were running around amongst the toys behind them.

A few of the women mumbled "Hello" in Georgia and the man's direction and then turned back to check their babies or reprimand their toddlers. Others just sat and stared. The man quickly assumed the leadership role.

"Well, I'm Simon," he said and held out his hand, which Georgia shook limply being the first hand that she had ever shaken in an adult setting. "This is my son Derwen, oak in Welsh," he added, as Georgia struggled to catch the name.

Simon removed his coat, revealing a full kit of hiking gear and Derwen was bounced around the room in his sling, with his mini jester's hat on, as Simon enthused the session into some sort of order. Within five minutes of his arrival, there were slides being slid down and dressing-up clothes being worn. The other mums had brightened up and were chatting to each other and to Georgia.

Georgia was asked a few questions about Jocey and where she'd been born and any horror stories about the birth. Georgia finally got the hint that now, as a grown-up, she was to ask a few questions back, which she did, although she had no interest in the answers.

Simon and Derwen swung by with a tray of hot drinks and the mums swooped on the chance for some more caffeine.

Georgia felt a fraud, an imposter, sat there in her pastel shades, sipping a cup of coffee made with powdered milk (as mother of twins, Melissa, had forgotten to collect some real milk on the way) and eating a pink cake (made by Emma and little Joseph the day before). She felt that they should all know that until last month, she'd been living in a squat and stealing or rummaging in bins for food. But mostly they should know that she *shouldn't* be sat wearing white trainers with glitter in the laces. They could if they wanted to, but *she* shouldn't be.

Simon and Derwen came back to join the throng and Georgia hoped that he wouldn't start a singsong. Instead, as he drunk his mug of hot water, he passed around a sponsorship form. "Sorry – me begging again, I'm afraid! This time I'm doing an abseil down the dam at the Elan Valley – to raise money for the homeless."

"Oh yeah?" asked Melissa, taking the form and adding her name. "What's the money going to buy?"

"Well," said Simon, slugging down the last of his hot water and bringing an emergency oatcake out of his pocket, "it'll go towards helping homeless people have outdoor experiences. We can bus them up to a woodland, say, and then they can learn some outdoor techniques. You know, empower people: the great outdoors is a very powerful place!" The woman nodded approvingly and passed the form onto the next person in the circle.

"They'd probably prefer a decent sleeping bag and a big plastic box to keep their stuff in…" mumbled Georgia, then declined the form, apologising as she did that she didn't have any money. The girl she passed it on to, poised her pen, thought a while, nodded and then passed it on to the next person without donating. As Georgia went to help tidy away the toys, she saw Simon stare at her, half in interest, half in annoyance.

Oh dear, she thought as she tossed Dora the Explorer into a cardboard box, I've pissed him off. Oh well, it was bound to happen sooner or later...

Chapter 17

Squatters' Rights

Godfrey sat at his office desk and yawned. He normally liked this time of day, a quick check of the headlines on the internet and a catch up on the cricket scores, but nothing seemed normal anymore. Even the faded posters on the wall about changes in council tax legislation that had been superseded fifteen years before seemed daunting and unfamiliar.

In fairness to Georgia, she was already extremely deft with Jocey and seemed to have none of the awkwardness and diffidence of the average new parent. But Godfrey would hear a gentle cry two or three times a night. Then he would hear Georgia pick Jocey up from her new Moses basket and coo as she settled herself against the headboard and began the long feeds. He would then hear two or three attempts to settle Jocey back in her cot and then the resigned chatter of Georgia as she snuggled the baby to her in her own bed.

At first he had gone in when the noises of a nappy being changed were made and had done the deed himself to let Georgia get her rest, but he soon stopped that and pretended that he hadn't heard. However, he didn't have the endorphins that a breastfeeding mother has to lull her back to sleep and instead he would lie awake for hours, unsettled but still tired and thus his sleep was nearly as disturbed as Georgia's.

He was also noticing the damage to his usual routine. He would come home to a form of chaos that all the women in the office would laugh about when he described it: "Oh, baby chaos is just the start, Godfrey, wait until she's crawling!" and they would cackle off into tales of when their little Davey pulled all the tins out of the cupboard and ripped the labels off – *"had pineapple on toast for weeks!"*

Sandra had looked at him fondly, "You really will just have to accept it I'm afraid, Godfrey. Looking after a baby is hard work and really, Georgia is doing very well. Just close your eyes to it; it'll get easier, honestly it will."

Godfrey had smiled and nodded, but it wasn't just the mess – a pudding of soiled nappy on the kitchen table or soggy breast pads on the arm of a chair he could deal with. It was the important stuff that he felt was slipping away from him. He'd already spent a few hundred pounds on so-called baby essentials, although admittedly, he would have been hit a lot harder if it weren't for Sandra's kindness. But it was the hidden extras that he fretted over – the heating turned up to a level that his particular system had never had to cope with, lights left on indiscriminately, hot water permanently in the tank.

Some evenings he would sit in his chair and feel his chest tighten as he sensed – sometimes even heard – the whirr of the gas and electricity meters as they raced round and round. His flasks were finding themselves redundant – although he was still careful to take them in his bag to work so as not to arouse suspicion. Also, it would not be fair to feed a malnourished, breastfeeding mother on Supernoodles and corned beef pasties, which in itself had added a whole new dimension to his fortnightly shopping bill.

Godfrey felt the need to have a little space, a little solitude. Perhaps he would go out tonight, leave Georgia to manage on her own. He needn't be long and he was sure that she would cope admirably. Perhaps he would just go for a walk – it promised to be a dry evening. And so, he felt it was just like the old times as he filled his flasks after work that evening and set off with a spring in his step and savoury rice slowly absorbing water in his Thermos.

Georgia thought nothing of it when he claimed he was going out with friends. She didn't really know him well enough to be aware that he didn't have any. "Good for you, Uncle God – I know that we are stifling your social life. Have a few drinks for me – God knows I could do with some!" Godfrey laughed; Georgia had always made him chuckle and he realised that actually, on the whole, he was enjoying have her and little Jocey to stay. He kissed the proffered Jocey and was still smiling as he walked off down the road, his flasks clinking gently in his rucksack.

He hadn't known where he was intending to walk to, but it was no surprise to Godfrey when he arrived at the back gate of Tŷ Mawr...

Once more, all was quiet and he was able to gaze into Jerry's study, lit up like a show home. He never meant to enter the garden, but found himself creeping across the lawn. He never expected that he would be imposing on people's privacy, but soon he had checked through the kitchen window for changes and ascertained that there were no vehicles in the yard. The abandoned Christmas tree with its fairy lights and tinsel wrapped around bare branches gave the house an eerie feeling of neglect, a full month after it should have been chucked into a corner of the garden with the intention of making a bonfire around it.

However, although he had barely any feelings of guilt as he unlocked the kitchen door and, listening intently, eased it open, he was still worried about detection; he wished that he had brought the book back that he had "borrowed" before – at least he would have had a legitimate excuse, albeit a slightly warped one, for being there.

This time Godfrey felt more at home; less of an intruder and more of a permitted, but unanticipated, house-guest. He sat for a while in the fireside armchair, stretching out his legs in the way that he imagined a man like Jerry Gloucester would do. He already had in his mind a picture of what Tŷ Mawr's owner would look like: Jerry would be tall and thin, an elegant man with expensive clothes and an easy manner.

In Godfrey's youth, his father had drummed into him the kind of man that he should seek to be, not even allowing factors such as Godfrey's natural height or hair type to alter the image. If only he just worked hard enough, did the right things, it would come to him eventually. He *could* be that man, and have all the trappings that went with it. Tŷ Mawr was the house that his father would see his son living in *if* he'd done what he'd advised and worked for it. It was this image of success with which Godfrey endowed Jerry, regardless of the evidence, or lack of same, he'd seen to support it.

Confidence would ooze from Jerry and he would be so

content in his own skin that he wouldn't notice Godfrey's occasional gaucheness; they would soon become firm friends. Jerry would seek Godfrey's opinion on many issues. First of local interest and then, as time went by, on matters of greater importance.

Godfrey imagined the two of them sat by the fire. Audrey would be fussing in the background and Jerry would be nodding his head intently, sucking on the stem of his pipe as Godfrey advised him on shares and ISAs. He saw himself swirling the fine whisky around the crystal glass, enjoying its peaty flavour in the way that the books said he should.

Godfrey smiled as he contemplated the scenario. In another, Jerry's friends were there too and they were all laughing at Godfrey's local anecdotes and saying how he was like a breath of fresh air. Yes, that was the kind of company that Godfrey wanted for his retirement: intelligent men with a bit of breeding, having interesting lives and careers – not the kind of clowns that were found in the local darts team or in his dreary history society.

However, that night, the kitchen was draughty and bare and Godfrey's reveries didn't last for long. Eventually his eyes fell on a stack of dusty newspapers next to the hearth. Surely it wouldn't hurt to have a little fire? He felt nervous once more as he crept to the pile and, careful to select a paper from the middle, he screwed up a few sheets and threw them into the hearth. With a match from the box beside Jerry's pipe, he lit the paper and sat back to enjoy the glow. The flames shot up, the draw from the yawning chimney was impressive and soon he found himself folding more paper into strips and winding them together just as he'd done as a lad in order to make them burn for longer.

After a while, he looked around, searching for something else Jerry-like so that he could get more into character. He walked down the musty hall to the main front door and picked up the huge pile of post off the mat. December 27th was the mark on the oldest mail at the bottom of the pile. That meant that they hadn't been since Christmas, and once more he tutted at the wasted resources – not just the lights and the fridge, but the house and its library too.

He settled back by the fire and started leafing through envelopes, being careful not to change the order – although Jerry was surely not a man to be bothered to check the order of his post pile? Noticeably, there was not a lot of junk mail. Godfrey reckoned you could tell a great deal about someone from their junk mail – he had pounds of it every day. Anything that offered competitions, vouchers or discounts had been filled in and returned and therefore he was a prime target for advertising, most of which offered services and products in vain. Jerry obviously didn't bother with coupons or loyalty card points; perhaps he had no need for the, in effect, free bottle of sherry and a toiletry gift set (which was sent each year for Annabel's Christmas present).

Godfrey had a sudden twinge as he thought of himself at the checkout earlier that week, rummaging in his wallet when his stack of vouchers – all of whose expiry dates and details were known and diarised – fell onto the conveyor belt. No, Jerry would probably just toss a platinum card to the checkout girl and not check the balance from one month to another. Well, Godfrey conceded, if he ever went shopping with Jerry, he'd leave his vouchers behind; it was as simple as that.

Towards the top of the pile, one envelope in particular caught his attention. An expensive cream envelope – but it was addressed to Eira and Mike Howard not to the Gloucesters. Godfrey fingered it lightly, turning it back and fore. Under his handling, part of the sticky panel came undone at the back – an old envelope, reckoned Godfrey, probably dust had got into the glue. By careful manipulation he was able to prise open the rest of the flap until he had a letter in his hand, written in the finishing school inkpen scrawl of Audrey Gloucester.

Dear Eira and Mike,

I trust this letter finds you both well and Tŷ Mawr in good order. Jerry has relinquished responsibility for the upkeep of Tŷ Mawr to me and has asked that I liaise with you in the same manner as he has done hitherto. My intention is to update Tŷ Mawr to a greater degree of efficiency and housekeeping and to this end, I would appreciate your help. I am having to rely on your eyes and ears as to the work needed. Jerry says he has chatted over some of the work he requires to reduce the costs at Tŷ Mawr and to that end I have enclosed £100 to start the process. Please address your correspondence to me as above.

Regards,

Audrey Gloucester.

Godfrey re-read the letter and paused. The lack of upkeep of the place had irritated him; there were so many little jobs that could so easily be done. Audrey herself had said how incompetent Eira and particularly Mike were. If only someone reliable were to take the job on.

Someone like him.

His mind ticked over as he sat fingering the ten ten-pound notes the mere sight of which warmed his soul. He thought of all the ten pound notes he'd had to relinquish to pay for Jocey's needs, and he suspected that it had only just started. He'd never fancied an additional job – but something like this with hours to suit – well, it could be the answer? Yet, how would he manage to convince someone he barely knew that he was a responsible alternative to people she had known for years – especially when he was sat uninvited in her house, having opened their mail? It needed thinking through.

As he pondered, Godfrey decided that he wasn't ready to leave Tŷ Mawr just yet. He desperately wanted to rummage a little more, get more into Jerry's persona. This was the man that he'd aspired to be since a boy of eight or nine and now that he had access to him, he wanted to find out what it was like to live like Jerry, to *be* Jerry. He was sure that he could be as good as Jerry was at being the elegant country gent; he just needed a little more practice.

He found himself standing at the door to the study staring with envy at the obvious and effortless class of the room and comparing it woefully with his own bleak little sitting room that would currently be swathed in babies' blankets, clothes and leaflets on breastfeeding and meningitis, being over-heated by a nineteen-seventies gas fire, and with some hideous celebrity television show blaring from the corner of the room.

"Oh, sod it," he thought and sat himself grandly at the fine old desk. He shuffled around in the chair like a guilty schoolboy in order to get comfortable and straightened his shoulders. He and Jerry must be about the same size, he thought; this desk is perfect for me.

He picked up a couple of old pens from an earthenware pot in the far corner of the desk. Both were dry of ink but Godfrey loved the weighty feel of them in his hand. He started opening and shutting drawers in the columns either side of his legs and looked at the contents, being careful to replace things after he'd inspected them. Old envelopes were mixed with fishing flies and the occasional ancient photo peered up at him.

Eventually he picked out a pad of writing paper and had an urge to write something. Something that needed copperplate writing like Audrey's. Something that needed an ink pen and embossed paper, not a spiral bound notepad and a stolen Argos biro. As he sat there, an idea unfolded in his mind…

Resisting the temptation to use the headed paper he'd found in a box – now that would be a surprise, he chuckled – he half-filled one of the ink pens with blue ink from a pot (having flushed it with water and cleaned it up for use in the kitchen) and settled down to compose. He practised a few words on the paper, sloping his writing this way and that until he was happy with the style. Then he took a fresh piece of paper and a deep breath:

Dear Mrs Gloucester,

I am writing to introduce myself. My name is Geoffrey Farmer,

He chuckled again at his own cleverness.

and Eira Howard has given me your details. Apparently her husband, Mike, has damaged his back and the doctor says that the only cure is rest – but being as diligent as he is,

Godfrey hugged himself as he imagined Audrey's snort.

he is reluctant to rest and not fulfil his obligations. Eira has asked that, if it is acceptable to you, I take over the maintenance jobs until his back is better. I am happy to do this for the same rate as Mike. She said that you liked to send the correspondence and payment to the house, and I am also happy with this as I live close by. She has also asked that you not mention this arrangement to Mike, who apparently does not agree with his doctor!

Eira said that you were keen to step up the maintenance and save money on the upkeep and, from her description of Tŷ Mawr, I have listed a number of things that might be worth you thinking about, as I could instigate these in a very short space of time, giving you immediate savings.

Godfrey listed two columns of suggested work: immediate ones that were close to his heart – such as energy-saving light bulbs, draught excluders, adjustments to time switches and the heating – and longer term ones such as fixing the gate hinges and painting the woodwork. He also left his mobile phone number (bought to use up the Council Tax section's budget and currently untouched in its box in his desk drawer) and made a mental note to charge the handset. He told Audrey to use that first as he carried it during work hours. He didn't want Audrey to ring Georgia on his home phone and have her give the game away. He signed the letter with a scrawl and rummaged for an envelope. To his delight, he found a book of stamps too!

He then squared himself for the more difficult task of a letter from Audrey to the Howards. Could he really just sack the pair of them for their poor performances? Perhaps he could take on the cleaning as well? Hmm, tempting though it was, hadn't Audrey said that they were old school friends of Jerry's? It might come back to haunt him in time if they ever met up. No perhaps just play it safe for the time being – he didn't really like cleaning anyway if he were honest; mucking about with the power tools that a chap like Jerry was bound to have, would be much more his cup of tea.

He flexed his shoulders and set about the task. Assuming that Eira would usually correspond with Jerry and therefore not recognise Audrey's writing, all he needed was a more feminine hand …

Dear Mike and Eira,
I trust this letter finds you both well and Tŷ Mawr in good order

Godfrey copied sections of Audrey's original letter explaining the relinquishing of Jerry's command and her desire to increase the upkeep.
and to this end I have enlisted the help of a local builder to assist with some of the heavier labouring. However, I still

*require a cleaner and hope that you, Eira, are still happy to
do this? I have enclosed*

And here Godfrey paused. He was not a dishonest man,
indeed his highly individual sense of integrity meant he was
cross with the Howards about the level of service they were
giving the Gloucesters, but he knew that the full one hundred
pounds was for cleaning *and* upkeep.

£50 for the remainder of the month.

Regards,
Audrey Gloucester.

Godfrey folded the remaining fifty pounds into another sheet
of paper and wrote, "Eira gave me this but I am returning
it to you in case you are not happy with the arrangement,
Geoffrey." This, he tucked into the Tavsham-bound letter.

He wrote a few more lines in Audrey's new handwriting
and tucked that into his pocket for future reference. He put
Audrey's new letter and money neatly into the existing
envelope and hoped that Eira wouldn't notice that the writing
on the envelope differed ever so slightly from that inside.

Feeling very proud of a good job well done, Godfrey
packed everything neatly away, replaced the post pile
with Mike and Eira's envelope amongst it and checked he
hadn't left footprints in the dropped pine needles around
the Christmas tree. He allowed himself a small rummage
through Jerry's well-stocked drinks' cabinet and then shut
up the house and ambled contentedly home.

*

Georgia was happy to see Uncle God back home, clearly relaxed after his evening with friends. His eyes were bright and the smell on his breath was that of a man having enjoyed a good night out.

Chapter 18

Nursing an Empty Glass at the Bar

Brian passed Ray a beer and sat down in the armchair. Ray nodded his thanks and took a swig: he had been saddened to see that Kathy obviously only brought out the Stella for special occasions, but he was getting used to their supermarket's own brand.

Brian shuffled uneasily in his chair and it wasn't only because Ray had taken the best seat in the house. He looked at the door and his instinct had been right – Kathy was hovering there and her expression told him to get on with it.

"See this guy here," Ray motioned at a forward in a yellow shirt, "he's got hellava left foot. I never realised it before, but if you really watch it – superb ball control."

"Oh, aye," said Brian miserably. He hadn't minded Ray coming to stay, a mate in need and all that, but Kathy was right, it really was time for him to go.

"Six bloody weeks he's been here," she'd exploded in a loud whisper in their bedroom the night before. "Six bloody weeks and he's not lifted a finger or paid a penny towards it." Brian had nodded, he too had been pretty unimpressed with his friend's attitude.

"I thought he was supposed to be a painter and decorator, but all he's done is decorated *our* bloody sofa with *his* fat arse."

"Van's off the road," Brian had mumbled in his friend's defence.

"And it'll stay off the bloody road if he doesn't do anything about mending it. Sorry, Brian, I know he's your mate, but he has to go." Kathy had folded her arms and that meant the end of the discussion.

"Well," began Brian, "it's quite difficult… He's a mate… Where will he go?"

"Don't care," said Kathy, her lips pursed, "but I do care that mum is coming at the weekend and Cynth from next door wants to come too, so we'll need *both* spare rooms." Kathy played her trump card with smug success.

"So sorry, but it's all booked. I'm collecting them from the station at four-twenty on Friday. He has until Thursday morning as I need to air the room; his feet are *revolting*." Kathy had then grabbed her dressing gown and gone for a bath leaving Brian to plan his strategy as to how he was going to dump on his mate from a great height.

"Oh, for fuck's sake, Ref, you're joking, aren't you? Did you see that? Come on, Ref-er-ree!"

Brian mumbled in weak agreement, "Er, Ray, me old mate, can we have a chat?"

"Course, mate, what's up?" said Ray, not taking his eyes off the screen. "Any chance of another beer, by the way? It's all right isn't it, when you get used to it?"

Brian scuttled away and was handed two more bottles at the door by a white-lipped Kathy.

"I'm afraid it's about your staying here, mate. I'm afraid, we, er, need your room at the weekend, well from Thursday actually. Kathy's got her mother and her friend coming down."

"Oh." Ray looked troubled, then reached over and patted Brian's knee. "That's fine, that's fine. No problem, I understand. Kathy's mother, eh? Woo! Fuck me – I'm glad to be out of it!"

Brian smiled, "Thanks, mate; I knew you'd understand."

"When is she off again?" asked Ray. "I'll just stay over at Andy's for a couple of nights until she mounts her broomstick."

Brian struggled to swallow his mouthful. *Come on, Ray, take the bloody hint, don't make me spell it out.* "No, look, I'm sorry, mate, you're not getting me."

For the first time, Brian saw Ray looking vulnerable. "I'm afraid you can't come back, Ray, mate," he said as gently as he could. "I know we're friends, but this is Kathy's and my home. We've had you for six weeks now – and we've been happy to – but it's time to sort yourself a place now. You know, get back to work, get yourself a flat. I know you've had a rough time, but it's time to, you know, move on, yeah?"

Ray nodded. "Yeah, course it is, mate. Yeah. Actually, I thought I'd go and visit a friend, Dan, in Tavsham for a few weeks – maybe set up down there. It's time I got my brushes wet again."

"That's the spirit. Time to move on – forget old Annabel, eh? Get out of Holsborough. You don't want to be sharing a house with a boring married couple now that you're single again – come on, spring's here! You want to be out flicking it about again. Dipping your wick. Sowing your wild oats!"

Ray cheered up, "Yep, you're right. Yes, there'll be a different side to 'getting the painters in' for the ladies in Tavsham shortly!" and he grinned as he imagined himself chatting to a bored housewife in a short red dress. Maybe with her twin standing next to her.

Outside the living room door, the nearest bored housewife gave a sigh of relief and wondered whether Brian would be cross when he found out that Cynth had died two years ago…

Kathy managed to find a friend, Teresa, who was willing to drive to a non-existent appointment in Tavsham on Thursday morning for fifty quid. "I need to be *absolutely* sure," she told Brian.

"Oh, come on," Brian had said, "he's not that bad. He's not some kind of rodent you have to drive across a river to stop him coming back in."

"Yes he is," snapped Kathy. "He'll stay with someone for a few days until they get fed up and eaten out of house and home and then he'll worm his way back in here," and she went to the kitchen to unpack a set of new phones that had the incoming number flash up upon a screen – mobile numbers too.

Brian had to admit he was glad to see Ray go as he waved him off that Thursday morning. He only had one suitcase of essentials this time, not having even opened the other three that Annabel had packed, so they were stashed in Brian and Kathy's garage until he was settled somewhere and ready to collect them. "He will *never* be 'collecting' them," Kathy had warned. "I will have a house fire before I allow him back here." Brian felt that he owed Kathy, so he'd muttered an agreement. To salve his conscience, he'd even slipped Ray fifty quid to see him right until he was working again. Although seeing as his van was sat slowly losing air from its tyres on Annabel's drive, Ray may need to live very frugally.

Brian was a sociable creature; he'd enjoyed Ray's company before he'd come to stay, but now he realised that much of that enjoyment had been on a "two naughty boys" basis. It had been on a sitting-in-the-garage-with-a-sneaky-beer-to-avoid-helping-with-the-salads friendship, or a listening-to-the-match-in-the-car-rather-than-help-with-the-washing-up thing. Kathy had said that she and Annabel had recognised this, but had felt it preferable to do the tasks themselves and let the fools think that they were being clever rather than having them cluttering up the place, making stupid comments and pretending to break things.

Brian now felt a little sheepish as he realised that the "lazy shit" tag that Ray had so easily earned, he'd worn too for many years. Kathy might inadvertently be thankful one day for the time that Ray had come to stay – but it wouldn't be for a while ...

Teresa had been given strict instructions to leave the stereo on, keep to bland topics of conversation and not, on any account, feel sorry for Ray or make any future arrangements.

"Be a lesbian who lives with her mother in a one-bedroom house if you have to, but do NOT tell him where you live or give him a phone number. Drop him at his mate's house, throw his bag after him and speed away. Don't look back, OK?"

Teresa had laughed, but after an hour and a half in the car with Brian's so-called mate, she was happy to do just that. Number thirty-four Gilbert Street was found. Ray was handed his one remaining suitcase and was knocking on the front door as Teresa frantically turned the car. She beeped twice and waved as she sped off down the road. Ray had waved back with an annoyed look on his face – bitch could have waited to make sure that Dan was in.

A young woman eventually opened the door. No, Dan didn't live here any more. No, she was sure. They'd only rented it since November – perhaps he'd been there before that? No, they didn't have any forwarding addresses – perhaps the landlord might have? One of the others had a phone number for the landlord that he could try – but they weren't back until after the weekend. And no, he couldn't leave his suitcase until then.

As Ray walked down the flight of steps leading from number thirty-four, he felt confused. It dawned on him that he didn't have anywhere to go and he was worried, almost scared even. He sat on the wall at the bottom, his suitcase at his feet. He presumed that the young woman was watching him and it didn't take much imagination to guess that Teresa would be long gone.

He instinctively felt inside his jacket pocket for his mobile phone, the modern-day comfort blanket, but the battery was flat. Damn, he should have given it one last flash at Brian's.

He was aware that his call payment plan would be sucking money from his bank account any day now, so he'd better get it charged – he'd only lose the minutes if he didn't use them. However, no one really rang his phone anymore. It had been useful when he'd been working, but the volume of calls had dried up as his work had. That bloody van; things would be so different if the van were on the road – he could have slept in it tonight; he probably could have made it quite comfortable.

Ray saw some curtains twitching across the road and felt jolted into action. Perhaps he'd get a bed and breakfast for the night; he'd feel better after a good meal and a bath –he could ring Brian for a chat once his mobile had been plugged in for a few minutes; perhaps he could borrow a charger …

Chapter 19

Splitting Multi-packs and Offering Them For Re-sale

Georgia was mooching along the road with Jocey gazing up at her from her pram. Jocey Willow was three months old now and Georgia was beginning to settle into her new role and her new life. She had taken on a few of the chores around the house and she and Godfrey were learning to live with each other without getting under each other's feet too often.

Georgia had found that as long as she could make the house look neater when Godfrey came home than when he'd left it in the morning, then he was happy. If it looked worse, then he was grumpy. If the fire was on high, he was even grumpier. And if the fire was on high, the television on and she was not in the house, then *look out* ...

She had got into the habit of having a walk in the morning and then the afternoon. "Good for you, good for the baby," the health visitor had beamed at her. "And if you do it at the same times each day, you'll soon be in a nice routine without even having to try!" Georgia liked the sound of not having to try at something too hard, especially if it meant that she might get a bit more sleep.

She turned down into Cysgod y Ffynnon's Parc Gwair, a hay field that Godfrey told her was hurriedly turned into a Victorian arboretum and which was now fast becoming a dark woodland infested with squirrels. Georgia liked Parc Gwair, she liked the little plaques that were here and there explaining things, she liked bumping the pushchair along little paths to see where they went and she was sure that Jocey liked watching the squirrels.

As they walked along the quiet paths, she enjoyed the wonder on Jocey's face as the trees rustled and created shadows above her. Georgia threw some of Godfrey's spare crumbs onto the ground in the hope that a few squirrels would come down from their branches. Jocey started to gnaw at her fist, a sure sign that she was getting hungry, so Georgia looked out for a bench so that she could sit down and feed her. A group of people were wandering around in the distance, but they wouldn't be a problem; she was getting good at feeding Jocey when out and about, she still liked her privacy, but once she was settled, she didn't really mind people coming over to chat.

Jocey was just beginning to gulp away, staring into Georgia's eyes as she struggled to cope with the flow, when the group started to potter nearer to Georgia. She watched them idly, trying to work out what they were up to. Most of them appeared to be in their sixties and seventies, but were dressed smartly as if for work. They had sheaves of papers to which they kept referring as a younger man in full waterproofs stopped to address them, pointing to the sky, opening his arms out to embrace the tree canopy and then ducking to the floor to draw their attention to some tiny little plant. They all seemed to be nodding enthusiastically at him. Then he turned to the side and the bulge swinging around in front of him made something click with Georgia. *Baby Derwen. Simon. Damn.*

A couple of the women in the group broke quietly away and walked off chatting. As they came near to Georgia, they stopped for a word and to have a coo at her baby. They asked all the right questions and made all the right noises, all at a respectful distance so that Georgia was happy to keep the conversation going. Eventually the rest of the group caught up, with Simon at the back of the procession.

"Look, Bron," said one of the first women to another in the group, "see this little one – just three months old. Isn't she beautiful?"

"Lovely," said Bron, taking a peep.

"And this young girl's doing ever so well, aren't you, *bach*?" Georgia glowed at the praise. "Hey, Simon, why don't we be representative? Let's ask this young girl her thoughts on your idea – it'll be Council money that's being pledged after all?" The others in the group generally nodded and muttered their approval, checking their watches as if keen to get back for afternoon tea.

Simon cringed a little, "Well, it's quite a complicated case that I've put forward to be decided upon by a lay person…"

"Nevertheless, let's see what this member of the tax-paying public has to say… My dear, we are county councillors and we have been asked to devote some of your hard earned taxes to this man's project. He wants to bus homeless people from around our county to Cysgod y Ffynnon, take them out into the woods and teach them things, to open their eyes to the beauty of nature and then show them how to forage for food. You want to *empower* them don't you, Simon? Teach them that there is something to fight for, to aspire to?"

Simon squirmed a little, "Yes, but…"

"So, love, if you were a homeless person, would you like to be bussed to Cysgod y Ffynnon and be empowered in the woodlands?"

Georgia considered Bron's question – not the idea, as her opinion of that was very clear in a millisecond, but how she was going to reply. Everyone leaned in to listen. "I think," and she could see Simon's expression move from enthusiasm to defeat as she spoke, "I would rather have a night in a hotel, a nice meal, my clothes washed and someone to help me phone my mum."

She could see the group as a whole let a breath out and smile at her simplicity and common sense. They thanked her and walked off, nodding and discussing whether they would have chance to stop for that cup of tea, or just grab a couple of biscuits and head off for their next meeting. It was as if Simon's proposal had been determined with no need for any further debate.

Simon marched past her and bid her good afternoon with a now thunderous expression that said, without the need for actual words, *"You cow, I've spent weeks trying to sort all this out and then you go and ruin it with one stupid comment…"*

Chapter 20

Talk is Cheap

Audrey sat at the table in the first floor kitchen. She enjoyed this time of day as the sun reflected off the smart house across the road, a replica of their own right down to the colour of the railings and the polished doorknob. The dogs had been walked round the park and were now farting quietly in their sleep. She poured herself another coffee from the pot. The doctor had said that she should cut down, but there was nothing wrong with her, so she didn't really see the point. Bloody routine checks – bloody doctors had to tell her something in order to justify their existence. She was the cheapest patient at her clinic; never bloody went – not like the other malingerers who filled the plush seating areas with their new-money crises.

Joanna came in, took the liner out of the pedal bin and replaced it. "See you tomorrow, Mrs Gloucester."

Audrey nodded. "Thank you, Joanna. Stairs then tomorrow, is it?" Joanna agreed. She had long since realised that Mrs Gloucester knew exactly what was planned for each day of her schedule; it was her way of keeping tabs and letting Joanna know that there could be no shirking. Audrey gave a curt smile as Joanna put her coat on. She really didn't know why they paid her to be there – didn't bloody do much anyway. Audrey was sure that she just turned the vacuum on and sat and read a magazine, but Jerry insisted on keeping her.

"You'd soon notice if she weren't here, Audrey. No, Joanna stays." Audrey found herself wishing she could have the cleaning to do – she would attack it with venom and have it done in no time. At least she would be accomplishing something. She used to be so *useful*. She used to have a role. Now she was merely passing the days; it was getting to the point when it was a big deal to take a suit to the dry cleaners. Rather than being an inconvenient two minutes involving parking on the double yellows and nipping in, she would plan it, leaving herself plenty of time to park, making sure she had her smarter shoes on and had combed her hair.

However, today she had the Tŷ Mawr file in front of her. She was going to enjoy this new responsibility. She'd lost her way a little over the last ten years or so, once the children had grown up. She'd been a Sister in a large hospital before the children were born and had run a damn tight ship – would never have had MRSA through shoddy cleaning staff on *her* ward.

She'd run playgroups, Brownies and then Guides as her girls had progressed through them and they had been the golden years as far as those institutions were concerned. However, once the children had matured beyond needing such things, she'd been a bit at sea. Just running a large Bridlon town house and two large dogs had kept her fairly busy for a time, but then even her housewife duties had been contracted out – Joanna did the cleaning, late meetings and dinner dates with friends had put paid to home cooking and hence much of the shopping. Jerry didn't seem to need her company as much as he used to either. It seemed that he was getting his support from chit-chat with his friends elsewhere.

She had been involved in a number of voluntary organisations, but had found the company of her peers a little shallow and frivolous. Unable to appreciate their excitement about a new diet or tanning treatment, she felt like a spare part at the occasional meetings over coffee or lunch that she went to. She'd always assumed that they were there to discuss the arrangements for a charity fundraising event – not to decide on what everyone was going to wear to it.

What Audrey possibly didn't realise, however was that in their turn, the other women felt that they had never connected with the charmless woman that smelt of dogs. Most committees considered her a pet project when they first met her, recommending their own hairdressers or beauticians, some even going as far as giving her a dress that they'd "bought in the wrong size". Eventually they'd realise that the nut dressed in raspberry tights and dog-walking shoes was not going to crack and then they would give up and talk around her.

What they had never come to realise was that this was Audrey Gloucester's Jerry Persona as she called it. It was the way she had to be when she was with Jerry or sorting out his affairs – be it organising trips to Tŷ Mawr or assisting with his friends' wives' charity events. She'd been that way when they'd met and although over the years, she'd allowed a softer version of herself, a more mellow person who was more in tune with nature and song, to be born and grow, she could never be anything other than Mrs Jerry Gloucester when she was around him or his circle. It would be like changing the language that you spoke to your mother in. The gentler Audrey who undid her sensible plait, took off her shoes and enjoyed life a little more, had to be saved for somewhere else ...

Jerry and Audrey had made a wonderful young couple; intelligent, handsome and dynamic. Jerry had somehow retained that status whilst Audrey had morphed into a dog lover, her energies being wasted on walking the labradors for six miles a day in three separate stints. She had made noises about getting another job, perhaps going back to nursing, or whatever the blasted term for Ward Sister was these days, but Jerry had seen it in just monetary terms, and hence there was no need and therefore no point. The extra hands that they would have to buy in, in terms of dog walkers and household help would probably cancel out any wage she might receive, so the notion had been put back in the box labelled "Other Life" and the lid shut tightly once more.

Hence the Tŷ Mawr file in front of her, consisting of three filed electricity bills dating back at least five years and a mound of loose papers, provided a twinge of excitement. Something to get her teeth stuck into, a project of her own at last, to manage and make better.

Audrey rifled through the pile and dismissed most of it as irrelevant and threw it out. Then, when the file was tidy and in date order, she returned to the letter she had received that morning from Geoffrey Farmer; this could be just what she was looking for. Sounded like a very sensible fellow.

She nodded at its courteous greeting and then scanned the list of works that he had suggested: the fellow could make a real impact on the place just by completing that list. However, that didn't stop her wincing as her finger stopped against so many of the tasks; *she* could easily do them – if only Jerry would just let her get on with it. It seemed strange that a woman of her calibre felt that she couldn't just do anything she pleased without her husband's agreement. It wasn't that he forbade her or that he wanted her doing nothing but drinking strong coffee and walking dogs, it was just that he had absolutely no interest in doing it himself and therefore he assumed that she didn't either. Therefore money was slung at each problem until it was solved: everyone a winner!

Audrey, however, was a doer rather than an instructor. During her days as Sister, a dirty floor would have seen her showing the cleaning staff how it should be done – and it would have been done to perfection. It therefore irked her to be idle and she had begun feeling pointless and inadequate. She had tried to muck in and do a few tasks that she had begrudged paying Mike Howard to smoke his way through, but the derision she had received from Jerry when the grout had hardened over the shower tiles before she'd wiped it off still maddened her. She remembered the shame of hearing Jerry laughing with Mike over the phone as he calmly and easily arranged to have it done properly and this made her blanch at trying again.

"Bloody inch icicles of grout; got a gash on my leg as if I'd slipped with my ice pick! Do me a favour, Mike, pop over and re-do it when you have a spare five minutes?"

Audrey had imagined Mike's chuckle and, "Of course, Jerry, consider it done. An easy job *if* you know how!"

Then there was the time when Jerry had found her trapped under the rose trellis. That had marked the end of Audrey's foray into DIY. He hadn't even said anything as he'd lifted the archway off her and watched with disdain as she'd crawled out, tearing her tights and filling her hair with dried bits of leaf as she went. He'd let it drop to the ground once she was clear and walked off, leaving Audrey flushed and frustrated. Sod it, she'd thought. Nearly time to walk the bloody dogs again anyway.

Yes, a project was needed and Tŷ Mawr could very well be it. She was heartily sick of Mike Howard, so him having a bad back let her off the hook from having to explain to Jerry why she wouldn't be using him. She would have to have a word with Jerry about releasing some funds so that Geoffrey could have a real crack at it. Go the whole hog, overhaul the sash windows, re-point the north wall and get the damp on the gable end sorted. She found one of Jerry's empty workbooks and started a list.

Chapter 21

Following Horses with a Shovel

Godfrey hadn't really done any work all day. To be fair, he hadn't done a meaningful chunk for years, but today he felt no guilt or qualms. It was his last day. After thirty-two years of hard, hard slog, he was finally free! Free to put all his plans into action; free to start being the *real* Godfrey. Perhaps he should change his name? 'Godfrey' had always seemed a bit dull, plodding perhaps. Some of his schoolmates had been Clives or Jasons – names that conjured up fast cars and exciting women. But his second name was Maurice, so perhaps he'd better just stick to Godfrey.

The department had a ritual on people's last days or special occasions – a big lunch out, the risqué rule-bending of not leaving anyone in the office to man the phones. Sneaking back in late just a little bit tiddly and then a light-headed afternoon with much more chat, flirtation and messing about than usual.

However, things hadn't really turned out as he had thought. During the morning of the appointed day one of the secretaries would come round to each person asking them if they wanted lunch out, in order to book tables. God would usually decline lunch, muttering under his breath about a haircut, appointment or the dentist and he would then join them after they'd eaten for just a drink. Why pay six-pounds twenty-five for a vegetable bake and fries when you could pay around thirty-seven pence for a home-made polony sandwich?

But today there had been no secretary peeping around the door cheerily asking what he fancied for his last supper. Perhaps it was to be a surprise? But, twelve o'clock came and went. Twelve thirty. Twelve forty-five. At one o'clock his stomach forced him to wander up the corridor and sheepishly peer through doorways.

"All right, Godfrey?" called Andy, phone to his ear, baguette in his hand.

"Oh, there you are, Godfrey," called Anwen. "Come here a minute!" His heart leapt, he knew the girls would make a fuss of him, he'd worked there for years. He sauntered through the door, barely able to conceal the grin on his face. "Sign these for me, Godfrey, Sandra's not in today and I need to get them in tonight's post."

His heart sank back again and he meekly signed the papers, noting with a sick feeling in his stomach the sight of empty lunch boxes and sandwich wrappers. Obviously lunch out wasn't going to happen. And the boss, who would normally oblige with a witty speech, wasn't even in.

He pottered for another couple of hours and miserably cleared his desk of his personal items – a comb, a few biros for his pocket, some out of date Rennies. Other offices had bunches of daffodils in them to brighten them up, but he had no plants, no pictures, nothing that made his office look like it had held the same person for nigh on fifteen years.

How was he going to play this one if no one else seemed bothered about his leaving? Should he just slip away at four p.m. or perhaps wait until his usual time – maybe even fill his flasks for a last time? Try and cancel out the cost of a couple of Georgia's numerous cups of tea (made with a full kettle each time!) a day. No, he had to do this properly. If his colleagues weren't going to make any effort, then at least he should remember his own manners and leave with his dignity intact.

Godfrey remembered the first time he'd walked in through the front door of the building. He had been eighteen and full of excitement for his future. He had a newly-opened account with the Principality and he was looking forward to filling it. He had moved from Holsborough to Cysgod y Ffynnon and was excited at the prospect of exploring somewhere new for a couple of years whilst he prepared himself for the next stage in life, and did what he had to do to attain his plans.

Somehow, that building had assisted in sucking the joy and life out of him. He was now fifty years old and had none of the vitality or fun of that handsome young man with his collar-length perm and his flares. He had had a clear plan, the first step of which was a decent job with the Council, in anticipation that his love might come and join him. Nowadays Godfrey had no real plans beyond what he might have in his lunchtime sandwich the following day. He was sure that it hadn't been his initial plan simply to get two promotions and move up a floor in thirty-odd years, but somehow, that was all that had really happened. Funny how life's quirks can alter your route – or how life sometimes doesn't have any quirks to alter its route…

That day had been so significant in his life, yet what had he let happen to the visions that were so structured and full of promise?

Never mind! Time to get back on track now! Fifty years young and still plenty of lead in his pencil, plenty of sausage in his roll and plenty of gas in his tank …

Three-thirty. Godfrey sat at his desk and sighed. He thought back to when Menna had left. Everyone (except him) had gone out at eleven-thirty and come back at three. They'd had a three-course meal and lots of wine before he joined them. Sandra had given a touching presentation and said how much Menna would be missed. The star turn had a large card signed by nearly everyone in the building (except by him – he hadn't had any change on him when the envelope went round). She also got a coffee-maker to make sure that she still drank far too much coffee in her next job, a large bunch of flowers, and then they all left for a night out. Godfrey had stayed behind; he hadn't fancied it. Indeed, he'd been able to fill his flasks early and leave by four ten.

Along the corridor, however, there'd been a great deal more consideration of Godfrey's departure than he suspected. Three days previously Sandra had groaned to a gathering on the stairs that it was lucky the taxpayer wasn't aware of the cost of the Godfrey Debate. The hours lost, the scale of the bitching and genuine soul-searching that had happened within that miserable little department as the public received bills addressed to Mr BSc Hons …

"Sod him," Anwen had said. "He's not put his hand in his pocket *once* for anyone else in this office. Ever. Not come out for lunch, bought cakes, put in for a present, anything. What goes around comes around." And then she folded her arms across her chest, her mind resolute.

"But he's been here for years," groaned Angie. "We can't do *nothing* surely?"

Anwen shrugged. "Why not? He manages it; thinks no one notices – but we do. No, this is his come-uppance – pity he has to learn his lesson on his retirement, but tough. Learn it he will."

Sandra pitied Anwen's children. "Well," she said, "I think everyone must do as they please – if they want to sign a card, take him out for a pint, then they should. If people don't, then they don't have to."

So the debate rumbled on. As Godfrey sat dreaming about being in a crowded bar with a load of friends after a history trip, no, a golf tournament, his colleagues tore his character apart.

As the day had gotten nearer, two camps had formed. The "Sod Him" camp and the "Oh, poor sod, give him some thanks for his thirty years of service," camp. The numbers fluctuated day by day with a hardcore in each.

The blokes, as usual, pretended to rise above such bickering, chuckling righteously to each other, "The cats are out today!" or perhaps more realistically, "Those women need a damn good shagging – give them something more important to talk about." But they lingered at the admin office doorways for longer than usual, enjoying the palaver.

Most, it had to be said, hoped that everyone else would have the guts to completely ignore Godfrey's leaving – perhaps just popping their heads round the door at leaving time to say, "See you then, Godfrey; all the best!" They weren't quite sure if they could be that callous themselves, but felt it was justified from others. On the whole they just found him a bit of a prat. A bit boring, a bit miserable, extremely tight, but he also didn't do any damage to anyone and therefore had achieved the status of "harmless old bugger". They'd be sad to see him go, but only for ten minutes or so. Angie's bum still needed watching and Eleri would still have to lean forward to push that filing trolley up the corridor.

Mansel looked on with disinterest. Early in the race, he'd put himself in the Harmless Old Bugger camp, just a little sad that Godfrey hadn't wangled it to leave a couple of days earlier on April Fool's Day: he, Mansel, would then have been able to make sure that he would go out with a bang! He'd always felt a bit of an allegiance with Godfrey. He felt that Godfrey was a little misunderstood, just like he was himself. In the same way that no one appreciated Mansel's jokes, no one really appreciated the reasons why Godfrey was a tight old git who wouldn't give away the steam from his early morning wee. Mansel hadn't quite worked out those reasons yet, but was always happy to pass the time of day with Godfrey; cricket, the football, golf were all mutually interesting topics that gave the kettle time to boil without having to slip in a bit of filing. Mansel felt that there was still a lot to learn from the older man in terms of wasting time without making it too obvious...

Chapter 22

A Stitch in Time

Four p.m. came. Godfrey watched the clock. At four ten he'd leave. No, better make it four fifteen. At four twenty-five, he got wearily to his feet and shook himself into his jacket. He was just brushing down his dated lapels when Trev peered round the door.

"Are you joining us then, Godfrey? We've got a, er, little something for your leaving."

God flushed with happiness. "Well, thank you, Trev, I'll be along now – just saying goodbye to the old office; I've sat here for ooh, fifteen years."

"Thought it smelt a bit fusty," said Trev brusquely and headed off down the corridor, alternately hugging and berating himself at what was to come.

A little crowd had gathered in Reception, none of whom could really look Godfrey in the eye. Godfrey didn't feel this was out of place – he'd never been able to look anyone in the eye at such gatherings either (but that was because he'd never really earned the right to be there).

Anwen was there, her face triumphant. Eleri lurked in the office, not able to face the event she'd helped plan – suddenly it all seemed a little small-minded and mean. Trev and Andy were there, both rocking back and forth on the balls of their feet in nervous machismo, wondering how it was that the women had cranked it up, yet the blokes were going to have to do the actual bad deeds. Mansel had taken his trousers off out of nervous comedy need. People had become fed up with Mansel's preparatory antics during the day, so they were pretending not to notice. A few other faces hung around, guiltily wanting to enjoy the show. Sandra was nowhere to be seen.

"Well, Godfrey, this is it then you lucky old bugger," said Andy wishing he'd rehearsed something to say – it always sounded so easy and genuine when Sandra had done these things before. "You've worked here a long time and, er, we have too and we've all enjoyed working with you." (It would sound silly to thank Godfrey for his hard work and loyalty to the team as a) he hadn't really done a great deal and b) Andy wouldn't have given a shit even if he had.)

"Apparently the average male lives for just two point eight years after retirement, so I'll be as quick as I can!" The crowd winced, not quite believing that he'd actually just said that. Such jaw droppers were more usually Mansel's style and no one would have considered him to give a leaving speech, even for such a tightwad as Godfrey. "We've had an, er, whip round and…" Andy started to get nervous. Even Godfrey sensed there was something not quite right. Eleri peeped out of her office doorway, her lips pursed and her eyes half shut to block out the forthcoming spectacle. Even Anwen was gritting her teeth.

Suddenly, the double doors crashed open and everyone turned to see Sandra struggling through with a couple of large carrier bags banging against her legs. A sigh of relief went through the air as she regained her composure, regretting her overcoat and trying to free up a hand to push her hair away from her flushed face.

"Ah," she said, trying to blow her fringe from her sticky brow, "I hope I'm not too late for the grand farewell?" A few people sheepishly exchanged glances, but it was Godfrey who went to her aid pulling the door open and collecting the flowered silk scarf that trailed down her back.

The group drew apart and gave Sandra her rightful position at its head. Andy muttered something about not really having started and said, "Over to you."

Sandra quickly assumed her role, her former fluster forgotten. Even her petticoat was re-absorbed by her skirt without any wriggling and hitching.

"Now then – Godfrey, Godfrey, Godfrey." The crowd tittered and Godfrey beamed – this was more like it. She did it all right. She recalled her first impressions of him when she came to the job. She thanked him for his hard work and diligence and his loyalty to the department. She picked a few of his least irritating foibles and allowed people a little chuckle and him a sheepish grin. She painted a lovely scene of him grubbing on a hillside for Stone Age relics whilst they continued to slog in their jobs and she finished by wishing him the greatest luck with his retirement – and the arrival of the new baby.

"And to show our friendship and appreciation of your time in the office," she continued, looking at the others in a school teacher manner, "we've had a whip-round and bought you a few gifts."

Out of her bags she conjured up a number of beautifully wrapped parcels and God was urged to open them so that others could see what their small-mindedness had bought. A hip flask for those early-morning fishing trips, a bobble hat in the colours of Cysgod y Ffynnon FC, an elegant book of old photos of the town that Sandra leapt forward to remove the half-price sticker from the back of and a bottle of fine malt – as it didn't matter any more if he had a bad head in the morning – and it may block out the sound of the baby crying!

Godfrey felt quite touched and almost emotional towards these people all of a sudden. He started muttering a speech about having enjoyed his time there, but realising that no one was really listening as they were all too intent on making messages and gestures to each other via their eyebrows, he settled for a quiet "Thanks." He had actually hoped for a lawnmower, as his own was just about through, but he realised that now was not a time to quibble, though he had made sure to mention it to most of them.

In a final act of generosity, Sandra took Godfrey's arm and led him away from the corridor, babbling aimlessly all the way down the stairs. She simply would not let him see that the carrier bag at Andy's feet contained two new Thermos flasks, a box of unopened tea bags and a key for an electric meter…

Chapter 23

Long Pockets and Short Arms

When Godfrey stepped out of the County Council building for the last time as an employee, on that warm April afternoon, he felt nothing. No sadness for half a lifetime passed in a dreary office, no excitement on being released from it. No poignancy about longstanding friendships that would be changing their footings and no eagerness to search for new ones. All he was thinking of was a twenty-minute walk home and then perhaps a jacket potato for tea – ten minutes in the microwave and then crisped up in the oven – and just momentarily about the missing new lawnmower.

But then Sandra changed everything. "So, Godfrey, a new life eh? Early retirement – you lucky thing! I'll be glad if I can crawl out of here before I'm seventy! Just think, all those things you must have thought of doing when you retired – you'll have to do them now. No excuses anymore – now you just have to put them into practice!"

Godfrey stopped dead. She was right. All those put-off dreams: friends, chatting with fellow members over a drink, a girlfriend, then a fiancée, then after two years, a wife. Children. A caravan – no, that *had* changed recently – a house in the countryside with two chocolate Labradors.

Alice. Alice Jefferson. No! Yes! All that time spent saving, refusing invites, going to bed early – *it all had to change* – there had been a reason for it in the beginning after all and now was the time in which it must all come to fruition. Godfrey's eyes were wide with unaccustomed excitement when he asked Sandra if she would like to go for a celebratory drink!

It was all so easy. They walked to the local pub. He bought two glasses of wine, then she did, then he bought a bottle – and it felt so good. His vouchers fell on the floor. She laughed as he picked them up. He gave her the one for fabric conditioner – he didn't buy it often and she laughed again as she thanked him and ferreted it away in her purse.

He took off his tie, she leant forward. He ran his fingers through his hair and she went to the ladies to remove the red wine from her chapped lips and to apply more scent.

Mansel Big Face stood by the bar. He was alone even though he was part of a crowd. His laughter was loud, his shoulders shaking just a little too regularly. For him it was a compliment to other people that he wished they would return. He was missing Lucy-Ann. He would much rather be sat with her on her sofa, even with that smelly chinchilla on his lap. She'd said that she didn't want to see him every night, as she liked her own space; he accepted this, but didn't really understand – he would have loved to be with her every hour of every day!

However, saying that, he was actually quite enjoying being out tonight with the boys. It was nice to sit with Lucy-Ann on the sofa, but it was also refreshing to have a few pints with his mates, especially after the stress of the Godfrey debate. Lucy-Ann was away on one of her occasional training courses. This time it was *Learning How to Deal with Rejection* – apparently essential de-stressing techniques for telesales people – especially ones that worked alone from home. "I could have written the notes for this one," Lucy-Ann had said wryly that morning as she handed him the keys.

She had asked him if he would mind looking after her animals for her. The lady next door usually did it and Lucy-Ann looked after her cats in return when she was away, but she was staying with relatives for a week and Lucy-Ann had been a little stuck. Mansel had sensed that she was a little uneasy about asking him, as if she wasn't sure that he could handle the responsibility. She had seemed a little nervous about having him in the rest of the house, as if she wasn't yet convinced that he wouldn't rummage through her personal possessions.

Mansel had taken the key with as much gravitas as he could and had clipped it ceremoniously to the belt hook on his trousers. He hadn't managed to get round there yet – he had planned to go on the way home from work, but he had met a friend in the car park who'd told him that their mutual friend Toby's wife had given birth to their first child earlier that morning. So, *voilà!* – in the pub! He felt a little guilty, but they were only gerbils and things like that – it wasn't as if they needed their daily walk by six every night! He'd leave the pub early and pop in on the way home and do it all properly then.

Until that time though, it was Toby's night, and he was

obliged to be there and wanted to share his excitement. Maybe the boys would be raising a glass to him one day? Alun handed round a tin of cigars, catching the barman's eye as he pretended to light it. "For later, boys, for later," the barman warned. Instead, they all raised their glasses to Toby and muttered a welcome to baby Jack.

Mansel thought that Toby was missing the perfect opportunity to hold centre stage. He, Mansel, would certainly capitalise on it when it was his turn. It was pretty weak, Toby just sitting there quietly supping his beer and saying, almost tearfully, "It was wonderful. Rachel did so well. Just wonderful. And baby Jack is so cute – little tiny tiny hands. It's like holding a little bag of crisps."

Mansel imagined himself standing in the middle of a circle waxing about how it was like trying to push a wet spaniel backwards through a cat flap.

They would shout, "You didn't!" when he told them how the midwife said, "I can see the head!" and he said, "Well, if it's ginger, it's going back in!" and how the midwife couldn't stop giggling. He imagined that even his wife would snigger at that one. "Does he ever stop?" the midwife would have asked Lucy-Ann – *in his wildest dreams, maybe* – and she would roll her eyes amid her pain and say, "No, not this one!"

Mansel wasn't unaware of the muttered "prat"s that would accompany some of his tales. He just felt that they were misdirected, that somehow they hadn't gotten the joke. He'd stopped the ones about cancer when he'd made someone cry and the ones about homosexuality had brought a few shudders since Adrian had joined the crowd.

He wasn't sure why his humour was wasted on these mates. They'd fallen about laughing at school at his one-liners. He remembered the hysterics at his Morris Minor joke in third year biology; that was surely his finest hour. Perhaps the others had just gotten dull and humourless as they'd grown older, their jobs, kids and lives wearing their spirits down. That was why he was still so buoyant, he thought. His job was a doddle and he was courting the lovely Lucy-Ann.

He dragged himself back to the conversation – what were they laughing at now? Had he missed something that he could have added a quip to? He was rather hoping there would be an opportunity for his tale of how he'd strimmed a toad at the weekend when he was cutting his lawn.

His eyes were also on the couple in the corner – could it really be Godfrey Palmer and Sandra Burton? Together in a "together" kind of way? They must have come straight from that cringing presentation to the pub and were still here. He'd *never* seen Godfrey in a social situation outside of the office and Sandra had stopped following Dave to the pub after he'd left her for Hayley.

That had not been right, Dave leaving Sandra and his kids just for a different view in the bedroom. It messed kids up, their parents arguing and separating. OK, so maybe Sandra did need to spice up a bit, take a *little* more pride in herself, but there was really no need to throw herself at Godfrey Palmer like she was. If she'd had a new haircut, a little less tummy and a chirpier disposition, then Dave probably wouldn't have gone for Hayley in the first place.

If Dave were honest, the only real difference between Hayley and Sandra was leopard print – they were the same age, both had two kids, a house, a car and a job. Dave might have found that it would have been a lot less upheaval for his poor children if he'd just visited a ladies' clothes shop and bought his wife a few presents instead. However, thought Mansel, having said that – in Lycra terms, seeing Sandra's sensible polyester blouse and comparing it to Hayley's fantastic leopard print strapless numbers, Dave had probably done the right thing.

But what was going on now?

A bottle of wine had just been emptied and a flush had entered both their cheeks. Surely they weren't going to become an item? How could that happen – Godfrey-tight-as-a-fish's-arse-Palmer and Sandra-ooh-I-mustn't-forget-my-umbrella-Burton getting together? No, not right at all.

Mansel had thought that Godfrey didn't have a sexual cell within him, yet seeing him sat there, drinking and laughing with Sandra – maybe he wasn't such a bad prospect after all. Perhaps Sandra's kids could use someone like Godfrey in their lives. A bit of stability and consistency was good for children.

The upshot was – everyone needed to find someone like Lucy-Ann! Someone who made them happy like she did him! Godfrey wasn't nearly as funny as he needed to be to have regular sex and a cooked dinner on the table every now and then – it had taken him, Mansel, years to get to this point. But now he was here, here was where he intended to stay.

"Ah, it was an incredible thing to watch," sighed Toby and a few of the other men nodded in agreement.

Mansel dragged himself away from his wise thoughts and

back to the conversation in hand. "I've heard it's like trying to push a wet spaniel back through a cat flap!" he quipped. "Hey, and guess what? I strimmed a toad the other day when I was cutting the lawn!"

"Prat."

"Jee-sus."

"Cock."

Chapter 24

Eating Blackbirds

Neither being used to dating rules or flirting games, Sandra offered to cook Godfrey a meal. He was enjoying himself so thoroughly, he said yes. They wandered home together, Sandra giggling a little at Godfrey's weak jokes and then clutching his arm for stability because she felt she could.

She fumbled for her key and he surveyed her house, garage and garden as he rubbed the life back into the hand that had carried the cruelly-heavy plastic bags. Nothing hugely expensive, but reasonable and well-maintained. The carpets were a little worn, but they were a quality floor covering and the coats on the racks were well made and of a durable nature.

Sandra clattered into the kitchen and deliberately set the lighting low. She was reaching a state of inebriation whereby an electric strip light was harsh and unforgiving.

"The kids are with their dad for once," she said, jolting Godfrey back from his tallying. Yes, that was Sandra's downfall – already having kids; it may be that she wouldn't want or couldn't have any more – but then, Jerry probably wouldn't at his age either, so maybe it would work out OK? If he was going to become a little bit more like Jerry and live the same kind of lifestyle, perhaps he needed to re-think the idea of a family. Sandra regained her place as equal top of his list of two.

She cooked him steak and he loved it. It had probably been years since he had indulged in such a spread. Oven chips, mushrooms, tomatoes, the lot. More wine. He started slurring; she started flirting. Her blouse's top button came undone and the neck slipped sideways to show her practical wide bra strap. Her petticoat returned to its usual position half an inch below her hem.

They retired to the lounge, sitting next to each other on the sofa in the big bland room. The lounge had stopped seeking any character many years ago. Too many photos of the kids in school uniform looked down from the walls, their oval brown card backgrounds set off by the run-of-the-mill gilt frames. (The smiles, which should have reflected innocence and youthful gaiety, had been induced by the photographer whispering, "Sex," at the required moment.)

Some may have sneered at the safe décor, the bland TV cabinet and the extent of the pelmets on the curtains, but Godfrey noted the sense of comfort, the warmth and the forty-two inch television screen.

Sandra had started pouting at him. From where he sat, he could see a fair chunk of her bra. He could also, if he chose to look, see up her skirt to the point at which her stomach met her legs. But, he was a gentleman, and so averted his eyes – most of the time.

A vision of a girlish woman flashed before him, her hair hanging around her face, a daisy looped behind her ear, her fingers playing with the wooden beads around her neck as she smiled at him. He compared it to the middle-aged woman sat across from him and wondered whether he should start moving on: he wasn't that young dude about to get himself another pair of zebra-print platform shoes anymore, and it wasn't fair to expect anyone else to have been preserved in amber either. If his retired life was going to be for living, maybe he was going to have to re-examine his ideals, as well as his cholesterol levels.

It was a jolt for Godfrey. The wine was making him lose his usual self-control – not only in his bodily actions, but also the connections with his mind. He surely hadn't avoided this kind of thing for thirty years in order to invest the price of a couple bottles of supermarket wine? *Surely?*

Godfrey felt his composure slipping away from him, and now the wine made him fuzzy and distant from the night's happenings. His lack of experience in such a situation made him embarrassed about what he should or could do next. It was moving too fast for him. The recognition of his life's limitations was momentous enough. Having Sandra pulling out all of her rusty stops – and doing a jolly good job of it in Godfrey's malnourished eyes – was almost an event too far. What would the eighteen-year-old Godfrey have done? He'd have known how to move the situation forward, make the best of such a scenario! However, the truth was that the fifty-year-old Godfrey didn't really know what to do next. He may have been saving such antics for his retirement, but he'd already bought two bottles of wine (and at pub prices too) and that was probably enough boundary pushing for one day.

If Sandra had had a foreskin, Godfrey could have cracked

on with confidence, having perfected his lonely technique over the years, but presumably she didn't and therefore it was best to start the next stage of his seduction on a clear head and an empty, gas-free stomach.

So, he got unsteadily to his feet, holding on to the sofa back for support. "Well, Sandra," he said slowly and carefully, aware that he was in danger of being a drunken buffoon. "I must go; I promised Georgia I wouldn't be late. Thank you for a lovely evening, a beautifully done meal and your kind company."

"Oh, are you going?" slurred Sandra, wiping some smoky grey eye shadow onto her temple. "You don't have to, the kids are out, you could even stay over if you wanted to, the spare room is made up; I'll just kick the cat off it." She felt her prey slipping from her blood-stained talons – *so near, so so near, surely?* With the whine of a drunken woman, she started babbling, "Oh go on, go on, it'll be fun. No strings; it wouldn't take long. I haven't really done it since Dave left and probably for a few years before that. Go on, you won't regret it in the morning. We can have some nice fresh croissants and orange juice?"

Godfrey thrust his feet into his shoes and started backing down the hall. Although he felt like sprinting from the house, his arms flailing above him as if he were shouting, "Fire! Run for your lives!" something within him told him not to close any doors behind him. He had had very few genuine offers in life and certainly none of this nature; he needed to keep his options open, think everything over with a sober head.

"Thank you again, Sandra. Come round to us one night.

Come and see the baby; Georgia would love it." He grabbed his bags and left as quickly as he could, scuttling down the pavement like a child who had been told not to run by his teacher…

Sandra watched him go, somehow finding the reserve to stop herself from running down the road after him. She just didn't want the evening to end yet. But as he rounded the corner and the sound of his leaving presents clonking into each other within their carrier bags disappeared into the silence, she shut the door with a sigh.

She drank three cups of tea down straight in an attempt to stop the room spinning, was sick twice and then fell into a deep slumber with her tights around her knees.

Chapter 25

Rummaging Down the Back of Other People's Sofas

It was eleven thirty and Mansel and five other blokes were winding their way along the high street. They were laughing and joking and one of them was kicking a Shandy Bass can along in front of him. Mansel felt on a high. He'd had a great evening, laughing and telling funny stories with his friends and obviously the beer had helped the night on its path. In a strange way, even though he'd known them most of his life, tonight he felt that he was much more accepted by them, that they now had much more in common.

They'd asked about Lucy-Ann and seemed genuinely pleased that it was going so well. Howard had muttered something about wasn't she the mad bint with the rabbit teeth, but the others had cried him down and said that they had thought that she looked gorgeous when they'd seen her on the night she and Mansel had first met. Mansel felt proud to drop her name into the conversation now and then and to be accepted finally as a "grown-up" amongst all his married or co-habiting friends.

So as he walked down the street, he felt he was invincible. As a teenager, he'd have had to have thrown a traffic cone through a shop window at this point, but as an adult he was trying to contain his exhilaration.

"Kebab anyone?" slurred Toby.

"Of course," cried Mansel, "it's a special occasion!"

They wound their way up a small back alley to the best kebab shop in town and stepped over other partygoers sat in the gutter scoffing chips and salad pittas, not noticing the chilli sauce dribbling down their new tops.

Mansel stepped into the Heavenly Kebab and greeted the men behind the counter like old friends.

"Hello, my friend! How are you?" one called to Mansel in his thick Greek accent. Adding, *That prick who was sick down the front of the counter is in again* in his native language to a colleague at his side. The three other men looked up and smiled at Mansel.

"What will it be tonight, my friend? Hot hot chilli sauce? Our most garlicky garlic sauce? What can we get for you?" *(You can give him the scraggy bits off the bottom if you want – he doesn't seem to mind.)*

"I'll have your largest doner kebab," Mansel grinned, rubbing his hands together in anticipation, "and *three* portions of onion rings!" He looked around for the admiring glances.

"Three, eh, my friend! Quite an appetite tonight, eh? *(Come on, let's make sure he's up all night.)* You want our hottest chilli on those too, eh? A big guy, eh?" Mansel laughed modestly and tried to suck his stomach in.

"They obviously think you're a fat bastard, too, mate," laughed Howard, "I'll just have a portion of chips please – with a little salt and vinegar."

The others placed their orders and soon they were winding their way back down the alley to the road where they would have to go their separate ways, juggling their greasy packs of food and flicking bits of lettuce and onion to the floor. "I never know why I ask for all the salads," moaned Fat Git, scooping a handful of grated carrot out of his pitta bread and throwing it on someone's car. "I hate bloody salad."

"You're tight," said Toby, a flap of meat sitting on his chin. "Don't want to risk missing out on something. Anyway, the night's still young – anyone fancy going back to my place after this? It's going to be my last night of freedom after all!"

Mansel jumped at the chance and the others agreed that they would too, just better text the missus first etcetera. Then Mansel groaned – he still had to do the bloody rabbits – he was already six hours later than he had promised that he would be.

"Don't worry," said Toby, "Lucy-Ann lives on Heol-y-Bryn, doesn't she? That's on the way; you can pop in on the way past." And they all wondered off in the direction of Heol-y-Bryn.

Mansel started to get a bit worried, he knew Lucy-Ann wouldn't be pleased with him being late anyway – apparently her animals were quite sensitive about their routines – let alone being pissed and bringing half a dozen blokes and their greasy fingers into her home.

"Look," he said, cramming the last of his onion rings into his mouth, "I'll run on and get it all sorted and I'll catch you up at Toby's, OK?"

"This 'running on' I've got to see," laughed Fat Git as

Mansel set off at a jog only slightly faster than their walking pace, weaving across the road as he went.

"We're be-HIND you!" called Toby and the others laughed and started walking as fast as they could, dropping chips and blobs of mayonnaise on their shoes as they went.

By the time Mansel reached the navy blue door of number thirty-two, he was exhausted. His head was beginning to spin and his movements were clumsy. He knew that he shouldn't be doing this in his current state, but Lucy-Ann need never know and he could make a solemn promise to himself that he would never be so irresponsible again.

As he fumbled for the key fob that he'd attached to his trouser belt loops, he felt his guts churn. Uh-oh, he shouldn't have had that Martini chaser, or that third portion of onion rings – and why the hell had he asked for another squirt from his friend the chilli sauce bottle? Surely one day he should simply *learn*: everyone else seemed to? With no time to spare, he got his key into the lock, burst in and charged upstairs, leaving the front door swinging open behind him. He just about made it to the toilet, where he sat with his head in his hands as his reputation as a hard drinking, iron-stomached man of steel ran from him in a painful gush.

Although his head was spinning, he was aware of a noise downstairs and much laughing and shrieking. He couldn't quite determine what it might be, but knew that it wasn't good. "Boys! Boys, m'n," he called in a pathetic whimper that barely made it to the bathroom door, let alone down the stairs. He daren't get up, as he was sure that Lucy-Ann wouldn't appreciate that either.

He heard one last crash through his fug and lots of laughing and a bit more shouting. Then he heard the front door slam and it went quiet. Thank God for that he thought as he turned to be sick in the bath. At last he could finish off in peace and then go and feed the animals. Lucy-Ann had said she'd left a list out and all the food in bowls, so all he had to do was make sure he gave the right bowl to the right critter. It surely couldn't be that hard…

Chapter 26

Watching Television in a Shop

Godfrey was pleased to receive a letter from Audrey on the first day of his retirement. He'd spent the night nursing a bad tummy and a sore sphincter and was keen to set some positive plans into place.

Dear Geoffrey,

Thank you for your kind letter. Your services would be very helpful and therefore I suggest we start forthwith. Your suggestions seem acceptable; please ring to give me a price for them and we can begin soonest.

Regards,

Audrey Gloucester.

Feeling decisive and positive, he phoned her number immediately.

"Audrey Gloucester," clipped the answer and he returned to being a local authority buffoon. At length he explained who he was, or rather whom he was impersonating, and thanked her for her letter. Sounding bored and impatient, she listened to his explanations and then cut through his waffle.

"Sounds just what we're looking for. You happy to price things up and then get on with it?"

Godfrey reassured her until she cut through him again and told him where the key was hidden – just this week though – and he pretended to clarify and take a note.

He packed a few items into his old work bag: a tape measure, notebook and pencil and then after a few seconds hesitation, his old Thermos flasks. Things may be changing since his retirement, but there was no need to let perfectly good habits slip.

He went into the sitting room and found Georgia sat amongst a chaos of muslin squares, breast pads and nappies wrapped into foul-smelling pasties. A morning debate ranted away on the box, the fire raged despite the fact that it was now April, the curtains were shut and the lights were on.

He felt his temper rising but then she smiled at him and his heart melted. "Sleeping?" he whispered. Georgia nodded carefully so as not to disturb the limpet on her chest.

He explained he was off to see someone and Georgia nodded, having no sense of incredulity that he might actually be visiting a friend. "Oh, Uncle God, you couldn't do me a favour on your way could you?" Godfrey nodded reluctantly, sensing another assault on his already ravaged wallet. "There's a load of washing on my bed – mainly Jocey's stuff. You couldn't take it to the launderette and get a service wash could you? They won't do just drying and it's been raining on and off for days. Jocey has nearly run out of clothes, poor thing!"

Godfrey winced – a service wash! Did she think he was made of money? And then he realised: yes, of course she did. She'd never been given any evidence to the contrary – not realising she'd been the only exception to his rule against generosity since her birth.

"Oh," he muttered miserably, wishing he could forget it, but well, perhaps it was his fault for being tight-fisted in the first place. Another few outfits would have given them another day's drying grace. However, he knew that this was all irrelevant to Georgia. All she knew was that she needed something washed and it was not in her easy reach to get it done.

Godfrey had already gathered the weary knowledge of every parent who knows that if they do not pick something up then it will never, *ever*, move. So he had taken to wandering around the house gathering up a cup here, a wrapper there, a tiny sock or a pile of tissues. The shelf above the radiator in the hall became a halfway house for all these lost souls and they would be left there waiting for him to complete their journey to the bin, the sink or Jocey's chest of drawers.

He knew that Georgia was oblivious to it all. She had said that the only time the squat would ever have been tidied was when either someone would lose their temper and chuck all the food wrappers down the stairs or when Danner was on speed. Godfrey knew that Annabel had always cleaned up after her when she had lived at home, so Georgia really had very little concept of the work involved in keeping things nice.

It was the same with money. Georgia seemed oblivious to the accepted rule that to have money, one has to earn it.

It is not finite and it is spent easier than it is earned. To him, a service wash equalled an hour's work, three meals or a week's electricity. To her it equalled, "I need a service wash. Will someone sort it please?"

So he set off to Tŷ Mawr in the car (see, now it meant that he had to use the car too!) with bad grace and Georgia's washing burning a hole in the boot. However, as he turned into the lane he felt his mood rise. He felt a sparkle of excitement that his legitimacy allowed him. Even if Eira was there, that was OK. Eventually he was bouncing down the farm track, enjoying swerving around potholes and scattering the idle sheep that lazed behind the fence.

He pulled into the yard and skidded to a halt in a style reminiscent of Audrey's. He slammed the door of his car, a satisfying bang that reverberated off the huge barn doors. His tool bag over his shoulder, he whistled his way to the side porch and easily put his hand on the key. The kitchen felt better for not being sneaked into and he put his bag onto the table with a confident crash.

To do the job properly, perhaps he needed to have a good look around? Taking his notebook and pen, he started to survey the house. He opened kitchen drawers and cupboard doors, alternately nodding or frowning at the contents – old Jerry was obviously a bit of a hoarder Godfrey chuckled, as he discovered a sideboard drawer full of tobacco-encrusted pipes.

A latch clicked open to show a utility room – however, it wasn't the broken pane of glass that caught his surveyor's eye, but the washer-dryer. It stood there, brilliant white and seemingly unused. He stared at it for a while – he couldn't, could he? He looked more carefully; it had a rapid programme, surely only half an hour, forty minutes at most? What if Eira came? But what were the chances of that? And if he locked the door from the inside, he'd have notice of her arrival? Sod it – why not…

So God collected the bag of fetid laundry and shoved it into the machine, wrinkling his nose slightly as the smell of sour milk and dried poo caused his still-fragile stomach to somersault. He poured a generous heap of powder into the drawer, followed by a glug of fabric conditioner – a nicety that little Jocey was yet to experience – and turned the machine on. It sounded deafening in the silent house and it shunted his guilt into place. He memorised where the off button lay, propped open the utility room door for a quick switch off opportunity and returned to lock the kitchen door.

He resumed his survey, now able to note the broken pane and the dripping tap. Room by room he pried, prodded and poked his way round. His notebook filled – in fairness to him – in a neat and methodical way. He drank in the old-money class. The furniture suites had been handed down from previous generations, expensive, solid but dusty. Mrs Howard certainly wasn't as house-proud as she might be. Clothes in wardrobes were dated but quality, books were hardbacks and Jerry's shaving brush was real badgers' bristle.

As he picked it up to see whether the handle was made of horn or not, he remembered his own father's shaving brush and the pitiful amount of bristles it had on it. Everything in their childhood house had been just about useable. Things were worn and used until they fell apart, and then they were repaired and used for a little bit longer. "You work hard enough, Godfrey, and you'll have everything that you want, but you don't have it until you've earned it, that's the ticket." So, because his parents earned very little, they didn't have things. So Godfrey had saved and saved so that he *could* have things – *and the person who wanted those things* – but still, he knew it was unlikely that he would *ever* have things like this…

Godfrey went into the second large bathroom, stepping down into it and admiring it as it opened out in front of him. This room had more of Audrey's touch; two thick towels, or bath sheets as his catalogue offers informed him such things were called, were hanging over a carved wooden airer. Baskets of dusty soaps sat beside jars of bath salts on the tiled surround and a wicker chair sat a respectful distance from the bath.

Godfrey thought of his miserable bathroom at home. Turquoise tiles chilled the user even before they got undressed. Small, worn towels flayed the skin from one's back and any cleansing product was supermarket's own with added abrasive qualities.

However, here was luxury. The window was of clear glass as it beheld no overlooking properties and Godfrey admired the view over the yard and the surrounding estate. He had the urge to live this life, to stand here and see his own fields, livestock and woodlands. He felt aches in his back that should have come from a day's fishing, but instead were from a lumpy mattress and a body not used to alcohol abuse.

He first heard then felt the drip that splattered rhythmically from the bath's tap – it was warm. "Christ," he muttered, "they keep the boiler on full time!" It would be pointless not to use the present tank-full before he turned it off – that small act of kindness would compensate for his use of the washing machine within a week. Hearing that washing machine complete its spin and reckoning he had a further forty-five minutes of drying time to pass, he put in the plug and turned the tap on full.

Godfrey laid his clothes out in the same way his parents had as teenagers during the war, so that he could easily jump back into them. He opened the window a fraction – he should hear any approaching car and have plenty of time to sort himself out before the occupants even reached the locked door.

He slopped in bath salts and bubble bath and selected a large towel from the airer. He felt no remorse as he sat naked on the wicker chair, his bare arse nestling into Audrey's silk cushion, instead pride at a job well done. As he lowered himself into the deepest bath he'd ever had, he felt happy and at home, and sighed his great contentment.

Chapter 27

Boiling up the Bones

Lucy-Ann's first clue to the fact that all might not be well was the sight of a pair of trousers dangling from the front door key in the lock of her front door and a large pair of shoes lying abandoned on the pavement.

She parked her car and crept slowly into the house, not knowing what on earth she might find. What she did find made her gasp in distress and fall to her knees with a cry.

Two cages were lying on the floor, the gerbils and hamsters within them huddled into the corners that had once been on their roofs. Plates of food were kicked over and bowls of water were lying empty beside stains on her carpet. There were handfuls of hay strewn around the place, lying along the mantelpiece and shelves like Christmas decorations. A bottle of half-finished wine that she had left, corked, on the hearth, was now empty and lying on its side.

She ran to her creatures and slowly checked each one, crooning gently to them. She righted the cages, refilled their food and water bowls and set the rest of the room to rights. Only then could she embark on her next job.

With her face set into stone, she checked the kitchen then stormed up the stairs in a furious rage. The smell of vomit hit her and a quick peep in the bathroom clarified the source of that and she turned away with distaste on her face. Her bedroom was as it should be, which left the spare room. A snore came from it and she strode in, fuming in anger. There on the bed lay Mansel. Face down. Dribbling on her spare pillows. Stinking like a polecat.

She watched him for a couple of seconds, trying to decide what to do. Should she just boot him straight out or listen to his story and *then* boot him out? In the end, she kicked the bed and he sat up, clearly disorientated and obviously not feeling well.

"You bastard," was all she could think of saying. *"You bastard!"* Her voice choked. "I trust you for *one* night. One bloody night, and you do this – this – to my house and my animals. How could you?"

"Wha'? Sorry? Lucy-Ann? Hang on, what's happened?"

"What's happened?" her voice rose to a cry. "You trashed my house. You knocked over my animal's cages. You threw up in my bath and you ask what's *happened*?"

Mansel lay back down and groaned. "I came by, I wasn't well. I think I just went to bed… Oh God, I can't remember…" He pulled the flowered duvet cover over his chest as if to hope that it would protect him from the onslaught.

Lucy-Ann folded her arms, and shook her head, trying hard not to cry. "I can't believe you would do this. I *trusted* you…"

"Are they OK? The animals?" Mansel tried to pull himself up again and the pain from his throbbing head showed in his face.

"They'll live. But that's not the point. *Not the bloody*

point! They're my pets. My *friends.* I wouldn't have gone on that course if you'd said you'd rather not look after them, if you said that you couldn't be trusted not to come round pissed and trash the place. I could have left the course last night and missed the evening workshop and meal and come home; it wouldn't have been a big deal." Lucy-Ann was shaking now, her petite features pursed in rage.

"Do you know, Mansel Big Face, that you're the first person I've trusted properly, apart from a few friends, in a long time? You wouldn't believe how long a time. And now this…" She turned away as if to wash her hands of him, then decided against it and turned back to finish him off. "No, actually, I'm not going to let you off lightly. I'm going to make sure that when you are sat on your big sofa in front of your big television with all your little mates around you, that you know what a shit you've been and why I'm *so* upset."

Mansel tried to sit up and look at her, but his face cringed in pain again as his head moved too quickly. He settled for resting his chin on his elbow and tried to look up at her, squinting at the bright sun that was streaming in through the window.

"When I was at school, I used to get bullied every day. Every-single-day. I would get my hair pulled on the bus – so I got it cut. It still got pulled. I was called Goofy, Rabbits, Bunny-Gob and Chomper. I got a brace, it got worse – then I was called Metal Mickey, Metal Rabbit, anything. My mum told me to ignore them. But, how can you ignore people who trip you up or make munching noises as you walk by. My dad said, 'Fight back,' but look at me – I'm five foot three and eight stone. How could I fight six girls who put carrots in my pocket? It was ridiculous. Even now, looking back, it was pathetic – I hadn't done anything. My only crime was being a bit small and weedy and having a toothy smile. It was hideous. Then one day," and here Lucy-Ann started to cry, "one day…"

Mansel hauled himself up as if to go to her, his face distressed at her pain. *"Don't you touch me!"* she screamed and got renewed strength from batting him back down. "One day," she continued, now calmer, "they were all laughing at me coming out of the cloakroom as I put my rucksack on and I decided that I couldn't go on the bus that night, so I walked three miles home. And when I got home, I found…I found a rabbit in my rucksack. The poor thing was terrified. So, I made him a home in a box, then got him a hutch and we became friends." It was as if she was talking to herself now, rather than ranting at him. "I never went on the bus again, I walked six miles a day, three miles there and three miles back. I sat on my own, ate on my own and avoided everyone as much as I could. Eventually I made a few friends, but my real friends were at home, so I didn't really need them…"

She looked at him, then looked around the room with its packs of spare hay, bags of feed, spare cages, drinking bottles and rubber toys. "I suppose it might have got a little out of hand. Maybe I don't need twenty of them anymore, but *that* is why they are so important to me. And that is why your disrespect of them is the reason why I am asking you to leave – and not come back."

Lucy-Ann stood to one side and looked out of the window. She was spent. She'd said her piece and now she felt cleansed and calm. Mansel didn't argue, he just stood up, clutching the duvet to him as he looked around him at the floor.

"Your trousers are on the front door," she said impatiently and rolled her eyes. He looked confused but followed her instructions. She couldn't look at him and held the door as he shuffled past. "*Leave* the bathroom," she ordered, as he saw the mess and blanched. "I'd rather do it myself than have you here another minute."

"Lucy-Ann," he whispered, looking pathetic with his hair all tufted and sticking up, duvet around his waist, "I'm so very sorry, I really am. I'm crap, but I would never mean to hurt anything, especially anything belonging to you. I'm just so sorry." She shrugged her shoulders and it dismissed him. He shuffled off down the stairs and Lucy-Ann was left alone.

She waited until she had heard him wrestle with his trousers and she heard a car beeping at him as it drove past and some young lads shouting at him out of their car window. Then the front door clicked quietly shut and her house was silent once more.

She went to the window and peeped out as Mansel walked painfully up the street. He turned around a couple of times to look at the house and stopped as if deliberating whether to come back and talk to her again, and she would lean back, tucking herself behind the curtains; she couldn't bear the look of pain on his face. She watched as he rubbed his hair and hung his head and slowly disappeared around the corner.

Then she sunk onto the bed and burst into tears, burying her head in his pillow. It smelt slightly of sick, but it also smelt of Mansel and it was the last scent of him that she may ever have …

Chapter 28

Charging your Mobile Phone at the Office

Toby was walking through town; he had a bit of a thick head, but was busy getting in a few provisions for his wife's return with the baby. It was mid-morning and the town was full of people gathering their goodies for the weekend.

He saw a familiar figure trudging along the pavement on the opposite side of the road. He had his work clothes on, but they looked as if he'd slept in them.

"Mansel!" he called and for a moment, he thought that Mansel had heard him. "Oy! Big Face! Over here!" Jeez – he looked rougher than he, Toby, felt! Toby crossed the road to greet him.

"Hey, buddy, how ya doing? Good night last night, eh? I've got a mouth like the bottom of a budgie cage – no, more like a gerbil cage, eh?"

Mansel glared at him and tried to walk past. "Hey, what's up? One onion ring too many for you or what?" Big Face turned back, still with a crumple mark on his face from lying face down on the pillow and with some dried saliva on his cheek.

"She dumped me, *that's* what's up. I fucked up, didn't I? I got pissed and forgot, didn't I? Instead of respecting her animals, I puked in her bath then passed out. And apparently all my friends…" (and the word was spat out) "…came in too and ransacked the house – and I let them, because I was comatose upstairs." Mansel's black stare and stale breath made Toby take a step back.

"What d'ya mean, dumped you? Because of what *we* did? Come on Mansel, we were only having a laugh."

"Some fuckin' laugh…" scoffed Mansel, "Pity my *ex*-girlfriend doesn't think so, eh?" and Mansel pushed past Toby and stormed off up the hill as fast as his monster hangover would allow.

Toby felt like he'd been winded. Mansel – dumped? Because of their arsing around? OK, so they hadn't puked in the bath - that had been *his* contribution – but dumped?

He leant against a shop window and sighed. Poor bloody Mansel, the first time in ages, years maybe that he'd seemed genuinely happy, rather than just acting happy and now his so-called mates had blown it for him.

Toby pulled out his mobile phone and started making a few calls – his celebration, his responsibility…

Chapter 29

Ironing Gift Wrap

Lucy-Ann flitted around the kitchen, tidying a bit here, moving a few things around there. The radio was on and she was humming and occasionally breaking into song – the wrong lyrics, but song all the same. She'd treated herself to a pot of fresh coffee and was about to go and sit, with a mug-full of it and a paper, where the sun was shining through the window when there was a knock at the door. She stopped dead.

Lucy-Ann rarely had knocks on her front door. She kept herself to herself with her neighbours, and friends knew to make arrangements far in advance and not to surprise her.

Mansel. It had to be Mansel back.

She hoped it wasn't as she wasn't quite sure yet as to what she thought about the Mansel situation. What he and his friends did should be unforgivable. He'd betrayed her trust, disrespected her, her animals and her house and that should be enough to say, "Sorry, no forgiving, no having another go: relationship over."

However, she had been so excited since meeting Mansel; it was as if her dreams had been answered. A handsome man, broad-shouldered and tall with a sense of humour to die for – and to die from, she giggled to herself, despite her heavy heart.

In the past men had never quite hit her spot, and she not theirs. They were drawn to her gregariousness at first, but then her comments and humour and animals caused puzzlement and finally disdain. People rarely bothered to finish with her formally, they just tended not to bother calling again. It was as if they felt that she *surely* wouldn't expect another date after the rather pointless last one that they had shared?

She'd never had anyone she felt she should fight to keep; actually, keeping someone had never really been in her gift. Yet, with Mansel, she'd felt that she had met a person with whom she could have a future and that is why when things like this happened, it was so important to get it right. If, with previous boyfriends, such a situation had arisen, it would have been the end. No discussion, just a final ending point. "Yes, that relationship ended on the Saturday morning, when I told him to leave after he'd thrown-up in my bath." She'd never had such a passionate argument before; never exposed herself in a way that actually mattered.

Despite this, inside she felt strangely calm. It was as if the row – well, it had been hardly a row, more like a rant – had been cathartic. Somehow, telling someone all that humiliating stuff that she had kept bottled up for so many years had made it over. Not that it made it right or that it didn't matter, but that it had happened to her as Lucy-Ann the girl, the teenager. Now she was Lucy-Ann the woman and she was a different person. At last she was no longer that skinny little girl with buck teeth that everyone took the piss out of for wearing old clothes and naff shoes. She was successful, she had her own home, she had been told that she was pretty and she could wear whatever she wanted as long as she paid for it.

Adults didn't put rabbits in people's bags. It had happened *in the past*. She didn't need to be ruled by it anymore. She wouldn't get teased if she went on a bus anymore, people wouldn't be cruel about her hair if she walked down an office corridor. So, although she still didn't relish the thought of seeing Mansel, she decided that she might open the door to him. See what he actually wanted. She didn't have to let him in. She didn't even have to listen if she didn't want to.

So she opened the door and outside were five men, each holding a large bunch of flowers. Lucy-Ann reeled in shock. One of the men stepped forward.

"Lucy-Ann? I'm Toby. This is Howard, Alun, Fat Git and Adrian. We're Mansel's friends and we owe you an apology."

Howard stepped forward and gave her his bouquet. "Lucy-Ann, we behaved like drunken tossers last night and we are really, truly sorry. Mansel had run on to feed your animals and we followed him. He didn't let us in; we let ourselves in while he was upstairs. I'm afraid we messed up your sitting room and we are so sorry. Mansel was just pissed. He didn't want us to come in: he said he would meet us at Toby's, but we were out celebrating Toby's baby being born and we'd had too much to drink and, well, we are very sorry."

Adrian muttered his apology and offered his flowers too. Alun did the same. Fat Git passed his to Alun and also a carrier bag with a few bottles of wine in. "To replenish what we drank of yours. None of us could remember exactly what it was that we drank, so we've bought a few and hope that we got it right. Don't blame Big Face, it was all us really."

Lucy-Ann stood stunned. She had four bouquets in her arms and another being passed to her. "Hang on," she said, trying to get to grips with what was going on and give herself a bit of breathing space. "Let me just get these inside." Toby nodded that he would help her and he gathered two of the bouquets and the carrier bag of wine. At a signal from Toby, the others muttered their apologies again and said that they hoped that they would see her again some time in better circumstances and then disappeared off up the road.

Toby followed Lucy-Ann into the house and through into the back kitchen. He hovered around as she busied herself with the flowers. Neither seemed to know what to say. Toby eventually broke the silence.

"I know it's not my place to say, but don't be too hard on Mansel, Lucy-Ann. He mucked up, but he really didn't mean to be disrespectful."

"Oh, I know," she replied lightly. "He was crap rather than malicious." She carried on looking in the cupboards for vessels that would hold all the flowers: she'd never had need for much more than a few daffs from the garden before. Toby nodded, and fidgeted with his collar. He still didn't know what Lucy-Ann was thinking. He desperately didn't want to blow it, say the wrong thing and make matters worse.

"Thing is," she said, relieving him for a moment longer, "I don't really know what to think now. We had a row this morning, a big one – understandable, I think, when someone trashes your house and pukes in your bath – but somehow, I feel a hundred times better than I did this time yesterday, before all this shit happened. You know – got something out of my system."

Toby nodded. "Yep, I know what you mean – my wife says that we all need a good blow out occasionally: get's all the dirty laundry aired, even if the things we are arguing about are actually still in the washing basket." Lucy-Ann poured him a coffee and motioned for milk and sugar. Toby took it gratefully.

"Thing is, Lucy-Ann – and this isn't to make any excuses for Mansel, as he can be a twit, plain and simple – he's not had an easy life. I've known him since we were kids together and he used to be just like the rest of us. Then his dad ran off, when Mansel was about nine, with another woman, then came back and then went again, and eventually his mother went off the rails a bit and had a string of boyfriends and Mansel just became an inconvenience. He was pushed from pillar to post, never really knowing where he was going to sleep that night.

"He was the kid not collected at the end of parties, who never had a PE kit on PE day and had to wear whatever was in 'the box'. He had to wait in the car for hours while his mum was "entertaining" in the house, or he would find a note on the door telling him to go to Aunty Elen's for tea, or an envelope with a couple of quid in for chips. As kids, we didn't really see how bad it was, but I've pieced it together over the years and I think he's just over the top as he had to be to make it through. He had to be larger than life to not get sucked into nothingness…"

Lucy-Ann listened, absorbing the information, but not giving anything away. They drank in silence. Eventually,

Toby finished his coffee and rinsed the cup under the tap.

"Thank you, Lucy-Ann, and thank you for allowing us to apologise – and for listening to me. I don't know whether Mansel will thank me for it – but sometimes, I think, knowing these things can help explain why sometimes *things* happen. And *things* often happen to Mansel. That's why he's called Big Face you know…" and he giggled a quick tale to Lucy-Ann and she chuckled in return, relishing it and tucking it away for future use.

"Now, if there is anything else I can do before I go to make amends, please tell me?" said Toby, pulling on his coat.

"Actually," said Lucy-Ann, with a smile on her face, "there is," and she rummaged in the cupboard under the sink and came out with a pair of rubber gloves and some bleach. "Go up the stairs and – actually just go up the stairs and follow your nose. It'll be good practice for the new baby…"

Chapter 30

Enjoying Life by Proxy

It is said that the young are very adaptable and it seems that, in Georgia's case, this is true. In the same way that she managed to go from living in a house smelling of bleach, with towels that were washed daily, to one which had plywood for windows and non-functioning plumbing, so she went from not lifting a finger to wiping her arse on damp newspaper. Therefore, she also managed to swap back without a great deal of either difficulty or gratitude. After a few days of saying to Godfrey that she would never take a hot bath for granted again, pretty soon she did.

Godfrey loved Georgia as much as he probably loved anyone, but he was a fifty-year-old bloke who'd lived alone for thirty-two years and change was not his forte. In fairness to Godfrey, it wasn't simply the kind of change that looking after a neighbour's cat for a fortnight entailed. It was a degree of change that rocked his whole existence. As an only child, Georgia had usually got her own way. Money had never been really short in her house and if it was, it had been Annabel that had done without.

Georgia had had a couple of magazines delivered each week; shoes were replaced just before she had thought they might need it. A clothing allowance had funded shopping trips with her friends most weekends and Annabel would have been as seduced by the adverts as Georgia, and therefore pester power was only a questioning eyebrow.

As Georgia got a bit more in control of her life in Cysgod y Ffynnon, so her expectations rose. She began to get a bit narked when Godfrey bought her a cheap weekly magazine, rather than the couple of glossy monthlies that she had hinted at. Breakfast was still own-brand cornflakes despite her questions about whether they still did Special K? Comments about her favourite conditioner were lost on Godfrey in a middle-aged male haze of "What on *earth* are you talking about?"

In addition, it wasn't just the materialistic differences between an unadventurous bachelor and a spoilt young woman, it was all the things that a person who lives alone can get away with. Weeing with the door open. Picking and rolling bogies in front of the television. Wearing a foul dressing gown. *Not flushing the toilet in order to save on the water meter...*

Therefore, by noon on Godfrey's first day not going to work, Georgia was already beginning to feel a little frustrated; was this how it was going to be from now on? Godfrey mooching about, getting in her way? She'd put Jocey to bed and found that Godfrey had not only not done the washing-up from breakfast as usual, but he had also used the last of the teabags before he left.

So when the phone rang as she was boiling a kettle for the sink – as he'd turned the hot water off *again,* she answered it without thinking. Bound to be him checking if she *really* needed that service wash done today? She'd picked it up out of its outdated cradle and said, "Hello," into it before she'd even thought.

The gasp on the other end of the line went through her and then a little voice asking, "Georgia?" confirmed her fears.

"Mum?" she whispered back.

"Georgia, is that you? Is it really you?"

Georgia burst into tears and all the toughness of the past two years, starting with the hideous embarrassment on her mother's bed through to not being ever really warm for weeks at a time in the cold, damp, miserable squat, fell from her in warm salty sobs.

Then she heard Annabel burst into tears. They wept for what seemed like minutes with no other communication.

Occasionally Annabel would manage an, "Are you OK?" or an, "Oh Lord, I've missed you," and finally, "The baby, how is the little baby?"

But when Annabel asked, "Can I come and see you? Will you… Will you come home?" Georgia had frozen. The tears stopped, the voice became stern and she returned to the streetwise version of herself.

"No, Mum. I'm not coming home and I don't want you here. Do you hear me? If you do, I'll run again and that won't be good for Jocey."

"Yes –Jocey," whispered the voice faintly on the other end of the line. "Such a beautiful name. How is…Jocey?"

"She's fine, Mum. Now I have to go."

"He's gone, Georgia," Annabel shouted at her as if it were imperative that she heard. "He's left. It's all forgotten Georgia. He's gone…" But Georgia clicked the phone down,

189

unable to cope with where the conversation was leading. She needed to think about how they might discuss the issues they had, not just deal with them on the hoof.

Georgia leant against the wall and let the tears flow. Hearing the voice that had always made things so much better brought a mixture of relief and anxiety. She abandoned the washing-up and instead made herself a coffee and went up to her bedroom.

She looked down at Jocey and as she felt the usual need to listen to the little one's breathing and re-adjust her blankets, she realised that her own mother must love her that much, but hundreds of times more powerfully as so much more time had passed in which that unconditional love must have grown. Once again, she saw her mother's face as she, Georgia, and Ray had been caught up to no good. How would she feel if Jocey did that to her one day? Once more she felt the shame rise and realised that she couldn't face her mum. Not just yet, maybe never.

The tears were a mixture of regret, embarrassment and despair and she knew that this just wasn't going to go away sooner or later. Something had to happen; the secret would be out. There was no way that her Uncle God could know what had happened as he would never have treated her as well as he had. He would have been ashamed of her, not benevolent and doting – and anyway, Mum could *never* have told him; she just wouldn't have been able to find the words.

The thought of the look on Uncle God's face as the truth was revealed brought fresh waves of despair as Georgia realised she might be about to lose her apple status in her treasured uncle's eye, and she laid on her bed and, with as little noise as possible, sobbed herself to sleep.

Chapter 31

Buying Day-old Bread

Mansel was slumped on his sofa. The television was on. He was wearing his Wales rugby shirt, Bart Simpson boxer shorts and crocodile socks and had a duvet with no cover on pulled up over him. There was a ball of chip wrappers tossed into one corner of the room, a Chinese takeaway bag filled with empty foil cartons on the coffee table and a half-eaten pizza was on his lap. He was manfully struggling through it, despite the recommendation that it was designed to feed a family of four.

He felt bloated and sick, but the desire to keep going in order to punish himself even more was stronger than his belt shouting, *Please! For God's sake, Mansel, you're killing me!* and his arteries wheezing, *Mansel...stop...only another micron of space to fill, then we'll be clogged! No more pepperoni – please!*

He was in a foul mood and engulfed in despair. He'd done some stupid things in his time – breaking his leg whilst doing a comedy stuntman antic for one, setting fire to his pretend aunt's shed after not listening to the instructions for the bonfire properly, for another – but never one with such dreadful repercussions. On top of that, the worst thing about it was that he didn't think that what *he'd* actually done was that bad. Annoying, stupid, juvenile, irresponsible and maybe even a little distressing for the animals who missed their usual mealtime, but surely forgivable?

The irony was that those wankers who'd spent the past fifteen years telling him not to be a prat had done the worst of it – and probably cost him his future wife, happiness and the mother of his five potential children.

They could go back to their cosy homes and luscious wives, feel a bit guilty for a few days, shrug and say, "Oops!" and then return to normal. They would still feel glad that if they ever wanted a night out, then good ole Big Face would be ever-ready, sat by a phone, waiting for someone to rescue him from being subsumed into PlayStation world.

Mansel was used to life dealing shitty hands to him and as a child there had been nothing that he could do to alter anything. He had gotten used to trying to look unobtrusive as he waited until all the other children had been collected from school. He would keep a pack of cards in his pocket and play solitaire as if he had planned to stay behind at school to do just that. Then when his mum rolled up, sometimes full of apologies and excuses, sometimes drunk or just plain snapping at him to get in the car and to stop dawdling, he could pretend that it had been fine.

He'd carried into adult life the passive childlike response to any argument or a difficult situation and would keep his head down and wait for someone else to sort it out. Somewhere inside him, he knew that he should probably go back round to Lucy-Ann's house and speak to her face to face when he was clean shaven, washed and didn't have his trousers hanging on her door lock. He needed to apologise, but he also needed to talk to her about what she had said – what she had shouted at him. Maybe even if she couldn't forgive him, they could part on respectful terms, rather than her last view of him being shuffling out of the bedroom door wrapped in a flowery duvet and smelling like a pub drip-tray; it wasn't the relationship legacy that he wanted to leave behind him.

However, there was something inside him that wouldn't let that happen. Instead, he took to his sofa, rang in sick to work and stagnated, quickly heading for being nocturnal and about two stone heavier. It was a coping mechanism – not a good one, but a mechanism all the same.

His phone had rung and his door had been knocked by all of the boys at some point, all shouting at him to open it and not to be such a miserable knob-end. He'd ignored them all, glad for the fact that they knew how much he was suffering, but then had been disappointed when they had got back into their cars: they couldn't know exactly *how* wounded he was if they hadn't kicked the door in to find him.

So, when his doorbell trumpeted the Welsh National Anthem at eight o'clock on the Wednesday night, he was glad and prepared himself to ignore it. His curtains were shut (as they had been since Saturday) and so the boys couldn't see that he'd got himself together enough to pop out for a pizza. As far as they knew, he was still sat on the floor in the kitchen, weeping and rocking back and forth. The anthem sounded again.

"Mansel!" called Lucy-Ann through the letter box. "Mansel! I know you're in there!"

Mansel dropped his pizza back into the box and as quietly as he could, he shut the lid.

"Come on, Mansel, I'd like to talk to you!" She didn't sound cross, in fact she sounded quite chirpy. "Mansel? Are you coming out or not?"

He sat there and pulled the duvet up to his chin, desperately thinking about what to do. He wanted to see her, to sort all this mess out, but he still needed her to know how hurt he was – but he didn't really want her to see him wounded in an unwashed and drowning in trans fats kind of way. It would have been better to have *lost* half a stone and be sat, all nice and clean, staring into space. She could have then hugged him, apologised to him and made it up (ideally in the sack) without being disgusted by what a slob she was apologising to, and probably feeling a little sick.

"Mansel – are you going to open this door or not? I'm not going to wait out here all night."

Still he sat frozen.

Then he heard the letter box slam shut and her heels clacking back down the drive. He dived out from under his duvet and ran to the door, trying to rub as much tomato puree off his face as he could in the time.

"Lucy-Ann!" he cried as he yanked open the door. She had just reached the end of the drive. He suddenly felt his semi-nakedness and tried to hide behind the glass door panel. "Please – come in?" She looked at him, laughed and walked back up the drive.

"I thought if I stamped my heels as loudly as possible it might make you get off that sofa!"

"How did you know?" he asked as she walked past him,

her face taking in the mess.

"Lucky guess." She stopped at the sitting room door. "Shall we sit in the kitchen?" she looked in the kitchen door, "No, out on the patio?"

"Lucy-Ann, I'm so sorry, I was stupid and rude and I abused your trust and so did my friends and I am so sorry for that…" He tailed off. He'd been thinking about it all week, turning it over in his head, but he still hadn't worked out exactly what he needed to say to her, apart from *anything* that made her know how bad he felt.

"OK." She said, taking it all in. "Look, you have a shower and get yourself dressed – I can't talk to someone who has pizza on his face and Bart Simpson on his shorts telling me not to have a cow."

By the time Mansel came back downstairs he felt a hundred times better. He felt clean, refreshed and a bit more confident. He had found a shirt that fitted first time, and had a pair of plain navy socks on. Lucy-Ann had scraped the worst of the detritus into the bin, had piled the dishes into the corner, had wiped the breakfast bar down so that they could sit and enjoy the pot of coffee that she had made. The sight of two clean cups sat next to each other and the smell of coffee nearly cancelling out the smell of man-fug, made it all seem better already. He thanked her and sat himself down opposite her on the high stool.

"Right," she said; she obviously *had* thought about what she needed to say. "I've had your apology and I've also had one from your friends, and they were actually quite nice!" Mansel raised his eyebrows in surprise and then pleasure –

perhaps they weren't such tossers after all. "Basically, I've decided that although it was a shitty and childish thing to do, there is no damage done."

Mansel's heart leaped – did that mean that he was forgiven?

"You're not completely forgiven yet," (*Oh.*) "and you have a little more grovelling to do – but that can be in the form of dinner out and perhaps a couple of treats banked, to be brought out at a later date. The good thing is that it has made me think about things quite a bit and I've realised that I might have got things a little skewed – you know, with the animals. I'm not twelve any more, I don't need them to hold me up, I can do that myself now. So, I've actually given some of them away – Skysie and Pheep have gone to next door's grandchildren, Tyler and Hamper have gone to the old-folks home and Waspie and Buzz are in the primary school – on the condition that they are looked after as per my instructions and if there *are* any problems, they call me straight away."

Mansel was amazed. Then he was embarrassed. Whilst he'd been sat on the sofa indulging his sadness with monosodium glutamate, she'd been laying her demons to rest and sorting the ropier bits of her life out: he couldn't wait to get tucked into that washing-up – show that he was capable of things too.

"So, there we are. Are we back on then?" She seemed quite matter-of-fact about it. Mansel's heart leapt.

"I suppose I could take you back," he smiled and then he ran around the breakfast bar, nearly breaking into a sweat at the distance, and gave her an enormous hug that lifted her from her stool.

"I've been thinking too," he said, snuffling his face in her beautiful hair, "I'm going to stop being such a prat – you know, grow up a bit."

"Course you are, Mansel, course you are. Now, in the meantime, can you get off my foot please, you're squashing my toe…"

Chapter 32

Pack a Picnic

Since Annabel's phone call, Georgia had refused to answer the phone and Godfrey had been made to say that she was in the bath or out with Jocey when Annabel phoned again. Annabel had quickly grasped what was going on and changed tack. She capitalised by quickly sending the traditional home for dust mites that was Teddy Boo and when Godfrey had told her how much Georgia had loved it, more presents arrived. Firstly a couple of outfits for Jocey, then a twenty-pound note in a non-controversial card, followed by a hurriedly crocheted blanket.

Then Annabel got a little more cunning and things arrived that were intended to encourage Georgia to miss the comforts of home. Bottles of her favourite cleanser and moisturiser were dived upon – Godfrey's soap had been as gentle as a scouring pad. A couple of photos of Georgia as a baby sat on her mother's knee – so that she could see whether Jocey looked like she had as a baby – had brought tears to her eyes.

Godfrey had beamed as he recognised his sister's handwriting popping through the door so regularly.

"Another parcel for you," he said cheerfully one morning

as he brought a large one to Georgia along with a cup of tea. She frowned as she saw the writing. "That's a few you've had now," he said. "Things going OK?" Georgia shrugged. "Stick with it, love," he asked, "family life is never easy; relationships are the hardest thing to handle in anyone's life. But, they also bring the most pleasure."

"Uncle God!" laughed Georgia at the obvious contradiction between what he had just said and the way in which he conducted his life. Then she saw a cloud darken his face and she regretted her insensitivity.

"I've not always lived like this," he said, serious for a moment. "I've had relationships, good relationships, and they're not all over yet. Some things take years to mature, to prepare for. Some people need, well, they need conditions to be right before they can move on to the next stage. Life isn't all lived in the here and now, you know."

Georgia shrugged. "You're right, Uncle God, and I'm sorry. It's just, well, it's just that I'm not sure if I'm ready for all this, you know, with Mum. It's like she wants to get back to normal – whatever 'normal' was – it's just that so much has happened, I don't know if I can do that." Georgia stopped, feeling that she had said too much, hoping that he wasn't going to ask *what* had happened.

"Perhaps you need to tell her that, love, tell her what you feel. She can't do it right if she doesn't know what right is."

Georgia nodded, and took the proffered cup of tea. "So," she said, thinking that they were both keen to change the subject, "what are you up to today?"

"Well, actually, I wandered whether you and Jocey might

fancy a trip out with me today?" With Godfrey's newfound spare time, he had decided that he might be able to do something nice with Georgia and Jocey. He realised that he'd been a little preoccupied with his own life changes since they'd arrived on his doorstep, and that had been fine up to this point as Georgia had no need to be dashing off on an adventure: peace and quiet would do very nicely, thank you. However, it had dawned as a beautiful May morning, and he had decided that this was as good a day as any. "So, how would you fancy going on a trip to the Elan Valley to introduce Jocey to eating worms and to have a look at the dams?"

Georgia had looked like she was about to groan and say, "Do I have to..." but then a smile broke over her face and she said that she thought it a great idea! So they faffed about for quite some time, considering that they were only going fifteen miles up the road, and eventually the clanking old car was filled with pushchair, carrier bags full of food, nappies, blankets and every other thing that a small baby seems to need. With one last de-cant of Jocey to change her nappy again, they were off and Georgia thought they looked like they were going on a trip of a lifetime, rather than a short day out up the road.

Godfrey stopped at the garage and put £12.37 worth of petrol in – just the right amount to get them there and back with not too many drops to spare, so as to save on weight in the car – and tried not to notice the roll of the eyes that the attendant gave Georgia when he rang the amount through. They rattled off into the countryside and Godfrey was very impressed, and pleased, when Georgia pointed out a couple of features on the hilltop and asked whether that was where he'd taken her on one of his history trips when she was younger. He was even more pleasantly surprised when she remembered many of the facts he'd relayed. "Yeah," she said, "I used to really enjoy our little adventures. There was a bloke, Danner, in the, er, place, I stayed at in Tavsham who used to love history too and he used to tell me all of these things – you know, about the Romans, the Vikings and all the Kings and Queens of Britain. Interesting bloke, Danner – when he wasn't off his head."

Godfrey was pleased (apart from the bit about being *off his head*) as this was the first proper information that Georgia had offered about her experiences in a conversational context. He muttered about enjoying the Viking period best himself and fell silent again in the hope that she would chatter some more. He was even gladder that she seemed to be remembering enjoyable things about her life *before* she ran away from home; it was important that it hadn't all been labelled bad.

Eventually the car made it to the Elan Valley and Godfrey parked it some distance away from the visitor centre to save the pound parking charge. "It'll be nice to have a walk," he mumbled, despite sensing that Georgia knew the real reason.

They unpacked all of their belongings and stuffed them into the basket under Jocey's pram. "I should have got one of these *years* ago," Godfrey laughed as he grasped the handles, "would have saved my back no end of trouble, carting shopping around in this!"

As they walked along the road, being forced onto the

grass verges by cars whose drivers *were* prepared to pay the parking charge, Godfrey told Georgia about the history of the dams, pointed out the old engine houses, told her about the long huts that used to house the workers and school their children. The grey stone dam was vast from their position under it and, having recently been a dry period, there was no water lapping over the top. Instead there were ropes and a few little figures dangling down from them.

They decided to unpack their picnic by the dam and to sit on the blanket in the sunshine and watch the abseilers sliding up and down on the ropes, listening to their squeals and watching their vertigo render them immobile with fear.

"Ever fancied abseiling, Uncle?" asked Georgia, her mouth full of a cheese sandwich. "I think I'd have trouble – you know, trusting some other fool to sort my ropes out."

"Yes, I suppose I have. I used to want to have a go at things like that – I always wanted to parachute, for example, or go on waterskis, yes, I really fancied a go on waterskis."

"Why didn't you then?" she asked. Godfrey shrugged. "You could surely have had a couple of lessons to try it? Don't you think that you *should* try the things you want to do, you know, hang the expense occasionally?" Georgia munched on, not looking at her Uncle's face, which had clouded over.

"It's not *all* about saving money; not just for the *sake* of it, Georgia." She shrugged again.

"What is it for then, the saving money?" She looked at him and watched as he struggled with his words.

"Plans, Georgia. I had *plans*," he whispered. He could see that she was interested and wasn't going to be fobbed off with just that. He took a deep breath: he'd never shared his plans with anyone – apart from the one that helped form them. "I was in love – I *am* in love. Alice, Alice Jefferson. That's what she was called – *is* called. I had a job I had to do to keep my side of the bargain. Her dad told me that. *That's* why I've been living like this. You know, not spending, saving the pennies. It's to keep *my side* of the bargain. Then, she'll keep *her side*."

"Christ, well, she'd better hurry up," Georgia said, obviously not appreciating the enormity of the conversation. "Otherwise, she'll have to include the cost of a Zimmer frame in her calculations!"

Georgia smirked and Godfrey smarted. He *knew* people would take the mickey if he told them what his life was really about, that's why it was easier to keep quiet. He had gotten used to people sniggering behind his back about him being as tight as a *gnat's chuff* or a *duck's arse*. He had thought it preferable to let them laugh and think the worst of him, rather than sully his actual plans and his fantasies with their questions and their derision.

He could imagine how the women at work would have cackled, *"Waiting thirty-two years for a woman! He's madder than we thought! Hell-o-o! God-frey! Perhaps she's changed her mi-ind! Perhaps she forgot to tell you!"* No, better to let them think he was just a fish's arse with well thumbed bank statements – and judging by Georgia's smirking, he'd obviously made the right decision.

"I'm going to go and have a closer look at the abseiling," said Godfrey frostily, not wanting to discuss it any further and he got up and started walking towards the foot of the dam to where the climbers had their camp.

As he walked over the grass, kept cropped short by the sheep that grazed throughout the estate, the breeze calmed his annoyed cheeks and ruffled through his hair. Somehow he felt that in outlining his life plan to Georgia, he'd held it up to scrutiny by his own eyes as well. Was Alice Jefferson ever *really* going to come? Had that conversation with her father so many years ago simply been the definitive statement of his life that he had followed so faithfully? What if those kind of smirks were justified? Was he just a fool? Had he *been* a fool for all these years?

He decided that it was too painful to contemplate at this time and he put it back in his mind to be considered again – when he was alone and could investigate the issues without interruption.

The dam loomed in front of him as he arrived at the piles of bags that sat at the bottom of it. Friends watched in excitement at their loved ones being winched up and down, banging their knees and elbows on the rough stones. A man in Lycra and a red helmet finished rummaging through a large rucksack and walked over to him.

"Looks pretty scary from this angle, doesn't it!"

Godfrey nodded. "I expect it does from theirs as well."

"No, not so bad when you're actually there – I've just been up and down. My fifth time, so I'm used to it, I suppose." Godfrey nodded again, shading his eyes from the sun as he looked up to the people roped on to the top of the dam. Another man joined them, also looking upwards and asking what was going on. "We're doing it to raise funds, you know: sponsorship," said the man in Lycra. Godfrey nodded, feeling glad that he'd left his wallet with Georgia. "Yes, we're raising money for the homeless. You know, homeless youngsters, to try and get them back on track."

Godfrey nodded, his earlier annoyance at Georgia gone again with the mention of homelessness and thoughts of what she must have been through. "Good for you; a good cause."

"Yes, a good cause," echoed the new arrival now standing beside them, "what actually will the money go towards? Rent? Finding them places to go?"

"Er, not exactly," said Lycra man, "we want to help people get back on their feet." He saw the new arrival reach into his back pocket, presumably for his wallet and so he launched himself in further. "Yes, we want to help people attain the bigger picture – you know, help them get jobs – interview suits, bus fares to interviews etcetera, etcetera." The man froze mid-rummage in his pocket while he considered it.

"I wouldn't have thought they would want those things," mumbled Godfrey. "Perhaps a decent hot meal first. Help to get a better place to stay?" Lycra man glared at him as the other man's hand came back round empty as he nodded in agreement.

Godfrey felt bad: the lad was only trying to help, and he, Godfrey, had probably just scuppered a donation. Georgia would have been grateful for any help, and he would have been grateful to anyone who had given it to her. "If you want to ask what a homeless person would really want, why not ask my niece – until three months ago, she was living on the streets in Tavsham." He saw Lycra's eyes light up. "Look, she's over there with the baby; I'm sure she would do anything she can to help."

"Wow, that would be great! A real homeless person! Fantastic!" said Lycra and he loped off in the direction of Georgia.

"It wasn't that fantastic," frowned Godfrey to the other guy. "I think she is quite pleased to be out of it …"

Georgia was sitting in the sun, having had her fill of cheese sandwiches and sponge fingers and she was now struggling to open the Thermos that had been dented and battered over years of clanking in Godfrey's bag and now needed a special technique to gain access to the contents. She had watched as Godfrey chatted to someone by the dam and now she saw one of the people he had spoken to loping towards her. What on earth did he want? She hoped that Godfrey hadn't sent him over for the last of the sandwiches, as she had eaten the remainder out of pure bored greed.

At about the time the Lycra runner slowed down obviously recognising Georgia, so she recognised him. Simon. Of course: he'd said that he was going to do some abseiling – this must be Caban Coch dam that he'd mentioned… What the hell did he want?

"Ah. Hello, Georgia isn't it? I've just been talking to your uncle."

"Oh. Yes. Simon, isn't it? Yes, that's my Uncle Godfrey. Where's Derwen today?" Somehow Simon looked a little different without Derwen swinging about on his chest, as if there were something missing.

"He's with his mother. She has him weekends, I have him weekdays. She works and I now work from home during evenings and weekends so that I can look after him in the weekdays. We're – er – separated you see."

Georgia nodded, feeling a tiny bit sad for him, as he did look less ebullient without his tiny pal. Somehow, although he was standing and she was sitting looking up at him and he was wearing Lycra trousers, she did think that he looked a little more normal today. The outdoor gear was a little more appropriate and he looked more in his comfort zone.

"I hope you don't mind me asking, but your uncle said that you used to be homeless – which I suppose explains your previous comments about my efforts – and indeed his, which I think *also* just cost me some money. He said that you might be able to give me some better pointers. You know, about what people might actually want. You see, I belong to a group that enjoys raising money, but to be honest, we're only guessing at what is actually needed." Georgia shrugged not really that interested. "You see," Simon bobbed down to her level and nearly whispered, "We don't actually know any homeless people. Never have. It would be great to speak to someone about it. Would you mind perhaps chatting to us about what happens, you know, what it's really like?"

Georgia shrugged again, "Well, it's just horrible isn't it. Cold, hungry, bored, bored, bored, miserable, bored, cold. And that's about it. Oh, and scary sometimes too, but not so bad in the summer."

Simon nodded and took in the information. Then he stood up and put his hands on the back of his hips, stretching his groin out towards Georgia, "Oo, I'm stiff!" he groaned. "Been up there twice today. Might try and do it again before they pack the ropes away."

Georgia tried not to look at the jacket potato that he had packed into his leggings and instead asked, "Why do you do it then? Raise money for things that you know nothing about? I don't get it."

Simon shrugged sheepishly. "I just enjoy the outdoors. You can get better deals on things that are done for charity. I'd never be able to afford to go abseiling by myself: you get it paid for if you do it for charity. Same with the 'Experiencing the Out of Doors' scheme that I tried so hard to set up – oh, and which you scuppered by the way. I used to work in an outdoor pursuits centre before Derwen was born, but I gave that up to look after him.

"I need to earn a living, and have been trying to access grant money to set up schemes – like the Experiencing the Out of Doors one – not just do these little charity events, but set up big projects that would pay an administrator – i.e., me! It would be great for me if I could earn a living doing things outdoors. I think everyone should be outside more; we all get things from it."

"Yeah. Cold."

"You'll think about it though? The talking to us thing – it'd be really useful? I'll be in touch: I've usually got a card, but I don't think I've got one with me today."

"No, I don't think you have either," said Georgia, "I think it'd be obvious if you had!" and for the first time, she smiled at him and he finally looked a little self-conscious and laughed back.

"See you soon then," he winked and loped back across to join his crew.

Georgia sat back into the sun, tickled Jocey's tummy, as

she'd finally woken up, and felt a warm glow inside her as well as one on her face. It was nice to finally *nearly* have a friend – a bit of a middle class arse perhaps, but still, possibly, a friend.

Chapter 33

Scrumping!

Jerry Gloucester withdrew his softening penis from the woman lying beneath him. This woman was at least thirty years his junior, but contrary to the controlled seduction that she'd planned, his flaccid age frantic to have even a small taste of her nubile youth, she felt surprisingly physically satisfied and even more surprisingly emotionally exposed.

Her intention had been to stop it before it had reached this far. Titillation and possibly a brief flash of flesh, and then she would withdraw and leave him frustrated and knowing that he had been toyed with. Her power would have been asserted and he would have felt both mildly humiliated and desperate for more. Instead, she cuddled into his greying armpit, her face a picture of submission and smiles and only just managed to stop herself whispering, "So, do you love me, Jerry?"

Having reached his climax, Jerry allowed himself five minutes rest and relaxation as he considered the rest of his day. Tamsin had been a bit of a diversion from his planned schedule, but hadn't made it irretrievable – back to the office for a couple of hours and then on to Gallagher's for a drink with Bramhall. However, his need now was to extricate himself from the soft flesh that until an hour and a half ago had been the ambitious Tamsin Holder, career-minded young woman whom Bramhall was sure wore clear-lensed glasses to make her look more intelligent. This bit was always so delicate – how to get out, dressed and gone, ideally keeping a toe in the door for future dalliances, while not allowing any expectations of loyalty or favours owed.

He excused himself gently and slipped from her embrace, tucking the hotel sheets back round her. He kissed her on the cheek and gently tucked a strand of her hair back behind her ear. She smiled instinctively and snuggled over onto his pillow and made as if to doze. Good, he thought, always easier if he could leave them sleeping; it saved on the difficulties posed by awkward questions that he never felt he could honestly respond to and answers that inevitably caused either raised expectations or angry remonstrations.

And so, as the powerful shower disgorged its contents over his body, he felt remote enough from the sleeping figure to concentrate his mind on his workload and the case in hand. He was skilled enough in the game of illicit love to leave the suite in a way that would pass a woman's critical eye. The shower was run for a bit longer to sluice out the hairs and arse gravel. The condom was hygienically disposed of and her strewn clothes put into a tidy pile on the back of a chair to make her feel that he cared. There would be nothing that she could legitimately ridicule him for with their mutual colleagues apart from his sexual prowess itself, and he prided himself that he was considerate and experienced enough in that arena not to warrant fair criticism.

He dressed quickly and quietly, combed his hair and

smoothed it into place. On the short walk to the office, he would buy a take-out coffee and sandwich for a late lunch and then any look of distraction he could put down to being slightly stressed.

Pulling the door to with a gentle click, he clipped confidently down the corridor and paid the discreet receptionist with his personal credit card; the one for which the bill went directly to his office address and was therefore immune to Audrey's scrutiny, and then he walked out into the lazy Bridlon sun.

After a good snooze, Tamsin opened her eyes and gazed around the smart but formulaic hotel room. It didn't take her long to remember where she was and how she got there. Surely he hadn't simply left? No, *"Are you OK?"* or, *"Where do we go from here?"* or even a, *"You're absolutely stunning and far too good for me, so I won't waste your time fawning over you, but thank you for the gift of your magnificent body."*

She sat up, holding the sheets up to her bust in case he should just be in the bathroom, but there was no sound. The bastard: not even, "Bye, then."

She scrambled from the bed and reached for her mobile phone, which had been turned to silent and tucked back into her bag – four missed calls and four answer machine messages. The first two were from her secretary, Jennifer. *"Tamsin, just making sure you know you have a two p.m., Mr Allinson, here at the office."*

The second was a little more concerned. *"Tamsin, Mr Allinson has arrived; can you let me know if there is a problem."* The next two were from her boss. *"Tamsin, can you ring the office immediately,"* and finally, *"Tamsin, for goodness sake, what is going on? I've just had to deal with Mr Allinson and he is not happy. Where on earth are you?"* Alison Hargreaves was a tough taskmaster and Tamsin had fought hard to win her respect and trust.

She felt sickened as she saw the clock – three-fifteen. She must have slept for over two hours – probably because she had stayed up so late the night before working on Mr Bloody Allinson's case. She looked at herself in the mirror that hung on the wall opposite the bed – naked and still blotchy from the sex. Bite marks were appearing on the tops of her breasts as evidence of Jerry's passion. Her hair tufted and tangled and her eyes smudged with make-up. What a state.

She turned to the side – the backside in lacy hipsters with which she had tantalised him and flaunted at him now seemed riddled with cellulite and the pubic hair that she had had tweezed into shape by a professional now made her feel like a would-be porn star.

There was another bleep as a text message was delivered to a different mobile phone. Tamsin turned with interest. She followed the noise and found its recipient under the bed – Jerry must have dropped it as he dropped his trousers and not picked it up afterwards. She looked at it and debated what to do. Perhaps he was trying to contact her; tell her that he was sorry he'd slunk away but he'd felt overwhelmed and could they meet again. He'd probably left his mobile phone there on purpose.

She gingerly pressed *show message* and settled back into the white bedspread. Message from Harvey Bramhall – one of the partners – ah, but Jerry would have needed to borrow someone else's phone to contact his own. It read. *Jer, when you've finished with Little Miss Saggy Tits, don't forget to book Roche's for Friday – & shower so as not to embarrass the wives, eh? H.*

Tamsin felt sick. She read it again. Bastard. Then again. She felt cheap, sick, stupid, foolish, everything. It had been a game for him, and just how easily had she allowed him to play it?

Knowing that it would do her no good to look, she turned to his in box and started reading its contents. Many were work related; many weren't.

Hotel Roehampton at usual time? asked one. Tamsin didn't really need to look at the headed stationary on the desk in the window to know that that was where she was now.

They ache for your magic touch x x exuded another. *I need you at my place – half an hour?* gushed *M*. She was horrified to see that that one was May 4th – only three days earlier. In fact *all* were relatively recent and all were discretely noted as initials so as not to identify the sender.

As she reeled down the list, her spirits sinking lower and lower, she spotted Alison Hargreaves's initials – no, surely not her too? *One more for the road? Leave your floozies at the door, AH x.*

Tamsin threw the phone to the floor and it skidded across the carpet until it hit the skirting board that had been dusted just that morning. Her own phone flashed to show it was ringing again and seeing that it was the office once more, she struggled with her temper for a few seconds more, and then burst into tears. There was no way that she could answer it

215

in this state.

How could she have been so stupid as to play into his hands; he was probably relating the event to Harvey Bramhall right now – how she had presented herself to him in a way that she felt was oh, so youthfully liberated at the time, but she could just imagine his clipped accent relaying to Harvey, *"...and then she thrust her arse at me – what on earth was I to do with the saggy old thing? Yep, she definitely looks better dressed that one, I'm afraid,"* and Harvey would laugh, as he always did at Jerry's tales, leaning against the door frame in his usual arrogant manner, looking forward to the moment when he could smirk at her as she walked past, shaking his head and chuckling with that knowing look.

She listened to the latest message on her own phone, again from Alison. *Tamsin, you have now missed your three-thirty appointment – Jan Charles. This is simply not good enough. You'd better have a bloody good excuse, or you can return to the office, in your own time of course, to collect your things.*

The tears flowed harder as Tamsin thought of all the late nights at the office, the years of study, the pride of her parents, all thrown away on one supposed ego shag with the wrong person at the wrong time. In the male dominated world of the Bar, she'd known that she'd have to work harder than her male peers and this she had managed and it was beginning to pay dividends. And now she had done exactly what was expected of her and they would close ranks, gossip and chuckle and things would never be the same again.

She threw down the sheets, showered excessively with much soap, and water as hot as she could bear and climbed quickly into her discarded suit, which Jerry had, so thoughtfully, hung on the back of the chair. The hotel didn't run to eye make-up remover and so she used soap and water to remove the mascara smudges from under her eyes and this made them sore and red. She was desperate to just get out of that room and so her usually shining hair was scraped tightly back into a clasp and her face shone with the harshness of the soap and her lack of make-up. She got into a tangle with her stockings – which had had no regard for future wear given to them in the act of removal – and gave up in frustration, instead thrusting her bare feet into her heeled court shoes. She grabbed her briefcase and both mobile phones and stalked from the room, trying hard to ignore the assessing stares of the reception staff who had been told by the previous shift that the Old Goat had yet *another* tasty blonde and just *how* did he do it?

The hotel suite had been her idea, but she'd never expected him to take her up on it. It had meant to be a flirtatious joke, but he had taken it at face value and steered her across the street and for some reason, she had followed. As, by the look of things, had so many others before her …

Jerry was a cool, confident man and the ball was always in his court. He had no need for "my wife doesn't understand me" conversations, he just did what he wanted to do and if a pretty woman was involved, well, all the better. His lack of need for her had made Tamsin just want him to need her all the more. Her flirting had become obvious, unsophisticated. If there had been a large white china plate with wheels on, she would have lain prone upon it and scooted herself into his office.

Tamsin perched herself on a counter stool and drank a long black coffee, ate a chocolate brownie and contemplated what had just happened. Then she had another coffee as she flicked back through a few more text messages. Eventually she made a decision and felt a little better. *No one screws up Tamsin Holder's career and doesn't have just a little of the same back.*

A cab took her home and the driver promised to return again on Friday at eight thirty p.m. prompt to drop her at Roche's Restaurant: that gave her two days to make sure her plan was carried out to perfection.

Chapter 34

Doing Your Own Dentistry

Mansel stood in his hallway with the slam of the front door still ringing in his ears. His heart was thumping and his hands were shaking due to a mix of strong caffeine and the anticipation of what he was about to do.

He felt he should change into a tracksuit and trainers to allow him the freedom of movement that his plan required, but his white shirt and Snoopy tie were part of the plot: she wasn't to know that he'd left work more than half an hour early to prepare …

It had been a stunt that he'd been considering for nigh on thirty years. He remembered its conception as clear as if it were yesterday. He'd been sat with four friends in the dry ditch that bordered the cricket pitch. The boys had been told to stop pestering the mums as they made cricket teas and the men had given them hard stares from their position on the benches at the edge of the field.

"Parents are *so* boring," Toby had moaned. "All my mum talks about is sandwich fillings and all my dad does is look for his cricket jumper."

"When I'm grown-up, I'm going to have a butler to find the keys for my helicopter," said Howard.

Mansel had thought for a moment, trying desperately to match the glow in the other boys' eyes as Chris had mentioned the 'copter. "I'm going to…" he started carefully, "I'm going to do things like lie on the sitting room floor with a pretend knife in me and cover myself in tomato sauce and wait for my wife to come in!"

The boys had laughed. Mansel had been encouraged. "Yeah, I'm going to hide the telly as if it's been nicked, knock over a few things and then wait for the screams!" There was more laughter as the boys tried to match his bravado, but failed: Mansel had done well that afternoon.

He'd borne that scenario in the back of his mind for all those years. Girlfriends had come and pretty quickly gone and none had seemed suitable for such a wondrous ploy. The right woman would scream, rush round crying and shouting, "Oh my God, oh my God," until he sat up and put that face on of his and then she'd scream again, probably slap him and then fall onto the carpet roaring with laughter.

He knew that he was in love with Lucy-Ann and this was her final suitability test before he declared it to her properly. He had decided that he would drop to his knees as she was just wiping the last of the laughter tears from her cheeks and state his love for her. He would say how he loved her beautiful eyes, her soft, soft hair and her warm little freckles. He would say that he loved how she made him feel, how secure and safe in her presence as if she weren't judging him – and finding him wanting. He loved her chatter and how he felt he could chatter back. He loved coming into his empty house and finding it warm because of the love in his heart.

The incident would probably reach the papers and the

article would start with "Funnyman Mansel has his own way of declaring his undying love – by pretending to be dying…" and end with his girlfriend being quoted as saying, "No, life is never boring with Mansel Batten!"

Tonight, he had decided, was the night for Lucy-Ann… He was in love and this was his way to seal it.

He hung his coat on the peg and then changed his mind and flung it on the hall floor. He opened the kitchen drawer and fingered his only sharp knife. He lingered over the bread knife but his fingers returned to the former.

He took it from the drawer and slowly and carefully placed it in his armpit and clamped his arm to his side. Mansel then realised that he'd never really trialled the idea properly before, but as he looked into the mirror he felt enthused once more: it actually looked quite good.

With his excitement mounting, he opened a cupboard and picked out a bottle of tomato sauce. It wasn't his usual brand; a slightly cheaper version that had more artificial colours and was, he felt, a better shade for blood.

He checked the clock: ten minutes to her arrival.

Back in the lounge, he carefully laid the lamp on the floor. He looked at the plasma television. He'd always meant to hide it to make it look like a burglary – but the idea had been hatched in the days of three channels and a tuning knob and he'd had no comprehension then of the amount of wires and sockets he'd need to reset on something like this. No, perhaps he'd leave the television alone – perhaps it could be a burglary that was disturbed *before* they got to the bit whereby they needed to undo wires. Mansel looked around almost in a panic. Eight minutes.

He took a shelf's worth of CDs down and carefully fanned them across the carpet – no point in losing the A to Z order on those if he could help it. He tipped up the dining table, then turned it round to hide the chewing gum on the underside – he remembered exactly when he'd done that, it had been the night that he'd hosted a poker session and he'd been trying to get into character.

Six minutes.

He took the lid off the sauce bottle, then replaced it and shook it vigorously; blood needed to be thick. He leaned back and, without hesitation, farted a generous splodge onto his shirt. He put the knife back under his armpit and looked into the mirror for the effect. He felt quite shocked at the reflection and excitement grew within him once more.

He looked round the room again. He needed a greater effect. He swung a splatter of sauce over the magnolia wall – the press would love that bit and would shake their heads in incredulity at the lengths he went to for his art! It looked good. More sauce on the shirt so that it wasn't outdone by the wall. Great. White shirt, red, red blood.

Mansel looked at the clock then raced to open the front door and left it ajar. He walked back to his spot and carefully noting the angle of projectile on the wall, he lay carefully on the floor and closed his eyes.

Lucy-Ann walked slowly along the pavement that led to Mansel's estate. For the last few months she had nearly skipped along the route, but now she was plodding, feeling worn out from the heat of the May early evening sun. She'd so enjoyed the last few months; it was great being part of a

222

couple after so many years of being on her own or having disappointingly short, or disappointingly disappointing relationships. She'd begun to think that it was her lot to be single and that she just wasn't cut out to have a partner and although she enjoyed her own company, there had quite obviously been things missing in her life.

But Mansel, well Mansel... He made her giggle as if she were a teenager at school. His joke in the Italian restaurant about the pine nuts looking like the ticks on her rabbit had made her giggle for the whole three courses and the waiter's disdain had just made her snigger all the more. His crocodile head jockstrap had diffused the tension the first time they'd made love and his hat with an axe through it made every walk by the river a scream.

And now she was going to have to ruin it all. Make it serious. A relationship that was built on comedy and light-heartedness would now need deep discussion and responsibility.

She felt sick, whether from the worry about what she was going to have to say, or from the hormones sent haywire by the little life inside her, she did not know.

It seemed so cruel: they'd spent, what ten nights together and now this. It was true, their efforts at contraception had been somewhat haphazard, especially when she'd put that Minnie Mouse dress on again, but surely a little spontaneity didn't demand a lifetime commitment to someone? She smiled again when she thought about the second time they'd slept together. He had told her that he used to have a large penis, but he lost it in a poker game ... He always made her laugh and now she might ruin it.

He'd gushingly told her he loved her on their second date and she'd laughed and said that he didn't even know her properly and that he couldn't say things like that. He'd gone quiet, embarrassed by his actions. He'd not said it since, and she felt it was because he wasn't always sure about how to conduct himself, so he had played it safe. Her pride had stopped her saying it to him - as she was an old-fashioned girl and surely the guy should say it properly first – but she knew that she loved him and the not saying it didn't mean that it wasn't felt. Although her instinct told her that he *did* love her, and love her a lot, now being in this position made her question everything that wasn't written down and signed by two independent witnesses.

She mulled over the past two days. Her periods were usually irregular and therefore she never usually took much notice of their timing. She'd been away on another business course (How to Chat Effectively on the Phone and Clinch the Sale) and instead of taking full advantage of the buffet breakfasts, she had felt sick at the smell of the first cup of coffee. The feeling that she needed dry toast had made the sickness better and an off-the-cuff comment by a diner at the next table saying, "Well, you know what that means don't you!" had struck a gong in her head and she desperately tried to remember when she'd had her last period.

She had felt sick again when she realised that it hadn't been for some time. She had been late to the workshop as she had rushed to a nearby pharmacy and had then done the pregnancy test in a hotel toilet during a comfort break. She'd made it through the afternoon and then excused herself from the evening's activities, and instead gone to her hotel room where she'd lain awake most of the night trying to come to terms with what she'd just learned.

She'd always assumed she'd have children, but thought it would be with a man that she'd been married to for at least two years. Although she was sure about her feelings for Mansel, it would have been nice to have spent time getting to know him properly and enjoy things happening at their own pace. He still refused to tell her why he was called Big Face. She knew from Toby of course, but had, perhaps cruelly, wanted to hear Mansel's version. He'd muttered it was something about him originally being called Big Cock, but the other kids hadn't been able to call him that in front of adults. However, something as fundamental as a nickname, surely she should know the real truth before having a child with him?

What if he didn't feel like she did about their relationship? What if he didn't want children – they'd not had that conversation yet either.

Then she smiled. She imagined the three of them sat on the sofa wearing monster slippers, a baby in a grey furry dressing gown with a hood and donkey's ears – she must cheer up: if this evening went well, life might be so much fun!

She looked up and could see his house. There was no way that it could be anyone else's! When she had first visited, she had known instinctively and hadn't bothered to look at the number. The golden mermaid fountain in the front garden surrounded by little stone men with their flies open, Welsh flags plastered across the windows in the upstairs bedrooms for curtains and an enormous satellite dish with a smiley face painted on the front of it planted on the side of the house.

She took a deep breath; she'd already rehearsed what she was going to say, how she was going to let him come to terms with it in his own time.

The front door was open, at least that meant that he was in and that she wouldn't have to press the doorbell that now chimed a police siren. Her heart began to pound and the butterflies in her stomach flapped harder.

She reached the door and pushed it open. "Hell-O-o!" she called. "Can I come I-in?" There was no answer. "Knock, KNO-ock..." Lucy-Ann saw Mansel's coat lying on the hall floor and automatically picked it up. Perhaps he'd come home in a rush, dying to go to the loo and had dropped his coat in his haste. Wouldn't it be a laugh if she caught him sitting on the throne with the door open!

Lucy-Ann hung his coat on the hook and walked along the hall. She peered into the lounge and then screamed a scream that would curdle the blood of a dead man.

She fell to the floor, still screaming. She saw the blood on the walls. She saw the CDs thrown to the floor by a man crazed with anger. She lurched to the phone that sat on the table by the door and punched in 999. She was far too busy shouting, "Help! Help! Someone help!" to notice a grin beginning to spread across her boyfriend's face. She was sick twice over her knees and the carpet, the sound drowning out the operator's urgent voice and then she ran...

Mansel turned to face his victim, but she was gone. She wouldn't have seen him sit up, a puzzled look on his face. "Lucy-Ann?" he queried. This wasn't supposed to have happened. The operator heard, "Lucy-Ann?" a few more times, then an, "Oh, shit!" She heard the phone being tripped over and then a man groan, "Oh God, what have I done?" The button was pressed for the police.

Mansel ran to the front door and looked out. He saw Lucy-Ann on her knees on someone's front lawn two hundred yards away. She was sobbing and pointing to the house. The woman she was with looked at him and Lucy-Ann screamed again. Lucy-Ann was pulled to her feet and hustled into the house. Mansel could imagine bolts being slid and the phone being grabbed – they must have thought that he was the murderer.

He felt sick and rubbed his hands through his hair – fuck – tomato sauce on his hair too, now. He ran back indoors and ripped his shirt off and pulled a jacket over his bare chest. He looked in the mirror and shocked himself. He found a clean section of shirt and wiped the worst of the sauce from his hair.

He then set off down the road as fast as he could, just as the sound of sirens began to drown out the sound of his chanting, "You-fuckin'-prick-you-fuckin'-prick..."

Chapter 35

Cold Baths

Mansel sat in the cell and hung his head. He could hear noises coming through the thick door – of phones ringing, people calling to one another and the occasional bang of files being dropped. They all just served to make him feel lonelier.

It had taken an inordinate amount of time for the situation to be sorted. His boss Sandra's ex-husband, PC Dave Burton, had interviewed him with a look of bewilderment on his face. Puzzled looks had followed discussion, had followed, "Hang on, talk me through this again?" Finally Dave had sniggered and left Mansel alone whilst he went to tell his colleagues what had happened.

Mansel hadn't been allowed to see Lucy-Ann and eventually he had been banged up in the cell whilst the officers chatted over a coffee and tried to get their heads round the events of the evening. He thought again of the smiles and raised eyebrows that the police had given each other as they led him into the cell. Lads who were too young to understand.

"Right then, Mansel, time for you to go home. I think we have now managed to ascertain that there has been no murder – although there might well be when your probably soon to be ex-girlfriend gets hold of you!" said Dave as he passed him his things and failed in his attempt to keep a straight face. Mansel could hear giggling from behind his old neighbour and another youthful face peered around the door.

"How, er, how is she? Lucy-Ann I mean?" whispered Mansel, wishing he didn't have to get the answer from a bloke who so obviously thought him a prat.

"Well, considering what she's been through…" started Dave, but then his face softened. "They think she'll be fine, a bit of a shock for her, but if she takes it easy for a few days, they reckon she'll be fine. As for the baby, well, she hasn't been for a scan yet, but they think that it should be fine…"

"Baby?" gulped Mansel, "what baby?"

"What baby? Well the baby inside Lucy-Ann, of course." Then Dave stopped as it dawned on him that Mansel may not know. "You did know that Lucy-Ann is pregnant?"

Mansel sank back onto the bench and put his head in his hands. Pregnant. Baby. Lucy-Ann. Who's was it? Could it… was it his? A baby…with his precious Lucy-Ann? He felt elated, then overwhelmed with emotion – shit, he could have killed it from the shock – he might still have. He groaned out loud and finally Dave took pity on him.

"Come on, mate, time to get out of here. Go and see her, she's resting in the cottage hospital. A policewoman was with her, but I think she's come back to the station now, so Lucy-Ann will be on her own."

PC Burton had been told by his superior to, "Give the prat a good kick up the arse. Tell him he's lucky not to be done for wasting police time. Remind him that he's a dickhead and that we'll be watching him." But Dave, for once, had the sense to know that any such words would be a waste of breath. Mansel had suffered enough and he might yet live to regret it for the rest of his life.

So it was a subdued man that was snapped by the local equivalent of the paparazzi, exiting the police station holding a clear plastic bag with a butcher's knife covered in congealed tomato sauce in it.

Headlines, along the lines of "Prat!" "Unbelievable, The Dickhead!" or "Would You Believe Just How Stupid Some People Are!" were inevitable.

Chapter 36

Taking the Pizza Out of the Pavement

Sandra had never had it so good. She had five neighbours, two of whom she had never properly met before, sat around her breakfast bar. Even her two children were hovering in the background feigning disinterest.

"Well," she said, shovelling some hastily arranged scones onto a plate and ladling on some jam, "she came screaming down the road; I only did what anyone else would have done. As it was, well, it was only her boyfriend – how ridiculous was that? What could possibly have been going through his mind?" Sandra's daughter, Sophie, looked in revulsion at her mother.

"Mu-um," she glared.

"Yes, love?"

Sophie rubbed her chin frantically and watched in horror as Sandra did the same. "Is it gone, love?" she questioned walking over to a mirror. Her daughter's snarl told her that it had.

"And when I found out about the baby, well, I could have wept for her. I sat her on a sofa and told her to put a towel between her legs to catch any discharge – thought it was bound to be a gonner after that fright." As a group, everyone shrivelled. Daniel walked out.

"Then, just as she sat down, we heard the sirens – see, the clever girl had called 999 from his phone and they must have heard her screams and come straight away. Well, Mansel had seen me take Lucy-Ann into the house when he came out of his door and he came running down the hill. Of course, the police saw him running, then stopping and sprinting back up the hill and presumed he was the murderer! What a palaver!"

The neighbours clucked and chuckled and wished Sandra would put the kettle on again – or maybe that miserable Sophie would?

"Then the police car screeched to a halt just as Mansel reached his front drive and four – would you believe it – *four* policemen and women jumped out and screamed at him to stop. Well I was watching out of this window by then..." and all of the neighbours dutifully looked at the window as if hoping to see a re-run, "...but Mansel wouldn't lie down – he was shaking his head and shouting, so they eventually charged at him and wrestled him to the ground! *Ever* so strong – I mean, Mansel is a big guy." The neighbours that knew him nodded.

"Then Lucy-Ann came to the window and started screaming over again – I think Mansel had got changed by then – he had a clean white shirt on when he was dead and by this time he had a dark coat, so Lucy-Ann presumed she was seeing the murderer. Then there was lots more shouting and running in and out of the house and then the ambulance came..." Sandra tailed off, her throat dry.

The audience nodded, they'd already heard the rest before.

What they now wanted was a detailed breakdown and to debate what happened in the police station. Was Mansel locked in the cells? Did they charge him? Strip search him? It would serve him right really: he kept such a ridiculous garden on an otherwise neat estate. Perhaps if they asked nicely, Sandra could phone her ex in the station and ask him to run through the events?

Sandra looked at the clock. Much as she was enjoying herself, she needed them to go. She wanted to wax her bikini line in case Godfrey popped round. Perhaps she could ask Sophie to help her?

Chapter 37

Think Yourself Warm

Mansel arrived at Cysgod y Ffynnon Cottage Hospital looking dishevelled. He was aware of the inappropriateness of his attire and his luggage (that see-through plastic bag and not *quite* so hilarious now contents), but his discomfort must come second to Lucy-Ann's health and safety. He just had to see her – and, if he looked a prat, well, she'd just have to get used to that, wouldn't she?

He mumbled something to the girl on reception who directed him to Lucy-Ann's ward. Her face told him that she knew some of what had happened and her curiosity followed him up the tiled stairs.

Lucy-Ann sat in bed propped up by a dozen pillows and sipped at her third cup of sweet tea. She had the ward to herself save for an elderly lady lying in a bed in the far corner. From her prone position she could see out of the window to the supermarket car park. She casually watched as people came and parked their cars, pretended to go into the supermarket and then sneaked off up into town to avoid parking in the main street and getting their cars sicked on or run over the top of by drunks. Fourteen people had done it

234

so far in the last hour and a half, and five cars had not been able to find a parking space in the car park. She had tried to work out the deficit to the supermarket coffers, assuming an average Thursday night shop might be forty pounds.

She had seen Mansel hurrying down the road towards the hospital with a pained look on his face. His jacket was undone from his exertion and showed his naked chest. In his hand swung a plastic bag the contents of which Lucy-Ann could only guess at. Perhaps he'd brought her some fruit.

She had been turning over in her mind how to play this one and she still had no idea. There could be no precedent for such an incident. The doctor had said that the baby should be fine and that such a fright, unpleasant as it was, needn't have affected it. She was to go for a scan the next day, but having thought seriously about her dates, and having had her abdomen prodded and pressed for some time, they'd worked out that she might be as far on as four months. She was to take it easy over the next few days and speak to a midwife about the "incident" as soon as possible, but apart from that, all should be well.

But the rest of it, well, she was at a loss. She would have to play it by ear and see what he had to say *this* time. She wasn't sure whether she wanted to see him yet, but she didn't suppose it would get any easier in time, and at least she had the support of the nurses around in case she wanted him to leave.

Mansel waved at a nurse down the corridor and she motioned him to go on into the ward.

Lucy-Ann looked up as he peered round the door and her

face began its automatic grin as she saw him. But, before it had chance, she remembered what she had gone to tell him and what the prat had done and why she was now here. She returned to her car park vigil – it was far easier to contemplate than the consequences of any of the above.

Mansel walked slowly to the bed, his face a grimace of uncertainty. Despite the notices, he sat on the end of her bed in what remained of his work clothes. He had not washed his hands or wiped his feet or used the alcohol rub on any part of his body. He coughed to indicate his presence and as he did so, little bugs scuttled from his throat, his shoes and his work clothes looked around and headed for pastures new.

"Lucy-Ann?" he whispered. "Oh, God, Lucy-Ann, how are you?" He couldn't fathom her look – was it contempt or confusion?

He groped for her hand, but she moved it away and turned back to the window. Mansel took a deep breath; he'd prepared what he would say on his way over – perhaps he should just say it. He took her hand again and this time she let him hold it.

"Lucy-Ann, I am *so* sorry. I'm such a prat, I cannot believe what I did to you – to anyone – but mostly to you – and they said you are pregnant – is it true? I had no idea – I'm just so so *so* sorry…" He took her hand to his mouth and pressed it hard against his lips. His warm tears ran over her cold fingers and he wished he could stop them trembling.

She looked at him and he could see that she was crying too. Was it rage or sadness? He couldn't tell.

"Mansel…" she wept and then turned away again, fighting to compose herself.

He took a risk and tried again. "I'm such a prat; I've always been a prat. They say you have to make your memories and, well, I thought - I thought it would be funny. It wasn't was it?"

Lucy-Ann's sobs broke into a smile. "No," she said, but she still hadn't taken away her hand.

"And the baby? Are you and the baby OK? And, and… Is it ..?"

"It's yours," she whispered, "I was coming to tell you tonight. I never… I never meant it to happen … I'm so sorry. I don't know what to do or what to think… I…just don't know. A bit of a shock. Another shock!" she smiled.

Mansel's heart allowed itself a tiny leap and his beam shone through his tears. "A baby! Mine? Oh, that's the most wonderful thing I've ever heard and I heard it from you! Thank you, Lucy-Ann, thank you!"

Lucy-Ann put her other hand up to join her first. "Are you OK with it? Really? It is a bit of a shock, isn't it? Maybe four months gone already apparently – that means its due in September. The doctor said that it's too difficult to tell on a scan or anything if the baby is traumatised, but it should be fine – it's the mothers who get the frights!"

"Bet there isn't much case history on this exact happening," grinned Mansel, unable to believe his luck. To his relief, Lucy-Ann giggled and his heart overflowed. He dropped the plastic bag with the knife in it onto the floor and fell onto one knee.

"Lucy-Ann, I was going to tell you things tonight – if it had gone as planned." He managed to ignore her eyebrows shooting up to her hairline. "I wanted to tell you that I love you, Lucy-Ann. I love you. I love the way you make me feel that I could do anything I ever wanted to do. I love your laugh, I love to laugh at the things you say. You're *so* beautiful – marry me, Lucy-Ann. Marry me?" He searched frantically for something ring-like, but knew from his earlier cell experience *exactly* what was in his pockets.

Eventually, he fell upon the pair of surgical gloves that the doctor had left behind. He bit the end off of one of the fingers and then chewed another small section away. He took the greasy improvised ring and held it to the tip of Lucy-Ann's finger, thankfully not noticing her flinch and looked into her eyes for the answer. With a resounding, "Yippee!" that would be the last one that the old lady in the corner would ever hear, he slid the latex band onto Lucy-Ann's finger.

The nurse discovered them an hour later when she came to discharge Lucy-Ann, lying together on the bed, sucking each other's thumbs and smiling into each other's eyes. The nurse, knowing that she'd still not really forgiven her Calfyn for farting in front of her mother at the weekend, felt a wave of compassion sweep over her and resolved to buy a chippy tea for two on the way home that night...

Chapter 38

Packing Away Your Red Nose for the Following Year

Georgia was looking for something nice to wear. She had piled all of her clothing onto her bed, which didn't really amount to much, and was desperately seeking something a bit more *her.* She'd been receiving benefits for a few months now, but they seemed to disappear on the practical things and didn't leave much left over for new wardrobes.

Sandra's daughter, Sophie, had donated a few things that she wouldn't be seen dead in and Sandra had added to the bundle with a few more things that *she* didn't want her daughter to be seen dead in; Sophie had inherited her mother's build and with some items, it was kinder to just take them out of temptation's reach...

Sophie and Georgia had been introduced to each other, on the presumption that because they were nearly the same age, they would automatically get on. Georgia had found Sophie spoilt, lazy and immature, quite forgetting that she had been happily heading that way herself not so long ago. It had given Georgia quite a boost to meet someone who she felt she was so much more switched on than. She felt more energised, capable and mature than the other girl, who lazed around scuffing her heels from bed to school to couch to bed each day. Georgia felt that she wanted to build on her experiences and make more of herself; she felt that she wanted to prove that she was more than just a silly girl who had gotten herself up the duff and then thrown herself on her uncle's mercy.

It was partly for that reason that she'd agreed to meet Simon and his mates – the *Adventurers Without a Clue*, as he now called them. He had called around her house a week before, with Derwen now squeezed happily back into his sling. Georgia had been surprised to see them, but had invited them in and Simon had made the tea whilst Georgia fed Jocey. They had chatted for a while, mainly about their babies and what they were doing. Derwen was a month younger than Jocey, was in a good routine and had slept through the night since six weeks. Jocey did what she liked and slept in her mum's bed. Derwen was now on three meals a day of organic produce; Jocey was still being fully breast-fed.

Whilst they were chatting, Simon pulled a plastic box from his immense rucksack and handed Derwen a finger of pear. He gave one to Georgia and soon Jocey was sucking away on it, thoroughly enjoying the mess. Weaning had seemed a little scary to Georgia, despite the health visitor's encouraging comments, yet Simon had sat there and made it look so easy. Jocey had been more than ready and since his visit had slurped her way through pureed apple, mashed banana and piles of strawberries (that had to be hidden from Godfrey's wallet's view) ground into baby rice.

Simon had asked whether she would come to his house

one Sunday afternoon to meet the others and just tell them a little about what she'd been through and what might be needed by other people like her. She was to bring Jocey and he would help look after her, as Derwen would be with his mother. It was to be very informal, and she was not to worry.

However, saying, "not to worry" was easy. The actual not worrying was a little harder. Finally Georgia realised that time was ticking by and she flung on an outfit with the least number of sequined logos on the front and grabbed Jocey, changed her nappy *again*, got Jocey's bag ready, changed her nappy *again,* and dived out of the door.

Simon's house was a surprisingly boring brick semi; surely he should live in a tree house at the very least? Once inside, she was a little more reassured that she had got the right place as there were coat hooks running one length of the hall filled with outdoor adventure kit: walking, cycling, kayaking and skiing. On the far wall, there were brackets with a canoe and three bikes strapped to them. Under the bikes ran a low shelf with at least a dozen pairs of sports and outdoor shoes and boots. *No wonder he's single,* thought Georgia, *there'd be no room for anyone else's stuff...*

She was shown into a sitting room with five men and two women sat in it. They all smiled in welcome at her and she was offered a seat and a drink. They were all older than her, but she felt fine as they chirped over Jocey. Two other young children were playing in the corner with a pile of ropes and caribina clips and a metal canteen of camping dishes. The others in the room seemed oblivious to the noise, obviously used to Derwen's unorthodox range of toys.

Simon came in with a tray of drinks; Georgia was the only one that had straightforward tea with milk. Everyone else had taken advantage of the vast selection on offer and he handed out mugs (mostly advertising North Face and Joe Brown's) full of green tea, Barley Cup, black tea, camomile and hot water. Georgia felt it was all terribly sophisticated and decided that she would try all of them some time soon.

Simon finally brought the chatter to a halt and introduced Georgia and Jocey properly and asked her to take over. Feeling suddenly very nervous in this room filled with pictures of ice-capped mountains and photos of gangs of happy people huddled together on rock faces, Georgia started talking, first mumbling with a shaky voice, and then talking with more confidence as she warmed to her theme and saw that her audience was genuinely interested.

She glossed over why she'd left home in the first place and they respected her privacy about that and asked no more questions. She told them about the horrendous first few weeks when she'd landed in a hostel and was too scared to leave her bed. Then she moved onto the next few days when she'd slept in a half-glazed link between two offices with two other girls and how people would step over them without acknowledging their presence. She described the squat and how it felt like a haven at first, safe, relatively friendly and a place that she could leave her few belongings and still find them there when she returned.

Georgia explained the misery of never having anything *nice.* Although it sounded a bit pathetic, she told of how she would have loved some body lotion, a hair-conditioning treatment or some nail varnish for her toes, just to make herself feel a bit better, just a little pampering treat to take her out of the damp misery in which *everything* had grit in, smelt of urine or was spotted with mildew. She had felt a bit shallow saying this, but one of the women said, "Well, we all know that a bit of pampering makes us feel so much better about ourselves, so I am sure we can all relate to that," and that made her feel much better.

The group laughed at some of the antics of hers and her fellow residents, but would be brought back to solemnity as the activities had usually ended in a fight or someone crying or "going off on one".

Jocey was cuddled and played with by every person in the room and Simon fed her organic avocado and star fruit – tastes new to Jocey *and* Georgia's palates. It was as if people wanted to transfer their sympathy and support for Georgia, but did it through Jocey instead.

Whenever Georgia faltered, thinking that she had surely said enough now, they would jump in with further questions.

"Why didn't you go to Social Services?"

"Didn't know where it was."

"Why didn't you just get a job in a bar or a shop?"

"Too young, plus I was dirty, had no address and no experience."

"Why didn't you go sooner to your Uncle Godfrey's?"

"Didn't know his number."

"What about Directory Inquiries?"

"Didn't think of that until after Jocey was born."

When the next round of drinks was offered, she tried a

green tea (not too bad, but not Typhoo), with a slice of carrot cake (didn't taste of carrots) and was quite glad when the focus went from her, back to the subject of homelessness and the gang's next fundraising venture – doing the Three Peaks Challenge: climbing Ben Nevis, Scafell Pike and Snowdon within a twenty-four hour period.

"So, Georgia," asked a tall, lean woman sitting on the floor in something that looked like running kit, "after telling us all this, what do you think we should spend our next pot of funding on?"

Georgia went silent: she didn't know. She couldn't speak for every homeless person's needs. Eventually she spoke very quietly, "What I really could have done with…"

"Yes?"

"What I *really* fancied…was a bacon sandwich…"

They all burst into laughter at her earnestness. "A little less complicated than we imagined I think!" laughed Simon. "Right everyone, I think Georgia's probably had enough of a grilling for one day?"

They all thanked her and one by one said goodbye to her and little Jocey and went back to their own tree houses. She was left with Simon who was spooning mashed kiwi fruit into Jocey and packing a few frozen ice cubes of pureed carrot and gravy into a tub for her tea.

"Actually, Georgia," he said tentatively, "I don't want to insult you, but hearing what you were saying earlier about not having anything 'nice'– my ex-partner, Rose, left a load of her stuff here when she left and she doesn't want it back; wants a *clean break* apparently. Has *moved on*. She's about your size and there are lots of things, nice things, which you might be able to use? I've bagged it up and you can take it if you want. What you don't fancy, either sell on, give it back or take it to a charity shop – it would be up to you."

Georgia's eye's lit up and she thanked Simon and said that she'd love to have a look. A smile burst over her face when she saw a few bin liners full of clothes and also a couple of carrier bags full of toiletries – nice ones, too – and things for her hair. "She had long hair, too," said Simon, a sad smile coming over his face. "She cut it all off when she left; said that she'd always hated it. I liked it though." Georgia didn't know what to say, so she kept quiet. "Anyway, what it means is, that there are lots of hair lotion things in there. See what you think of it." Simon gathered all the things together by the door and offered to drop them round straightaway whilst Georgia walked back with Jocey.

They thanked each other for a good, productive afternoon and said that they looked forward to seeing each other at the next Parent and Toddler group. Simon waved as he drove past Georgia in his camper van with roof and bike racks sticking out of it like a hedgehog's spines and she had to try hard to stop herself breaking into a run to get home and have a rummage through those bags…

Chapter 39

Carpet Insoles

Annabel hadn't been able to help herself. She was speeding down the motorway with her new jumper on. Her hair had been cut and coloured and her wardrobe had been thinned out at the same time she had emptied Ray's.

She couldn't believe how wonderful she felt and had done since Ray had left. It had actually taken very little time to get over him: she'd shed a few tears as the taxi had driven him away, but those had stopped as soon as the kettle had clicked off and she realised that she could make Earl Grey again.

She'd tried to avoid Kathy and Brian Hansford for the weeks that Ray had stayed at their house, and then treated them both to a slap-up meal out as a thank you once Ray was safely spirited away to the West Country. She'd spent the rest of the time cleaning, redecorating and re-asserting her personality on the house. She was amazed how much free time one has when it is not spent pussyfooting.

After she had whirled through the chores, she had stopped at Georgia's door. The room behind it had been left as a time capsule, so that Georgia could just pick things up as she'd left them when she returned home. It got dusted and vacuumed every week and then the door would be gently shut on it. With her new broom in hand, Annabel eased open the door...

It was a real little girl's bedroom. The funky bedspread should probably have been changed a couple of years before Georgia had left. The outfits on the band members on the posters were dated and faded: they probably had paunches and children of their own by now.

Annabel had taken a deep breath and set about it with a raspberry and ginseng-inspired energy. The posters were ripped off leaving imprints in the mauve paint where the sun had been unable to reach. The lampshade was removed and the duvet and bed stripped. All Georgia's pre-teen clothes were heaved into a pile and her trinkets were packed neatly into a box. Once clear, Annabel had painted it all and by the end of the weekend it was a fresh guest room with a refurbished cot in the corner.

Annabel had cried as she scrubbed the cot that she brought down from the attic. She painted over the old lead paint and bought a new mattress and bedding. She propped a small teddy in the corner and hung a mobile overhead.

All the room needed now, was Georgia and Jocey.

She hadn't been able to sleep she had been so excited with the plan that was formulating in her mind. She'd go and surprise Georgia. Bring her back home. It seemed so simple, a straightforward process - but she hadn't stopped to think about what Georgia might want...

Godfrey handed Georgia her seventh cup of tea of the day and she accepted it with a smile. She was wearing some of

Rose's clothes and Simon had been right, there *was* some nice stuff in there. She had new jeans, tops, jackets and skirts. She also had a dressing table's worth of toiletries, perfumes and bath products. She even had a hairdryer and some straighteners. At last she sat in her chair with glossy hair and smelling of something a little more feminine than a biochemist's version of pine needles.

She had also been touched by a voucher for a cut and blow dry given by one of the women in the group and some things for Jocey by one of the men, with a note to say plenty more to follow if she were interested as his daughter had grown out of them. She felt like she was getting back to being the person that Georgia Harrow was supposed to be. She was strong and fit and now she felt happier about the way she looked and dressed too.

Godfrey sat into his armchair and gave a sigh in the same way that the armchair did as he eased himself into it.

"You're still looking good too, Uncle God…" Georgia smiled with a wink at him. Her own transformation had inspired Godfrey to let her have a go on him. So, she'd spent the previous afternoon giving him a "make-over" as he allowed her to call it. She had cut his hair, got him to shave off his beard and she had given him a few tips about clothes, accepting that he wouldn't go out and buy a new wardrobe in a hurry, even for a Georgia make-over. Hence a new Godfrey sat in his sighing armchair. His clean-shaven face looking several years younger than it had done the morning before, his hair a little more in tune with what other people's hair looked like in this decade and his shirt out over his trousers, rather than being restrained by a waistband pulled up almost to his chest (though it would have looked a little better had his shirt tails not been quite so long).

"Yes, thank you, Georgia," he smiled. "I nearly didn't recognise myself – or you – this morning! I feel like a new man!"

"Yeah, I do too…" Both he and Georgia sat in silence, smiling as they watched Jocey on the blanket on the floor. A pile of toys surrounded her, but she had her eye trained on Godfrey's slipper.

"She's nearly there," smiled Godfrey as Jocey stretched to reach it.

"Go on, Jocey!" said Georgia, willing her on with maternal pride.

Jocey sensed the importance of the occasion and the need to impress the two people who loved her most in the world and with one huge heave, she rolled her chubby self over and grabbed at a toy, beaming at her achievement and the joyous clapping that was going on around her.

Amongst the celebrations, they almost didn't hear the knocking at the door...

Annabel had stood there for five full minutes. It had seemed the obvious thing to do, yet now she was here, it suddenly seemed an uninvited intrusion. She deliberated about going back to her car, returning home unseen, but that would be ridiculous.

Her new highlights and colourful clothes felt fake and uncomfortable and she dabbed at what suddenly seemed excess lipstick with a tissue.

No, get a grip, she told herself. The people inside are your brother, your daughter and your granddaughter: what could be more natural than to pay them a visit. She braced herself and knocked – just as a cheer went up from within.

Godfrey opened the front door and with a small puff of surprise, waved her into the hall. Georgia had got up and come to the sitting room door to see who their rare visitor was. "Mum," she said and her face fell flat.

"Georgia, love!" wept Annabel and tried to hug her, but Georgia turned to the side and Annabel turned the action into one of taking off her coat instead.

"Thank you," she said quietly as Godfrey took her coat and a proffered tin of cakes and received a peck on his cheek out of habit, rather than love. Annabel looked flustered for about three seconds and then couldn't contain herself any longer and squeezed herself between him and the door frame and exclaimed in delight at the beaming Jocey on the carpet in the lounge.

"Oh," she cooed, "she's beautiful! Oh, hello little one, aren't you beautiful!" She fell to her knees beside the rug and stroked the downy head. Annabel failed to notice the thunderous look on Georgia's face as she stood and stared at the unexpected bonding session.

Georgia felt surprised at being so cross in that way. She hadn't asked her mum to come; she hadn't prepared herself for the shock. Yet, now that her mother was here, she felt angry that she, Georgia was being ignored. Didn't her mum want to see *her?*

"Don't touch her head; it's still soft," barked Georgia to Annabel.

"Oh, I know how to handle a baby, love, I brought you...

Oh, yes, sorry, love. Yes, you know best." Annabel had turned and at last saw Georgia's look. The scowl of contempt hadn't changed much in two years, then. Annabel got to her feet, her earlier confidence gone. She felt out of place. She shouldn't be here: how on earth had she thought that she'd be welcome? She thought back to earlier that day as she had sat at her dressing table knotting various scarves around her neck and trying on all her old earrings – more like a teenager experimenting for a night out with friends than a forty-five-year-old woman who'd worn the same colours for years. She had sat there imagining herself on Godfrey's sofa with a beautiful baby in her arms. Georgia would be about ten years old and sat next to her drinking in the wisdom her mother was imparting.

Godfrey was in his armchair smiling at the three of them and then he would hug them all goodbye and accompany them to the car. They would all wave at each other until they rounded the corner and then she and Georgia would chatter all the way home, putting the past behind them and setting a new pattern for the future.

At the sight of her new room, Georgia would squeal with delight and Jocey would fall asleep in her cot and sleep for the first time until seven-thirty the next morning, simply from being in the house with her grandmother.

However, Georgia's look told Annabel that the oft-imagined scene would probably not be turning into reality any time soon …

Godfrey was not so astute and disappeared off to make tea.

*

251

The kettle was filled – *hang it!* – and Godfrey tinkered with mugs and even found a few biscuits. He was pleased to see Annabel. He had enjoyed having Georgia to stay and of course little Jocey, but it was about time that they headed back to their real home. A girl needs her mother at a time like this, not some dusty old fart who still feels silly cooing at babies. Yes, he had been glad that he had been able to help, but it would be good for things to get back to an even keel.

"So, love," said Annabel, clapping her hands together in a way that irritated Georgia to the core. "How's motherhood treating you?"

Georgia looked at her mother in amazement, her grimace so deep it contorted her face. It was quite a shock to Georgia just how quickly she'd changed from feeling that she'd moved on and was growing up and enjoying her life, to suddenly realising how much she held her mother responsible for everything, yes, actually *everything*. For every cold night in that stinking squat – her fault. For Ray making her feel uncomfortable in her own home – her fault. For that fucking idiot who had pissed in her box of magazines as she slept – *her fault*.

And then, she asks that stupid question in the way one might ask if you like your Chelsea bun!

"What do you mean, Mum?" she blurted. "I'm sixteen years old, I've no idea what to do with her, I get no help from anyone, I've no friends, no money and I'm sleeping in my uncle's spare room. Oh, and I've no idea who the father is…was…is. So there won't be any money or support coming from him. What do you think I should say?"

Annabel welled up again and covered her sobs with her hands. "I'm sorry, love, I just don't know what to say really. I – just *so* wanted to see you, and little Jocey of course, but you especially – it just *ached.*" She dabbed at her eyes with a clean white tissue from her sleeve.

"Big deal," mumbled Georgia, the fourteen-year-old in her returning as her relationship with her mum seemed to have stalled at the point that it had been when she left; her mum was still naff, uncool, embarrassing, and selfish. Tight, old, fat and a bit musty into the bargain – even Uncle God paled in comparison.

But as she sat frowning and immune to her mum's tears, Georgia began to mull over some of the feelings she had been aware of since Jocey's arrival. Annabel would have hugged her and loved her and been worn out by her. She would have felt drugged from the lack of sleep, felt her toes curl as she breastfed through the pain barrier and had every conceivable bodily fluid splattered over her and her clothes time and time and time again.

Georgia had mulled over how she might feel if Jocey ran away from home at fourteen? She had quickly dismissed it as she would always be a good parent: *her* child would never have a need to run away. But, she'd already been guilty of sitting in front of daytime TV whilst Jocey festered in a caustic nappy. The toddler equivalent might be feeding Jocey crisps rather than a roast and the fourteen-year-old equivalent, well, maybe she could imagine herself in Annabel's position after all – although hopefully she, Georgia, would be taking photos of Jocey's boyband-fit boyfriend rather than the other way around – but, yes, perhaps these things do happen.

Yet she was also cross with Annabel for making her feel so angry. She wanted to get back to the feelings that she'd had earlier – the feelings of being capable and confident. Why had she returned to being a petulant little madam as soon as her mother arrived on the scene? She *had* received help from the armies of health visitors and their like who had spent *hours* of time with her, let alone the mounds of help that she had received from Uncle God. She had a bit of money coming in. She *had* sorted herself out. She *could* look after Jocey and now, she even had friends …

She looked up once more at her mum. Annabel caught her eye and choked a smile. "I'm so proud of you, Georgia, you've done a fantastic job – she's so beautiful!" It was *exactly* the right thing to say and Georgia dissolved into sobs and buried her head in her mother's breast as they each cried the tears that had been battened down for two long years.

Godfrey took his time in the kitchen. He measured out the tea leaves after swirling a minimal amount of hot water inside the pot. As the kettle *nearly* made it to boiling, he filled the teapot and poured the rest into the plastic bowl in the sink in order to rinse the lunchtime sandwich plates. He fetched a milk bottle from the fridge and poured a splash of milk into the mugs, then he thought a little and poured the most chipped mug of the three's milk back into the bottle: perhaps he should leave them to it?

He took the tea-tray into the lounge and rested it gingerly on his school woodwork project. Annabel managed to stop crying for long enough to say, "You haven't still got that bloody thing have you, God?"

He started to bluster, but soon realised that it had been rhetorical. Instead he looked at mother and daughter. No, grandmother, mother and daughter and smiled. They didn't need him cluttering the place up – perhaps he'd just head out for a little peace and some fresh air.

He zipped up his coat as he passed Annabel's gleaming car and noted with surprise a baby's car seat in the back: he hoped she'd kept the receipt.

He walked slowly towards Tŷ Mawr. He no longer felt furtive or guilty, it was more as if Jerry had just asked him to nip out for some milk – no, some avocados or asparagus. He popped into the corner shop and bought himself a pasty and a butterscotch dessert – there would be no need to rush back then. He quite fancied a night in by the fire.

A quick check round was all Godfrey felt was needed on arrival at Tŷ Mawr and then he shouldered the door. The kitchen smelt of polish and the Christmas tree had gone; Eira must have picked up her ideas a little – or maybe had just popped by to spray a little polish into the air to make it smell as if she had.

He fell straight into his recently established routine and lit a little twig (from the handfuls he'd collected on his journey from home) and newspaper fire and settled back in the armchair to read one of Jerry's five-month-old papers, a tumbler of whisky at his side.

Jocey lay sleeping on her grandmother's chest as Georgia described her birth. The relationship between the two women seemed to have moved onto a different plane as they delved into perineums and mastitis.

Annabel had cried once more as she had realised that she didn't know how her daughter took her tea; she'd mainly drunk strawberry milkshake when they'd last shared a drink together.

Godfrey had been pleased to find a bottle of brown sauce to go with his oven-warmed pasty. Feeling slightly light-headed from the whisky, he decided to take a bath, since Eira had carelessly left the immersion on after her visit.

Annabel whispered as she told Georgia about Ray. Both looked at the carpet as she said how easy it had been to give him his marching orders. Jocey's wails broke the silence and no more needed to be said.

Godfrey stayed in the bath until it grew cold. His state of relaxation was intense and as he retrieved his hairs from the plughole and flushed them down the toilet, his mind wandered to the bedroom at the end of the hall.

It was a magnificent room: a huge bed made snuggly by a fat duvet and duck-down pillows. The lack of personal belongings in it led him to believe that it was a guest room. Could he? Possibly. In fact, he probably *should*. Georgia and Annabel needed this time alone. And anyway, he could hardly roll home half-cut, flushed from a hot bath and smelling of juniper muscle relaxant. Questions would no doubt be asked. Ones he wasn't quite ready to answer...

Godfrey padded around the top floor wrapped in a towel;

he didn't feel ready to go to bed yet. He found what must be Audrey and Jerry's bedroom, a medium-sized room at the rear of the house stuffed with chests of drawers and wardrobes.

He saw a thick dressing gown hanging on an elaborate hook on the back of the door. He felt its quality and then, unable to quite stem a sense of stepping into the clothes of a dead man, he slipped first one arm and then the other into it. It was too long for him and a little snug across the shoulders; obviously Jerry was taller and leaner than he. It smelt faintly of smoke and dust and perhaps a little aftershave, but it was beautifully warm and after some parading in front of the mirror, he decided to keep it on for the time being.

Godfrey was a decent enough man to know that borrowing a fellow's dressing gown was one thing, but wearing it next to naked, albeit clean, buttocks was another. So he rummaged through Jerry's drawers until he found a nightshirt that seemed to fit and so he popped that on too.

His evening attire complete, he combed his hair with Jerry's comb, cleaned it on his dressing gown pocket and returned to his chosen bed.

He sat in the middle of it and became one with comfort. He leant back against the padded headboard and felt absorbed into its luxury. He compared it with his own faded counterpane and stretched towelling sheets and realised that he really should do something about them; perhaps Jerry had a spare pair of sheets that he could borrow?

He clicked off the tulip lamp and sank back into the down pillows. No sheep needed counting that night: they didn't even come to look through the gate.

Chapter 40

Shopping From the Damaged Goods Shelf

Audrey roared her Rover down the M4, tears of rage converting into pressure applied to the accelerator. How could he? How *could* he? She'd been a good wife. Yes, she had. She loved him, she gave him his head and didn't interfere – but the *bastard* had taken advantage and run off with a filly half her age. She'd spent her days trimming beef and walking the bloody dogs and he'd spent his womanising and clocking up bills in bloody hotels.

She turned the radio off as she realised that she wasn't listening, but feeling frustrated with the silence, she turned it back on. Perhaps some music? She pressed the buttons in a random way and far harder than they required, "Bloody rubbish!" she cursed as some interminable "modern" jazz failed to improve her mood.

She looked down at the speedometer: one hundred and four miles per hour. Better slow down, she thought; it wouldn't do to get any more points just when she needed her independence. Damn Jerry for managing to persuade her to take his last three. The thought of him made the rage well up in her once more. She hit the indicator and roared off onto a services' slip road – time for a coffee and a calm down she thought, her sensible head returning; it would make life far too easy for him if she wrapped herself round a crash barrier.

Godfrey slept. Beautiful sleep unhindered by Jocey's cries or next door's cats. It would have been enhanced by having a beautiful woman at his side, but maybe it wouldn't be long now…

He dreamt dreams that unfurled the frown on his brow and unclenched his fingers. Occasionally he would wake and check his watch and feel so pleased that the night was still early. To feel so refreshed after just a couple of hours of sleep boded well for him when he awoke the next morning.

Audrey crashed into the kitchen and dashed straight for the downstairs toilet; that coffee at the services had been a mistake. As she sat and let go, her mind felt much the same relief as her bladder.

She had done the right thing coming here. By rights, Tŷ Mawr should be Jerry's domain. It had been his family home for generations, but Audrey felt that in this case familiarity bred contempt and he did not appreciate the old house sufficiently. Whenever they came to stay at Tŷ Mawr, it was their usual practice for Audrey to come on the Wednesday morning with the dogs. Jerry would leave work mid-afternoon on Friday and get there in time for supper. Audrey would love those two days before her husband arrived. After she had opened a few windows and done the dusting that Eira had been paid to do, she could sneak off for the rest of the time, to a place where she could be herself and not at anyone else's beck and call. Jerry's mother had bequeathed that place – plus a sum of money for its cleaning and upkeep, to her, saying in her Will that a married woman needed freedom – a female domain – in order to retain her sanity and sense of self, and Audrey used it, and loved it, simply for that purpose.

As long as by the time Jerry arrived Tŷ Mawr was fresh and aired and there was supper cooking in the range, he would never ask what she had been up to. He never noticed how much work she put in to anything, because that was how it had always been at Tŷ Mawr when he was a boy – old, dusty, but with the smell of a roast. In hindsight, however, perhaps if they'd spent a little more time together at Tŷ Mawr and a little less time pursuing their own little worlds, they wouldn't be in the mess they were in now?

Audrey shuddered as she washed her hands thoroughly, using the thick block of functional soap that sat by the cloakroom sink. The house already felt different to her – smelt a little different perhaps? This place needs some serious airing, she thought to herself. *The towel feels damp.*

The dogs were scratching at the kitchen door having just performed against the corner of the house, being of the same mind as their mistress on arrival at Tŷ Mawr.

"Come in, boys," clipped Audrey, glad to have their company. Although she'd spent many nights there alone, somehow it seemed different as there was no impending Jerry. A loneliness crept over her that she was completely unused to – but one that she knew was likely to be around for a while yet.

The dogs piled in and flew around the kitchen sniffing

and snuffling, knocking chairs and shifting dust as their tails wagged their whole bodies.

They both ran expectantly to the door leading to the rest of the house. It annoyed Audrey – that was bloody Jerry being soft with them. In Bridlon, dogs were only allowed in the kitchen, but here he let them upstairs sometimes, on the bloody beds even. Ridiculous, absolutely ridiculous.

Audrey went back to the car to collect her handbag, and noticed that the dogs didn't accompany her – usually they were constantly around her legs, tripping her up even, but not tonight – perhaps they sensed something was amiss between her and Jerry; dogs were very astute, particularly these two.

She dumped her bag next to the table irritated that the dogs were now scratching at the hall door. "Lie down!" she bellowed. The dogs shrank to the fireplace rug and lay down. They looked peeved, but they knew their place in the pecking order and it was well below Audrey.

She busied herself with a bag of groceries – even in her dash to leave the Bridlon house, she had still been quite methodical. Semi-skimmed for her with a couple of inches popped into Jerry's full-fat to make sure that there was enough for his morning cereal. A slab of butter and half of the remaining loaf of bread.

She'd read stories about wronged women cutting the sleeves off their rotters of husband's suits, pouring his wine down the drain or emptying his bank account – but that wasn't really her style. Rise above it, act like a lady and hold your head up high.

She lifted the kettle to fill it for a late night drink – strange, it felt the tiniest bit warm... *must be imagining things*. She patted it and moved her hand round the outside. No, it couldn't be; she *was* imagining it. It must be the shock. She filled it and patted the side again – did it feel cooler now? She couldn't decide, so clicked it on anyway. She stood for a while, the tiniest bit spooked. The dogs had been strange earlier – *and was that a drop of water on the draining board? Surely that should have dried weeks ago?*

She scanned the room as if looking for a clue – a swag bag next to the door perhaps? A striped black and white jumper hanging on the hook? No, of course there was nothing. She pottered about doing the things that she always did when she arrived, wiping the dust from the table, winding up and setting the old grandfather clock and putting her groceries away in the fridge.

Finally she tutted, cross with herself. She shook her head and made a cup of tea. "Come on, Audrey, pull yourself together!" she said out loud, as if saying it would make it happen.

She went to sit in the fireside chair but stopped in front of it – *surely the bottom mark that had been imprinted in the leather by the last person to sit in it was bigger than Jerry's?* His lean buttocks were like two small bags of water; they would never leave such a fleshy dent? She shook herself again and sat down: how ridiculous. But it was enough to tip her over the edge and, surprising even herself, she began to whimper at the thought of her situation...

She'd been sat there in the restaurant, quite happy listening to Bramhall telling some story about the case he'd been dealing with earlier in the afternoon when that woman had come in. Audrey had watched her coming through the door of the restaurant and somehow had known that she meant trouble. Beautiful, in a power suit sort of way, she had scanned the room until her eyes had settled on their table. Audrey had thought her rude and watched as she had brushed away the waiter and strode over. Was she one of the other guests they were waiting for?

"Mrs Gloucester?" the girl had clipped. Audrey had replied, "Yes," as one would in such a situation. The phone had been almost thrown at her.

"Look at it," the suit had demanded. Audrey had turned it over, yes, a nice phone as phones went – it was rather like the one Jerry had. Jerry had a strange look on his face, but hadn't tried to stop the girl.

"No, you fool," the girl had shrieked, "look at the message on it!" Audrey had turned it again, not really knowing what to do.

"Tamsin…" Jerry had stood up, warning the girl, but it was too late. Carol Bramhall had taken the phone from Audrey and looked at the message. Audrey had seen Carol's eyebrows lift and had taken the phone back from her. "That's enough, Tamsin," said Jerry, but it was too late now. Carol showed Audrey how to look at other messages and her first lesson in mobile phone usage beyond the simple "call" function had been to find out about her husband's myriad sexual dalliances.

Audrey had looked up in disbelief to see Tamsin, stood in her short white dress and jacket and contrasting spike heels, gloating at Jerry as his wife's life fell apart. Audrey knew immediately that she was a mere pawn in some sordid revenge attack. Carol took the phone from her and kindly found some more texts for her to look at.

Audrey remembered little else as she took in the look on Jerry's face. She remembered bumping her head as she picked her bag up from the floor under the table, and then getting her chair stuck as she tried to push it back over the carpet. She cringed as she recalled herself trotting through the restaurant, bumping into waiters and groaning quietly like an animal in pain. Jerry had come after her, walking briskly, not breaking into a run, calling her name as quietly as he could so that she knew he wanted her to stop, but without being loud enough so as to make more of a scene than there already was.

He'd caught her in the lobby, and grabbed her arm. "Audrey," he'd ordered, "let me explain." However, by that time people were watching. The doormen in the corner had paused their conversation, a couple of waiters had stopped what they were doing to stand by the door. Even Carol had left their table and followed her out and something told Audrey that it wasn't for sympathy and support. She'd wanted to whisper, "Not here, Jerry – at home. In private," but that would have sounded as if she were giving him some slack, so instead she jerked her arm from him.

"I don't want your pitiful explanations. What possible explanation can there be for something like that?" she managed to spit at him. Then she'd braced her shoulders and walked out of the lobby, remembering through her rage to thank the doorman as he opened the door for her.

Somehow she had arrived home. Jerry hadn't followed her or even had the grace to hail her a cab.

*

Sat in the kitchen chair in Tŷ Mawr, she deliberated about how Jerry could have done such a thing? And been so careless as to have been found out? He must have known she wouldn't have been able to ignore it, forgive him or simply take a lover in revenge. Now everything had to change – *everything.*

She thought about her recently single friend, Moira, who would dab her eyes and say that what she missed most was not being able to talk about the children to anyone who was anything more than mildly interested – no one to reminisce with, or to laugh at how Johnny had painted his bed red at three or how Sophie had zipped the puppy into a suitcase. Who else would find it so funny that their children, when small, had told visitors that one dog was called "basket" and the other "bloody dog"?

Nancy had said that she still hated filling the car with petrol even after two years and Irene continued to sleep downstairs despite Ted having been gone for some three and a half years. And now she was going to join their club – estranged wives, bitter about the final straw that threw their previous three decades or more of marriage into a box labelled "sham".

Audrey took a pressed handkerchief from her sleeve, wiped her eyes and dabbed at her nose. There. Wallowing over and done with. A good night's sleep should see her back on her feet – perhaps tomorrow she could tackle the rubbish that had been dumped in the far barn. Productive activity was by far the best medicine for what ailed her – for the time being at least.

*

Godfrey lay motionless under the bed, trying to calm his breathing, which had turned into a wheezing pant from the fright, the exertion and now the dust. He'd awoken with a start and had lain there wondering what had jolted him from his luxurious slumber. He had lifted his head slightly from the pillow to allow clearer hearing and his heart had missed a beat as he heard the toilet flush. *Someone was downstairs.*

He looked over at his watch sat on a bedside table that was no longer his bedside table. Eleven fifty-five.

He sat up in fright trying to get his bearings. Yes, he *was* wearing another man's nightshirt and was sat up in another man's bed in another man's house – and no, he had no right to be there.

He heard Audrey's roar at the dogs and this spurred him into action – they were still two floors below him, so no one should hear the boards creak. He jumped out of bed and quickly re-made it. He flipped the pillows, brushing them first – just in case Jerry didn't have wiry browny-grey hair.

He whipped the curtains open and was glad of the moonlight as he gathered his discarded clothes and Jerry's dressing gown and slipped under the bed with them, pushing shoe boxes and suitcases out of his way.

Godfrey mentally ran over his movements since he'd been in the house that evening – had he been careful enough? He'd washed and put away all the crockery he'd used – but what about the tea towel? That could still be damp? And the kettle still warm? And the sink still wet with droplets? He groaned at his carelessness. What if Jerry and Audrey were aware that someone had been there? The first thing they would do

266

would be to send the dogs upstairs – he'd be torn limb from limb, or at least licked into submission whilst Audrey tore him metaphorically limb from limb for his damned cheek.

He tried to remain rational; he'd just have to brave it out. What was more likely was that the house's rightful inhabitants would just go straight to bed without stopping to feel tea towels and then he could slip out when they took the dogs out first thing in the morning.

He felt a little better for that thought and took the liberty of even allowing himself a little chuckle as he wiped dust from his face – not the most comfortable night ahead for him, he'd be bound!

Audrey screeched at the dogs to bloody behave and squeezed through a crack in the door to try and stop them pushing past her and racing up the stairs. They were getting out of control already. She sighed another inward sigh as she realised that the dogs were now solely her responsibility. She'd always done everything for them, but Jerry had somehow always been the boss. She could imagine that they might begin to get naughty now that Jerry's last glare of discipline was nearly a hundred miles away.

She climbed the stairs feeling determined to pull herself together. No need to leave the first floor landing lights on tonight, but perhaps she would do just for her own comfort.

By the time she had reached the second floor she was beginning to feel much better – onwards and upwards, she clipped. In the bedroom that she had shared with Jerry for thirty-two years worth of occasional weekends, she looked at the solid double bed and its dusty counterpane – that bloody Eira, she never even *thinks* to do anything else apart from vacuuming – and she doesn't do that very often...

"Actually," she said out loud, "Sod it. Why would I want to sleep in *his* bed on the side that *he* doesn't like, with blankets rather than a duvet because *duvets don't feel right?*"

She rummaged through her drawers and pulled out a nightie and headed for the principal guest room.

Jerry Gloucester's shoes clipped along the remainder of the route to his large town house in Anchor Road. They were going a little slower than they would normally since their owner wasn't really ready to go home yet. Jerry was a confident man, usually correct in what he said and always with the courage of his convictions. It was said that he won so many cases simply because of the way he spoke, judges and jurors alike just assumed that he must be right.

However, tonight had been a little different and he felt like the shit that he in all likelihood was – at least so far as the females of his acquaintance were concerned. Half of him was cross. Audrey knew that he loved her at least as much as any other middle class professional husband of thirty years or more does his wife; why had she made such a scene and run out like that? It wasn't really very becoming, especially as that little bitch Tamsin had caused it. He could have understood it if it had been Madeline – now she was worth running from, but Tamsin Holder? No, she'd got the wrong end of the stick there.

He had stayed a while at the restaurant, to save face mainly and to give Audrey time to calm down and come to her senses. Bramhall had been a bit smug and Jerry hadn't wanted to give him the satisfaction of knowing the depth of the upset. Plus, Madeline had been at a table in the corner with a group of friends and he had wanted to catch her for a few minutes, arrange that next trip to London. After he'd left the restaurant, he'd just walked – walked for miles through the late night streets of Bridlon. The coolness of the night had soothed his temper, and, if he were honest, hopefully Audrey's too.

He slowed down further as he rounded the final corner before home. The imposing town houses looked down on him and mocked their disapproval. He checked to see if the house had any lights on; it was in darkness. The wife's car was gone from the drive – good, that meant she had gone somewhere to calm down.

He let himself into the house and wasn't bowled back into the corner by the dogs as he usually was – that meant that Audrey had taken them too. Probably gone to Tŷ Mawr then.

He turned on a few lights and mooched around. The house seemed very large. The kitchen was sparkling as it usually was, but no note. Jerry nodded. Probably meant that she was still angry and irrational. Rational people left notes. He hung around and realised that he was waiting for Audrey to make him a cup of tea. She was nearly always at home when he was and she looked after him in that way that meant that he never really felt the need to hint at anything. A hot drink would be proffered at certain times of day, after work it was usually something alcoholic. His coat would be spirited away onto a hook, being checked for cleanliness as it went.

He walked into the sitting room and idly looked to put the

television on. Where was the bloody remote? He looked in the coffee table drawer – no. On the bookshelf – no. Had she hidden the bloody thing out of spite? He sat down with the newspaper but soon threw it across the sofa in frustration. Where the hell was she?

He picked up the phone and phoned a number from memory. "Hello, Madeline!" he said. "How are you? Can you talk? Yes, I can." He nodded a couple of times and smiled. Madeline always made him feel good. "That weekend to London we were talking about – you don't fancy bringing it forward do you? Tomorrow? Yes, I'll pick you up at, say, nine? No, it's OK, I'll come to your flat. All right, my love, I'll see you tomorrow. And you. Goodnight." He clicked the phone off and then phoned his office number so that the redial function wouldn't give him away. Old habits died hard…

Godfrey had been practising breathing quietly, but now his breath was sucked into him via a squeak as he heard footsteps padding his way. He had already ascertained that Audrey appeared to be alone, which had been a relief, but he still tensed every slack muscle in his body as the door clicked open and the light switched on.

He made a quick decision as to which breathing method was quietest – quick small breaths – but then he wasn't letting as much out as he was sucking in and so he began to swell, his heart thumping harder with the effort – surely she would be bound to hear that?

He felt the dusty Hessian under cloth of the bed press closely to his stomach as Audrey sat on the duvet and the springs groaned beneath her. Godfrey began to feel claustrophobic: *please, please don't stay in here…* If she moved at all he'd risk being suffocated – or, worse, discovered in some sort of farcical princess and the pea scenario.

He felt the bed shift slightly and could see Audrey's hands reaching down to undo her shoe – don't put them under the bed, *please don't try and put them under the bed…* To his relief, he heard one, then the other get thrown against the skirting board. He could see the navy leather lace-ups lying there – yes, they were surely a style that Audrey would wear.

The bed creaked as Audrey stood up and he allowed himself a deeper breath. He listened as she unzipped her trousers – bloody hell, he was going to get an erection at this rate! But then he thought rationally and realised that it was quite unlikely, even if his old French teacher lookalike was sitting above him; it was a scenario he would have taken great pleasure in thirty-five years ago, but now? Well, it was a little more complicated than a fifteen-year-old would have made it…

He heard her fold her clothes and hum as she put them on the same chair that he'd sat on earlier to remove Jerry's dressing gown. The light clicked off and then the bed creaked onto his face.

He lay motionless as she tried to get comfortable and he tried to time his breaths to fit in with her creaks. Then he lay, less than twelve inches below her, listening to every huff and puff. She plumped her pillows, he moved his left foot. She rolled over, he twitched his right. Godfrey thought that she sounded very uncomfortable – *good, perhaps she'd go back to her own flippin' bed.*

Eventually she sat up, turned the lamp on then got out of bed and went to the door. Godfrey breathed an enormous sigh of relief and allowed himself a wriggle. But then he heard footsteps padding back his way – oh, bloody hell, what did she want *now*! He heard Audrey winding up a clock and then another groan as she sat back on the bed. He could see the cracks in the hard skin of her heels that were just inches from his face – *what would she do if he just grabbed them!*

Dark hairs curled from her legs as he observed the toned ankles with interest – not at all puffy, unlike Sandra's which were nearly spilling over her shoes! All that dog walking, he suspected, kept Audrey nice and trim. Again, he felt another potential flutter in his loins – was she sat there in a lacy negligee, like the one he was sure Madame Laurette would have worn? He wished that he'd had a bit more of a rummage in her drawers – found out what kind of woman it was that would be sleeping on top of his face!

Audrey set the alarm clock taking the time from her wristwatch, winding it up and putting it on the bedside table; the tick-tock was reassuringly loud. Somehow, Tŷ Mawr should have a loud clock at the bedside – funny really, they had an electric one in Bridlon, but Tŷ Mawr had just seemed so wrong and quiet without ticking – it was as if it were holding it's breath!

Back in darkness, she lay in the bed. It felt so comfortable, as if it had been aired and warmed for her. These pillows smelt slightly different from the usual Tŷ Mawr pillow smell – a slight smell of juniper perhaps? She tried to think who

272

had slept in the bed last – goodness knows, could have been months ago, Christmas probably.

Audrey felt reassured by the ticking and wriggled back into the pillow, squeezing out a small fart – another benefit of not having Jerry around: he didn't really tolerate women farting. He hated nighties too – especially this old thing. Said she looked like an escapologist wrestling to get out of a pink flannel sack. She felt sleep coming and embraced it with open arms…

Annabel unlocked her front door and although she was alone, her heart felt light and the smile on her face was involuntary. She felt such joy at the thought that she would be going back to see them again so soon – three weeks was nothing! No time at all when compared to two years!

She was perhaps a little sad that Georgia and Jocey hadn't come back with her, but maybe that was ok. One step at a time.

Georgia put Jocey back into her cot and slipped back into bed. She felt emotionally drained from the tears that she and her mother had shed that evening, but she was pleased. Yes, on the whole she was pleased with what had happened – perhaps it might be the first stage of her having a little bit of her own life back if Annabel were around to babysit every now and then. Georgia didn't know where the hell Uncle God had got to though – perhaps he'd gone to Sandra's – lucky old git must have wangled himself into her bed!

Jerry sat up in bed, leaning back against the leather

headboard. It was actually quite nice to be there on his own for a change, a rather large tumbler of whisky at his side and no Audrey to frown at the size of the measure. He had tossed his clothes onto the floor without a thought that they actually might now have to stay there and he had taken himself to bed in his vest, pants and socks without bothering to brush his teeth. No one to care either way!

He picked up a book from the bedside table, an old fishing one that he had brought back from Tŷ Mawr and he flicked through it, looking aimlessly at the pictures as much as trying to ascertain what the expert was trying to get over to him. He wondered what might happen now. Scenario A: Audrey would come back tomorrow and apologise for having fled like that and they would sort everything out. Or Scenario B: she had gone for good and left him like Pat's wife had done just a few months before – apparently glad that an excuse came up to allow her to do so and still get sympathy from the courts during the divorce proceedings.

Jerry made a mental note to cover scenario A: leave a letter in the kitchen to say that he had gone away for a few days to think about what he had done and that he was terribly sorry – just in case Audrey came back whilst he was banging Madeline in London.

Audrey should know that he had never meant to hurt her. It was just that his home life and his love for her took up a different mental and emotional compartment to his work life and his dalliances with women such as Tamsin and Alison. Everyone knew that they were just for fun – Tamsin needed to wise up if she were going to survive a life in the law. It was important to treat each other well; discretion was of the utmost importance; no ties, no promises and no expectations. He had been courteous and pleasant with Tamsin, but the silly girl had expected his undying devotion – and that was never going to happen after one lunchtime liaison.

Madeline, however, dear Madeline, was a different matter. They had been lovers for nigh on twenty years and she occupied a silk-lined compartment all to herself.

Madeline was a beautiful intelligent woman who was independent and sought no more from him than his trust and the occasional pleasure of his company. There had been times in the early days when she had asked that he leave Audrey and be with her, but he had always said that that could never happen and eventually she had accepted it and carved a life for herself elsewhere.

Reading was her passion and wonderful nights were spent in her flat when Audrey had gone to Tŷ Mawr in advance of him. Madeline would have planned a delicious dinner that she would cook for him and he would sit with a glass of wine and watch her. After a beautiful meal, they would retreat to the sofa where they might just sit and chat, or she would read him poetry in her silky voice. Sometimes, he had work he had to finish and then she would just sit near him and read.

Her flat was immaculate without being sterile. It was decorated with Madeline's typically tasteful sense of understated quality. Nothing clashed, everything was in the correct place at the correct angle, even if it were a mere pile of books on the corner table.

Jerry never saw the workings of the house. He never saw piles of washing, washing-up to be done or even Madeline vacuuming. Even the dinner detritus was somehow removed, cleaned and put away without Jerry being jarred by the clank of crockery or a crash of saucepans.

Madeline's attention to detail with regard to her personal appearance was the same. He never knew her stubbly, or dog tired. Even when they woke in the morning, she was always bright and any ruffled hair made her look even more gorgeous. She was *never* too tired for sex.

To compare that haven with his life with Audrey was to compare a holiday in the sun with a weekend cleaning the car and unblocking the downstairs toilet. Audrey was wonderful, but she was warts and all. He'd seen her so tired that her face was positively crumpled. He'd seen her pre-menstrual, menstrual and post-menstrual. He'd heard her have a cold and he'd heard her have the trots. She didn't have the option of postponing and rescheduling.

Jerry wasn't stupid. He knew that if one wanted a clean house, rested dogs and an ironed shirt each day then someone had to do the work – but he really just didn't want to be bothered watching it. He wasn't a bad man: he'd seen his male friends and colleagues taking a more active role in household chores and childcare, albeit often under duress, but he had simply never been asked. So, he'd gone along with the status quo, never complaining – as in his friends' experience it was usually a complaint and then a row that started the changes – and Audrey had just worked away on her end of the bargain.

So, in twenty-four Anchor Road, the twenty-first century had started pretty much the same way as it had in the twentieth century with the lady of the house quietly toiling away within, as her husband toiled in his chambers and had stress relieving affairs with beautiful women. There were obviously differences that made Audrey's life a little more pleasant than that of her forebears – electricity, deodorant and pooper scoopers for starters, but the roles were the same and the wives none the less devastated when their husband's dalliances were revealed.

Jerry put down his tumbler and rolled the whisky around his mouth as he considered his position. Bollocks, he thought, as he swallowed and cleared his throat from the burn, I may have actually blown it. He knew Audrey would be devastated by what had just happened. He could imagine her heading off, probably to Tŷ Mawr, or maybe the other place, crying or perhaps livid with rage. She had a very strict moral code, a relic of her nursing days, and he knew that he had just shot it to smithereens. This code would not allow her to share his bed again or even to live under the same roof. He had friends who were routinely found out and they just grovelled and laid low for a few months, spent more time with the children and were eventually cursed then forgiven. Not Audrey. No. There would be changes afoot.

Jerry yawned, slugged down the remaining whisky, acknowledged that a smaller, Audrey-overseen measure would have been better for his head, then settled down to a good seven hours' sleep.

Chapter 41

Using Your Vest-Soaking Water as Stock

Ray walked up the street for the twentieth time that night. Where the bloody hell was Tommy? He'd promised to introduce him to some bloke who wanted a painter and decorator for a bunch of houses that he was refurbishing, but that was supposed to have been at half six – it was now gone midnight. Ray was cold and pissed off. He had met Tommy in the pub a few weeks before and had done a couple of weeks of work for him. It had been good getting himself back together again, doing a bit of labouring, enjoying a camaraderie similar to that he enjoyed before the van died and Annabel kicked him out.

The boys at the B&B seemed to manage on odd jobs and days of work here and there, but Ray really fancied getting something a bit more regular and getting himself a flat. Living at the B&B had some advantages – like a big breakfast plonked on a plate in front of him each morning, and no washing-up – but it was only ever intended to be a short-term thing.

He'd had a few laughs there and that night when they'd gone back to June's place had been fantastic – him, John and June and her mate, Heather. He'd never had a proper foursome before and it had been bloody *amazing!* It was just how he'd imagined life in the city would be, far more cosmopolitan than his small town friends would manage and he'd taken a deep breath, determined to go with the night.

They'd sat in the sitting room and thrown their car keys (although he hadn't had any and had to borrow June's spare set) into a box and then taken in turns to draw them out again. He'd been with Heather twice and June once. He'd even pulled John's transit keys out the box at one point, but as the women disappeared upstairs together for a good time, he and John had popped a couple of cans and chatted quietly about the football for a while.

He felt like his life was coming together – Brian had been right, *that's* the real reason he needed to come to Tavsham and not stay with him and Kathy. Nice bloke, Brian, but he was never going to invite Ray back to his place for a foursome with Kathy and one of her mates!

Ray walked past the Builders Arms once more – could Tommy *still* be pissed off that he'd been a bit late for the last few mornings? Tommy still owed him money – even if he'd been late starting, he'd still done the equivalent of a full day and Shirley at the B&B wasn't going to let him back in if he couldn't pay her in advance *and* for the past three nights when he'd been completely skint – there weren't any rooms she needed decorating in lieu, they'd all been done several times over by other blokes who had been left short. Bloody Tommy.

Ray tried to get into the Builders again, but was stopped by the same bouncer as earlier. "Sorry, mate, still can't let you in, I'm afraid. Your friend's not in here and I can't let you wait without buying a drink, can I?"

Ray tried to look over the bouncer's shoulder, "But I think I can see him over there – look he owes me money, I can buy loads of bloody drinks then! Come on, mate, let me in – just to have a look."

The bouncer shut the door and turned to his accomplice and Ray was back in the cold. He threw his kit bag to the floor in rage and kicked the door. The bouncers opened the door again, so Ray gathered up his bag and ran. The last thing he needed was a belting.

Ray walked the remainder of the street. He felt sick from hunger and anger. How *on earth* had this been allowed to happen? A few months ago, he'd been sat with his feet under Annabel's table eating a roast, now he was walking along a dark pavement in Tavsham with nowhere to go and no money. *Right, think,* he told himself. *Where can you go?* But the answer was nowhere. He'd even tried June's house earlier that evening – but the door had been opened by her daughter and June had scowled at him and not let him in, saying she was busy. "You weren't too busy to let me in the other night though, were you," he'd shouted after the door shut, "nor my bloody mate. Slag!" That was probably when he had missed Tommy – bet he had come in during the twenty minutes when he had popped over to June's.

He watched as a group of drunken revellers climbed into a taxi – he wondered whether they would let him join in the ride, but then he realised that he didn't really have a destination.

Reality hit. He was literally homeless. He had no money. He had no real friends in Tavsham and he had nowhere to go. What was he supposed to do now? He couldn't go to one of those hostel things as he wasn't a down and out or anything – a good week's work would see him back in a flat of his own. But what about tonight? He sat on some steps and wondered whether to cry. Instead, he found half a kebab and he picked out the bits of meat from the unchewed end. Eventually, reluctantly, he ate the lot.

Right. Tonight he would have a kip here on these steps, then first thing he would get up and have a bit of a wash and shave in the nearest public convenience and then go and get a job. Ah, it was Saturday tomorrow. Right. He'd get a job on Monday. Perhaps he'd try and ring Brian tomorrow if he could borrow a charger to get Brian's number from his mobile phone and then if he got some money to use a phone box. There seemed to be quite a few "ifs". Eventually he fell asleep, after having climbed into his painter's overalls for extra warmth, feeling glad that this would be his only weekend sleeping rough.

Chapter 42

Harnessing the Steam From Your Pee

Godfrey heard the clock in the kitchen strike three; he was beginning to get *really* fed up now. His initial terror had turned into a thrill of adventure once he knew it was just Audrey: even if he was discovered, she would hopefully be terrified enough to allow him to escape and he had worked out that he could probably shift the piles of mail and dive out the front door and be away before Audrey had got herself together enough to get to the kitchen to set the dogs on him.

He'd tried to move, ever so carefully, to slither out at the side of the bed. Perhaps he could creep downstairs and maybe jump through Jerry's office window, or at least hide somewhere a little more comfortable for the rest of the night. However, he was well and truly stuck with the underside of the mattress resting on his highest points. He didn't have the arm room to lever himself across the carpet, nor the stomach muscles to slither. In addition, there was a pile of plastic bags of things that he was lying against and every time he moved, he produced a terrifying rustle.

However, after an hour of lying there with Audrey sleeping quietly above, he began to get uncomfortable; dust, lack of movement and then his bladder. *Don't think about needing the toilet* he reminded himself, thinking about it. He tried distraction techniques – clenching first his toes, then his feet, then his thighs – oops, next it would be his groin area *And you know what lies around there…*

He recited his school song in his head, he tried to remember poetry, he tried to think about what Georgia and Jocey's next move might be. But Jocey needed nappies…*and what wouldn't he give for one of those right now!*

He tried to think about his own future – he'd been quite pleased as to how his life had picked up since retiring, just like he'd thought it would. Perhaps a few more hours at Tŷ Mawr might allow him to meet Jerry properly – being invited for supper rather than being introduced across a police interview room table, as it would be if he tried to get out and *go to the toilet.*

He was afraid to sleep – he still didn't know whether he snored, but he suspected that he did. Snoring would give Audrey plenty of time to wake, gather her thoughts and then stick a breadknife between his eyes before she got the dogs to rip his *bladder* from his body.

At five forty-five, he started trying to leak just a little urine – just to take the pressure off. The carpet was a quality one and the only possible positioning of the bed probably meant that the last person to have stepped where he lay was the carpet fitter in the mid-sixties, so it should be absorbent rather than worn. So, just like his mother before him, he tried to sneak out a few drips, an egg cup full perhaps. But his sphincter had other thoughts and a gallon of ageing gent's urine unstoppably spilled forth.

Firstly it settled within the nightshirt and then Jerry's dressing gown. The quality pile of the dressing gown worked its magic and the flood began its passage into the carpet, stopping only to soak into Godfrey's chinos rolled neatly at his side. The warm fluid began to seep into the weave of the carpet, trickling into a large ring (where over the next couple of weeks it would dry, leaving a fetid smell that would set Audrey onto her hands and knees, sniffing the carpet in puzzlement).

Eventually Godfrey felt relieved. A little sheepish, but relieved. He had to fight to stop himself falling into a warm damp sleep, so great was his state of relative relaxation. Getting up to go to the toilet always left one slightly more awake – perhaps there was future mileage in this method… As dawn broke, the relief began to wear off and the wet warmth turned to a damp and smelly chill.

Jerry woke feeling bright and refreshed. The whisky had been enough to help him sleep without giving him a thick head.

As was often his way, he had gone to sleep with a problem and woken up with a solution. He'd pretty much decided that Audrey would not be coming back and therefore he had to consider his options.

His clients would regularly complain to him that he wouldn't be as pragmatic in his advice if he felt even a fraction of their anger or sorrow, but he'd always felt that rants and tears were a complete waste of everybody's time and energy. He wouldn't be wasting any of those emotions on this situation. Move onwards; don't look back.

As was usual, Audrey's eyes snapped open at 0700 hours. The sleep had done her good and she lay and contemplated the weeks ahead. She presumed her first call would be a solicitor? Oh, it was so unfair – Jerry had all these things at his fingertips. But she had no money to pay a solicitor. Jerry always paid a sum into her account each month and this was used for household expenses and the occasional haircut. It had been generous and plenty for that – but surely not enough to pay for solicitors – she knew from his conversations what sharks they were.

However, despite her anger at Jerry, she knew he was also a fair man and she had no doubts that he would support her adequately. She would phone him on Sunday night to discuss the matter. Hopefully by then she would have pulled herself together sufficiently to have a mature conversation.

She swung back the covers and sat up – she was sure that she heard a sigh of relief coming from the bed. She circled her feet round a few times and set off for the bathroom.

Audrey walked along the track, the ten minutes down to the public road and back had done her good. The dogs still seemed a little excitable, but then they were so intelligent, they were bound to be a bit wound up. Although it was her usual walk, this time she noticed things as if she were seeing them for the first time: fences with the barbed wire hanging loose from the posts, rotting gate posts, unkempt hedges; who would have to pay for all these? Was it her or the farmer that rented the land? The ruts in the track seemed huge, with great potholes that could hide a badger, which might then pop up and take off her front bumper. Ditches spewed out onto the track, resulting in the water eroding the surface. Damn Jerry: couldn't he have taken a little more care with the upkeep of the bloody place?

As they reached the yard, the dogs started barking again and raced to the side door. She trotted after them cursing anew. They flew at a man standing at the door and her roars just stopped them from ripping his throat out and then they sat, three feet away from him, waiting for the command to kill. The man was dishevelled and somehow sheepish and he had his hand on the door knob. He looked like he had slept rough and had a big damp patch on his fawn trousers as if his bed had been a puddle.

"Can I help?" said Audrey. The man looked strangely familiar, but she couldn't recall from where she might know him.

Can we eat you? smiled the dogs.

"Mrs Gloucester?" he asked, smoothing down his hair and trying to regain his composure. She nodded. "Um, Geoffrey Farmer. Your odd job man?" Audrey nodded in recognition, but it was obvious that she was still dubious.

The man began to gabble. "Sorry to come so early, but I wanted to get started. I have knocked the door, but no one answered. I didn't realise you were back – sorry, I should have told you I was going to be coming." The man realised that Audrey was looking at his damp patch. "Sorry, I am in a bit of a state aren't I? My niece is staying at my house with her new baby – I had to, er, sponge something off my trousers. That's why I'm so early actually, I thought it was better that I left her to it!"

That was enough for Audrey and she smiled and motioned to the dogs that the man was accepted. "Well, you'd better come in. Cup of coffee? No doubt you haven't slept much if you have a new baby in the house." The man relaxed and smiled.

"Thank you. Yes, I am in need of sleep, and a cup of coffee would be wonderful."

Audrey filled the kettle to the brim and to try and cover his discomfort, Godfrey made a stab at small talk, trying to be a little different from the babbling Council official that he had been when he visited in his Council Tax capacity, and feeling desperately glad for Georgia's recent make-over. Hopefully Audrey wouldn't link the dapper man before her with the bearded official of six months previous.

"So, how are the family? Will they be joining you?"

Audrey looked at him flatly. "No. They won't." She busied herself looking for tea bags: Godfrey knew exactly where they were kept. "Actually, I don't really know if I have a family any more. I don't know if we could be described in that way now."

Godfrey groaned inwardly – *please don't go into detail*; he wasn't good at intimate conversations.

"Yes, I'll have to start telling people soon, so I might as well start getting used to it. My husband of thirty odd years, Jerry, has been having affairs. With women from work. I've been walking his dogs and shopping for his tea whilst he's been having it away with young trainees." Audrey turned to Godfrey. "One of whom very kindly told me so in front of all my friends – just last night in fact." Audrey grimaced as she thought back to the evening before.

She still felt embarrassed that she hadn't realised that the girl was talking to her. Audrey thought of the people whom she had called friends enjoying the spectacle. Seeing the posh old trout being humiliated by a beautiful young woman.

Godfrey was at a loss and muttered that he was very sorry to hear that as he threw back the scalding tea.

"Yes," said Audrey, "I've now got to learn to live on my own for the first time ever. I married Jerry at eighteen, went straight from my parents home to his home. But soon, I'll be a divorcee. Me, a bloody divorcee? No, I didn't see it coming, sir, I certainly did not."

Godfrey mumbled again about it being a terrible thing. His concern was genuine, but his reason might have been more for the potential loss of his haven than out of sympathy for the woman standing by the kettle. Audrey coughed uncomfortably and said, "So, er, Geoffrey, what about you? Are you married? A family man?" It was as if she needed to start practising small talk after so many years of saying exactly what she wanted and no more or no less.

Chapter 43

Going to a Party via the Perfume Counter

As Jerry glided to a halt outside Madeline's flat, the front door opened and Madeline looked out and gave him a wonderful smile. Her hair caught the light as she turned to lock the door and then bent to pick up a small case from beside her feet. She strode down the steps, her sage green trouser suit and flat pumps perfect for a day's exploring in London.

Jerry jumped out of the car to greet her. It was what he loved about Madeline – she was always appropriate. Audrey faffed so; cluttered by dozens of bags to go the shortest distance, usually having to return indoors for a hairdryer or some such trivia. Madeline was just there, ready, effortlessly prepared.

He took her case and placed it beside his slightly larger one in the boot and then kissed her on the cheek. "Good morning, my dear, wonderful to see you." Madeline smiled and climbed elegantly into the car.

They purred to the motorway where Jerry asked whether she would like some music. Madeline nodded and so he selected CD number four and she settled back into the cream leather and let *La Bohème* wash over her.

Jerry turned to watch her; he loved the way her eyes closed

allowing her to enjoy the richness of the music. As if sensing his gaze, she smiled her beautiful smile.

"My dear," said Jerry, "I have something to say to you." Jerry didn't feel the need to wait for the right moment or plan what he was going to say, his confidence and assumption that it would be well received was enough. Madeline opened her eyes and looked at him and he felt the love spill from their depths. *All these years,* they said, *all these years…*

"I've decided to leave Audrey."

Madeline's eyebrows shot up but then she nodded her acceptance.

"I know I said that I never would but, now the children have left home, I feel that the time is right. I will, of course, be supporting Audrey, but it's you that I love and therefore we should be together. I suggest that Audrey have Tŷ Mawr, bloody great barn of a place; we can sell Anchor Road, as it will be far too big for just you and me; and then I can move in with you. Then, at a later date, we can decide whether we want to buy somewhere else together, or stay in your flat."

He watched as Madeline absorbed the information. "Oh Jerry," she whispered, "can this really be true after all this time?" Jerry smiled and squeezed her hand.

Madeline leaned back once more and turned up the stereo as a crescendo washed over them both. *Fuck me, she thought, Audrey must have shat the bed or something. How the fuckin' hell is this going to work? Well, it'll have to be goodbye to Tom and Jeano, that's for fuckin' sure…*

Chapter 44

Drying Out the Coffee Grinds

Audrey gathered herself together and sat in Jerry's chair in the study. She picked up the phone. Then she put it down again; she couldn't phone him from here – it was still his study, even if he may never use it again. She retreated to the kitchen where she felt more comfortable and sat with a pen and a pad of paper. She needed to be practical and looked at the list of questions she had in front of her. Maybe they didn't all need answering tonight.

"Jerry Gloucester," said the voice on the other end of the phone. Audrey was somehow shocked to hear that it sounded the same as usual.

"Jerry," she clipped. "Audrey."

"Ah, hello, my dear, how are you?" the voice was sensitive, shaky even.

"How do you bloody well think I am?" screeched Audrey, her self-control leaving her. "You've been having an affair – lots of affairs. How do you think I'm going to be? You humiliated me – in front of my friends – our friends. How do you bloody well think I'll be?"

There was silence. Audrey began to feel her grip loosen; she could never argue with Jerry, his silence just made her feel silly and hysterical.

"Well say something! Tell me, for the sake of our thirty-two years together, why you have done what you have done and what the bloody hell I am expected to do now!"

She could hear Jerry's sigh, but to her relief he didn't belittle her screeching or patronise her into feeling foolish. "My dear, I am truly sorry. I shouldn't have let that happen."

"What, the affair, or the finding out?"

The silence meant to Audrey that the finding out bit was the crime.

"That girl meant – nothing."

"Nothing! You throw away our thirty-two years on a fling with *Nothing?"*

"It was foolish and it was wrong and for that I am sorry. But it has happened and you have found out about it and we need to move on."

Audrey could feel her right to be angry being taken from her and she felt the tears coming. "Well, what do we do now?" she said, her fight spent.

"Well, that depends on whether you can forgive me and take me back?"

Audrey felt that she hadn't been given enough time to reach this point. She hadn't said her full piece. He hadn't begged for forgiveness – she knew that she wouldn't be able to forgive him, but he didn't sound as if that was what he was really after.

"Jerry, are you really asking me to forgive infidelity of that magnitude and carry on living with you as man and wife?" she tried to sound as incredulous as she could.

"I didn't think that you would be able to," he replied, as if it were now all sealed.

And that is how Audrey found herself the owner, in sole name, of everything the Gloucesters owned in Wales – property, land and effects – and in receipt of a lump sum of five hundred thousand pounds, two thousand pounds per month living allowance and custody of two chocolate Labrador males. She'd driven him up from fifteen hundred a month, by quoting a number of widely reported court settlements to abandoned City wives, and scoffed at the idea that he might keep the dogs, but she later felt that he'd probably anticipated that and had started low to allow for the increase in allowance. Even though it touched her heart, she also felt that he probably wouldn't have wanted the dogs really, either.

However, she put the phone down feeling as if she had agreed the ingredients on a shopping list for a forthcoming dinner party, rather than the spoils of a long and hitherto successful marriage. It was typical Jerry. He'd probably spent an hour working through the figures on one of his pads and had it all ready to discuss with her, with his best and worst case offers circled in red pen. She felt cheated and angry – not for her settlement, which she agreed was a living allowance, but from her lack of any sense of retribution. Her upbringing would never have allowed her to forgive and forget such a cardinal sin, in the same way that it wouldn't see her squabbling about money, but it would have been nice to have had at least a little bit of snivelling from him to crow over on a wet Sunday afternoon.

Chapter 45

Growing Your Own

It was a bright August afternoon when Georgia and Annabel walked through Cysgod y Ffynnon to the lake. Although people these days can't promenade half as well as the Victorians could, the lake was surrounded by families walking in the sun, riding pink bikes with tassels on the handlebars and feeding pounds of white sliced to the constipated swans.

Jocey loved the swans and Godfrey regularly lamented the amount of perfectly good bread that ended up blocking their colons instead of his. Annabel was pushing Jocey in Sandra's old pram and adjusted the new sun-shade. "There," she cooed, "that's better! Would you like to go on the swings, Jocey?"

"Yes, I'm sure she would, you love the swings don't you, Jocey?" cooed Georgia. "We do this most days now, don't we my love?"

Annabel looked at Georgia and smiled, "You used to love the swings too, Georgia. 'Faster' was one of your first words!"

"Well, we like it here; I've got some friends now that I meet in the park occasionally."

Annabel felt warm inside seeing her daughter doing so well as a mum and really seeming to be happy. She had visited a couple of times since her first surprise arrival at Godfrey's house but she and Georgia were still finding their feet. She felt that they had not gone back to where they used to be, but instead it was like meeting a penfriend that you knew so much about, but were still sorting roles out in relation to being in each others' company.

She knew that Georgia would have grown up – simply because sixteen-year-olds are different to fourteen-year-olds. However, the new Georgia was a different person entirely to her younger self. She was not just a more confident and mature version, but confident and mature in a different kind of way. Annabel would feel the occasional twinge when she realised that Georgia was not "hers" anymore. She was her own person and a person who did what she wanted to and what she felt, in her opinion, was best. The relationship that was growing was more of one between two recently acquainted adults rather than a mother and daughter.

Annabel felt a little nervous; she wanted to broach the subject of Georgia coming home. Before her first visit, she had been quite sure that she would be returning with the both of them and that she would go back to being the queen bee of the household, looking after her child who just happened to have a baby of her own. But the more she saw of Georgia, the less sure she was about it ever actually working out that way.

Jocey was put into a baby swing and swung the smallest arc possible and Annabel and Georgia laughed at the look on her face. In their burst of joint maternal happiness, they both watched a couple walking towards the lake. The woman was heavily pregnant and wore a T-shirt with a printed speech-bubble saying, "Let Me Out!" The man was tall with a T-shirt reading, I'm not really fat, I'm just in sympathy with her. They laughed because he had stood the wrong side of her and his arrow was pointing to a group of fat ladies across the street.

The couple opened the gate to cut through the children's play area. They laughed together as the woman pretended to squeeze through the gap. They held hands again as soon as they were able and strolled over to where Georgia, Annabel and Jocey were next to the swings. "Oh, she's beautiful," cooed the woman about Jocey. "Hey, just think, Mansel, we're going to have a real live one like this one day!"

"Hope so!" he quipped looking at Annabel for appreciation. "Pushing a dead one on a swing would be a bit pointless!" Annabel was horrified, but the woman laughed.

"Mansel!" she chided playfully. Then added to Annabel, "Don't mind him! He's a bit nervous around babies, I don't know what he's going to do when this one comes out!"

"Run for it, probably!" the big bloke laughed.

"When's it due?" asked Annabel, keen to divert the way the conversation was going.

"Just a month to go!" she said, rubbing her hands unconsciously across the swelling. "It's our first. Not really sure what to do with it!"

Annabel nodded in sympathy just as Mansel quipped, "All I know is that I'm not allowed to bake it in a quiche!"

The woman grabbed his arm, "Come on, you! Let's get you out of here before you do some damage!" and the bloke was dragged off after he had made a zipper impression over his mouth.

Annabel shook her head in disbelief. "My goodness, they'll let anyone be parents these days."

"Oh, they're OK, I've seen them around before. The bloke always says something stupid to Jocey, and the woman always laughs and then apologises for him! I'm sure they'll be fine when it comes out…" Unluckily for Georgia, she had to eat her words when she saw the couple scuttle off as one of his skimmers very nearly took a duck's eye out on its third bounce…

"You're really settling in here, aren't you?" said Annabel. "You seem to know a few people; you know your way around."

"I like it," said Georgia. "I like the way people stop and chat to each other; it was hard being ignored all the time in Tavsham, especially when I could have actually done with a bit of friendly help. I suppose here I'm with Jocey, I'm not a threat to anyone, or anyone's conscience, whereas I was before."

Georgia went quiet. Annabel was near to tears at hearing just a short sentence that suggested that her daughter had not been looked after. "Come and stay for a weekend would you?" she gushed on impulse. "It would be lovely to see you – just for a couple of days?"

"OK," said Georgia. "Just for a couple of days."

Chapter 46

Going to the Doctor's to Read the Magazines

Ray's bottom was beginning to hurt. He had been sat in that bloody chair for three hours. The woman on the desk was now trying to avoid his gaze, but he knew if he kept it up, she would have to help him. She said that she had given him all the help that she could, but – as far as he was concerned – if it was the Job Centre, then she should be getting him a job. Simple as. Sending him over to the newspaper section was pointless. He just wanted a job and he needed one today. So, if that meant he had to sit and stare at her for the rest of the afternoon, so be it, but he was going to get a job.

He smirked as she caught his eye again whilst looking up after another client left her desk. Ray enjoyed her discomfort. She got to her feet and walked out the door signalling to the next person in the queue that he was to take a seat and that she would be back as soon as she could. Ray sensed that she was doing something about him, and about bloody time too.

The woman returned to her chair and pretended to get stuck in to her next applicant. A tall, gawky man walked towards Ray, a file clutched to his chest.

"Mr Haddon, can I be of any more assistance?" said

Gawky, sitting down on the chair beside him. "My colleague says that she has helped you all that she can. Apart from helping you go through the newspapers, there is nothing else we can realistically do."

Ray took a deep breath and looked forward to being as patronising as he felt Gawky was being to him.

"Yes, you *can* help me. I am looking for a job. I need a job as I have no money at the moment and nowhere to live. This is the Job Centre, so find me a job." He sat back and folded his arms. He'd said his piece, now they had to help him.

"Mr Haddon, if only it were as easy as that," began Gawky and Ray felt like punching him and saw the man flinch as he uncrossed his arms: yes, he knew he had B.O., but let Gawky try and smell nice on just two T-shirts. One was still damp in his bag as he'd washed it a few days before in a Marks and Spencer's toilet, but he'd started getting funny looks when he hogged the hand-drier for so long and eventually he had stalked out, red with embarrassment as nice clean shoppers queued behind him.

"I can't just give you a job. It doesn't work like that."

"Well how *does* it work?" said Ray, beginning to raise his voice in frustration.

"Well, you need to find one that you like the look of, take down the number in the corner, then go to the telephone area and—"

"I know!" shouted Ray, finally losing his temper. "Then it takes two weeks for them to interview me and then it takes two weeks to tell me that the job doesn't exist and in the meantime, I've spent another month sleeping on a flight of fuckin' steps!" Ray jumped to his feet, hot with temper and red with the shame of what he had just shouted out.

"You're all fuckin' rubbish. That's what you are, fuckin' rubbish," he yelled at the workers all furiously ignoring him behind their desks. He pushed a stand of leaflets over and they fluttered to the floor in his wake. A security guard opened the door for him and he was led outside.

"Come on, mate, this way," the bloke said in a voice that Ray would have used to young drunks in the pub just a few months before and he allowed himself to be led out of the door past queues of people sitting with nothing better to do than watch him. "Best to try the Crossroads Café each morning if you're looking for labouring work? That's where the developers go when they want labourers – get there for seven thirty and you're bound to get something."

"I'm a qualified painter and decorator. I had my own business," yelled Ray, "I'm not a fuckin' thirty quid a day labourer!"

"Sorry," said the security man. "I was just trying to help."

"Well…" Ray felt stupid. Some own business. His van was rusting on Annabel's drive and the only brushes he had left were those two one inch ones with the splayed bristles squashed in the bottom of his bag. "Sorry, mate," he said, all deflated. "I didn't mean that. I just got so frustrated in there." The man shrugged.

"Where was that café again?"

"Crossroads Café. Down on the corner of Baker Road? Just buy yourself a breakfast and sit and wait. You'll get something."

"Thanks," said Ray, trying to make amends. "I'll do that. Thanks."

The guy shrugged and went back in, leaving Ray standing with his damp holdall in his hand and a long weekend ahead. How the hell was he going to '*Buy* himself a breakfast and wait'? He shuffled off to nowhere in particular. It was Friday. Perhaps it might be worth going back to that pub, the Builders Arms and see if Tommy might be there – perhaps he'd got the Friday wrong and it was tonight instead of a couple of weeks ago. Maybe he'd let him stay in one of the flats that he was doing up – he could do a bit of extra painting in repayment. That would work.

He set off at a leisurely pace. His shoes were wearing thin on the soles; he must have walked for miles in the past couple of months. There was nothing else to do really except for walk when you have no money and no place to sit down. Ray shook his head. How…*how on earth* had it gotten to this point? He just couldn't believe how easily it had happened. Six months ago he had been a cheeky, upbeat kind of guy. He had an eye for the ladies and they had one for him. He had a nice house to live in and plenty of clean T-shirts. Now all he possessed was a cracked holdall with some damp clothes in.

His bank card had been swallowed. No one would give him a room to rent. He didn't know anyone who might give him a job. He had no mates and no means to get out of here. He had thought about hitching, but he had nowhere to aim for. Nowhere else was necessarily going to be any better than Tavsham. At least he knew where the Job Centre was and he had tried to get some benefits, but he hadn't filled in the forms properly yet.

He had been told to take them back and fill in *all* the boxes when the assistant saw that he had not filled in his address. "I haven't got a fuckin' address," he'd shouted then too, "that's why I'm fuckin' here isn't it?" Security had led him from that room then too, but that guy hadn't been so friendly.

"They're not paid enough to get shouted and sworn at, mate," he'd spat.

"Well, I'm not being paid anything at fuckin' all," Ray had retorted to the security man's back.

Ray limped along. He was depressed by everything around him. Tavsham was a shit hole if you had no money. Everything cost and there was no way he was going to sit in the library all day. He drew the line at going to services for homeless people. He wasn't homeless, he just didn't have a place to live. There was a difference.

The offices were beginning to empty and people were meeting up to start their nights out. Friday nights. He used to love Friday nights. He would go out with some of the boys down to the local and they would have a few pints after work. Sometimes they'd phone the wives and they'd all go out for a curry. Sometimes even Annabel would have come too – those were in the days before she had a face like a smacked arse.

Music started pouring out of open doors of pubs and chairs had people sat on them chatting on their mobile phones. This was more like it. Tavsham looked like a good place to have fun.

He spotted a group of hens out for a party. They were all clutching bags of chips and bottles of Bacardi Breezers. The bride was a gorgeous blonde in a basque and fishnet tights. There were pink feathers everywhere. Ray felt his lust rise to his throat, "All right, girls? Having a good night are you?" He saw their horrified faces when they looked up to see who was talking to them. Six months ago, they'd have stopped for a laugh with him, maybe he'd have joined them for a drink. Now they were scared of him, disgusted by his smell and week-old beard. His heart sank again and he slunk back into the shadows. Perhaps he'd just follow them at a distance; girls on the razz usually didn't finish their chips…

Chapter 47

Re-using the Tea Bags

Godfrey had his feet firmly under Sandra's table, literally, and he felt, metaphorically too. It was the third time that month he'd been around for dinner – and this time the children were away for the night. He had met Sophie and Daniel when he'd brought the car around to collect their old high chair for Jocey, but they had pretty much dismissed him as insignificant. However, he was quite used to this, having been on the end of the public's sneers as he'd pursued their hard-earned wealth for his council tax coffers for so many years.

For Daniel, just seeing Godfrey's car rattle onto the drive had been enough. Sophie waited until she'd seen the cut of his suit, then looked at her mum in disbelief. Sandra, however, seemed smitten.

Godfrey wasn't surprised; he'd planned it this way. He was actually quite sad that he'd left it so long; this socialising lark was quite good fun. He'd made a bit more of an effort tonight, under Georgia's direction, although she'd told him that he had to give her a little more to work with as one couldn't make a silk purse out of a horse's arse. Something had definitely happened to the girl's vocabulary since she'd left home!

Godfrey had always found Sandra pleasant enough company and this was becoming more so as she relaxed a little more in his presence. Although it wasn't a slur on Sandra, he would actually be quite pleased to have his feet under any single woman's table – he was just quite pleased that this table's owner was relatively attractive, had a big bottom and liked cooking steak. Alice had had quite a big bottom *and* she always used to choose a steak …

He watched Sandra as she flitted around the kitchen. She was obviously comfortable cooking in front of him rather than having prepared it all beforehand and Godfrey had been sat with a glass of wine and a small plate of Marks and Spencer's canapés and told to relax – as if stress had been an overwhelming element of his day.

Sandra was multi-tasking in a way that had Godfrey in awe. She was chatting about some tips for Georgia in dealing with Jocey, frying the steaks, stirring some pepper sauce and slugging wine from the glass beside the hob. Godfrey made a mental note to check out the prices of those large wine glasses. They made his garage voucher ones look a little lame.

As Godfrey felt the wine taking effect, he allowed himself a few more generous glances at Sandra's buttocks: great big things that wobbled out of sync with the rest of her body's movements. He was finding her quite attractive these days, her sense of fun and desire to look after everyone in her world were appealing traits to such a self-contained man and he was finally looking at his own life and wondering whether he'd had the balance wrong all these years. He found that he now liked the way the kitchen was lit by under-unit lighting, whereas on first viewing he found such things excessive and unnecessary. He appreciated the fact that she had cracked open two packs of canapés simply to allow him more choice. He wasn't expected to eat them all – although he was giving it his best shot – and the remainder may not even get frozen for another occasion. It didn't really matter. Godfrey was finally grasping the point of hospitality.

These thoughts also brought into question the Audrey/Sandra debate. At first Audrey had been the out and out winner – neat, intelligent, monied and not prone to extravagances – all the things he admired in anyone, but especially a woman. Her figure was proof that she didn't overindulge in excess; her clothes were expensive, but plain and hardwearing. Sandra in comparison was extravagance personified. She delighted in frills and fancies and was draped in costume jewellery and scarves, immersed in perfume and her hair was coloured and teased into shape with what must be a *range* of gadgets. And her figure, well that was a monument to excess – in fact, monumental excess.

It had been mainly her availability, in addition to her pleasant disposition that first drew him – but now he was beginning to appreciate all of her traits. Her hair looked – nice. Her beads suited her and her scarves disguised her fat neck. However, on top of this jumble of new feelings, he also could add that of disloyalty, as if he were betraying the one he was already pretty much betrothed too…

By the time Sandra had put two plates of steak, chips, onion rings, tomatoes, peas, pepper sauce, carrots, salad and coleslaw on the table, he'd abandoned such nonsense as disloyalty: the woman in front of him had turned into a buxom wench, and he tucked into the evening with abandon.

Sandra on the other hand, had had a long hard think about her plans for the evening. She'd been embarrassed and shamed by her behaviour on the evening of his leaving "party". She knew that she'd frightened him off and therefore needed to take a more traditional approach with this traditional male. He was obviously not a chancer: a fly-by-night would have taken the opportunity to sample her wares that night and never have been seen again. Therefore she must let him make the moves, let him think he was in control.

So, she slowed down her wine consumption and stepped up his. She dimmed the lights to reduce the sight of her thread veins and undid a button on her blouse. She kept her heels on, even though her corns were causing her to limp like a sheep with foot rot. She hadn't quite worked out how her girdled tights with a capacious pair of black pants under them might look at a later hour, but she'd play that bit by ear.

And so the night moved on. Godfrey seemed to love his main course and only didn't continue until rupture because she said that he must take home the leftovers. They had a small slice of cheesecake each and Sandra fed him a couple of strawberries from the top. By this time, she knew that his thoughts had moved on from food and so she tried to make it easy for him.

Godfrey was obviously completely inexperienced in matters of seduction and Sandra felt that, at this rate, he would soon be making a move home due to ignorance, indecision or both. Finally, it was the downstairs toilet light that made the move for him. The bulb pinged on his seventh visit and she told him to use the one upstairs.

He, quite understandably, asked her to show him where it was.

She showed him and then hovered outside, trying not to think that she was hovering around a door that had a pissed man weeing behind it, probably leaning with his forehead against the wall as he did so. As she stood there, she suddenly became very aware of what lay under her clothes. Her body had never been the same since having the children. Things had drooped, dropped and to her horror occasionally dribbled. With Dave it had never seemed to matter that much. It had been a gradual process and because she had carried his children, it would have been a bit unfair of him to have moaned about it. She had known that he fancied fitter, more attractive women, but she'd never had the commitment or urge to become one, but here she was about to embark on a grand unveiling to a man who may have little or no idea about what in reality lay beneath the normal female trappings.

She was aware that Godfrey was no Adonis, though he did look better without the beard, but she felt particularly bloated tonight; she'd drunk a lot of coffee earlier in the vain attempt to calm her nerves and she always retained water when she was stressed.

It was that dilemma that so many women had faced before her, be confident with a *Well, you're lucky to have it, mate, so enjoy it while you can…* attitude or go for the alternative *turn off the lights and hope to distract him from noticing* angle. What she neglected to remember was that as one who never had the heating on after nine thirty, Godfrey would surely love to be enveloped, on a cloudless summer evening, in something that felt like a warm ball of pliant bread dough.

Outside again and with the bit of strawberry skin removed from his left incisor, Godfrey made pathetic references to it being a big house upstairs and what size were the, er, bedrooms.

In the end, she put him out of his misery and led him to her room. She shushed his tapping on the veneer of the wardrobe doors and stopped him checking the view. Instead she lay on the bed and asked him in her lowest voice to join her.

He squeaked and bounced to her like a schoolboy offered an underwear catalogue. Then he remembered his manners and sat on the edge of the bed and took his shoes off.

Sandra laughed and grabbed him to her and they got stuck in.

Godfrey didn't seem to mind the white belly flab spilling over her tights. Nor did he notice that if you touched her ankle, the skin stayed dented. Stretch marks were accepted as nature running its course, but he was a little over-intrigued by the black mole on her nether regions for her comfort – anyone would think he'd never seen such a thing before.

They rolled around like two hippos, his briefs needing immediate incineration by the fashion police, her bra needing to be two sizes larger if it wasn't going to leave such a welt.

Godfrey was a little concerned by the sight of Sandra's red toenails and thought that she had at the very least dropped a brick on her foot, until Sandra sheepishly admitted that she wasn't as agile as she used to be and reaching her toes with a tiny nail varnish brush was a bit hit and miss.

There was chafing, vaginal wind and a nasty burp from Godfrey. There was reciting shopping lists, counting backwards and then revving back up a little with visions of Westlife *sans* shirts from Sandra.

Neither made it to a wave crashing climax and it sort of petered out into a slightly drunk cuddle, but that was just fine with both of them and a sweet sleep gave the bedsprings a rest and allowed Sandra's neighbours to unplug their ears and stop saying, "I can't hear you, I can't hear you!".

Godfrey walked home the next morning with a spring in his step and a pull in his groin. He'd had a wonderful evening and felt very pleased that it had ended the way that it had. It had been years since his private parts had had such a work-out, how many years…well, since that conversation with Alice Jefferson's father. That day had certainly changed things for him, that was for sure.

But today, the sun shone and his willy ached and he had no need at all to think about Royston Jefferson. Think of Sandra, he thought. Think of the delicious breakfast that followed a cup of tea in bed provided by a, thankfully, showered and dressed Sandra; he hadn't known whether he could have gone through it all again sober. He was very aware that instead of a ramrod leaping out from under the sheets for her sexual pleasure, something resembling a walnut whip left too near to the radiator would have peered round the duvet in fear.

They'd chatted and laughed about the antics of the night before and it had broken the ice. Sandra had held his hand as she sat beside him on the bed, but it had been a friendly gesture: no pressure.

He'd had a delightful power shower, with a range of products to choose from that actually foamed up, and he'd spent a wonderful twenty minutes lathering, shaving, washing and, damn it, conditioning too, whilst Sandra made breakfast. Georgia's influence was obviously beginning to make its presence felt.

He dried himself in a bath sheet with deeper pile than his own best carpet. He put on Daniel's aftershave, Sophie's deodorant and Sandra's moisturiser and went down to breakfast a red, shiny pompom. Sandra had laughed and laughed, but had then kissed his forehead and said that he smelt like an explosion in a perfume factory – but it was said in fun, not as a criticism.

They had both been keen that he left before Sophie and Daniel were dropped off by their father – the children didn't need to see the poodle that had spent the night porking their mother.

"They'll be here on the dot of ten," said Sandra. "He's always late picking them up, but by Christ, he can manage to drop them off on time."

They were very aware that Sandra's face was red from snogging a man who usually shaved with a blunt razor and the man sat at her breakfast table had obviously strained his groin. These were clues enough to send teenagers screaming to their bedrooms, declaring that they would saw off or sew up their private parts by the age of thirty-five and it would be right and proper if everyone else did so as well.

Therefore at nine-thirty prompt, Godfrey had been waved goodbye by a coy Sandra peeping around the door. He lifted the arm that wasn't carrying a Tupperware box with a half-eaten steak in it and waved back. Then he set off along the road with the wind lifting his conditioned hair in a way that it had never had the energy to do before.

Godfrey was just drifting back to how different his life might have been had he not had that never-to-be-forgotten conversation with Royston Jefferson, when he saw a large familiar face walking towards him. He turned to look behind him, but there was no escape and short of diving into a bush, the meeting had to go ahead.

"Good morning, Mansel, lovely day," he said, hoping to get through it unscathed.

"Oy, you dirty old goat – what are you doing along this road? Don't tell me… Hey Lucy-Ann, I know where this old goat has been – and it's not just in the *house* at number forty-seven!"

Lucy-Ann cried, "Mansel!" but it was enough to send Godfrey blushing to the roots of his newly fluffy hair.

"Oh, I've just been for a morning stroll," he muttered. "What are you doing?"

"Morning constitutional," said Lucy-Ann, trying to suppress her giggles and she patted her pregnant stomach in case her meaning wasn't obvious. "Only a few weeks to go now; I need to get my exercise in."

"Looks like *he's* been exercising all night!" laughed Mansel and he started doing his shagging impression when a police car purred past with two horrified teenage faces at the windows. They'd recognised Godfrey, seen Mansel's pointing finger and thrusting hips, put two and two together and got a queasy stomach for their efforts.

Lucy-Ann was laughing so much she had to hold her bump until Mansel quipped, "Better get going – we don't want to have it here do we? Hey, Godfrey, just think – it can be mates with yours nine months from now!" He was led away by a leaking Lucy-Ann, beaming in pride at his hilarious performance.

Godfrey shook his head and walked on, but his mood wasn't to be deflated. He felt virile, strong and indestructible. If he'd done it once, well, he could do it again! Why, oh why, had he waited so long?

He got home and turned down a cup of tea from an intrigued Georgia. "I'm a bit tired," he mumbled, "had a bit of a late night last night. I think I might just have to go to bed for forty winks."

"Uncle God!" shouted Georgia. "What *have* you been doing?" He did the decent thing and said nothing, but he couldn't resist a little lift of his eyebrows and he heard her laughter as he shut the bedroom door.

Once in his room, Godfrey's mood changed. He seemed to suddenly see his bedroom for what it really was. A dingy, miserable, worn room that had never seen any fun, laughter or even companionship. In fact the only other person to have spent any time in it had been the bloke that had helped him bolt the second-hand bed together.

That bed could have had a wife in it. It could have had children sat between them on a Sunday morning. And it bloody well might have had, had he not listened so attentively to Royston Jefferson.

Almost in tears at his newly awakened sense of loss, he kicked his shoes off and climbed fully-clothed under the sheets, pulling the itchy blanket up to his chin. He fell quickly asleep, his mind played wonderful tricks on him and he soon forgot his sorrow and dreamt that he was lying on silk sheets looking at a dark mole somewhere on Alice Jefferson's naked flesh…

Two stony faces met Sandra's welcoming smile as she opened the door to her children. Sophie gave her a look that suggested that Sandra must have, at the very least, skidded on her guinea pig as it took its weekly constitutional across the kitchen floor and Daniel looked as if he might be about to be sick. Both brushed past her on their way to their rooms, Daniel stopping only briefly for a foray into the fridge for a stomach-settling slice of cold pizza.

Sandra felt helpless and humiliated. Her mood wasn't improved by catching the eye of Dave the Dart as he slapped the steering wheel of the patrol car in delight.

She slammed the door and went back in for a spot of comfort-eating and last night's few leftover canapés, wishing that Godfrey had filled up on a bit of toast before he'd arrived…

Chapter 48

Wiring up to Next Door's Satellite

Two miles away from where Godfrey slept with a wide smile on his face, Audrey Gloucester put the phone down in a rage. Her hands were shaking and she was nearly in tears. A woman – *a woman* – had answered Jerry's phone. No, *their* phone. Her and Jerry's phone. And she'd taken her time when going to find him. *And* she thought that she heard Jerry say, "Thanks, darling," as it was passed to him.

"Who the hell was that?" Audrey had barked to him.

"Madeline Dreyfus," said Jerry factually. "Anyway, how are you Audrey? Well? How are the dogs? How's Hamish's hind paw?"

So, they'd chatted about the dogs, the cost of the scaffolding, and the mix of cement that the labourers should use. She'd jotted a few points down, then listened in amazement as he'd rattled off a few details about the divorce and the need to change his will. However, she was not to worry, but it might be good for her if she started to look for a bit of work. Part-time would probably be fine – would need to fit around the dogs. There was another instruction about when to return to the vet, should Hamish need it. Then she found herself saying goodbye and wishing him a pleasant remainder of the weekend.

She'd sat down in shock afterwards. Solicitors? Wills? *Madeline bloody Dreyfus?* What the hell was that about? She was that tart from the secondary-modern surely? The one who used to do things with the boys on the bus? Audrey's friends had dreaded walking past the secondary-modern school wall as the plebs would flick their cigarette butts at the posh girls in their burgundy blazers. Audrey, however, had always thrown the butts back and told them to grow up.

She remembered Madeline Dreyfus as a busty girl in a bursting white blouse, lots of black kohl round her eyes and a skirt six inches shorter than would have been allowed in Audrey's school. She'd been younger than Audrey and she hadn't heard of her since she'd left school herself, but would have presumed, if she had thought about her at all, that she would be living in a distasteful flat somewhere with eight children all fathered by different men.

Perhaps she had taken over the cleaning at Anchor Road? Maybe she was delivering, oh, Audrey didn't know, pizzas perhaps?

But the *Thanks, darling,* played on her mind and a picture of a more mature Madeline crept into her mind. Instead of leaning against the school wall with her tight blouse and black eyes, she was leaning against Audrey's cooker. Her hair would be brushed instead of tangled. She may have had a mouth like a sewer, but looking back, she had been a beauty. She may also have done all those things on the bus, but it would have been to boys that yearned for her.

No one had ever really yearned for Audrey. Jerry had been

316

a friend of the family and all who knew the couple had been delighted that their efforts at pairing them up had worked. A parent pushing for a particular suitor didn't really want to know if desire was part of the package.

Audrey felt herself tremble and then steam rose within her. She had been dignified, pleasant, understanding and fair. She had not burned Jerry's ties nor had she smeared dog shit on the inside of his briefcase. The whole separation process had seemed a farce. There had been no screaming arguments like Moira had had, no crying rages like Hester. Not even a little hysteria – any of which would have been perfectly justified.

Instead, there had been perhaps a dozen conversations – granted, uncomfortable conversations, but only conversations. She hadn't had her fifteen minutes, and suddenly it was time.

The redial button was stamped on. This time the shrieking started as soon as Madeline purred her greeting.

"How dare you! How bloody dare you! Where is my husband? I *demand* to speak to him now! Get out of my house – do you hear me? Get out of my house!" But only dogs could hear her as her voice sounded higher and higher as her hysteria rose.

"Mrs Gloucester, if you'll…"

"Mrs Gloucester, just one…"

"Mrs Gloucester, can you…"

Audrey was glad that she was finally saying her piece, venting her anger on someone, even if it were a little misplaced. During a breath, she heard Madeline walking across a wooden floor – good, she must be going to get him at last. Audrey now felt warmed up: now was her time.

A door clicked shut in her Bridlon home - sounded like the dining room. Excellent, Jerry must now have the phone and had asked Madeline to leave the room.

"Right, you fuckin' bitch, now you just listen to me…" Audrey gasped as Madeline dropped the Mrs Gloucester routine and sounded as if she had been possessed by the spirit of her Secondary-Modern self.

Audrey whimpered as the tirade swept over her "…you fuckin' slag…affair for twenty fuckin' years…hear that? Twenty fuckin' years…send someone over to break your legs…you hear me? Now get out of my life you stuck-up bitch. Not fuckin' better than me now, are you? Posh bint." The door clicked again. "OK, Mrs Gloucester, I'll tell him you phoned. Good day to you too."

Chapter 49

Cooking With the Gristly Bits

Audrey got out of the car, not really bothered that she was on a single yellow. She was up for a fight and any passing traffic warden would just be a vent for her steam, until she remembered that the traffic wardens only patrolled in Cysgod y Ffynnon every other Thursday. Her rage was written over her face as she stormed up the pavement.

"Morning!" called a shopkeeper as he re-arranged the bags of birdseed outside his shop. Audrey nodded curtly and stomped past, giving an unnecessarily wide berth to the goods on the pavement.

"Well, hello…" began a lady that Audrey recognised from a neighbouring farm.

"Morning," spat Audrey and paced on.

However, by the time she had been obliged to wave to a baby in a pram, had patted two Great Danes and asked about their diet, she began to feel a little better despite herself. Chairs had been set out on the pavement outside a café and she thought, *hang it,* and sat down. A young girl brought her a mug of hot chocolate with a generous squirt of cream and Audrey settled back and decided to make a fresh start to the day.

She'd always liked Cysgod y Ffynnon; a town that she felt suited her, that was steeped in her preferred era. She'd never really got on with the supermarkets that she was pretty much forced to shop in in Bridlon. Progress, they'd called it as the bakers, butchers and greengrocers one by one shut their doors, despite a huge local population. She was much more of a *I'll have that chop, no,* that *one, and that one, yes on the left* kind of person and buying four chops when she only wanted three, chosen for her by someone who didn't even know her, and then sealed in a pack so that she couldn't check the underside of them, was something she had never really come to terms with.

She liked the fact that there was a queue out of the door of the bakers; it showed that it was worth buying from. She liked having blackboards on pavements with the offer of the day chalked on. She even liked the fact that some of the shops still closed for lunch – arrogance in the face of impatient custom that her Jerry's Wife (make that ex-Wife) Persona fully understood. Her softer persona liked the friendly touches that such small shops could give and if she were in that persona, she loved to stop, browse and chat.

Like many market towns, Cysgod y Ffynnon had lost its way somewhere in the late eighties and there had been many empty shops and those that were open were in need of a little tender care. However, it was now thriving, with shops selling everything that you might want, and quite a bit that you couldn't imagine ever wanting and Audrey enjoyed the buzz of the to-ing and fro-ing townsfolk. She appreciated the effort that shopkeepers had made to keep the Victorian features on their shop facades, some of them, she was sure still sold things from that era, too. She liked the fact that the ironmonger sold nails by the pound and that the electrical shop still did repairs.

She sat stirring her hot chocolate and then wedged a serviette under the wobbly table leg to curb her increasing irritation. She calmed down again. She felt that she needed to have a good hard think. Not a think as she walked the dogs, where she might be distracted by a limp or having to check the texture of their stools, but a proper concentrating think.

She needed to accept the fact that she had been left. Not high and dry maybe, but left nonetheless. Regardless of the rights and wrongs, she was now on her own and dwelling on it would hurt only her. She could not *make* Jerry feel bad for what he had done and if he had chosen to live with Madeline Dreyfus, no doubt in due course his comeuppance would smack him in the face like a mouthful of jumped-up tramp's spittle.

Therefore, she must be calm and decide what she wanted to do with the rest of her life. Although she half joked about her personas, her Jerry one had rather taken over her other one, as she had so little time to be the person she really wanted to be. It made her realise the amount of time she had spent spinning around his world instead of creating her own orbit. When things were busy and the children needed her time, her job had been to sort out everything they needed and Mrs Audrey Gloucester was far better at it than Audrey the gentle soul curled up with a book. Since they'd left home, she could have become a little bit more of the Audrey that she felt that she was deep inside.

This was now surely the time to think about the kind of life she wanted and the person she actually wanted to be. Jerry obviously hadn't given her a second thought when he had decided that what he wanted to do was a little additional servicing of his colleagues and clients and perhaps now was her time to do the same...

However, it was never that easy; one couldn't change one's opinions about acts such as adultery in just a few hours. Audrey had always had a very clear moral code about such things and perhaps what Jerry had been taking advantage of *really* was her pride. He would have known that she had her standards and this had always been referred to when friends of theirs had taken their wayward partner back. "I wouldn't let him back into the house," she would shudder, "not after that. No, that would be the end for me."

Yet, now it had happened to her, was it *really* such a bad thing he had done? If she hadn't found out, especially in such a humiliating way, she would still have been quite happily pottering around. He always came home at night; he never left any evidence lying around the house or his person. In France, what he'd done would be acceptable. Perhaps discretion, not fidelity, was the key? The moral code was beginning to be a little less clear cut. Would the softer Audrey have handled it any better?

Although she didn't want to admit it, she *did* miss Jerry. He was always dependable even though he was so busy. He gave her access to an interesting life through him – even though she didn't necessarily know the whole story, she would still have an opinion on each topic he brought home. He was a very sociable man and her friends tended to be thanks to him – his friends' wives for example and her life was now suddenly very empty.

However, time had moved on and discretion was a lost cause and her current position did not seem to be negotiable. And that conversation with Madeline Dreyfus, well, that would have put the last nail in the coffin lid of any reconciliation.

She needed to keep herself busy; that would help. However, her busyness at Tŷ Mawr would usually be in readiness for his arrival, even if he never commented on what she had been rushing around to do. She sometimes snatched a night or two at her retreat – her folly, as Jerry called it – but if she hadn't had time to sort Tŷ Mawr out, she wouldn't have allowed herself to go. Now it was all different – what was the point in her pulling up the carpet in the spare bedroom to find out what that smell was, when she could just shut the door on it and use another room? There was no hint of expectation of someone coming to stay now – no last minute colleagues arriving for a weekend that she would tutt about, but then enjoy. She was finally able to do *exactly* what she wanted, when she wanted, but in a way, it was quite a daunting prospect.

Maybe she needed to try a different tack? Perhaps she'd grounded herself in a decade where she'd been best suited and everyone else had modernised around her. If she were to move forward half a century in her outlook, perhaps she'd understand it all better – maybe even start to enjoy life a little – something she hadn't really done since the children were small.

Audrey looked at her appearance in the café window. Her hair was set in a style that her rather old-fashioned mother had helped her with when she went for her first job interview; hair swept back from her face and secured in a stern plait. She'd always told hairdressers, "No, thank you, I know what suits me," when they suggested something different. Whereas actually, she didn't know what suited her, she just knew what she had walked out with last time and the time before that. When she finally had the time to be the softer Audrey, she simply undid her plait and let her hair fall around her face. Admittedly though, even *that* hairstyle was thirty years out of date …

She took a good look at her mushroom-coloured slacks – elasticated at the back, good roomy pockets and sitting at a length to meet her sensible shoes. Audrey didn't even need to look at her navy sweater to know that it was nothing other than functional. Her Gentle Audrey clothes had all been stuffed away in that other house, which didn't even allow her to get into character unless she were there, which was next to never.

She thought about Tamsin: looking fantastic, albeit a little slutty, in that dress, spilling all over the place. She imagined Madeline, still in her school uniform, all sultry and full of feminine guile. Obviously neither of them had to walk Barney and Hamish three times a day, but maybe something could change?

Madeline Dreyfus. The thought of *that woman* brought a black cloud back over her mood and she snarled at the waitress who asked her if everything was all right with her hot chocolate. "Well, it's only bloody hot chocolate, how bad could you possibly get it?" she'd snapped, then immediately regretted it as the young girl retreated with a rather surprised look on her face.

"Mind if I join you?" someone said and indicated the chair opposite her. It was the local bobby, PC Dave Burton. He didn't wait for an answer, but eased himself down and put his hat onto the table. "Thank you; needed to rest my legs. Audrey Gloucester, isn't it?"

"Yes," said Audrey, wondering how he might know her.

"I know your husband, Jerry, he was in the sixth form when I was just a little first former. Great chap, great chap. How is he?"

"I've *absolutely* no idea," said Audrey. "No idea, no desire to know."

"Oh dear," said PC Burton, "caught you on a bad day, have I?"

"Not really," clipped Audrey, "it's just that he will soon be my ex-husband and I have no wish to discuss him with anyone." She hoped that that would be that and that he would move off and rest his legs somewhere else. But she had not bargained for PC Burton's lack of motivation to get on with something police-like and useful.

"Well, I'm very sorry to hear that," he started, although his face showed otherwise, "very sorry indeed. Happened to me, you know – divorce and all that. Nasty business." He looked meaningfully at Audrey, a cue to continue that wasn't taken up. "Yes, it's never one hundred per cent the right thing to do and never one hundred per cent the wrong thing. You know what I mean?"

Audrey's frown suggested that she neither knew nor cared.

"Affair was it? With Jerry?" He took from Audrey's glare that it was. "Yes, I left my wife for a fantastic woman. Thought that she was everything I could ever want. Turned out that I'd seen the best of her already. You know, lots of fun in the pub, but you can't do twenty-four hour fun can you?"

Audrey shrugged her shoulders as if *she* could.

"Yes, there is a place for a good home, tea on the table, washing done, chat in front of the television – playing with the kids, you know? I miss it. Yes sir-eee, I miss it."

Audrey was getting bored. It was *her* day of misery; she didn't want to be listening to someone else's. Especially from some bloke who thought that Jerry was great. That was the last thing she wanted to hear.

"You'll have the last laugh, though. You may not think it now, but you'll have the last laugh. He'll feel bad about it soon enough. Regret – it's a terrible thing. Eats you up, it does. But you know what you need to do now?" he said.

"No," said Audrey, but she had a feeling that she was going to find out.

"Get back on the horse!" said Dave. "Move on; the best revenge is good living and all that! That's what's made me miss my ex-missus recently; realise that I'd made a mistake. I can tell you, seeing her moving on, when here I am doing my own ironing and eating cold takeaways, is all the revenge that she'll ever need." He settled back pleased at having imparted his wisdom. *This community-policing lark came in so many different guises…*

His lecture was interrupted by a crackle from his radio.

"342 come in. 342 come in."

"342 receiving," he said winking at Audrey.

"Can you give your location, 342?"

"Oh, I'm er, walking down Victoria Street, then I'll do a round of the park."

"The Gov' says to look up and to your left. He's in the window above the architect's office. He says for you to get off your arse and do some work. Over."

Dave blushed and looked up. Audrey followed his gaze. There standing in a bay window was a uniformed man standing with his hands on his hips glaring at them. Dave jumped to his feet, bid farewell to Audrey, did a half-hearted salute to his boss and scuttled off down the street.

Audrey laughed out loud and gave a little clap in the direction of the officer at the window opposite who nodded back and returned to his business.

She sat back in her chair and smiled. Suddenly she felt better. Happier maybe. Even when things were gloomy, there were still things to smile about. Perhaps that fool of a PC had been right in a way. Perhaps she did need to get on with life? There was no point in sitting around being miserable, waiting for philandering Jerry Gloucester to feel sorry for her. And would she want his commiserations even if he did?

But how did one go about getting back on one's horse? A job perhaps? Perhaps she should inquire at the local hospital. Make some new friends maybe – starting with apologising to that poor lady that she had shunned ten minutes before. Male company? Probably a little early for romance, but maybe she could get to know a few local chaps, get to know them as friends. What about Geoffrey for example? He seemed pleasant enough and he wasn't married. Perhaps he would like to come to supper one night? In an Audrey Gloucester kind of way, she paid for her drink, gave a large tip to make up for her rudeness, thought *no time like the present* and scuttled off to the butchers to select a couple of chops for supper.

Chapter 50

Staycations – or Holidaying at Home

Godfrey was woken from a dream about a giant that had Alice Jefferson's bare feet and was swirling Sandra's chunky gold bracelet around his head, by his old office mobile phone, which lay on his bedside cabinet. Being someone who has few phone calls, he bothered to sit up and answer it, hoping it wasn't somebody from the office trying to find out what had happened to their out-on-site emergency mobile.

"Geoffrey?" clipped a voice.

"Er, yes," he replied, quickly stepping back into his alter-ego.

"Audrey. Audrey Gloucester, Tŷ Mawr."

"Hello, Audrey, how are you?" She'd never phoned him before and he felt a little uncomfortable that he'd brought the deception into his home with such innocents as Georgia and Jocey in it.

"Very well, thank you." Audrey seemed nervous; he wouldn't have thought that she would have had the capacity for nerves. "I'm ringing...well, I'm ringing to ask whether you would, er, like to come to dinner tonight?"

Godfrey was in shock. Then his new virile socialite persona kicked in – of course she wanted him to come to supper – didn't everyone? "Well, yes. That would be lovely. Thank you very much. What time? And can I er, can I bring anything?"

"Just yourself. Seven-thirty?"

The phone clicked off as God was still muttering his appreciation. He put the phone down and looked into the small mirror on the hall wall. His hair was raised an inch from his head after his sleep. He thought he looked devastating.

Better get back to bed for another re-charge, he chuckled to himself and slipped, grinning, back under the covers.

Chapter 51

Getting the Best from Your Doggy Bag

Godfrey walked the back way to Tŷ Mawr along the cycle path. He had left with plenty of time in hand and was happy to enjoy the journey. There were still some bright yellow flowers out on the gorse and the coconutty scent added to his feelings of all being right in his world. He had no qualms about walking back in the dark – there was to be a full moon to light up his route and his love would keep him warm! Although, after last night's romantic success, he was rather hoping that he might not have to walk back until the next morning…

The dogs welcomed him into the garden and he was pleased to see their tails wagging; even with their liver-scented slobber, it was a better thought to be licked by them than it was to have one's leg ripped off.

Audrey came out of the side door with her pinny on and wearing a long Indian cotton skirt and a pair of sandals over her white bare feet. She looked rather awkward, though, with her navy jumper on with a little pair of white collars peeping out of the neckline. Godfrey wasn't sure what to make of her attire but he hoped that the outfit meant that she'd made an effort for him. "Hello!" she called, looking a little flustered. "How are you?"

"Very well," he replied, "and you?"

The pleasantries over with, she darted back indoors assuming that he would follow. "Sit down, sit down," she said, waving her hand towards the fireplace. Godfrey dived into Jerry's chair: he had made it! He was sat, invited, in the fireside chair at Tŷ Mawr! Godfrey had always wanted a house like this and felt he'd been destined for it. A house that befitted his personality, the real Godfrey who had been sat inside a dull, mean facade for so many years.

And even better, he now had the features of a face that could present the roasted duck and the carafes of wine to guests. Perhaps it should actually be *Audrey's* face that would smile at his jokes and touch his shoulder as she walked past. Her face that he could make shout out in passion as he made powerful love to her outdoors in their beautiful garden...

All he needed now was a—

"Whisky?" enquired Audrey. "Jerry usually had one at this time of the evening."

"Wonderful, thank you," said Godfrey, glad he hadn't watered down the remainder of the bottle when he had had a tipple on his previous visits.

"Can I do anything to help?" he asked, his new socially aware self coming to the fore.

"Actually, you can lay a fire if you want," said Audrey, "even though it's warm outside, this place still feels terribly damp inside. It's after being shut up for so long. It's not right: houses need to be lived in if they are to be expected to stay in good condition."

Godfrey jumped at the request. He hadn't really wanted

to help, but sitting next to a lit fire, in Jerry's chair, with Audrey opposite – well, it was how it was supposed to be. As for Sandra, well perhaps she could go back on the back boiler for a while until he'd thought it all through; weighed up the pros and cons of each option.

"Of course," he said, "I'll go and get some sticks."

He trotted out of the door and much to the dogs' delight gathered a load of twigs and dried moss. After another swig of whisky, he settled down on all fours to lay the perfect fire. He twisted some newspaper then surrounded the pile by twigs, larger ones at the bottom and then a little moss on the top.

He could feel Audrey's impatience mounting as he blew on the embers, willing his little turret to jump into flames. As he knelt back to assess his success and get some blood back into his brain, Audrey took her chance and nipped past him and placed the old chop bag over his turret. "There, that'll get the bloody thing going; plastic burns so well, don't you think?"

Godfrey felt like crying as green and yellow smoke curled over him and the plastic melted into drips of flame that settled over the twig construction and secured its future. "There she blows!" said Audrey, wiping the raw meat juice onto her skirt. "Save all that ridiculous messing about with twigs."

The meal was pleasant enough in an anonymous boiled potato kind of way and although the hospitality wasn't up to Sandra's standard, the conversation was bright and intelligent. Audrey was fascinated by Godfrey's knowledge of local history and he regaled her with all the facts that he had brushed up on for the next history society meeting.

"Yes, I believe we have a book here on the Elan Valley," said Audrey, making as if to jump to her feet to go and get it. Godfrey shrank in guilt. Miracles notwithstanding, he was pretty sure that the book was still on his shelf at home – and his suspicion was probably more accurate than Audrey's belief...

He brushed the need for the book aside and told her the story of how the Elan Valley had been earmarked as suitable for flooding to provide water for the Midlands in the late 1800s. He told her how the strong but disparate community tried to fight to save their homes and livelihoods, but in the end was forced to leave the village and live elsewhere as an army of workers flocked to build the series of enormous dams. He playfully asked her to guess how many cubic tonnes of stone were used or what the reservoir's capacity was, but he saw her eyes glaze over and had the sense to quit whilst he was ahead.

"Funny, really," said Audrey with a look in her eyes that suggested that she was thinking back to happier times, "I've spent a lot of time up at the Elan Valley – I used to love playing at the water's edge with the children – but I feel guilty to have enjoyed it now, knowing all the hardship it caused."

Godfrey felt guilty that he'd never given it a thought. He was still excited by the newly-read fact that fifty-thousand men had worked on the earlier scheme, but only four-hundred and seventy on the second phase because the technology was so much better by then.

An apple crumble followed, out of a bowl big enough

to feed an army of sheep shearers and Audrey was bagging it into portions for the freezer before Godfrey had even finished his.

They had another whisky at the fireside and Godfrey popped back to the log store and filled Audrey's basket. It wasn't that she was incapable of such a task, he just felt that he wanted to look after her a bit. It was a new feeling for him, this caring lark, but he felt that before long he might even start to enjoy it!

After a discreet yawn from Audrey, Godfrey got to his feet and made to leave. "I'll walk with you for a way," said Audrey, "the dogs will need a late night visit."

And indeed they did, just as Godfrey leaned in to give her a goodnight kiss on her cheek. It was a thank you peck, as opposed to a hopeful peck, and it would have been a pleasurable experience if the silhouette of Barney straining hadn't been setting the scene. "Poor boy," said Audrey, looking over Godfrey's shoulder at the crucial moment, "his digestion's all out of kilter. I need to up his grain."

"Goodnight!" called Godfrey as he walked off into the darkness, tramping inadvertently through Barney's offerings as he went.

It had been a pleasant evening, Godfrey mused as he reached his own front door and sat down to remove his soiled shoe. Next door's Sooty had left a dead frog on the doorstep and he flicked it away distastefully. But, better than a live one, he smiled as he remembered Georgia's screams the week before.

Ten minutes later, he settled into his bed and considered his game plan: Sandra had been fun and exciting and obviously the sex bit, after such a long drought, was worth a number of points, but Audrey had been interesting and intelligent – and she brought with her the Tŷ Mawr lifestyle – which had to be a bonus. But then, there was deciding where Alice Jefferson, for whom all his savings had been made, fitted into the picture. Well, he chuckled, she'd better arrive soon, otherwise she'll find that she's missed the boat!

His last thoughts before he drifted into a whisky-enhanced sleep were a) damn, that own-brand soap hasn't quite got rid of the dog-do on my finger and b) perhaps I'll leave all three options open and make a more informed decision in a couple of weeks' time.

Chapter 52

Driving in the Slipstream of the Bus

Mansel Big Face pulled the last pair of trousers out of the bottom of his wardrobe and put them on the pile, which was now about twenty pairs high – eighteen of which he hadn't worn for at least the last seven years. The local Red Cross shop welcomed him and Lucy-Ann with glee now; they had already struggled in with two sets of golf clubs, fifteen coats, twelve pairs of Council work boots and twenty-two shirts. Apparently the Mansel rail was selling well – "Good quality men's clothes are fantastic for our building labourers," the woman had gushed. "They don't mind that they're fifteen years out of date – they're only going to get dirty or ruined anyway!"

Mansel had been a little hurt at first – he'd worn the ski jumper that night he'd done the juggling trick with those women's handbags – the one where one had been unzipped and the tampons had gone everywhere! The zigzag jumper had gone through the car wash with him whilst winning that dare from Joz Morgan and the white puffa jacket had survived the James Bond impression when he'd rolled down a flight of steps.

However, Lucy-Ann was right, they both had to have a

grand clear out if it were going to work. Two full houses did not make one nice not overfull house without a great deal of culling – and clothes were a good place to start. In turn, she'd agreed to get rid of her feather boa collection, and the younger four of the six guinea pigs, so it seemed fair do's.

As he thought of Lucy-Ann, Mansel's face broke into a smile. How had he been so lucky as to attract such a wonderful woman? He looked around his bedroom and saw a functional space that no longer had too many clothes in it. It had a television hanging from a bracket on the wall, navy blue curtains and a flattened area of carpet next to his bed where his pile of *Auto Traders* used to sit. Soon, it would have perfume on the dressing table next to his aftershave, perhaps a pretty make-up bag or a pair of hair tong things that he could moan about with his mates after they'd burnt a mark on the wood.

He stuffed the surplus trousers into bin bags and, with only a little hesitation, chucked three out of his four dressing gowns after them. How wonderful to soon have Lucy-Ann's dressing gown hanging on a peg next to his – although in time, they would obviously have to get matching His and Hers ones – perhaps Disney did an adult range? Things that other couples took for granted, he never would, he thought.

He looked at the clock again in excitement – just enough time to pick up the van that he'd arranged to move Lucy-Ann's stuff in and go to the Red Cross shop on the way. No, perhaps he'd go and get the van first – he bet that the women in the shop would laugh like mad when they saw what he had organised to do the job …

*

Two miles down the road, Lucy-Ann zipped up the last of her suitcases and left it where it lay, as instructed. Her belly got in the way of her bending, now, and her back was beginning to ache. She put her hands on her hips and stretched back, feeling the life inside her turn as it shifted position. Without realising it, she rubbed her hands over her stomach, as if reassuring her baby for the adventure ahead.

She was excited to be moving in with Mansel and had no qualms about selling her own small house – his was bigger and was the more obvious choice for all of them to live in and she had no worries that she might need to keep a bolt-hole. Not that her friends were fully convinced, not since Mansel had secretly poured a whole bottle of lighter fluid over the barbeque while someone had popped off to get the matches to ignite it, and had followed that up by passing someone a hotdog doused in onions and tomato sauce, but with a raw sausage in it.

"You'll be hospitalised – again – within weeks," her best friend had warned. "He's nice, but, well, he's just…" There wasn't a word for Mansel and Lucy-Ann knew what her friend had meant, but she wasn't concerned. She knew she loved the whole Mansel package, pratfalls and all, and she knew that her life would be wonderful and full of love and laughter. Her main worry was what she was bringing to him – could such a light-hearted and fun man cope with a wife and child without being stifled? She so hoped that this unintended pregnancy wouldn't change him.

As she packed the last of her toiletries into her vanity case, Lucy-Ann considered the disservice to mankind of smothering such a character. How dull life in Cysgod y

Ffynnon would be if there weren't a person like Mansel to swim in the lake with a plastic duck on his head or to line a wheelbarrow with a blanket in readiness for a baby's afternoon walks?

Lucy-Ann sighed and put her vanity case on the bed. Then she looked up as she heard something from outside and then lumbered to the window. What *was* that screeching noise?

She stared, then clapped her hands to her mouth in joy. Thomas the Tank Engine complete with two carriages had pulled to a halt outside her house. Mansel stuck his head out of the window of Thomas's engine and waved a green flag at her. It was the road train that chugged around Cysgod y Ffynnon's lake each Saturday and Sunday carrying piles of children clutching ice creams and moaning that it wasn't going fast enough. Mansel'd said he'd be able to sort out something – perks of the job, he'd laughed. She'd imagined a white van with the Council's logo plastered over the side. Instead she had this, complete with Adrian, Toby and Fat Git sitting grinning in the carriages, ready to help. No, she thought as she waddled down the stairs, life is no way going to be dull with this one…

Chapter 53

Forgetting to Return the Argos Pen

Annabel unpacked shopping bags overflowing with the evidence of her excitement. *All* of Georgia's old favourites were there, plus a few anticipated new ones. There were magazines, toiletries, cereal variety packs and Walnut Whips. She had another stack for Jocey – talcum powder, wipes with aloe vera, eco nappies with elasticated sides and aromatherapy bubble bath – damn, was she sure that Jocey was going to sleep well at Nana's house!

She had time to make a cottage pie for lunch and also to prepare a smoked salmon salad in case Georgia's tastes had matured over the past few years. She sang as she chopped vegetables and peeled potatoes. For the tenth time that day, she checked Georgia's room and was just re-arranging the flowers in it when Godfrey's car shuddered to a halt outside.

Annabel gave her hair one last prime with her bristle brush and ran down the stairs. She swept the occupants out of the car with an intensity that rattled Georgia, who muttered, "Calm down, Mum, for God's sake."

A sleeping Jocey was scooped out still in her car seat and put gently into the lounge. Annabel picked up a few plastic

341

carrier bags with Georgia's and Jocey's belongings in and ran them inside, making a mental note to buy Georgia a nice holdall and Jocey a cute little bag – she'd seen some nice ones with fairies on in Brown's near work: she'd get her one of those.

Georgia got out of the car and stood looking at her old house as Annabel began her assault on her daughter, her aim being to make it impossible for Georgia and Jocey ever to leave, starting with, "Who wants tea? Viennese whirls or apricot flapjacks?"

When Georgia had accepted the invitation to go to her mother's for the weekend, she had felt overflowing with love and good will to all around her. It had seemed a harmless enough invitation to accept, to come over for the weekend and let Jocey spend a bit of time with her Nana, but as the day got nearer, Georgia had felt increasingly uncomfortable.

To go "home" would be to go back in time. Not just to the place that That Ray Thingy had happened, but back in time as a person. Would it mean returning to the suburban prissy Georgia who would moan about anything and everything and for whom the more her mother did for her, the more she would expect her to do and the more she would despise her for it? It had even started getting a bit like that at Uncle God's until he'd found a new reason to get out of the house, and she'd felt a little more settled about the life she was going to lead for the foreseeable future.

To go back home would be to deny the experiences she'd had in the years since she'd left. After having lived in a damp squat, she couldn't allow herself to moan that the towels were a bit crusty, knowing that Annabel would rush out and get the deluxe fabric conditioner that cost twice the price. Or to whinge about the fat on her steak when she had eaten nothing that hadn't come out of a bin or had been nicked off a shelf for so many meals.

She had no desire to tell everyone about her experiences just to satisfy their inquisitiveness, but she *had* been there, and therefore to re-assume her old life would be a bit of a kick in the teeth for the new streetwise and self-reliant Georgia, a wilful giving up of the skills and strengths that she had learnt – from rummaging through the right bins at the right times of day, to kneeing the occasional bloke in the nuts because he thought that different rules applied to women who weren't on the electoral register and hadn't washed properly for three weeks.

Jocey would be washed and cared for and she would be too if she allowed it. Her body yearned for the rest that the house promised – the clean bathroom, those thick towels and the cupboards full of treats, but her sense of independence urged *caution, caution*.

So it was a subdued Georgia that walked up the remainder of the path and was dragged by Annabel into the kitchen. New cupboards, she thought, new paint too. Annabel was like a child at parent's evening – so desperate to show off her work that she didn't know which piece to point to first.

She opened the cupboards to show Georgia all the things she'd bought. "God, Mum," said Georgia, "I'm only here for the weekend; do you want me to put on twenty stone or what?" She was glad that she'd got that bit about it being only a weekend, but was still sad about the look that flashed across her mother's face. Annabel gave a nervous laugh and looked as if she was trying to calm down.

They sat like three great aunts in the lounge with platefuls of cakes and biscuits to choose from, drinking tea from Annabel's new mugs with their funky patterns, which, of course, Georgia felt obliged to comment on.

Godfrey was in his element. Coming to Annabel's was always a hospitality lesson that he was happy to run through again and again and then ignore in his own life. This was the first visit he'd made since Ray had left and he revelled in it. He and Ray would never have been friends in any walk of life, let alone one in which Ray didn't treat Godfrey's sister or niece very well, or in which Godfrey was a tight buffoon who kept on eating all the best biscuits.

He was pleased to see Georgia and Annabel chatting easily, albeit mostly about Jocey, and that Ray or any sign of him was well and truly gone. The fact that there was no longer a stack of those bloody fig rolls that no one else was allowed to touch in the cupboard was good news; to Godfrey, it meant that Ray was gone in soul as well as in body. Annabel was obviously neither pining for him nor expecting him back.

"I sold his van and his golf clubs in the end, well, gave them away really considering the price I got for them!" she announced triumphantly. "Well, he'd not come for them for three months – what else was I expected to do? Brian and Kathy haven't heard from him since he left them, so he's probably having a ball in Bath or wherever it was he went. Probably shacked up with a floozy somewhere, painting *her* hall and stairs, if you know what I mean…"

344

Chapter 54

Sewing Newspaper Inside Your Jacket

Georgia wandered out of her bedroom at eleven-thirty, having woken from the only undisturbed lie-in she'd had in the eight months since Jocey had arrived. She was wearing a pink playsuit – well, at least that was what Annabel had called it, seemed more like a velour tracksuit to Georgia – and had a new pair of fluffy slippers on her feet.

Jocey had been whipped away at her first murmur and Georgia had barely had time to open her eyes and nod at her mother; she must have been waiting outside the door to have acted so quickly.

She'd had two cups of tea brought to her bedside, one was cold by the time she'd awoken to find it and the other had been sipped joyously as she leant against the headboard and flicked through a magazine from the pile on her bedside table.

Georgia had re-connected with mainstream society now – daytime television had quickly seen to that. She knew all the celebrity's secrets, tips and foibles and so the magazines were just updating her knowledge. As she'd sat in her playsuit, the last of the squat and the damp and the drunken shouting matches floated away in a haze of warmth and idleness.

Eventually she manoeuvred her new slippers downstairs and went into the kitchen. She wandered over to the kettle and clicked it back on, then turned with a start as something dropped to the floor behind her.

"Sorry, love," said a man kneeling where the washing machine usually sat, "did I scare you?"

"A bit," she smiled. "Are you here to mend it?"

"Yes, your mum said that you were coming and that she desperately needed it for the baby – and that another bloke had let her down, so I said I'd come this morning. She said to tell you that she's taken the baby out to let you sleep in. I'm Graham by the way."

"I'm Georgia," said Georgia. "Do you want a cuppa?"

Graham? That rang a bell. Hadn't Mum blushed a bit yesterday when Uncle God crassly tried to pass the time by asking about any new boyfriends?

"Yes, I will thanks," said Graham, straightening himself up and brushing himself down. He seemed keen to start a conversation to pass the time whilst he was watching her chest. "So, you're back for the weekend? How long are you staying? Back to see your boyfriend is it? I expect a pretty girl like you has a boyfriend in every port, hey?"

Georgia's hackles went up and with them her squat-induced guardedness. She suddenly felt vulnerable in her ridiculous playsuit and she wished she'd put a bra on before she came downstairs.

"Are you calling me a slag?"

Graham blushed to his roots, "God no, sorry, love, I was just having a laugh, making conversation, you know. I didn't mean anything by it."

Georgia was pleased that she had retained her knack of making people feel small and it felt good.

She finished making the tea in silence as Graham returned to the washing machine. She put a cup down on the floor beside him as if nothing had happened and walked through to the lounge.

She slumped onto the sofa and clicked the television on. She felt sick. *This* is what life would be like if she stayed here. Lie-ins, Jocey out of the way, and avoiding her mum's boyfriends in case they fancied her instead. That wasn't the life she'd wanted at thirteen years old and, she realised somewhat belatedly, it wasn't the life she wanted now.

She looked in disgust at the debate about how to hang drapes and flicked off the television and went upstairs to dress. She would say goodbye to Graham before he left in case he did turn out to be her mother's boyfriend – in hindsight, she'd probably been a bit over the top in her reaction – then she'd leave her mum in peace to enjoy him. His eyes would just have to drop a couple of inches lower to reach the desired view on her mother, she thought spitefully, that was all.

Yes, back to Godfrey's house. She'd known really that she couldn't come back here to live and the washing machine man had just made her mind up for sure. Perhaps Uncle God would help her sort out a flat for her and Jocey; he had spent thirty years working for the Council for goodness sake, which ought to stand for something. They could make a proper start in Cysgod y Ffynnon, just the two of them. Get to know her new mates a bit better, get a job even. Perhaps Jocey could stay at her great uncle's house occasionally and then Georgia could work in a shop or a hotel or maybe go to an evening class or something for a couple of nights each week.

Georgia dressed and tidied her room (making a bed in her mother's house for the first time in her life). She needed to grow up and take a bit more responsibility for herself now she was back on her feet. She would pack all her things later tonight and then she would be ready for Annabel to take her and Jocey back the next day. She would take the toiletries and magazines with her – that was on the level that most children take the piss out of their parents; that, and getting their washing done. She'd sneak a few of those goodies from the kitchen too, get Uncle Godfrey's cupboards looking a little less like the crushed and expired goods shelf at the supermarket.

By the time Annabel wheeled Jocey along the pavement clutching a balloon and dressed in her new pink coat, Georgia was standing looking out of the window feeling calm and resolute.

Chapter 55

Furnishing From Skips

In a dismal room in Tavsham, Ray Haddon peered through the gloom. He now felt like he appreciated the concept of Chinese water torture as the rain drip-dripped from the ceiling.

"Someone should put a fuckin' bucket under that," said Barry, opening one eye and returning to his stupor.

"Well, why the fuck don't *you* then," retorted Ray, his irritation overwhelming him. These useless bastards, he cursed. Barry just sat there in a pissed haze and Danner just sat and stared. Barry didn't move.

"Well, *I'll* fuckin' get something then, shall I?" snapped Ray and he ridiculously hunted around in the pile of rubbish on the floor for a bucket. Eventually he found an old pizza box that Danner had brought in with real pride two nights ago. "Found it next to a pile of puke!" he'd gloated and had proceeded to eat the remainder in front of him, without offering to share, and whilst humming *Zipedeedoodah!* Ray had felt so angry that he could have killed him.

Ray put the pizza box lid under the drip and sat back on the sofa. The *drip drip* changed to a *splat splat*. "That'll go soggy," said Barry. "It'll never work."

"Who fuckin' cares?" screamed Ray, standing up. "Worried that it'll spoil your carpet? Ruin the artexing in the room below? Look at this fuckin' place! Who gives a shit?"

"Fuck off then," said Danner quietly, "no one's making you stay." Barry nodded and started to drum a rhythm on his thighs. Ray sank back into the sofa spent and near to tears.

He'd been so grateful, just two months before when Danner and Barry had found him crying on his steps. It was cold and raining and he had reached the end of his tether. He had woken to find some smartly-dressed young men urinating over him and laughing. They were drunk and looked like they had had a great night out. They were surrounded by a group of women who were dressed for clubbing. They must have all been freezing cold, but they stopped scuttling along for long enough to have a laugh at the tramp being pissed on.

Ray had struggled to wake from his sleep and by the time he was able to move, he was soaked in rapidly cooling urine. He swore at them, and they all ran off laughing, someone chucking their half-finished burger at him as they went. It wasn't so much *what* they had been doing that had made him despair, it was more the fact that they thought him completely non-human. They didn't stop to think that he might actually be a nice guy; someone with whom a few months ago they might have passed the time of day with whilst standing in a queue or waiting at a bar… It was the fact that ten yards up the road, their conversation had moved on to something else – and that stung. He was utterly unworthy of notice. Irrelevant.

Then Barry and Danner had walked past. They had heard

him and had asked if he was OK. When they saw that he wasn't and that he had piles of bags next to him, they had asked if he wanted to stay at their place; someone had left a few months before and her old room still had a mattress and a blanket in. He had been so grateful that he'd felt like kissing them both.

They had led him to the squat and he had barely noticed that to get in, one had to squeeze past a sheet of plywood. He didn't care that it was pitch black and that the only light in the whole place was one candle in the sitting room. He was just so pleased to be there, to be safe and under a roof, that he embraced his new home as a palace. He was settled on the sofa and someone passed him a bottle of cherryade and gave him a bread roll. It felt like a banquet.

He chatted for a while with his new friends and they didn't seem surprised by what had happened to him that night. "Kids they are, little bastards. They haven't got a fuckin' clue. It's all all right when daddy has a big bank balance, you see."

Their lack of drama made the experience seem a little more bearable and soon Ray was shown to his "room". Danner left him with a candle and some matches and Ray collapsed onto his new mattress with delight. He thanked Danner again and wedged the door shut.

His little room was a haven. It had a mural on the wall and a box of clothes in the corner. A large wooden sheet over the window kept the noise of the city out and he felt content and at peace. He took his wet clothes off and settled into the damp sleeping bag without a thought about what might be living in it and read a couple of pages from a magazine in a box at his side. The previous occupant must have been female he thought, as he flicked through the pile of *Glamour*s and *Closer*s.

It was almost like being back home at Annabel's, with Georgia leaving her bloody magazines all over the place…

But his gratitude hadn't lasted. He had soon got fed up with the state of the place, the fact that *everything* was filthy. Grit and broken glass got *everywhere*. The house smelt and its occupants smelt. And they didn't *do* anything.

He'd promised at first to do a few jobs around the place, tidy it up a bit. He gathered together a load of rubbish, but there was nowhere to put it, no bundle of bin bags under the sink. In desperation he threw it outside and felt bad as a mother walking past with her child glared at him as paper blew across her path. He tried to fix a few things, but he had no tools and no materials, so he soon gave up. Also, no one seemed to be bothered if he did anything or not. They certainly didn't join in and help. In fact that snooty bitch Hannah in the next room to him asked him to stop it as he was creating a dust. Creating a dust! In that place!

So now he spent his time much as the others did, sat in that disgusting 'sitting room' bickering or making stupid plans that would never happen. Some of the more active residents went out shoplifting or pickpocketing, so they could afford to go out in the nights to pubs or clubs. The older ones like him, Danner and Barry couldn't be bothered. They mooched about foraging for food during the day, sometimes tried to wash themselves or their clothes, but mainly they just lay in their sleeping bags or sat on that bloody sofa reading old newspapers and moaning.

No, Ray had had enough. He couldn't stay any longer. He would gather his things up tomorrow and leave this shithole: perhaps Brian could convince Kathy to let him stay a couple of weeks until he got his van back on the road again?

Chapter 56

Giving "Love" as a Gift

Mansel Big Face opened his eyes and smiled. Life was good. Every day it was good. He looked around his bedroom, now a fetching shade of lilac, but that wasn't to be helped. He felt warm as he saw Lucy-Ann's make-up bag on the dressing table; no one had ever put make-up on in front of him before and he loved being in the same room as Lucy-Ann when she did hers. He saw her hairbrush with the lovely long brown hairs entwined around the bristles and he saw her panties in the corner, flung that way in a dramatic gesture as she'd pleaded with him the night before to *Take me roughly and get this damn baby on the way.*

"Lucy-Ann?" he called, "Get breakfast on the phone. I think I'll just have the croissant today, with a little apricot jam."

He heard a chuckle from the corridor. She was pacing again.

"Are you OK?" he asked, getting out of bed and popping some Mickey Mouse boxers on. "Still got backache?" He rubbed her back and she groaned and leaned back against him.

"Oh, that's better," she whispered. "I've been up since

five, I just couldn't get comfortable."

"You should have woken me. I'd have shown you how to get comfortable – I've been comfortable all night!"

Lucy-Ann grinned. "Thank you, Mansel, that makes me feel much better."

"Breakfast?" he asked. "What would you like to eat this morning? A scouring pad? Coal? Or just a little raw minced pork?"

"I don't feel too good actually; I've got a bit of a bad belly."

"Erk. Bad belly in a baby way, or bad belly in a too much kebab after downing six bottles of white wine kind of way."

"Don't know," she mumbled, stretching out her stomach. "I know it's supposed to be another few weeks off, but perhaps this could be *it?*"

Mansel swallowed hard. He'd been so excited about the whole pregnancy thing. He'd loved having Lucy-Ann come to live with him and they had gotten on far better than he could have ever hoped. He'd had a great time at the pre-natal classes; just as he had predicted, he had been the class wag. They'd loved it when he'd turned up with a balloon filled with water under his jumper *to see what it felt like*. Their comedy T-shirts had provided much hilarity and he thought that he'd only overdone it the once, when he kept on making popping sounds when the midwife was explaining about the waters breaking.

Lucy-Ann now had a signal for when it was time to shut-up and it seemed to be working. It was usually at least one comment before Mansel felt it was strictly necessary, but perhaps that was where he had been going wrong all these years. Yes, Lucy-Ann was a fantastic addition to his life and many people had shaken their heads in disbelief when they'd met her.

But now, it seemed that the wonderful new opportunity for japes that was Lucy-Ann's pregnancy thing might be nearly over. The reality of a baby at the end of it might be on its way.

"Shall we call a midwife? Do you want to go to hospital? Shall I get some towels or something?"

"Mansel!" she laughed, "I've only got a bit of a tummy ache and I am sure that for the next month I'll have plenty more. No, you get breakfast on and I'll just wander around for a while longer."

Chapter 57

Taking more Sugar Sachets than your Current Drink Requires

Georgia was lying on her stomach in the garden of one of the women in the Adventurers Without a Clue. The big groundsheet was attracting the sun and she felt deliciously warm and happy. Gwen came out of the kitchen carrying a large glass jug of brownish liquid with lots of bits in it.

"Pimms," she grinned. "No garden party is complete without Pimms!"

"Oh, a garden party now is it?" laughed Simon, "I thought it was a 'come round for a cup of tea' afternoon? Is Jocey all right in the sun, Georgia – she can have this little sun hat if she wants, Derwen has plenty."

"Thank you," smiled Georgia and plonked it on Jocey's head and everyone laughed at how cute she looked with her North Ridge floppy hat over her fair little curls. Georgia took her glass of Pimms and sipped at it, trying not to get any of that flippin' cucumber that someone must have dropped in by mistake. She scooped it out and flicked it into the bushes.

"It's supposed to be in there," whispered Tomos, Gwen's younger brother, who had wondered out into the garden to join them.

Georgia giggled, "It may be supposed to be in your drink, but it's damn well not staying in mine."

Tomos laughed and pulled some out of his own glass and flipped it in the same direction as Georgia's. "Yeah, you're right – who really wants veg in their drink, I ask you!" Georgia thought Tomos was gorgeous. She'd met him once before when he'd sat in on one of their get-togethers and had made amusing comments from behind a newspaper on the sofa. He had Gwen's athletic build, without any of her sportswear. He was tall and lean and had bushy blonde hair. Jocey crawled over Tomos on her way over to Georgia and he laughed and tickled her toes, "Oy, you! Have some respect! You could at least say *excuse me!*"

"Actually, folks," said Simon pulling out a notebook from a large pocket on his knee, "now that there's a few of us here, I thought I might just run a new idea past you?" The others nodded in agreement and Georgia rolled onto her back to absorb a few more rays. "Don't go to sleep, Georgia, this one includes you…" he added and Georgia rolled back, concerned.

"Sorry, but you're not getting me wedged in a pothole or clinging to the side of a mountain – and can you imagine the response I'd get if I asked my Uncle God to sponsor me?" The others laughed; they enjoyed hearing about Uncle Godfrey's little ways.

"No, this is a bit different," Simon continued. "We don't want you up a mountain – although I am sure that you would enjoy it and get an awful lot out of it…"

"You wouldn't," whispered Tomos, "it's hell. Believe me!"

"What I need you for is the legitimising of our fundraising." Georgia's look was enough to encourage Simon that she hadn't dismissed it out of hand. "That last project that you scuppered in the park? Well, I have rewritten it and put in another bid – and you are the mouthpiece, the *Ambassador!*"

Georgia looked concerned. "Don't worry," he said, "we just need someone to do things like talk to the people who we'll bid to for money; to let them know that it is a legitimate and a useful programme – and I would make sure that you are happy with all the things that might be happening within the project. Also – within the bid, there is an element of funding for such a post, so we would pay you for your time."

Georgia looked stunned. "What, me? Paid to talk to people?"

"Well, they'll listen to you, with your experiences – as I well know, and to my financial detriment!" The others sniggered; they had heard about Simon's various trials for funding.

"You'd be great, Georgia," said Davey, a lanky mountain biker in full Lycra lying on the grass with his SPD shoes at his side. "You know what you're talking about and the way you talked to us lot, well you can put it across so that people understand and that's important."

Georgia considered it for a few moments. "OK," she smiled. "But you'd have to make sure that I know what I am to say, what I'm not to say and when, all right?"

"Yeah," said Tomos, "best not mention the one about being off your face and walking along the central reservation of the motorway, eh?" Georgia threw one of Jocey's fluffy toys at him.

The others then went on to discuss the bulk of the project, the things that they would actually do. She heard words like *yurt* and *empowerment* and was content to let the rest flow over her head. She was just happy to be lying in the sun and making plans; thinking about the things she might be able to do.

In the squat, people had made plans all the time, but they never came to fruition. They would be grand, convoluted things that relied on so many other factors falling into place: it had mainly been a way of passing time and nobody felt foolish when nothing happened – in fact it was never really expected that anything *would* happen. But now Georgia was beginning to feel that some of the little ideas she was having were actually coming to fruition.

God had let her have a barbeque for her new friends, albeit one with just value sausages and burgers, but it had been a great evening. She had taken Jocey swimming and had mended the rain cover on her pushchair. These were small things, but quite important steps towards becoming independent.

It was great to have friends again, to be lying on a clean blanket – especially one that weighed only six ounces and rolled up to fit in a beanbag-sized parcel (although why it needed that attribute when Gwen had a massive great garage to store it in, Georgia had no idea).

It was all working out for her, at last. Jocey was well and happy and the health visitor was pleased with her and with Georgia. Uncle God had promised to take her to the Council housing office next week to see if there were any benefits that she might be entitled to, to get Jocey and herself a flat. Just think, her own place. Maybe even with a tiny little bedroom for Jocey? If she had her own place, well, then she might be able to have her own guests?

She looked up at Tomos who caught her eye and winked. "Hey," he said jumping to his feet, "I promised that I would introduce young Jocey here to ice cream didn't I? Start her on the route to additives and trans-fats. Coming?" Jocey looked up at him and started crawling over. "Good girl," he said, "she knows that caving and bungee jumping are foolhardy things; she knows that ice cream is far better for her, don't you, Jocey?"

Georgia hauled herself up too, blushing at the invitation in front of her friends. She brushed the grass off her jeans and collected Jocey and her toys to put in her pushchair.

"Have a good one," smiled Gwen.

"Keep your sun hats on," called Davey.

"Oh, and *try* and make it organic," said Simon, "it's *so* much better for them..."

Chapter 58

Warmth From a Library Radiator

Godfrey walked along Cysgod y Ffynnon's main shopping street enjoying his stroll in the late summer sun. All felt good with the world. He had come out for no reason in particular except to share his good feelings with all that cared to partake of them.

It was Victorian Week and people were promenading in long dresses, their plastic carrier bags knocking against lacy parasols. Shops had barrows outside selling the things that Victorians would have sold, the shopkeepers delighted at having another chance to try and sell the stuff that great-grandfather had stockpiled in the basement.

There was a poster inviting him to a music hall night. Another offered him the chance of catching the vintage car rally on its route around the lake. If he waited another hour, he might see the highlight of the week, the Victorian procession. Health and safety prevented the oompah band playing too loudly on the bandstand, but the atmosphere was one of joviality and pleasure.

He popped into the butcher's and the butcher welcomed him, surprised to see Godfrey at such an early hour; he normally would pop in five minutes from closing time to see if there were any last minute bargains to be had. Victorian Week made it the week for displaying innards and cheap cuts but the butcher hadn't sold any until that point. It was Godfrey's lucky day and he managed to come out with a bag full of trotters, faggots and liver for the freezer. In the baker's they were surprised that he wanted to buy today's bread at full price.

The assistant in the chemist didn't even recognise him. A value bottle of shampoo can last an awfully long time.

He bought a newspaper and sat on a bench by the railway station. He'd always liked trains as a boy and used to watch them come and go, learning about engines, capacities and ticket prices. Trainspotters have to have a great deal of patience to spot on the mid Wales line – if one loco is missed, the next might be some hours away – but Godfrey felt he had the luxury of time. He'd been working for the past thirty years to get this amount of time, and this afternoon it felt worth every petty criticism of his midterm reports.

The station's signal house museum was packed with new Victorians wondering what all the excitement was about. There were flags along the length of the station welcoming visitors to the town. The rail staff were also in Victorian costume. Ah, no they weren't: they were in their current uniforms.

With a nod to Mrs James from Waterloo Road, he conveyed his pleasure at sleeping over at Sandra's again on Thursday night. A smile to old Mrs Dawson transmitted his gratitude at an afternoon on Audrey's sofa on Monday. John Michael got a very mixed message regarding an afternoon walking Hamish gently round a field on the lead.

Audrey was away this weekend, gone off to get up to some folly or something similar: he hadn't been sure what she had been on about, but imagined it was something that women did now and then. Godfrey – or Geoffrey – had felt very supportive about her current situation and had actually enjoyed discussing the matter. Audrey had thanked him for listening and told him, with a grasp of his shoulder, that he would have made a good and caring father. He had been touched and regret had burned within his soul.

The guard came out of his little room, the icing sugar on his chin showing that he had just been having a pleasant little moment too. He chatted to a couple of people who had gathered on the platform and they began to collect their bags together and stand up as if the train might rush past them in anger if they weren't completely ready. Children were called back from the edge and threatened with holding their mother's hand if they didn't stand *right* here right *now!*

Godfrey leaned forward in anticipation as a little two-carriage anticlimax chugged around the bend. He watched as it groaned to a halt and the people on the platform waited politely for the exiting passengers to get off. He could see them searching the train, trying to bag their seats before they even got on – but there was plenty of room for all, so they were able to help each other on and off without much scrummaging.

He watched a couple as they helped a lady struggling to get off the train with her two sticks. Good, thought Godfrey, someone else who can benefit from the love I have to share.

On further investigation, the woman wasn't as elderly as

her gait and the sticks suggested, in fact, she might not have been much older than him. She was helped from the train and her case slung after her by a bored guard. She took her time to sort her bags and coat out as they kept slipping down around her sticks and landing on the floor. Her helpers had disappeared and Godfrey felt that it wouldn't be right to just sit and watch. He'd seen enough of the train and felt able to spare her as much time as she needed to help sort out the next stage of her journey.

He walked up to her and asked if she wanted any help. She looked up and tried to push the hair out of her eyes. "Can I help?" he repeated, "you look like you have too many things there!"

"Thank you," she said, grateful for his assistance. "Could you just hold my big bag for me, I need to get to the bus stop."

He picked up the bag and made sure that she was free of the train as it dragged itself off for the next stage of its journey. He could sense that she was in a lot of pain as she walked gingerly on her sticks, each footstep making her wince. Godfrey soon realised that she was still struggling. "Here, let me take your other things," and he took her coat and smaller bag from her arm. She was finally able to wipe the drip from her nose without a bag falling to the floor and she turned to thank him again and looked at him. Something about him obviously caught her eye.

"Godfrey?" she asked. "Godfrey Palmer? Is it really you?"

"Sorry?" said Godfrey; he still hadn't seen her face properly through her hair.

"Alice. Alice Jefferson, that was!"

Godfrey's heart stopped momentarily and when it started again it was crashing against his chest wall. "Alice," he wheezed. "Alice Jefferson."

He carried her bags a little further with her hobbling after him. His mind was in turmoil. He had spent the past thirty-two years not doing things for Alice Jefferson and now here she was, this hobbling harridan at his side

"Godfrey," she called. "Godfrey, slow down. Look, let's have a coffee. I'm in no rush. Would you like a coffee? A chat? For old time's sake?"

Godfrey nodded, still in his stupor. He didn't know what to think – whether to be happy to see Alice full stop, or whether it was better that his dreams remained filled with the young blonde girl with the gypsy skirts and bare feet. He led her painfully to the nearby café as she chattered about coming to Cysgod y Ffynnon for Victorian Week to visit a cousin whose husband had died recently. He shepherded her through the door and sat her at the nearest table. He went to the counter and pretended to survey the produce. He needed time to think. How was he to deal with a situation like this – blow his top or laugh away decades of misery, of waiting? Of waiting for something that in hindsight was never going to have arrived.

He carried a tray with two cups and a teapot. He knew exactly how she had her tea and he poured out a dash of milk in preparation. He finally got a chance to look at her; she had taken off her beret and brushed her hair back from her face. Her hair was like straw, bleached to buggery and with an inch of greying roots. It was a mess that looked like it had been cut by a well meaning but impatient neighbour. Her white top was greyed by years of washing and her ruby lipstick bled into the lines around her mouth. From the marks on her fingers, Godfrey surmised that she still smoked too much: it didn't seem such a sexy trait anymore.

Her eyes were watery and had been affected by years of pain. They no longer held his in a dance of light and life; he could barely bring himself to look into them. She smiled under his surveillance and her teeth were tobacco-stained and unkempt. He felt cheated. His dreams and his purpose in life had been a sham.

"So," she began, as if they'd been mates who'd met up each week, "what's the news? Gosh, it must be, what, twenty-five years?"

"Thirty-two…"

"Thirty-two, eh? So, what have you been up to?" It was obvious that she was a little uncomfortable with her appearance as she kept brushing her hair with her hands, trying to tame its dry wildness.

"Er, nothing much really," said Godfrey truthfully. "What about you?" But he wasn't sure that he actually wanted to know.

Alice shrugged. "Well, I still live in Holsborough, but on the estate now." Godfrey nodded. The estate? What the hell was Alice Jefferson doing living on the estate? "I got married, had four children, but that all went a bit wrong. I've lived with a few people, but I'm on my own again now. It's quite difficult – with this pain." She winced again as she tried to shuffle in her seat to get comfortable.

"What's the matter?" whispered Godfrey, still not really

wanting to know. "The pain? What's it from?"

Alice laughed a bitter laugh. Her laugh never used to be bitter. "I was quite an adventurous young thing! It all went a bit wrong."

Godfrey's quizzical look gave her the go-ahead to carry on. "You remember Barry Claxton?" Godfrey felt sick. What had that thug done? Had he run her over perhaps? Chucked a bucket of rocks on her feet? What? "Well I married Barry Claxton – that's my name now, Alice Claxton. Not as nice as Alice Jefferson, eh?" Godfrey's head was spinning. *Married Barry bloody Claxton. No! Surely, no!*

She accepted the tea that he poured and laughed that he had got it right. No, not laughed – cackled. Alice Claxton no longer laughed. "Yes, Barry and I were, well, a little bit on the wild side!" She waited for him to goad her on, so he did with a shudder. He wasn't sure that he needed to hear this.

"Sex. Vegetable sex!" she whispered at him over the table, her breath stale in his face. "We threw our house keys into the ring and I picked up the bloody greengrocer's!" Godfrey was shaking his head: he couldn't be hearing this – couldn't imagine what her disability might have to do with greengrocery... He watched in horror as she threw her head back and laughed, her tongue yellow and her teeth missing or brown.

"Yes, nearly killed me! Barry couldn't handle it. Left me with the kids and barely able to move. Dad had to move in – he wasn't happy I can tell you…" She misjudged Godfrey and took his shock for amusement, and cackled, her laugh turning into a hacking cough.

Godfrey pushed his chair away from the table. *Vegetable*

sex! Vegetable sex? He looked at Alice in disbelief; the discrepancy between his imaginings and the reality was just absurd. The laughing woman beside him was starting to look concerned. "Sit down God, don't be so sentimental!" she wheezed between coughs.

It was too much. He saw the plump glossed lips of his dreams turning dry and thin, twisted with pain. He saw the hair that he used to love to run his fingers through being ruffled by potato peelings and scented by sprouts. The breasts that used to be brought out for special occasions were pitta breads flapping under her thin jumper...

Godfrey ran for the door. He felt out of control, but knew that he just needed fresh air. He burst through it and leant retching against the window, unaware of people just inches from his face watching him through the glass as he almost lost his lunch. He looked up and back into the shop as if giving Alice Jefferson one more chance. But instead he could still see Alice Claxton desperately trying to pull herself to her feet. "Godfrey!" she cried. "Come back. I can't get out of here without you!"

Godfrey ran up the street and sprinted around the corner into the main street; he needed a physical barrier between him and that woman. He pushed two Victorian children out of the way and leant against a wall, breathing wildly. A woman looked at him in distaste and pulled her elderly companion away as if he might hurt her. He struggled upright and set off, trying hard to control his walk.

He staggered along the road, somehow getting absorbed into the Victorian procession. A one-man band crashed his cymbals too near his face and Godfrey stumbled again. He

369

stepped on and crushed a dropped parasol and the language that came from the owner's mouth certainly wouldn't have met with Queen Victoria's approval.

The crowds were intrigued by him. Many recognised him, by sight if not by name. What *was* that man in the tweed jacket doing stumbling around in the middle of the procession? Was he in costume? They couldn't quite tell, but he hadn't made much of an effort if he was. Was he drunk at this time of the day? Or having a heart attack? Shouldn't someone else be calling an ambulance – he was a bit of a funny colour? Eventually Godfrey burst through the other end of the crowd, knocking a man on a penny-farthing over as he did so.

"What the…" said the man as he crashed to the floor, buckling the lovingly restored bike and losing him his deposit from the Victorian Costume Shop.

The crowds watched Godfrey stumbling along the pavement. His socks had disappeared down the backs of his shoes and his face was red from exertion and shock.

Anyone who looked, knew that they saw a man in torment. It wasn't in sadness for his former love, a love who had had pain in her life. It was for himself. It was for the nights spent at home saving money so that it would be enough for Alice bloody Jefferson. It was for the holidays and outings passed over so that he could be worthy of Alice bloody Jefferson and it was for the women and the friends that he had never got to know because he was trying to make a life that would be good enough for Alice Jefferson.

But while he, Godfrey, was doing that, braving the cold and living on own-brand spaghetti hoops, she went and married Barry bloody Claxton! That good for nothing thug who wouldn't know an ISA if it bit him on the nose. Barry Claxton had never pretended to be anything other than what he was: work-shy and a chancer. Godfrey'd been busy wearing his dead father's socks and Barry had been taking his beautiful Alice to wife-swapping parties. Then when Barry had ruined Alice, turned her into that cackling harridan Godfrey had just left in the café, he did exactly what Barry Claxton was always going to do and ran off and left her stranded. Abandoned. Just like Godfrey had done in that café. However, despite the overwhelming shock to his system Godfrey still felt guilty – Barry Claxton probably never had.

As Godfrey turned into his road, something clicked inside him: he had a lot of catching up to do. And he had to do it *now*.

Chapter 59

Dining From the Allotment

Dave Burton walked into the police station at the beginning of his shift. He hated Victorian Week. Town would be full of petty incidents, traffic snarl-ups and the need to build community relationships.

To make it worse, the sergeant had decided that a more embedded presence was needed – and had got some bicycles. "Bikes! I ask you," cursed Dave as he clicked the kettle on. "Bikes – with these bloody hills!"

"It's for visual *and* practical purposes," Sergeant Davies had explained. "They can make you visible to a lot of people in quite a short time. And anyway," he had added, with a pat to Dave's stomach, "a bit of fitness training on your behalf wouldn't go amiss…"

Dave hadn't been able to retort and was only glad that a shirt button didn't ping off at that very moment. Living with Hayley may involve leopard print, but it also included an awful lot of beer and takeaways. The last three years had been like living in student digs again. He now knew how Hayley managed to spend so much time out enjoying herself – it was because she did bugger all else.

Credit where credit was due, Sandra had kept a tidy house

and there had always been regular meals on the table and shirts in the wardrobe.

He'd found that if he actually wanted to see Hayley after a shift, then he had to go to the pub to find her. Sandra used to complain that that was the only way she could ever spend time with *him* on a weekend, but now it seemed that he was the one telling someone to get themselves home and spend some time with the children. Not fair really…

Sergeant Davies interrupted his bad mood by throwing a fluorescent vest at him. "Make sure that you wear that – and your helmet – at all times. It'll make a good impression *and* keep you warm in this heatwave!" The sergeant smiled, then looked pointedly at his cup of coffee, "Come on, Burton, child chimney sweeps don't arrest themselves you know!"

Dave swore under his breath then scalded his mouth as he took a big swig of coffee, then poured the rest away. "Has anyone mended that rubbing brake I reported," he asked, trying to delay the inevitable.

"Dunno," said the Sergeant as he wondered off, whistling.

Dave cursed again and set off to the compound and the hated bike. Why couldn't one of the younger lads take the bloody bike out? They liked people more than he did too. He'd been in the job too long, he rued, he would have loved a bike when he started twenty-five years ago. Now he wanted to just sit in lay-bys being a visual statement in speeding blackspots – especially when he'd had a night like he had last night.

He'd met Hayley after work at the rugby club and she'd obviously been there a while. He'd had a few, but it wasn't like it used to be. It used to feel cheeky and exciting, sneaking out for a few beers after work, sitting on a bar stool next to Hayley, laughing and joking. He'd always be persuaded to stay half an hour longer than he meant to and then would return home to Sandra, where there would be something on a plate in the oven covered by tin foil that he would wolf down and then crash into a clean bed, knowing that his uniform for the next day would be hanging, washed and ironed in his wardrobe.

Now that he could stay out as long as he wanted, he was finding it all a bit tedious. Hayley was actually quite rough and a bit of a soak – and probably a bit of a slapper too, having found out that free drinks don't buy themselves. Now that she was aware that Dave's generosity at the bar was actually coming out of their joint household income, she'd stopped flirting with him for drinks and had started chatting up others and he was beginning to see that he had been taken for a fool with a full wallet.

He used to find her kids turning up at the pub wanting money for chips quite funny – much more "real" life than his Daniel and Sophie who had everything they needed presented on a plate. Soft as jelly those two, whereas Hayley's were able to look after themselves. University of life, Hayley had said they were going to go to, but somehow, coming home a bit tanked up and finding them asleep on the sofa in front of a horror film with school in the morning, was beginning to concern him. Another thing he had been meaning to have a word with Hayley about – *if* he could ever get to see her awake and sober…

The gate of the compound slammed behind him like a

cell door and Dave sighed again. He could see the two bikes propped up against the far wall. One was the one with the inferior saddle that had bruised his buttocks two days before – and the other now had a flat tyre. Therefore, he had no choice but to take the one that had caused him so much pain previously.

He lifted the back wheel and spun it: at least it spun for half a rotation, then stopped dead. No – it looked like no one had bothered sorting that. Double shift too. He was going to be knackered before he reached half way.

So as Dave swung his leg over the saddle and whistled in agony as he sat down, he cursed once more. He'd not ridden a bike for twenty years, then twice in three days he'd been on a twenty mile circuit up hill and down dale: his arse was killing him. Just as he was about to ride off and find some quiet corner of the festival to chat to a few mates on the Rotary Club stand, the sergeant put his head around the gate.

"Dave – bit of a fracas at the Corner Café. Someone has apparently run off without paying and his ex-girlfriend is in there refusing to pay – or budge – apparently. Just stick your head in and see if you can calm it down – it all sounds a bit out of hand."

Bugger, thought Dave. Up the hill it is then; not only will my arse be in tatters but my knees will be knackered as well.

Godfrey saw his house as he puffed along the pavement and his heart both dropped and leapt. Solace, a place to think. *A miserable, dismal hole in which he had sat in the cold as life passed him by.* He rounded into his garden and felt for his door key. There it was, not even on a key ring. *If it wasn't for Alice bloody Claxton, he would probably have a Winnie the Pooh key ring, bought for him by his kids as a joke for his birthday.* As he stood by the door something caught his eye on the step: two piles of cat sick and one had a little shrew in it.

He recoiled in horror. He wasn't particularly squeamish, it was just that cat sick, with a shrew in, could so easily be the last straw.

He raised his hands in rage. Who the hell was going to clear *that* up? No wife to discover it first, no children would want to make kitty better, and Georgia would just step right over it, it not being the worst pavement pizza she'd ever encountered – no it would be *him,* wouldn't it? Him, just *him.* He would have loved to have had a dog – but dogs cost money. Seven pounds forty two a week according to his calculations; three hundred and eighty-five pounds, eighty-four pence per year of money that had instead gone into a high interest savings account that used to be referred to as "For Alice", but had turned over the years into one that was mutteringly re-labelled "For Retirement". A big bloody great Alsatian wouldn't let that damn cat throw up on his doorstep, or leave half-frogs on his patio, or limping mice lurking in his lounge. How much fun would he have had over the years walking a lovely big Alsatian every night? Sometimes with his wife or a child at his side, sometimes on his own, chatting with fellow dog walkers about how he was escaping from the madhouse for a bit of peace and quiet.

It was too much. Still enraged, he turned and stormed

back in the direction he'd come, then he turned and started in another direction. Then back again. He saw a public footpath sign and dragged open a gate. It scraped his shin, so he abandoned it, not bothering to slam it shut. He struck out, embracing the difficulty in striding through long grass. He saw that the path was heading up a mountain to a telephone mast perched on the top and he relished the distance. That would give him space to think.

And, when he reached the summit, think Godfrey did. He allowed himself to dig from his memory the conversation that had moulded his adult life. He dug it out and spread it out on the grass to see it for what it really was...

He had gone to Alice Jefferson's house a flash eighteen-year-old with a proposal on his mind. He'd bought himself a new shirt and the town's loudest tie, ironed his bell-bottoms himself and then bathed and smoothed down his moustache. He'd ordered a bunch of red roses from the florist and had bought a special box of Dairy Milk that had a purple ribbon around one corner.

He'd felt invincible as he strutted down the street. He'd seen a terraced house that he thought that they might just be able to afford on his clerk's wages and then they could use her secretarial wages to tidy it up and furnish it before they had babies.

He had thought it all through and was sure that she would bite his hand off. They were in love and that was all that mattered.

But Royston Jefferson had answered the door and changed *everything*. Godfrey had been a little taken aback as he'd assumed that Royston would be at the football. In the way that Royston did, he had stood barring Godfrey's entry with his massive frame. His six-foot five-inch presence blocked Godfrey's view of what was happening within. There was no way that he was going to get past unless Royston wanted him to, and Royston didn't want him to.

"Good afternoon, Mr Jefferson, is Alice in please?"

Godfrey always felt intimidated by Mr Jefferson; he was pleasant enough, but Godfrey knew that he was watching his every move. When he was trying his luck up Alice's shirt, it was Royston that was overseeing his technique. When he told Alice that he loved her, he would be sure that it was Royston's sneer in the background that made him feel seven years old. When they were alone together they would laugh about Royston's protectiveness, Alice in an indulgent way and Godfrey with a scared titter.

It had always been obvious to Godfrey that he wasn't good enough for Royston, but he had thought that he was good enough for Alice and he knew that he could make her happy. Once she had accepted his proposal, he could ask for Royston's permission knowing that it would be OK, because it was what Alice wanted. Until then, he had decided that he could put up with becoming a jabbering idiot every time he was in his beloved's father's presence.

"What's with the flowers, Palmer?" Royston had barked.

"Well, they're for, they're for…well, Alice – is she, er…?"

"Chocolates too eh? What's going on, Palmer?"

It was then that Godfrey very nearly proposed to Royston. He told him what he had bought the roses for; he told him that

Alice loved these particular chocolates. He told him where he thought they might live and he ground to a defeated halt after he had said how happy he would make her.

Royston listened to it all with an unreadable look on his face and waited until Godfrey had wilted into a mumble. Royston stared at him for five seconds more to seal his discomfort and then put his arm around Godfrey's shoulder and gently marched him back the way he had come.

"Now, you see, Godfrey, like any father I want what's best for my daughter and I need to know that you are a serious prospect before I let you ask her a question like that." His grip silenced Godfrey's protestations and he was able to continue. "You and I both know that Alice is very special. She's not like all the other girls around here. She *is* special and, as her father, I need to be aware of that when considering her future happiness. Don't you agree?"

Godfrey managed to mutter something that was taken as agreement.

"You'll take no offence then, Palmer, when I say that your proposal can't be a serious one at this time, can it?"

Godfrey now felt as dejected as the roses that hung buffeting against his knee as he was trotted along the pavement: six-foot-five legs cover a lot more ground in one stride than five-foot-eight legs, especially when concerned with Alice Jefferson's future happiness.

"No, you go away and prove yourself for a while. There's no rush; Alice won't be going anywhere. Move away for a while, live in a different country perhaps. Get yourself a better job. No daughter of mine will be living in Alfred Terrace, I can tell you. Save a bit of money and then come back to me and we will talk again."

At eighteen, Godfrey had been a trusting soul and although a little miffed, he felt that Royston might have a point – Alfred Terrace was probably a little shabby for a girl like Alice. In addition, he sensed that there was no way around Royston's blockade and therefore he might as well agree.

The Godfrey sat puffing on top of the mountain next to the mast could now see exactly the card Royston Jefferson had presented and how he had played an absolute blinder. Using his bulk and strength he had bullied a young man into moving away and starting down a life path that he had not intended to take. Godfrey had known that Alice had relatives in mid Wales, and presumed that she'd asked them to send those Cysgod y Ffynnon newspapers with jobs in that he had applied for – because Alice had wanted to live there and she had been helping him on the next stage of the grand plan. Now it made sense. The distant family that Alice Claxton was now visiting would have been asked by *Royston* to send the newspapers.

It also made sense that Alice had suddenly gone away for the few weeks whilst he was moving to his new job. *Perhaps Royston was the reason why she'd never replied to his letters, too?* Godfrey sat looking out over the spa town he had come to call home and salty tears slid down his face. In truth, he had probably known pretty soon after he had moved that he had been disposed of, but he'd never quite made the announcement to himself that it was all over. His letters had got shorter and drier as the months had passed and the final few had weeks between them. Not once had he had even a postcard in return. However, he had gotten into the habit of visiting the bank each week and emptying whatever was left in the spending money tin on the mantelpiece into his "For Alice" savings account. He soon started making a mental note of the things he didn't buy that he would have liked to have bought and put that money into his tin when he got home. It actually added up quite quickly.

In hindsight, he could have returned in a couple of years with quite a healthy sum and legitimately whisked Alice away from her father having done just what Royston asked him to do. However, by then, he had started to enjoy his savings and had a complex system of not spending that had become quite absorbing. If he sat in the cold of an evening rather than putting the electric fire on, he would have saved x and if he eked another week out of a haircut, he would save y. Sat on that hill, he could shamefully admit to himself that after that first couple of years, he had become reluctant to let another person scupper that system. Alice Jefferson couldn't be expected to sit wrapped in blankets of an evening to save the equivalent of the price of a sausage; it was a ridiculous scenario. Therefore the pretence of planning and saving for Alice was overtaken by the reality of being a tight git who was the only person on his road, if not in town, who looked forward to his bank statement coming through the door.

Dave was sat at the counter in the Corner Café, drinking a hot chocolate and tucking into a Welsh cake. He was passing the time of day with the owner, whose faith in the police force had been restored due to the inclusion of an additional £3.70 in his till, and a restaurant emptied of a screeching harridan and an abandoned carrier bag full of liver and trotters. *The sergeant is right, thought Dave as he shovelled a few stray currants in; it's all about community relationships...*

His radio crackled and he cocked his head to hear it. "Come in, 342, come in?"

"Receiving," he replied.

"Can you pop to the end of the parade in Victoria Street? Bit of a problem with a man on a penny-farthing. Someone pushed him over, then ran off. Broken his arm and his penny-farthing. Ambulance is on its way, but will be twenty minutes. Can you go and settle it down."

"Received," said Dave and then cursed again as he eased himself off the high stool, put down his hot chocolate and went outside to put his smarting haemorrhoids back on the saddle...

Godfrey felt empty. He shook his head at the waste of a life spent in self-imposed poverty. He still knew how much was in that savings account to the exact penny and he was ashamed. The best things in life were supposed to be free, but he had put a price on all of them that he had not been willing to pay.

He looked at his watch. Five thirty. He'd been out for hours. Perhaps he'd better get home and have some supper. Then he thought – No! No – it was not time to go home and have some supper; it was time to go out and adventure. He stood up and eased the creaks out of his joints. From his vantage point, he scanned the town – where should he go? He could see colourful dots that were people sat on benches outside one of the pubs. He could see others walking around the lake. Then his eyes fell on Tŷ Mawr, standing grand and empty amongst the woodlands and fields. Audrey was away, there was no one there. *Perhaps tonight – even if it were for one night only – he could live the life that he should have been living all these years?*

He set off with a spring in his step and a grimace on his face; he had loose change chinking in his pockets and for once he wasn't afraid to spend it...

Chapter 60

Pretending to be on Antibiotics on a Work Night

Ray was sat trying to read the paper in the fading light. It was a few days old, but news about someone or other's boob job didn't really date that quickly.

"What's that?" asked Danner, coming into the room and sitting at the other end of the sofa. Ray ignored him. Danner was driving him insane at the moment. The very sound of his footstep through the broken glass in the hall made Ray tighten up.

Danner started drumming his fingers on the arm of the sofa. The velour had long since been encrusted into submission and the result was a hard surface that was perfect for tapping.

"Can you stop that, please?" asked Ray through his teeth. "I'm trying to read."

"Big deal," said Danner. "Surely me moving my finger isn't enough to stop you reading. People are moving their fingers all over the world, but people are still reading."

"Yeah, well it's just annoying me."

"How can me moving my finger six feet away from you be annoying? You can't even see it."

"Yes, well I can hear it."

"Well, I've stopped, so you can't have been hearing it."

Ray pursed his lips and tried to get back his article.

"Barry'll want that after you; he likes to wank over the girls in the chatline ads."

Danner had changed to scraping now as he ran his fingernail across the matted velour. Ray felt as if he might explode. He just *had* to get out of this place.

He'd been to the café that the guy in the Job Centre had told him about every morning, well, nearly every morning, for the last two weeks and he'd had three days work. It had felt *great* to have money in his pocket and to be doing normal things again.

One of the men had subbed him to join them at the chippy for lunch and he had scoffed his pie, chips and gravy with a sheer physical pleasure that he hadn't known since that foursome at June's.

He'd then joined a few of the boys for a drink after work and he'd had a great time. After the boys had finished their pints and left for home, he'd got chatting to some other blokes at the bar and had stayed a couple of hours longer, ordering food from the menu to try and soak up some of the beer.

Actually, that is when it had got a bit sour. His new mates kept trying to nick his chips and he'd gone a bit over the top. Eventually they'd told him to fuck off and he'd taken his beer and his curry and chips to a table in the corner.

He'd bought two cans of Coke as he swerved his way back to the squat and that was the end of his forty-five pounds wages, but he'd had a great day and it felt wonderful to be back in a crowd again. He'd missed the next couple of days because of his hangover, but then went back and had worked two more.

He'd been more careful with his money this time and had allowed himself some more chips for tea on the way home, making sure that he'd eaten them all before he got anywhere near the squat.

Therefore, upstairs in his jacket pocket was sixty pounds. Another couple of those and he could start getting himself a room and sorting himself out properly. He couldn't wait to get out of this shithole and get away from those irritating morons. They might be happy living in the scent of fresh urine, but he was not.

Just before he was about to put Danner's head through the wall, there was another sound on the stairs and a jubilant Barry came through the door.

"Boys," he said, holding up two white carrier bags with a big smile on his face, "this is your lucky day!"

"Yahoo!" yelled Danner and he jumped up to check out the goodies. Curry! Fantastic! Ray put his annoyance to the back of his mind to brood over later and dived to make a "table" out of an upturned cardboard box and two old pizza boxes to hold the side dishes.

"Right, we have a meal for three persons," said Barry. "We have chicken tikka masala, three naan breads, um, onion bhajees..." The fare was unloaded onto the table and Ray and Danner were like children ripping off the lids, trying to situate the best dishes near their own seats. "And I've even got cutlery!" finished Barry through a mouthful of poppadom. Ray desperately wanted to say, hang on, share the poppadoms out properly, but managed a more gracious,

"This is marvellous, Barry, thank you ever so much."

"Where d'ya get it?" asked Danner.

"Best not to ask!" replied Barry with a knowing wink and a tap of the side of his nose. Ray and Danner laughed and then all three dived in. They discarded the cutlery to start with as they dredged out great piles of curry with their naan breads and pushed them down with a crunch of a poppadom. Barry even had a bottle of dandelion and burdock. It was the best meal that Ray had ever tasted.

He was enjoying it so much that he wanted to slow down and savour it, but was keenly aware that if he did, Danner and Barry would eat his share. He had suggested that they share it out evenly to start with, but neither Danner nor Barry gave any hint of listening. Their faces showed that the more Ray talked and they didn't, the more of his share they would manage to stuff in. So, he shut up and carried on eating, deciding to concentrate on spooning up the communal dishes and save his own private naan bread until the end.

It was delicious. Little bhajees, pilau rice and a great big dish of prawn korma. Eventually the eating slowed down. It wouldn't be the end of the world if Danner ate one more scoop of chopped onion than his share now; Ray was nearing satiation and could afford to sit back and take a breath or two.

"That was bloody marvellous, Barry. Thank you again, my friend."

"Yeah, cheers, Barry."

"You're very welcome: it's always good to share what little we have with each other."

Ray's ears pricked up – something wasn't quite right. He

looked closely at Barry: what was different?

"New shirt, Barry?"

"Yeah, do you like it? I got this and, look, a new pair of daps. My old ones had just about had it."

"Must have cost a fair bit, Barry? All this and new togs?" said Danner, mopping up the last of the korma with his naan bread.

"Yes," and then Barry looked at Ray with a smug smile on his face, "I'd say about, ooh, sixty quid in all?"

Ray jerked up – sixty quid? *His* sixty quid? He saw immediately in Barry's face that it was indeed his sixty quid and he had just treated these two bastards to a meal and Barry to a new wardrobe.

"You fuckin' bastard…" roared Ray as he launched himself at Barry, all his anger from the weeks of frustration exploding from him and being used to wipe the smile from his housemate's face. The upturned wooden box that Barry had been sitting on shattered under the weight of Ray landing full on him and they fell to the ground taking the curry table with them.

"F'fuck's sake, be careful," shouted Danner trying to rescue the remaining food. He had enough cunning to hide the rest of the vegetable sag behind the sofa before trying to pull Ray off.

Barry had been strong in his former life, but years of malnutrition and poor living conditions had sapped his strength. Ray, however, had lost the soft belly that had blossomed under Annabel's table and had hardened up, but he still had a good three stone weight advantage over Barry and also the strength of absolute rage.

"You...bastard!" he screamed as he punched him in the side of the head. "You fuckin' bastard!" The fighting wasn't good. They were so entwined in a confined space full of rubbish that their punches didn't have any swing, but they were relentless. Mice ran from the rubbish in all directions, distressed at having to abandon the buddy that was now squashed under Ray's right knee.

Danner cackled as he stood on the sofa and watched. "Go on!" he roared to no one in particular. "Hit the fucker!" Eventually he decided on his allegiance and dived onto Ray's back just as he was beginning to tire. He managed to roll Ray off, and then Barry was able to start his assault. He gave Ray a couple of punches in his face as Danner was now holding Ray's arms above his head.

The blows stunned Ray, giving Barry time to sit astride his chest and regain his poise. Blood was dripping from Barry's nose down his new shirt and onto Ray's chin below. "Hold him properly," he grunted to Danner, who was happy to do just that as he gave another cackle.

Through his haze, Ray saw Barry pull a knife from his jeans' pocket and heard the click as the blade snapped open.

"Shall we?" Barry laughed. *"Shall we?"*

Danner egged him on whilst Ray choked on a tooth. "No, no," he tried to say through a gurgle of blood. Oh my God, what are these nutters going to do now?

Barry held a handful of Ray's hair and sliced it off from the top of his head. Then another and another, but only from the top. Danner continued to scream with laughter as Ray weighed up the dangers of wriggling versus staying still and putting up with it.

Every time Ray tried to heave Barry off, he got another punch, in the eye, on the cheek, or a surprise one in the crotch. By now, there were other people in the room. Someone was sat on his feet. "I always hated this tosser," said someone else as they knelt at his side. "Here, give me that arm to hold."

Eventually Barry finished Ray's "haircut" and started on his clothes. His jeans got sliced up the sides from heel to hip, occasionally cutting his skin as well. His shirt was cut into fraying tatters and his buttons cut off one by one.

Finally Barry rolled off, his anger spent and he stepped back to view his handiwork. Everyone was laughing far more than was needed, as Ray was dragged bleeding and battered to his feet.

Danner held Ray up as Barry went right up to his face. "We took you in and gave you a home. We shared our food with you and taught you how to find it. We gave you drink when we had it and Danner found you that blanket. But you haven't shared a single thing with us, *not one single thing*.

"All you have done is look down on us and tell us how much better you are than us. But we used to be normal too. I had a wife and kids, my own shop – yes, I did. Danner here has got four kids, haven't you, Danner?" Danner nodded. "But, we fell on hard times too, just like you did, OK?

"I went bankrupt and we lost the house and my family went to my mother-in-law's, but she wouldn't let me stay. Danner's wife went off with someone else, wouldn't let him see the kids. Isn't that right, Danner?" Danner nodded again, staring into Ray's eyes and quiet at last.

"But you didn't see any of that, did you? You never once asked. You just thought we were born crap and pissed and that this is all we ever dreamed of? Well, I had a caravan once. I did, our own bloody caravan, and we would go for weeks at a time to the seaside. But now, well, all we've got is this – but it doesn't mean we've stooped so low we don't help each other, OK?

"So, I reckon we were due that money, isn't that right, boys?"

There were general nods of acknowledgement from round the room, "So, now you can fuck off, ok? Fuck off." Danner spun Ray around and pushed him towards the door. Barry gave him the biggest kick up his arse that he'd ever had and it brought tears to his eyes. He stumbled to the stairs then staggered down them.

Ray tripped through the plywood "door" and fell onto the pile of urine-soaked rubbish that was the front garden. He got to his feet and tried to walk sensibly down the pavement. He was aware that a couple of people standing on the opposite side of the road were staring at him. He turned and glanced in an empty shop window and stared in disbelief at his reflection.

His jeans were covered in blood and curry and were flapping in the wind. Ditto his shirt. He looked how David Banner looks when he has turned from the Incredible Hulk back into himself, his clothes in tatters. His hair was missing on the top which made the two remaining tufts at the side look ridiculous. A front tooth was missing and he had blood running from his mouth and nose.

His face was swollen and his eyes were closing under the

weight of their bruises. He burst into painful tears and fell to the floor. He was just going to lie there and wait for someone to help him, take him in, give him a bath and some good clothes and a job. Rent him a room, or a studio flat and give it to him for free until he got back on his feet.

However, through his sobs, he realised that the road wasn't really busy enough for anyone to see him and help him, perhaps he'd better shuffle round the corner to a busier stretch: otherwise he might be here all day…

Chapter 61

Swapping Gift Tags

By the time Godfrey reached Tŷ Mawr, he was nearly running. He was so desperate to get on with his new life that he felt he couldn't waste even a minute by dawdling down the farm track; no time to enjoy the birdsong or to stop and watch the caterpillar inching across the dust.

His hair was damp with sweat as he abandoned all his usual caution and crashed into Tŷ Mawr looking for something exciting. He rampaged around the house, opening drawers and rummaging through them for inspiration. He messed up the airing cupboard and felt through all Jerry's jacket pockets. He was saddened by the cotton-ness of Audrey's underwear drawer and bored by the contents of her magazine pile. He took a swig from Jerry's whisky bottle, then started to run a bath. After fifteen seconds of waiting and having poured in a cocktail of bath products to enhance the experience, he pulled the plug in disgust. Who had time to waste lazing around in a bath?

Dave was sat by the till in the Victorian Shop. The mug of tea at his side was fresh and piping hot. The plate of biscuits held two of his favourites. He'd calmed everything down, the guy on the penny-farthing had gone off in the ambulance and Dave had wheeled the bike back to the shop and explained the situation to the owner. A good result all round. An hour of textbook community policing.

"Control to 342. Respond."

"Control, 342 receiving."

"Give location, 342."

"I'm in the Victorian Shop, Victoria Street, over."

"We've got reports of cows loose on the Bryn Coch road. Someone left a gate open and there are bullocks on the road. The farmer's been called, but a car has hit a bus in the process. I've got a unit heading there, but it's a way off. Can you get there? By Craig Mawr Farm. Know it? It's only a mile away from your location. Over."

Dave sighed as he put his tea down and popped a couple of biscuits into his pocket – he'd need those after getting up that bloody hill.

Godfrey sat at Jerry's desk and started writing a letter to an old aunt, but that went no further than hoping that she was well? He took another couple of swigs of whisky, then threw the pen down and headed back out of the study. He stripped two panels of peeling wallpaper from the hallway, then grabbed his bottle and dived outside.

Right, he thought looking around, what next? He saw a pile of logs in the corner of the yard that needed splitting – perfect. He had no fears about chopping a foot off and in his mood he had the back of the twenty-five-year-old Godfrey. Now, where might Jerry keep an axe? His eyes turned to the large barns across the courtyard – of course, axes would be kept hung up in the barn! He'd never walked across the yard before and it dawned on him how far it was. By the time he reached the barns, they seemed enormous. Great stone constructions with huge wooden doors fifteen feet high. There were no locks at all, just two large bolts at foot and shoulder level. He put his whisky down and wriggled these until they were released from the dirt and the rust and he grated them back. Then he braced himself and dragged one of the doors free. It scraped across the slabs, occasionally jolting to a halt on a stone. He would wriggle it free again, kick the stone away and brace himself once more.

He could feel that the whisky had affected him as he lost his balance a couple of times and misjudged his pressure on the door, but the feeling of being slightly out of control excited him and he took another swig.

When the door was finally open, he wiped his hands over his face, leaving dirt tracks through the sweat. He stood back to catch his breath and peered into the gloom.

There were the usual things one expected to find in a farm barn; a few old bales, some rusting machinery and some empty feed drums that might come in handy one day. What Godfrey hadn't expected to find was a speedboat, poking its bow out from under a filthy tarpaulin.

As he walked towards it, he felt his heart beginning to beat. Not the half-hearted *pa-pa, pa-pa* that usually ticked his body over, but a *bang-bang, bang-bang* that sent adrenalin searing through him. *Now,* he was finally beginning to feel alive!

He tugged at the tarpaulin, relishing the dirt and dust on it and then dragged it off, sending nests of mice cascading to the floor. This is where that bloody cat should be, he growled, keeping this place sorted – not bloody throwing up on his doorstep. The thought of his doorstep brought back the cackle of Alice Claxton and he bundled up the tarpaulin, glad of the twinge in his back as he pulled the last bit free.

He stood back rather unsteadily to take in the scene. *Flight of Joy* read the name painted in red paint at the stern. Who'd called it that, he mused. Not Jerry, surely and certainly not Audrey? Jerry would have called it *Fair Result* or *Judgement Day* or something and Audrey, *The Boat* or *Labrador. Awaiting Alice,* that's what he, Godfrey, would have called his boat, he thought, depression sinking his shoulders. Not anymore though. No, his new boat would be *The Adventurer* – actually, *Flight of Joy* was fine.

He climbed around the back of *Flight of Joy* and kicked a few boxes and tools out of the way to free the trolley that she sat on. The trolley seemed in quite good condition – then he remembered Audrey grumbling about the money Jerry spent on *having that bloody boat serviced* every year – *never uses it, mind, just thinks he does.*

Godfrey climbed back and went to the front of the trolley and picked it up. He was pleased to find that it was actually quite manoeuvrable. Perhaps he'd get that other door open and get it outside to have a proper look at it.

As he was juggling with the other door, he found a set of lights and clicked them on. Huge floodlights lit the range of barns and the yard outside making him realise that he hadn't noticed dusk falling. People could play a football match under those lights he thought, unaware of his illuminated presence throughout the valley.

The light gave him further confidence and he set about dragging the boat outside. He couldn't help but look over the engine, nor could he help priming it and fiddling with the key. To his amazement, it roared into action first attempt and the grin on his face widened as he revved the throttle – the stadium now full of sound as well as light.

He set off through the other barns looking for something else. He didn't know what he was looking for, but as soon as he saw the big green tractor, he knew that that was it...

The John Deere had massive wheels and a yellow light on the roof. The door was unlocked and after he had struggled up the steps to the cab, Godfrey wasn't surprised to find the keys in the lock; country folk – always leaving the keys in the ignition, in case someone needed to move something! Well, today, he, Godfrey Palmer, did.

The tractor spluttered into life and he jolted back and forwards until he had familiarised himself with the controls. He felt very grand as he slowly drove the tractor from its home, through the big double doors and down a slight slope into the yard.

He drove it round and round the yard for a while to get used to its size and then without much forethought, reversed it back towards to the boat.

If anyone had seen the spectacle of the tractor and the speedboat trailer being manoeuvred through the yard gate by the slightly pissed middle-aged man, they would have pulled up chairs and cracked open their picnic hampers in glee. After four attempts, Godfrey finally managed to get a nearly straight line and took a run at the gap, a job made slightly easier when his rear tractor wheel dragged the gate from its hinges and bumped it a hundred yards down the lane.

He didn't dare look back as he would have ended up in a field, but if he had, he'd have seen a scene of devastation, a teenager's bedroom on a farmyard scale. The floodlights lit up the whole yard, picking out all the things he'd dragged from the barns. Tools were scattered across the flags as he'd hunted for something to help him hitch the trailer to the tractor. A petrol can had been emptied into the speedboat tank and then flung to the side. The tractor had crushed a few random objects and they lay flattened in its wake.

The kitchen had been re-ransacked for goodies for the journey and the unwanted contents of cupboards lay across the floor. The fridge was overheating, struggling to cool the whole kitchen as its door swung open, and its shelves stood bare.

The back door was open wide, the key still in its lock. Also, a man who rarely drank more than a single glass of low-alcohol lager had pillaged the drinks cabinet...

Godfrey bounced along the track, feeling a little more confident in his driving capabilities – once he had lost that gate the tractor handled much better. He practised a couple of hill starts and even tried a reverse, but the trailer made that nigh on impossible, so instead he just hoped that he wouldn't need it.

He finally reached the tarmaced road full of confidence. Another swig of whisky would help hone the driving skills. *Now, where to?* Cysgod y Ffynnon town centre possibly wouldn't be the best idea; a badly driven tractor dragging a boat would be too much of a spectacle for a town that could grind to a standstill thanks to an inexperienced caravan tower. Also, he didn't have enough friends to warrant driving around trying to spot and wave to them – not like in the old days, when John German used to drive them all round Holsborough, squashed into his dad's Triumph Dolomite. Apparently that used to really wind Royston Jefferson up as they sped back and fore past Alice's house, beeping the horn as she hid in her bedroom and Royston stood at the door bellowing threats and obscenities. Godfrey had kept his head down, but had enjoyed the fun. *Fun.* There hadn't been much of that around since Alice Jefferson. *Alice bloody Claxton.*

The thought made the rage rise again and he took another swig of whisky and set off left instead. *What about the Elan Valley?* It was only about fifteen miles away and he could go on the back roads… He checked the gauge, yes, plenty of fuel for a little trip like that. So, off he set.

Dave was leant on the gate with the farmer, agreeing between them how irresponsible bloody ramblers were.

"It'll be my insurance that has to pay for this," cursed the farmer. "I'll have to fill in the bloody forms and lose my no claims. Me!"

Dave nodded. Bloody ramblers; he'd never seen the attraction in hacking about in fields, that was certain.

PC Burton's radio broke into the silence.

"342, come in. 342 are you receiving?"

"Yes, 342 here, receiving."

"Give your location, 342, are you still with the cows?

We've got a suspected break-in at Tŷ Mawr farm. Repeat, break-in at Tŷ Mawr farm. Cleaner has reported it from across the valley – lights on all over but the owners are away. It's only about half a mile from where you are now. Can you attend? I'll send another unit over, but they'll be a while. They can give you a lift back to the station. Over."

"Agreed," groaned Dave. He'd been hoping to slowly make his way back to the station and sit in a car and rest his arse for a while. And he needed a pee.

He checked with the farmer where Tŷ Mawr was. "Well, you see where that tractor towing a boat is coming out from? Well turn there and go straight to the end of the lane, don't turn off. See the lights? Can't think why we didn't notice them before; lit up like a bloody beacon."

Dave looked where the farmer was pointing and saw the big John Deere drag a speedboat off up the hill. Damn, there must be two hundred yards of hill to climb before he even reached the turning. Half a mile to the house? *Oh my aching arsehole…*

The locals were used to seeing tractors on the roads, although they usually dragged trailers piled up high with hay, rather than speedboats, but they gave Godfrey a wide berth as he bounced up the road, looking over the hedges and seeing Tŷ Mawr in the distance, with its Millennium Stadium-standard lighting.

He made it to the back road without a police escort and set off along the narrow lanes, bumping off the hedges and gouging out great swathes of mud from the banks. At the first gate across the road, he stopped, climbed down and opened it. He had such trouble getting back into the tractor that he didn't bother stopping to shut it. The sheep either side of the gate skipped in excitement as they dived through to go and shag the neighbours that they had been admiring through the fences for so long (and so a new breed was born).

The second gate was a rickety wooden thing and God remembered the hassles he'd had with it in the past, fiddling with knotted string on a cold day, so instead he jammed his foot on the accelerator and piled through it. "Yippee!" he whooped. Now *this* was the life!

By the time he'd reached the first dam, he'd killed two sheep and a Jack Russell, but had been completely unaware of anything untoward – well, apart from one of the sheep, which had caused quite a bump, almost dislodging the boat from its trailer.

Godfrey pulled in, sat in a lay-by and set the tractor idling. The dusk was settling over Caban Coch, the first in a series of five huge dams. He pushed open his window and listened as the water trickled over it and fed the river below. He marvelled at the technicalities in making such enormous and efficient structures.

He was calmed by the sound of the water and felt the need to be on it – maybe even *in* it. That would cool him down and make him feel better. He set off again, this time at a slower and more enjoyable pace, allowing the sheep around him to live to chomp through another day. He swigged another mouthful of whisky to keep the wind out and set off higher and higher into the Cambrian Mountains, winding along the roads that linked the dams and the few farms that remained untouched by the reservoirs. There was no traffic around despite it only being eight o'clock. Even the packs of motorcyclists that had raced around the hairpin bends during the day, had eaten their fill from the ice cream and burger vans and headed back to their other lives.

It had always been Godfrey's intention to explore these mountains now that he had a bit more time. Striking wild expanses were crossed by bridleways that had linked the old community to its neighbours and services, and were now used by walkers for pleasure rather than as a necessity for those going about their daily business. The rising moon lit the tops of the mountains and Godfrey's headlights picked out a few hardy sheep lying chewing in the grass at the roadside.

He'd once told Audrey how some joker had tied a *For Sale* sign to the chimney of a flooded house that had been revealed during a drought when the water levels had dropped, and she'd laughed a rare real laugh. Ah, beautiful Audrey. But beautiful Sandra too: they were all beautiful, all ripe for the taking. Perhaps he could go and live with all of them. In Tŷ Mawr. Sandra, her kids, Georgia and Jocey, Audrey too. He could take it in turns with his ladies to make sure that it was fair. They'd be fine with it; they'd get on together well. Even Jerry could come and stay and they could go fishing, no, go and play golf together. Maybe, maybe he'd have just *one* wild night and then he'd go back and sort everyone out. Be sensible. Sort out Tŷ Mawr, and then start a life that didn't involve thoughts of that cackling harridan and her dubious sex life. First, though, he might just have a little swim…

Chapter 62

Roadkill!

Jerry let himself into Madeline's flat, no, *their* flat and closed the door behind him. He wiped his shoes on the mat and hung his coat and keys in the closet. He immediately felt the weight that was everyday life roll from his shoulders. A tumbler of whisky and a read of the paper before Madeline came home to absorb him and his woes into her soft folds, would make everything better.

One of his daughters had just called him a "callous bastard". He'd tried to be candid with her, but daughters don't want the facts. Even though she'd flown the nest several years before, Jessica still wanted Mummy and Daddy living together in the same house and doing the same things in case she should wish to come and stay with them whilst visiting friends in Bridlon. Even less did she want to hear that she had to come quickly and collect all her old toys and tennis rackets and school projects and dolls' house and thick jumpers unless she wanted the lot skipped. She didn't want that kind of crap in her own house, but she really wasn't happy that her dad didn't seem to want it in his either. *How could he? He couldn't have a sentimental bone in his body!*

He was never usually bothered by her tantrums, but this

one had struck a chord. Jerry was normally confident about every move he made in life, but this last couple of months had been uncharted territory. At Audrey's request, he'd put their house on the market – and accepted an offer for the asking price that very same day. Audrey had arranged for him to move all his belongings out a week before contracts were exchanged and she was due up on the Monday to fetch what she wanted and the rest would go to the house clearance people.

Therefore, the man who'd never had to so much as pack his own suitcase for his holidays found himself very cross with Audrey for not choosing exactly what he wanted to take and packing it into boxes for him. He'd taken the past two days off work and had spent them dusty and in a bad mood. How *exactly* did one pack twenty-five shirts and fourteen suits without crumpling them? After he'd spent most of the morning swearing at the ridiculousness of it, he'd found the three cardboard wardrobes supplied by the removal firm. He'd kicked one across the room, then stamped on it, skinning his shin then falling onto his back. It was all very ungainly and he'd been ashamed of his childish behaviour.

Instinctively, however, he'd known not to ask Madeline to help. Madeline did things like telephone the removal company; she did not do other people's shirts or dust. So although Madeline was out to the theatre with Lavinia, one of her work colleagues, and wasn't expecting him at her flat that night, he felt the need for her warmth and ability to make all seem right with the world. Her gentle presence would turn him back into the usual Jerry: someone who is gracious and makes good conversation, not an arse who is lying on his back sweating with a cardboard wardrobe stuck over his foot.

Jerry had even bought her a gift. He wasn't a regular gift buyer, although he was generous with treats and surprises. However, Jessica had also said that, as well as not having a sentimental bone in his body, he also didn't have a thoughtful one. She hadn't liked his smug comment about having so few bones, he was surprised that he could stand up, but hers had struck a chord – even though he didn't really believe it. She obviously didn't know him as well as she thought she did.

Therefore he had brought with him a silver bag with silver cord handles. In it was a beautifully wrapped velvet box containing an antique pearl necklace and earrings. He'd felt rather proud as he'd gone to the jewellers to choose it himself, rather than sending his secretary. It had been one of those shops that the staff have to unlock the door to let people in and he could see them looking at him with uncertainty as he was still wearing his packing clothes. But, they must have been glad that they had as fifteen minutes and a few thousand pounds later, he'd stepped out the door with his little silver bag and a mind to ring his daughter and tell her.

Back in Madeline's flat, he went into the kitchen to fetch a tumbler, but then ran his fingers through his hair and felt suddenly filthy. He'd never been anything other than squeaky clean or about to get squeaky clean in Madeline's company, and to be otherwise just felt wrong. He'd not bothered showering last night but had since packed all the towels so he couldn't have showered before coming here even if he'd felt like it. Yes, he'd have a shower, then when she did arrive home he would be clean and fresh; he didn't want Madeline thinking that he'd let himself go the day before he was to move into her flat!

He loved Madeline's bathroom; it was elegant and luxurious. The large shower cubicle was next to a chaise longue and he sat on it to undress. Educated by the last three months of not having Audrey clearing up after him, he put all of his clothes into the wash basket and closed the lid.

The shower encased him in gentle rain and a selection of appropriate products washed the trauma of the day away. He found a razor in the cabinet and shaved and then did a bit of tidying with the scissors and the tweezers.

By the end of his personal grooming session he felt wonderful. Surrounded by the aroma of Madeline's favourite fragrance, he felt relaxed and tired. He didn't like the thought of sitting on the sofa wrapped only in a bath sheet, so instead picked up Madeline's thicker dressing gown and put it on. He knew that he looked a little ridiculous with white ruffles stretched across his chest and it pulled a little at the back, but it suited his mood and his need to look vulnerable enough to encourage Madeline to sweep his troubles away.

He tidied the bathroom after himself, washing hairs down the sink and wiping the shower screen with the used towel. He padded up the hall back to the lounge where he fixed himself a large whisky, fetched his newspaper, and then settled himself into the chair by the lamp to wait for Madeline's return.

Dave was leaning on the roof of the squad car assessing the mess in Tŷ Mawr yard. He and the other officers had had a good look inside, but whomever it was that had made the mess must be long gone.

Between them they had sealed off the premises and done all their necessaries and were now chatting over the bonnet before returning to HQ to start on the paperwork. Couldn't do much until the owners were able to come and say what was missing.

"All units. All units receiving."

The younger officer jumped to the radio, "Yes, 556 receiving."

"We've got a major RTA, on the B4373 between Cae Gwyn and Maen Du. Can you attend?"

"Agreed. We're on our way."

The man jumped into the car and his colleague jumped in through her door. "Sorry, Dave," she said, "no time to sort your lift. You'll be OK? "

Dave waved them off, knowing it would be pointless to disagree. At least he had time to roll a cigarette and to take that leak – perhaps if went out the back way, he'd get on that new cycle path and take the short cut back to town; cut off at least a couple of miles.

Instead, "342, are you receiving?"

"Receiving," he groaned.

"342, we have a problem. We have an incident with a tractor. I repeat, a tractor. It's gone on a rampage through the lanes. All units are out. 342, you will have to get to Llanerch Farm. I repeat Llanerch Farm. Know it?"

Dave spluttered. It must be five miles away!

"I know, 342, I'm aware of your bike. However, we need to stop him. The farmers are going to meet you at the end of their lane. Two miles for you. Maximum. You need to make sure that it doesn't come back that way. Report back, 342, when you have news on the situation."

Dave was now really fed up. He pedalled off up the lane, his legs aching, his buttocks chafing and sore. A text from Hayley saying that they were off down the club and for him to pop by if he had a spare half hour, didn't help his mood. Spare half hour? What planet was she on?

Jerry woke with a start two hours later, as the front door crashed open. He took a couple of seconds to realise that he was still sat in the armchair in the lounge. He had gotten a bit cold and needed to un-crick the stiffness in his neck. Oh good: Madeline was back. Perhaps he'd wait, all curled up and vulnerable, and surprise her. He listened to the sounds of a coat being hung on a hook and a bag being tossed onto the dresser. He could just imagine her unravelling a beautiful silk scarf from round her neck, releasing her soft hair back onto her shoulders.

"Hang on, hang on, I need a piss," screeched a woman and he could hear the sound of her heeled shoes clattering up the hallway. He froze, unsure of what to do. What was going on? Who was this woman? Could it really be Lavinia come back for a late night coffee and a quiet chat?

He heard the bathroom door crash open and then surely the sound of a horse urinating into a tin bucket.

"Oh, shut the door!" laughed a man, "I don't really need to see that, do I?"

"Oh, fuck you!" slurred Madeline's voice. "Fetch me a drink or I'll have a shit!"

Jerry didn't know what to do. He was sat in a winged chair with his back to the lounge door wearing a frilly white dressing gown and not believing what he was hearing.

"Oy, Mad, got any of that nice red?" said another male voice.

"In the rack," called Madeline amidst a resounding fart that made them all laugh.

Jerry could hear glasses clattering out of cupboards and the sound of a cork being uncorked. He pulled his feet up onto the chair and gripped his knees: what on earth was happening?

"Here, Mad," shouted second-voice, "drinkies!"

"Ta," she replied, "I'll be in as soon as I've washed me clout!"

The men laughed again and Jerry could hear them chattering as rustling and running water came from the bathroom. He then heard the clacking of high-heeled shoes on the wooden floor. But this time they were slow and deliberate down the hall.

"Hey, boys, where's my drink?" drawled Madeline. Ah, thought Jerry, that was better. That's more like the Madeline he knew, her low silky tones coming in waves of smoothness from the hall. He must have misheard the rest. He allowed his feet to drift back to the carpet and embraced feeling a little foolish at being found in her dressing gown. Perhaps he'd wait for her colleagues to leave.

"So, boys," she cooed, "where d'ya want to take it?" That was fine too; she'd returned to being a hostess and was passing round the drinks.

"Fu-ckin' hell!" said voice one. "A whip and all!"

"I'll take it…" said voice two, "um – yes, up the rear I think!"

And so it was that Jerry Gloucester, QC, spent the next forty minutes sat curled up into a tight ball as he listened to the woman of his future dreams being banged into next week, barking like a dog and finally giving a symphony of fanny farts that sent arrows ricocheting through his soul.

Jerry shook as the voices retreated towards her (their) bedroom clinking bottles and glasses as they went.

"Oh I'm going to miss you!" said voice one. "No one else is *half* as dirty as you are!"

"Yes, you make sure that you ring us when you need a bit of a break from being a barrister's wife and we'll be straight over. Just you tell him that you, oh I don't know, need a pearl necklace to go with an outfit!"

In fairness to Madeline, she wasn't disrespectful about Jerry, but instead gave a non-committal laugh, but then ruined it by screaming and running down the hall after a noise that could only have been a male member being slapped against a female posterior.

"Calling 342, come in, 342."

Dave groaned. He was sat at the kitchen table at Llanerch Farm. The farmer's wife had stopped crying and he had managed to ascertain that it was just a Jack Russell and two sheep that had been flattened by the tractor. Bad if you like Jack Russells and sheep, but not the end of the world in his eyes. He dunked another custard cream and responded with a weary nod to the farmer.

"342, we know that you are on the bike, but we have an incident at the Elan Valley. There have been reports of the tractor and speedboat and we believe the driver to be under the influence and we think it's the same tractor that killed the sheep and dog. We're worried it's going to escalate, so we need you there. I'm sending units from Bryn Du, but they will be some time. We need you up there. It's about three miles to the hill above Caban Coch. Radio back with any information. Having you pinpoint to the oncoming unit where the tractor is will save a lot of time. They'll give you a lift back to the station. Over."

Dave couldn't believe his ears. "This is *not right,*" he spluttered to the farmers. "Ridiculous. This is *not* how modern-day policing should be. I've done at least, ooh, fifteen miles today on that bloody bike."

"In my day," said the farmer doing up his waistcoat, "*all* policemen were on bikes. Everyone just helped them where they could. Come on. I'll give you a lift to the top of the hill; I've got to check the cattle anyway."

Dave thanked him grudgingly. He felt miffed about the retort suggesting that he was moaning, but also felt slightly sick at the thought of going back into the farmer's Land Rover. It was probably forty years old and he didn't think that it had *ever* been cleaned out. Crusts, bits of pasty, chocolate wrappers and dog hair formed a coating over everything. Also, it smelt as if all the farmer did all day was sit in his cab emitting cheese and onion crisp fumes.

Dave's bike was still in the back of the van so he, and the four remaining dogs, piled into the front. The ancient Land Rover coughed into life and the farmer chugged off along the lane, the dogs taking it in turns to put their paws and then their heads on Dave's trouser-knees. Hayley'll never get this slobber out, rued Dave, even if she bothered to try. Sandra would have; first time too. And he could have rung her to come and give him a lift. If he rang Hayley, he'd have had to arrest her as soon as she got here...

Chapter 63

Befriending Neighbours With a Pool

Mansel Big Face sat in his new people carrier and wept. He was happy beyond words and he had just left the most beautiful baby lying in his beautiful fiancée's arms. Little Bethany had been born a few hours earlier and it had changed his world. Lucy-Ann had been wonderful, all that pushing and screaming, she'd been so brave and now they had Bethany. Bethany Joanne Big Face. No, Bethany Joanne Batten.

He hoped that he'd played his part well; he certainly had bruises developing on his arm where Lucy-Ann had grabbed him to try and get through the pain of the contractions. The part that surprised him most was that he hadn't wanted to be a comedy genius for a single minute of the birth. He hadn't mentioned anything to the midwife about wanting the baby to go back if it were ginger, or about them naming it Behind the Kebab Shop or IKEA Disabled Toilet as a reference to where it might have been conceived.

He had done what the midwife had suggested and he had done what he thought would help Lucy-Ann, and when she had cried in his arms as little Bethany was taken away to be weighed, and told him that she couldn't have done it without him and that he had been wonderful, he had felt the best he had ever felt in his life.

He felt the weight of fatherhood heavily on his shoulders and yet he was ready for the challenge. As a child, he'd seen it as his mother's fault that his life had been so difficult. He had seen his father as a struggling hero, having been driven from the family home, trying really hard to see his little boy, but failing at the last minute due to some unforeseen crisis. His child's eyes had blamed his mother for being rubbish, for forgetting the simplest of things, for not turning up and for making his life a difficult and miserable affair.

However, as an adult, he'd finally begun to reassess it and seen the more likely scenario of a father who became embroiled in his new family and couldn't be bothered to try a bit harder with his old one, and a mother that had made excuses for him and then drowned under the demands of being a worn out, skint, single parent.

Therefore he knew how he *wasn't* going to be as a dad and he hoped he knew how he *was* going to be. He was going to be there, for a start. Bethany would have her PE kit ready in a bag at the beginning of the week. He would always be five minutes early for collecting her rather than a hour and a half late. And if she were going to Aunty Elen's for tea, it would be because she wanted to go and not because he and Lucy-Ann were on a drinking session in a pub somewhere and weren't likely to make it home for bedtime.

Mansel knew that he didn't want to be the prat anymore; he'd done his fair share. He wanted to be a good bloke, a good dad, to get things right for a change. He didn't feel the need to go to the pub to meet the boys to tell them that it looked like Lucy-Ann had been hit in the crotch with an axe or to sing Natalie Imbruglia's *Torn,* as had been his intention. He wanted the warm glow to last. He could see now why Toby had seemed so sentimental that night in the pub and he had no desire to risk losing the glow for the sake of some silly comments.

After he had helped Lucy-Ann into the bath and held little Bethany whilst her mother got herself washed and dressed, the midwife had advised him to leave them to it. Lucy-Ann had had a long day and needed all the sleep she could get. Mansel had kissed his fiancée and daughter goodbye as they were taken off to the ward in a wheelchair and he had watched as they disappeared down the corridor, already looking forward to when he could see them the next day.

He felt that to go home and do the dishes from earlier would be to burst the bubble too soon. He wanted to hold that feeling. Perhaps he'd just drive around for a while. It was a beautifully warm, still night; he might be able to go and sit somewhere scenic for a while.

He settled back in the car and removed the shoe horn from his pocket: that was a potential joke that really hadn't been needed given that Bethany was a little on the small side, being a few weeks early. He found a classical station on the radio and set off slowly, enjoying his trance.

Mansel cruised for miles before he remembered that he had promised to phone Lucy-Ann's parents to tell them the news, and he supposed he should phone his own as well: see if they could listen for long enough for him to get the details across. He pulled over in a lay-by and found himself parked up behind a tractor and, hang on, was that a boat on the trailer behind it and.... *Blow me if that isn't Godfrey Palmer ex of Council Tax, one floor up from Ducks and Slides trying to wrestle it off?*

"Godfrey?" called Mansel, jumping out of his car. "Is that you? What on earth are you up to?"

"Mansel? Big Face, is that you? Thank God for that, I thought you were the police."

"Police? Why would I be the police?"

"Well, I saw their blue lights going down the valley a little while ago, I hid for a bit – but I think that they are gone."

"Hang on, Godfrey, what's going on here? Is this nicked or something? Why would the police be chasing you? And how can you hide in a bloody great tractor?"

"Well, I haven't had too good a day. Knocked a couple of gates off their hinges, left a few lights on, that kind of thing."

Mansel walked over to Godfrey, still not really understanding what was going on. Aside from the fact that Godfrey was squinting into the headlights, he still looked a little weird and seemed to be staggering a bit. "What are you up to? Am I missing something here? What are you hoping to do with that boat?"

"I want to go in the water," said Godfrey, as if it made perfect sense. Mansel could smell the whisky on Godfrey's breath, and there was a look in his eyes, that wasn't quite right. His cardigan was buttoned up wrongly and he had blood dripping from a finger, too.

"Are you OK, Godfrey? Has something happened?"

Godfrey sagged visibly and then thought a while. "Yes.

Actually, something has happened. Have you ever realised that something about your life has been wrong? For many years? Well, today I did and I must change, and to do that, I need to get this boat into the water."

The parallel struck Mansel. "Well, actually, yes I have. Today, too, in fact …"

"In which case you will know that I *have* to get this boat into the water and therefore will you help me please?"

Mansel saw no argument to this in the face of their obvious common experience and therefore rolled up his sleeves and assessed the situation. How were two men – one slightly the worse for wear – going to get a boat across a road and into a reservoir that was down a slope of large boulders, in the dark?

"There's a little track that leads into the reservoir down there," said Godfrey as if sensing his concerns. "If we unhitch the trailer and wheel it down the road for fifty yards, we can cut across the path and down the slope into the water."

And it was like the old days of Godfrey making stupid suggestions in the Council's inter-disciplinary team meetings and Mansel not really thinking about them, but just carrying them out. And if there was anything Mansel liked, it was to feel comfortable and at home: being ordered about by Council officials (even retired ones) was well within his comfort zone.

Together they pulled the trailer along the road and then manoeuvred it through the gate that Godfrey had pointed out. Mansel was glad to get it off the road; he was concerned about the police that Godfrey had referred to and didn't fancy trying to explain this one to them, so soon after his last outing to Cysgod y Ffynnon police HQ. He was a bit worried that he hadn't hidden his car; this far out of town, it would be too much of a coincidence for it to just be "parked" and not involved in any misdemeanour.

Mansel and Godfrey did their backs in wheeling the boat across the path and then wrenched their shoulders trying to act as human brakes as it dragged them down the scree slope. It hit the water with a crash and it was only a lucky dive that allowed Mansel to grab the rope attached to the bow, stopping them from losing the boat across the lake. There was a glug as the trailer disappeared under the water and Mansel feared that they may not get that back tonight.

"Christ, Godfrey, that boat wasn't fastened on to the trailer; you could have lost it on the way!"

Godfrey started giggling as he strode back out of the water and pushed his hair off his face. "That would have put the tin hat on it, wouldn't it!" he laughed.

Mansel shook his head. "What are you going to do now?"

Godfrey didn't answer, but instead looked into the distance towards the dam, "Did you know that this dam, Caban Coch, is thirty-six metres high? Or that it holds over nine million litres of water? Or that many men were lost during the thirteen years of making it?"

Mansel shrugged. No, he didn't know the exact details, but knew of it, but that really wasn't the information he was after.

"Godfrey. Hang on a minute. Listen to me. What are you doing? What are *we* doing?" The pain in this shoulder was bringing him back into reality.

"Please come with me, Mansel? Just a little ride round the reservoir? Let me do just one exciting thing in my life and then I'll put everything else right. Will you help me? Please?"

The old Mansel would have dived in fully clothed, then splashed Godfrey, then probably tipped the thing over. However, the new Mansel had responsibilities. He wasn't a prat any more: he was actually quite helpful. He felt that he understood Godfrey's need for this, no matter how bizarre it might seem to be taking a spin in a small speedboat in the moonlight. Because he too felt that he had reached a turning point in his life, he thought he should perhaps help someone else realise theirs.

No one could ever envy what seemed to be Godfrey's life – a tired, boring existence that probably relied on putting buttons into collection boxes to get his kicks. Mansel's life had never been short of kicks, but they were usually physical rather than emotional and from people he had annoyed, pushed over or offended in some way. If Mansel could help Godfrey change his life from one of tedium and misery, towards one that included just some of the feelings that Mansel had enjoyed that day, then perhaps it was his human duty to do so.

"OK," he said slowly. "I'll come in and we'll have a quiet chug around the reservoir and then I will drive you home and we will sort this mess out tomorrow? Understood?"

Mansel had thoughts of a gentle punt around a lake as he wallowed in fatherhood and memories of his gorgeous baby girl. He could still smell Bethany on his shoulder, where she had laid snuggled up to Dad whilst he had smiled delightedly at her mum; he could give Godfrey ten minutes of his newly precious time whilst he basked in those warm *cwtchy* feelings. He climbed into the gently rocking vessel and then held out his hand to Godfrey. He was just looking for a torch to light their careful journey when his thoughts were shattered as a naive dream and the motor roared into being.

Flight of Joy shot out across the lake, sending a wash over Godfrey's jacket back on the shore.

"God!" shouted Mansel over the noise and he fell back from his seat and landed with a thump at the bottom of the boat with his legs in the air.

Godfrey started laughing and he leant over to help pull Mansel up, but the boat rocked alarmingly. "Don't do that!" screamed Mansel. "You'll have us over! Here," he said dragging himself back to the bench and leaning towards the engine, "let me do it."

Godfrey put his hand out to stop Mansel, "It's OK, I've got it now. You just sit there…" Godfrey did a little rev and the boat started forward again, then a little turn. It was as if he were just practicing; Mansel watched him carefully, ready to pounce as soon as he went too far.

"I used to really fancy trying waterskiing," muttered Godfrey, more to himself than Mansel who he seemed to be losing awareness of. "You know, doing those jumps and turns?" He revved up again and sped off across the lake, moving the rudder back and fore as they swung in zigzags across the water. "I used to be quite a speedster in my car you know? Really used to rev the guts out of it…"

Godfrey looked at him and Mansel was suddenly scared.

420

The old Godfrey didn't seem to be there any more. He had been replaced by a manic piss-head intent on destroying them all.

"Godfrey, I've got a baby girl!" he shouted above the noise of the engine. "Be careful will you, I'm needed now. Slow down!"

Instead, Godfrey had turned to face the blackness, no longer listening to Mansel. This was it! This was the pinnacle of his adventure and it felt good. The warm air rushed past his face and a thousand midges pinged off his cheeks. The water smelt good and the breeze and the roar of the engine made him feel alive for the first time in years.

"Not too good for me now, are you, Royston Jefferson!" he shouted into the darkness. "Nor your bloody daughter! See me now in my speedboat, why don't you! Bet your daughter's never been in a speedboat, has she, Royston Jefferson?" He swung the rudder and the boat changed direction and headed off again into the night. Godfrey was aware of a blue flashing light somewhere in the distance, but it didn't matter; they couldn't stop him! He was invisible as well as invincible!

He was aware that he had a passenger, but only as someone on the borders of his adventure. He wished that Mansel would just keep quiet for a while and stop shouting – let Godfrey enjoy the most important night of his life. Therefore every time Mansel reached for the controls, Godfrey would rev the engine harder, sending Big Face crashing back down to the bottom of the boat.

Mansel lay on a pile of tools and mildewed raincoats. I must think of something to do, I *must* think of something to do, he told himself. No, not in the lying on your back, wiggling your feet and shouting "Dead Ants!" kind of way, like one does in football after someone scores a goal – but he knew that he would struggle to find a sensible alternative. He had never had a situation that required such concentration. All his life he had floated from one easy option to another. In fact, walking across the bar to speak to Lucy-Ann on that first night of the rest of his life was probably the most pro-active thing he had ever done. He had stumbled into jobs, into buying a house, buying cars, choosing friends. Nothing would truly prepare anyone for the situation he was now in – stuck in a speedboat with a madman intent on going out in a blaze of glory, or so it seemed – but Mansel had not even had a taster session with a slightly giddy aunt on a carousel.

The Mansel of yesterday would have thought, sod it, and wriggled his legs and shouted, "Dead Ants!" at the top of his voice and just hoped for the best, but the Mansel of today was different. He had just had the most wonderful experience of his life and two people needed him to make their lives worth living. Actually *needed* him. The headline "Local Funnyman in Boat Adventure" was no longer enough to warrant seeing how this current adventure might turn out. No, he *needed* to get out of this. *Needed* to, before the maniac at the helm smashed into the rocks or turned them over in water cold enough to freeze solid and snap off what had just made Mansel a dad.

He looked at the silhouette of Godfrey crouched at the front of the boat, like a spaniel sticking his head out of the car window that was enjoying the wind rushing through his ears, but had no means of anticipating of the narrow bridge ahead... Mansel tried shouting again, but Godfrey was oblivious.

So, for Lucy-Ann and for Bethany, and for the life that was ahead of them in Disneyland, Cysgod y Ffynnon, Mansel counted to three, hauled himself into a sitting position, then dragging every last ounce of memory from his stomach muscles, flung himself over the side of the boat into thirty-six metres of cold, dark water.

Godfrey barely noticed, save for a splutter in the engine as Mansel rocked the boat and part of him caught on the sharp blades of the propeller, altering his person for ever. HEADLINES: *'Local Idiot Gets Caught in Boat Propeller Shock!*

PC Dave Burton was in considerable pain. He was sat on his cross bar, his chest was heaving and he was struggling to suck in the amount of oxygen that his body required. He had finally reached the top of the hill. The farmer of Llanerch Farm had obviously taken a dislike to him as he had stopped only half way up, pretending that he could see his cattle from that particular gateway, even though it was as dark as the inside of one of those cows.

Dave hadn't realised that there was still a couple of miles of hill left when he had had his bike tossed out after him. By the time he had put his helmet and vest on and sorted out his lights, the farmer had grunted at his cows, flung a bale of something over the gate and turned his vehicle around.

The Land Rover had farted out a cloud of red diesel at him

and PC Burton was left alone in the darkness.

Dave was still cursing the farmer by the time he reached the top of the hill, not to mention Sergeant Davies, the bloke in the control room at the station, Hayley for not being able to drive him places when he wanted, Sandra for being happier than he was and the chef in the station kitchens for making such nice jam puddings.

As his heartbeat slowly dropped below one hundred beats per minute and his haemorrhoids began to hurt more than his lungs, he looked out into the darkness where he thought the valley should be. There were three street lamps in Elan village itself and he knew that that was south of the Caban Coch dam. No sign of movement there. He could hear the gentle rush of water coming over the dam, but was that an engine sound on top of that? It didn't sound like a tractor; it sounded more like a large lawnmower. Could someone really be mowing their lawn in the dark at this time of night?

"342 calling Control. Come in Control."

"Receiving, 342. Where are you?"

"I'm at the top of the hill overlooking Caban Coch dam. I cannot see any movement of the tractor. I repeat, no sign of the tractor or other vehicular movement."

"Oh, it's OK, 342. We have the tractor. There are two units at the side of the reservoir and they have impounded the tractor. The suspect is in the speedboat in the reservoir and they are ready for intervention. We tried to contact you, 342. You must have had a problem with your radio. The guv says you might as well come back to the station. You won't be able to be much more help at the scene, so probably not worth you going any further. The units need to get back as soon as. We think we have a case requiring immediate psychiatric attention.

"As soon as another unit becomes available, I will send it to meet you. Do not divert from the route you are on. Over and out."

"Oh, for God's sake!" Dave shouted in rage and he threw his bike to the ground. They had to be joking! Was it April the first or something and he hadn't noticed? His legs were wobbling from the effort of getting up the hill and his backside was throbbing more than anything had in years.

After all that, suddenly a little, "It's OK, we have the tractor"? Pathetic, absolutely pathetic. This was the last straw. Time to hang up the badge, he thought, how can they treat someone like this?

In a rage of frustration, he gingerly picked up his bike: damn, now he had broken the front lamp. He checked his mobile to see if he could phone someone to fetch him, a bloody taxi if need be. Sod it, no reception. He turned his back on the noise from the dam and started back down the lane, rattling in the dark over stones, sticks and clumps of mud. He skidded through cowpats, sheep poo and slime from the blocked ditches. Aside from this, what his broken lamp made him miss were the cuttings from a hedge of mature blackthorn…

Mansel knew that something wasn't right, although he couldn't work out what. Get to the blue lights, get to the blue lights, then it'll all be OK… He swam on his side with his right arm scooping at the water and his left flailing weakly. He was shouting for help above the sound of the speedboat.

He was terrified that Godfrey was going to swing around again and crash over the top of him.

He was sure that he'd lost an arm – or at least his hand. How was he going to hold Bethany if what he thought had happened had happened? How was he going to push the wheelbarrow pram? He knew that his arm, if that *had* happened, would be gently dropping thirty-six metres to the bottom of the reservoir, surely no one would be able to find it, and stick it in a bag of frozen peas and take it to the hospital with him? He remembered that amputees could still feel the limbs that they'd lost, and so he was terrified to check what was missing at this point: wait until he was safe on dry land. He *needed* to get to dry land: that was all that mattered.

"Help ME! Help ME! I'm in the water!"

He could hear some shouts and he yelled back again in reply. The blue lights cut out occasionally which meant that someone was passing in front of them. He heard more shouts and then the car headlights were turned towards him. He tried to wave with his right arm, but sank. He spluttered back up to the surface and spat the water from his mouth. He was beginning to feel faint and knew that if what he thought had happened had happened, then he would be losing lots of blood. The water was *so cold.* He couldn't believe that he could be so cold so quickly. His teeth were chattering so violently that he was unable to shout. *What if they lost sight of him and never found him again?* He still hadn't confessed to Lucy-Ann why he was really called Big Face and as his intended and the mother of his child, she had to know truth.

Just as he started to feel dizzy and unreal, he saw two

people splashing through the water towards him. They were stumbling and falling, but kept getting up. They were shouting at him to stand and he finally comprehended and put his legs down and felt such relief as his feet hit stones at the bottom. He wobbled upright, reassured by a woman's voice, "You're OK now, mate, we've nearly got you." He finally felt able to investigate and see what had actually happened and swung his right arm around to where his left was supposed to be. As he put his arm round, he saw blood shining in the moonlight. He screamed. "Don't look now, sir, just hold me. We'll sort it." The woman finally reached him and grabbed his right arm to steady him. "Come on, we need to get out of here. Hold onto me." Mansel felt himself beginning to faint and heard the man that had now reached them too shout, "Stay with us Mansel, come on. Don't you leave us, Mansel; come on, the world needs comedy…"

As Mansel allowed himself to be dragged from the water, he felt that it was indeed his finest hour…

Godfrey spun the boat again, heading off in a different direction, the moon now behind a cloud and covering the lake in an eerie darkness. He was enjoying the sway that his movement caused and his ability to concentrate now that Mansel was gone. He was busy thinking: if on average, men live for two point eight years after retiring (though he wasn't sure if that was all retirees or just those who went on until sixty-five), that meant that he had another twenty-nine months to live. If he could live them at this level of excitement, then it would all have been worth it. Thirty-two years of blandness for twenty-nine months of excitement –

it was almost a ratio of twelve to one? But then, he hadn't drunk or smoked since his early twenties, so perhaps he'd be healthy enough to make it to thirty-two months or more and that would make it a bit better? Perhaps he could take up paragliding or oyster diving or something?

He thought of Sandra sat with a picnic hamper waiting for him to emerge from a deep pool with a pearl or perhaps a fish between his teeth. He thought of Georgia, smiling and waving goodbye at him standing in the doorway of her new flat. Jocey was in her arms and the hall behind her was newly decorated in bright colours. He thought about Audrey waiving away the damage that he had done to her home. "I would have done the same in the circumstances," she'd smile. "Just make sure that you come over after that gold rush trip that I've sponsored and tell me what you found!"

However, what he hadn't thought about was the design of Caban Coch reservoir and dam. The fact that the dam was thirty-six metres high, he had already acknowledged. The fact that the water gently cascaded over the top of it had escaped him. Faster and faster he piled the boat into the darkness. He was aware of the two police cars on the road alongside the lake, but he couldn't distinguish the words they were shouting over the tannoy. Hopefully they had pulled Mansel out of the water and had sat him with a blanket and a cup of hot cocoa while they waited for him, Godfrey, to finish his adventure.

His hair streamed backwards, the dandruff and cheap shampoo finally dislodging from his follicles with the force of the wind. His face was set into a smile, a peace exuding from his features in a way that had been missing for so long.

Flight of Joy finally hit the top of the dam, crashing into the wall and exploding into a haze of fibreglass shrapnel. The engine went silent as it crunched into the stone and then began its journey to the bottom of the reservoir. Godfrey was catapulted the fifteen feet of the length of the boat and then onwards into the darkness.

Godfrey heard Mansel screaming from the roadside, but his words were irrelevant. He was feeling exhilaration as he was launched from his vessel into nothingness.

He thought about his shares, finally looking as if they might recover; the pension providers that would be hugging themselves with glee at such an early demise. He thought about Georgia cuddling little Jocey. Then he thought about Alice, beautiful beautiful Alice – and then he thought, "Oh, bollocks," and then he thought – nothing – at – all.

Chapter 64

Save on Groceries, Eat Hospital Food

Mansel woke in a clean white bed: instinctively he knew that it couldn't be his own. He felt groggy and strange and the lights shining from the strips on the ceiling were hurting his eyes. He heard a little snuffling noise from his side and he strained his head to see what it was. It was an angel wrapped in a white gown, with a baby at her breast.

"Mansel?" the angel whispered, "you're awake!" It was Lucy-Ann's voice and it filled him with love.

"Lucy-Ann? Is that you? What's happened? Am I in hospital?"

"Yes my love, you are. Cysgod y Ffynnon hospital, now. Are you OK? You've had a bit of an adventure!" Mansel nodded, some of the memories were coming back to him in a haze. He could see Lucy-Ann's face, surrounded by a haze of sunshine from the window. It was beautiful and it was crying – for him.

"The boat? I jumped into the water, didn't I? My arm – has it come off?" He struggled to sit up.

"No," she smiled, "just the top of your finger! Hardly a fish's nibble of a piece! But you're fine – you had hypothermia. Apparently it was quite serious for a while –

they had to fill you with warm fluids intravenously as you spent so much time in the water – warm you from the inside out. Apparently though, the hypothermia helped as all your blood went to your organs rather than out of your finger – good, eh?"

"Bethany!" Mansel suddenly saw whom it was that Lucy-Ann was holding. "She's here!"

"Yes, she said that she wanted to come and see her daddy! We've been discharged to here too and we can stay here until you are well enough to go home – well, unless they have a rush on!"

Mansel pulled himself up onto his elbows just as Bethany removed herself from Lucy-Ann's breast and rolled on to her back, milk-drunk like a little fat puppy. Mansel reached out his good hand and stroked her.

"Oh, Lucy-Ann, she's beautiful," and tears came into his eyes. "Do you know, it was thinking about you and little Bethany that made me decide to jump out of the boat – I knew that I had to get back to shore, back to see you …" Then a shadow crossed Mansel's face and he rolled back and groaned, "Godfrey, he couldn't have got out of that alive – is he…? Did he make it?"

Lucy-Ann shook her head. "They haven't found a body yet, but they don't think he could have made it. The boat was in smithereens; he either got caught on and sank with the engine, or was flipped out over the dam wall and has washed down in the river. Everyone is out searching for him, but it doesn't look good. I'm sorry, Mansel. It must have been so scary for you…" Mansel shook his head and dissolved into tears and Lucy-Ann went to him as fast as her stitches would allow her to and hugged his head to her, crying quietly with him. Only Bethany was content and unmoved by her father's plight.

Later that day, Mansel was sat up in bed with Bethany snuggled on his chest, with her little knees drawn up and her hand grasping tight to one of his remaining fingers. Lucy-Ann was dozing in the chair next to the bed. The curtain drew quietly back and a nurse popped her head round.

"Everything OK?" she smiled, checking Bethany and taking Mansel's pulse as she flitted around the bed, setting the sheets and blankets to rights. "Mansel, there is a man here from the local newspaper, he would love to have a chat with you – do you think that you are up to it? I've said that I would *ask* but I wouldn't make any promises. It's entirely up to you – if you don't want to, I'll send him off again."

Mansel shrugged. The Mansel of old would have "Wha-heyed" and "Bring it on"d, but the new Mansel considered it, conferred with his fiancée and then said, "Yes, for Godfrey, I'll do it. It would be good for his memory to set the record straight. OK, send him up…"

Chapter 65

Getting High on Life

The sun streamed through the windows as the primrose-coloured muslin was pulled to one side and fastened with a band of plaited raffia.

"Good morning," whispered a gentle voice, and a man in a bed responded with the hint of recognition. "I've brought you a drink – some more hot water with a squeeze of fresh lemon. It'll give you a good start to the day." Her voice was a singsong and it soothed his passage from sleep. He managed to mumble his thanks, but didn't reach out to grasp the cup and instead watched as it was put on the wooden table beside him.

He felt safe in this tranquil room with its wooden floors and dreamcatchers fluttering peacefully in the open window's breeze. The smell was of clary sage and it helped the man to feel rested and at ease.

The gentle hands with strings of beads wound round long, elegant forearms, pulled the quilt slowly from his shoulders and they helped him to a sitting position, supported by large patchwork cushions. The woman fetched herself a drink and then sat in a wicker chair in the corner of the room and watched him. She had all the time in the world.

The man shuffled around a bit, plumping up the cushions here and smoothing them down over there. Eventually he reached for the drink and sipped at it, holding the earthenware mug in both of his shaking hands.

"How are you feeling today?" asked the voice and it soothed him and he felt no need to reply. "You're looking better. How is your drink? It's not too hot I hope?"

The man tried to shake his head a little, but his response was more of an acknowledgement than a reply.

There was a silence once more, save the sound of rustling as the woman reached for a sketch pad and looking alternately between her model and her page, started drawing with a soft-nibbed pencil, stopping every now and then to dampen her finger and smudge the line.

Soon, on her page, was the drawing of a man sat in a bed, leaning against a wicker headboard that fanned out behind him.

The man sipped and the woman sketched, pausing every now and then to tuck her long hair behind her ears or remove a piece of fluff from her bare feet.

"My perfect muse," she smiled as, over a few days, she watched the man slowly getting better.

There was a noise from outside and the sound of a gate clicking. "Oh," said the woman, "I'll just go and sort that out: it's the man from the village shop bringing the delivery I rung through." The woman unwound herself from the basket chair and glided out of the room. The patient watched her go with a slight smile on his lips. As the van drove away and rummaging sounds came from the kitchen, he carried on sipping his drink, his eyes staring into the beautiful scene outside the bedroom window. A woodland of deciduous trees running down to reach a tranquil body of water with an identical folly nestling in trees on the far side of the shore; what could be more therapeutic to a person who had been so traumatised?

The noises in the kitchen stopped. There was silence. After a few minutes there was the soft padding of footsteps coming back into the room.

"Geoffrey," came the soft voice, "it's me again, Audrey, I think we've found out what happened to you..." Audrey lay the local newspaper on his lap and he looked at the headlines, although they meant nothing to him. *TIP-ical! Man Loses Tip of Finger as Friend is Catapulted to Death*! The picture of Mansel sat looking very serious on a hospital bed with Bethany in one arm and his bandaged finger held up in the air, brought a flicker to Godfrey's face. "The boat..." he whispered.

"Yes," said Audrey, "it looks like you were in a boat – look, you must have crashed as this is all that remains of it." The picture she pointed to was of a pile of shards of fibreglass with a few odd bits of rope and a waterproof jacket in a pile next to a police frogman on the side of the reservoir.

"The adventure of a lifetime for one man turned out to be an adventure that might well have cost him his life...

Mansel Batten (known locally as Big Face from the years when he carried his Under Elevens' football trophy everywhere and the reflection made his face look big) thought he was going for a gentle drive to get used to the idea of being a new dad, when he came across his friend,

435

Godfrey Palmer, on a mission of self-destruction..."

"Look, Geoffrey," smiled Audrey, "they've spelt your name wrong! *Godfrey Palmer!* Typical local rag!"

"Godfrey seemed anxious and was determined that he wanted to go out in the boat. I thought I would help him, but it was the worst thing I could have done," said Mansel, still recuperating in his hospital bed."

"Yes, I remember now," said Godfrey very slowly, "I was in the boat – and Mansel jumped out – and then I don't know what happened." He stared more at the pictures as if they were jogging his fogged memory. "I woke up lying on a wall, it was running with water, so I walked along it and then went into the woods. I remember seeing lights – and I was so cold and so wet, so I walked towards the lights. I can't really remember anything else…" He tailed off. Audrey laughed quietly, grasped his hands and rubbed them gently with her soft, cool ones.

"Geoffrey, I think that you are the luckiest man alive today! *I* think you must have crashed your boat, been propelled into the air and then *landed* on the top of the dam! You must have walked along an eight-foot-wide wall with water trickling over the top. You had a hundred-foot drop to one side and a hundred-foot depth of icy-cold water to the other! It's amazing that you are still alive!"

Godfrey nodded. "I remember that now, it wasn't until I had gone some way that I noticed – keys fell out of my top pocket and when I went to get them – I realised that the wall wasn't there…I crawled the rest of the way…"

"That'll be why your knees were through! Well, and I thought that you'd just fallen in the water on a careless fishing trip!" she said. "I will need to phone the police and let them know that you are safe and sound-ish, anyway. And apparently you trashed some poor soul's house, but I am sure we can put that to rights! They are only possessions after all; possessions can be replaced, people can't. But until they arrive, we can do some more of the stuff that helps make you the luckiest man alive today…"

Godfrey squinted through his haze at the scene around him and saw a face framed by long, loose hair, a body clothed in a cheesecloth blouse and a long Indian skirt with a pair of bare feet emerging from the bottom. He smelt a fresh smell of soap wash over him. And, just as he'd been planning for thirty-two years, an elegant lady climbed onto the bed, lay down beside him and tickled a tendril of long hair over his face…

The End!

More from Lorraine Jenkin

Chocolate Mousse and Two Spoons

Lettie Howells has hit a new low. This is the last, the very last, time her soon to be ex is going to leave her counting the bruises. Her housemates and supersorted sister persuade her that she's not going to find the man of her dreams among the tourist traffic in Lyme Regis and she duly sends off her ad' to the Lonely Hearts columns. From a motley crew of respondents she selects Doug – a jolly but 'once-bitten' hunk of a Welsh forester.

But the path of true love does not run smooth: there's two whole communities of friends and relations to muddy things up – from Lettie's dominant mother Grace (who takes up with one of Lettie's cast offs), to her ditzy lodger Lisa (who flirts with Lettie's boss).

Though her day job sees her serving tea and cake, Lettie yearns to paint. Then a trip to Doug's home town provides new canvases and an unlooked-for brush with fame…

"Witty, clever, fun and sad - couldn't put it down!"
Miranda Krestovnikoff (BBC's Coast)

"This sweet romantic story is flavoured with an unexpectedly strong cast of characters... a case of expecting light fluffy chocolate mousse and getting so much more" – Chick Lit Club

"The various twists and turns of each plot meant that I

*could hardly stop reading each night, desperate to know
how one of the characters would react to the chocolate
mousse incident!"* – Western Mail

*"Fun and witty...with many twists in the tale that all women
can relate to"* – County and Border Life

978 1870206 95 2   £6.99

Lorraine Jenkin now has her own great Blog at:
http://lorrainejenkin.blogspot.com/

Other titles from Honno

More than Just a Hairdresser, by Nia Pritchard
Mobile hairdresser Shirley catches the boyfriend of friend
and assistant, Oli, in a compromising position and gets the
evidence to prove it. Others in relationship straits become
keen to enlist her help, and with her mobile hairdressing
business taking off in a new direction, Shirley's little pink
diary is the keeper of surprising secrets.

"Enjoyed it loads. A good juicy read!" Margi Clarke

978 1870206 85 3   £6.99

Headhunters, by Claire Peate

A girls-own adventure for grown-ups: ambitious young journalist Kate and newly appointed Dean, Archie – more Converse All Stars than socks-and-sandals – find themselves thrown together to solve the mystery of the disappearing skulls.

978 1906784 02 7   £7.99

Praise for Claire Peate's previous novels...
"More substance than your average chick lit" – Big Issue

"The suspense and humour will keep you gripped" – Western Mail

Back Home, by Bethan Darwin

Ellie is brokenhearted and so decamps home. Tea and sympathy from grandad Trevor help, as does the distracting and hunky Gabriel, then a visitor turns Trevor's world upside down...

"A modern woman's romantic confession, alongside a cleverly unfolding story of long-buried family secrets" – Abigail Bosanko

"Lively, fresh and warm-hearted – an easy-going and enjoyable read" – Nia Wyn, author of *Blue Sky July*

978 1906784 03 4   £7.99

Sweets from Morocco, by Jo Verity
Gordon has to go... Tessa and Lewis decide that something must be done when the arrival of baby Gordon threatens their, so far, perfect childhood. A bittersweet story of sibling love and rivalry.

"A richly detailed and absorbing narrative journey" –
Andrew Cowan

"A ripping yarn and pitch perfect evocation of childhood and sibling relationships" – Daily Telegraph
978 1906784 00 3   £7.99

The War Before Mine, by Caroline Ross
A brief wartime romance leaves Rosie heartbroken and pregnant, not knowing if Philip – on a suicide mission designed to stop the Nazi invasion – is alive or dead.

"More than a war story, more than a love story...
A slice of living history" – Philip Gross.

"A bright new star of Welsh writing" – Sunday Telegraph

978 1870206 97 6   £6.99

About Honno

Honno Welsh Women's Press was set up in 1986 by a group of women who felt strongly that women in Wales needed wider opportunities to see their writing in print and to become involved in the publishing process. Our aim is to develop the writing talents of women in Wales, give them new and exciting opportunities to see their work published and often to give them their first 'break' as a writer.

Honno is registered as a community co-operative. Any profit that Honno makes is invested in the publishing programme. Women from Wales and around the world have expressed their support for Honno by buying shares in the co-operative. Shareholders' liability is limited to the amount invested and each shareholder has a vote at the Annual General Meeting.

To buy shares or to receive further information about forthcoming publications, please write to Honno at the address below, or visit our website: **www.honno.co.uk**

Honno
Unit 14, Creative Business Units.
Aberystwyth Arts Centre
Penglais Campus
Aberystwyth
SY23 3GL

All Honno titles can be ordered online at
www.honno.co.uk
or by sending a cheque to **Honno**.
Free p&p to all UK addresses